"COME, LET US HAVE AT IT," SIENA SAID "MANO A MANO. WINNER TAKE ALL!"

She whipped off her shirt and flung it at Lord Kirtland's feet. Amusement warred with arousal as he stared at her bared breasts. "An interesting figure of speech."

"Defend yourself, sir." Siena dropped to the other side and came at him from behind.

He whirled. Their weapons clashed. Siena's kick nearly took his legs out from under him, but he had anticipated she might not fight fair. Kirtland twisted and pinned her up against the unyielding wood of the bench, crushing his heat hard against her. The feel of her long legs was exquisitely enticing, like steel sheathed in velvet. He must try to remember that all he wanted from her was a confession. But that was proving damnably difficult.

"I'm afraid you have no choice but to concede defeat, madam."

The blaze in her eyes took on a different glow. It was not the flicker of surrender, but some light he could not begin to define.

"Pax," she sighed. Then her lips were on the corner of his mouth, a gossame

For Melanie Murray,
my wonderful editor,
who believed in the Merlins
and helped make them so

The Spy Wore Silk

Chapter One

Steel clashed against steel, the blades flashing like quicksilver fire in the afternoon sun.

But this time, there would be no errant sparks, no flare of flames. This time, the wolf-faced Italian would not goad an explosion of temper—

"*Porca miseria!*" Spinning with deceptive quickness, *Il Lupino* punctuated his curse with a flurry of lightning slashes that sent the opposing saber clattering to the courtyard cobbles. "*Non, non, non*—is all wrong!" he snarled. "You must slide to the left, then counter with a *punta sopramano*."

Damn.

"And your thrusts must be deeper and faster, *Volpina*. Like so . . ." The Italian's swordpoint cut through the air with a lethal whisper. Soft but deadly.

"*Grazie.*" *Volpina* watched its sinuous dance.

"Like a man making love to a beautiful woman." Finishing with a flourish, he raised his weapon to the *en garde* position. "Now try it again—this time with more passion." A smile flashed, the crescent curve a mocking reflection of the hard-edged steel. He was being deliberately provocative. "Unless, of course, you are too tired to continue."

"Not bloody likely."

As intended, the challenge prickled, like daggers dancing on tender flesh. For an instant, anger blazed, sparked by wounded pride. But then, *Volpina* recalled the master's own words.

Fight fire with fire.

Snatching up the fallen saber, *Volpina* crossed swords for only an instant before lashing out with a furious lunge that drove *Il Lupino* back to the edge of the chalked circle.

The Italian parried the attack with ease, but as he set his stance and angled his blade to block the next blow, *Volpina* suddenly whirled around and drove a knee into his groin.

Woof. *Il Lupino* doubled over, then dropped to the ground with a leaden thud.

Silence descended over the courtyard, save for the twitching scrape of leather against stone.

"*Bella! Bella!*" After several moments, the Italian recovered enough of his breath to speak. "*Magnifico,* in fact."

Pushing the steel away from his throat, he uncurled his legs and managed to sit up.

Several of the onlookers winced in sympathy, while one or two bit back a titter of laughter.

"Machiavelli would be proud of you." A note of humor blunted the rasp of pain. "A lady should never fight fair."

"No hard feelings, *Signor* Da Rimini?" The darkhaired beauty known only as Siena set a gloved hand on her hip and shook the sweat from her brow. Fire still tingled through her tensed muscles, but its burn curled the corners of her mouth into a small smile. Finally, she had bested the wily wolf at his own game.

"On the contrary. It gives me great pleasure to see one of my pupils begin to master the art of war." For an instant his grin appeared to angle to a more serious tilt. "It seems you have been born with natural talent, *Signorina* Siena. My job is to hone it to a fine edge."

Siena stared down at her sword. Her real identity had long since been lost in the stews of St. Giles. But like all the students at Mrs. Merlin's Academy for Select Young Ladies, she had been given a new name on entering its world, one chosen at random from the ornate globe in the headmistress's office.

A new name for a new life. A new meaning for the savage skills learned in the primitive school of the slums. Once inside the ivied walls, she had been determined never to look back at the twisted alleyways of her past.

"Now, girls, pay close attention to my words and not my manly thighs." Her musings were cut short as Da Rimini resumed his cocky drawl. "*Signorina* Siena has just given us a perfect demonstration of why it is important to keep a cool head in the heat of battle. The point is, all of you will need to rely on wits and imagination, rather than size and strength, to prevail over an opponent. As you have witnessed, brains can be a more potent weapon than brawn."

Siena reached down and helped him to his feet.

"Fire and ice," he murmured. "Once again I commend you, *signorina*. Now that you are learning to fight with your head as well as your heart, you present a deadly challenge. God help the enemy."

A shiver ran down her spine, hot and yet cold. Was she ready to test her mettle in the real world?

In the distance a bell chimed the hour. "The lesson is over for today, girls," announced Da Rimini.

Siena stripped off her padded doublet and shook out the knot of curls coiled at her neck. Tall, slim-hipped, and lithe as a rapier, she could pass for a boy in her fencing gear. But the thin linen shirt, dampened from her exertions, revealed curves that were decided womanly.

Da Rimini gave an appreciative leer as he watched the raven tresses spill over her shoulders. "On the morrow I teach you how to execute the *botta dritta,* eh?"

"Assuming you have the ballocks to step back onto the field of battle," quipped the student known as Shannon. The class wit, she was always quick to unsheathe a sharp tongue. Sometimes too quick. Her penchant for challenging authority had recently provoked a disciplinary warning. A second might result in expulsion.

"Nonnie," cautioned Siena, hoping to keep her roommate out of trouble.

"Like my sword, my *testicolos* are made of steel, *Signorina* Shannon." The Italian waggled a brow, his slitted eyes still aimed at Siena. "Indeed, all my equipment is honed to a fighting edge. As the lovely *Volpina* would quickly discover if only she would accept my offer of more intimate instruction in the nuances of hand-to-hand combat."

Ignoring his lascivious looks, Siena handed her gear to a first-year student and gathered up her books. "Come, Shannon, we had better hurry and change, else we will be late for our next class."

Her friend, however, could not resist a parting retort. "Indeed, *signor*? I heard your equipment was in danger of growing dull with disuse." Exaggerating a flourish, she tossed *Il Lupino* a scrap of chamois. "But if it needs a bit of polishing, you will have to do it for yourself."

With his laughter ringing in their ears, the two of them cut across the fencing yard to the graveled garden path.

Siena slanted a sidelong glance at her friend as they rounded the tall privet hedge. Shannon had the same willowy height, the same loping stride—and the same stubborn set of the chin. Indeed, they might have been taken for twins, save that her friend's hair was the color of autumn wheat and cut several inches shorter.

"You are lucky. Da Rimini was in one of his better humors today," she said. "But he's unpredictable. The next time you try to pick a fight with him, it may not go so well."

Shannon shrugged off the advice. "The lecherous old goat. His nickname ought to be the Snake instead of the Wolf. Only yesterday he tried to slide his hand up my skirts as I was cleaning my pistol in the armory." She made a face. "Why the headmistress hasn't given him the boot ages ago is still a mystery to me."

"Because despite his alley cat manners and advancing age, he is extremely good at what he does," answered Siena. "I doubt there is a more skilled fencing master in all of England."

"As long as he keeps his sword to himself—"

"Rumor has it he was forced to flee Milano over some incident involving a blade." The student known as Sofia, who shared their spartan dormitory quarters, caught up with them in time to hear the last exchange. Falling in step beside Shannon, she added a wink. "As well as a contessa and a cardinal. And for Italians to express outrage, it must have been shockingly scandalous."

"It isn't as if this is an ordinary institution of higher education. Nobody here at the Academy—including ourselves—is remotely respectable." Siena flashed a sardonic smile. All of them were orphans who had been left to fend for themselves in the slums of London. Alone and homeless, they had quickly learned the cardinal rule of the rookeries—only the strongest survived. Not that she cared to recall those early days, save to remind herself that she was tough enough to stand up to any challenge.

She darted another glance at her companions. The three of them were more like sisters than school friends. Shared adversity was, perhaps, a stronger bond than blood.

Unperturbed by the oblique reminder of their desperate past, Shannon laughed. "You have a point. How many schools for females include a Negro boxer, a convicted cardsharp, and a former courtesan to King Carlos of Spain among its instructors?"

"You neglected to mention the Indian fakir," said Sofia.

"*Fakir?*"

"An expert in disciplining both the body and mind. He must be bloody good at it, too, for he arrived this morning in a spitting sleet, wearing naught but a saffron loincloth and two bloodred rubies in his earlobes."

"We are already doing an hour of yoga a day." Spinning to a halt, Shannon bent over and touched her forehead to her toes. "Lud, what will Mrs. Merlin think of next?"

"Since you asked, a Turkish belly dancer is coming next term to teach a special class in the art of seduction." Siena set aside her momentary melancholy and forced herself to join in the banter. She was one of the lucky ones, she reminded herself. If Lord Lynsley had not witnessed her beating off three boys twice her size to protect the gold watch she had just stolen, she would likely still be eking out an existence as a thief. Or perhaps a whore.

Sofia shimmied her hips. "I don't mind surrendering my virtue in the name of England, just as long as they don't expect me to bed the Prince Regent. I draw the line at sleeping with a man who wears a corset."

"There are no lines, Sofia. Not here, not in our world." Siena turned abruptly and resumed walking toward the quadrangle of Georgian brick buildings that housed the classrooms and dormitories. "We'll do whatever they ask of us, whether it be slitting a man's throat or seducing the Prince of Darkness."

Pressing the tips of his well-tended fingers together, the Marquess of Lynsley looked out the window of his ministry office. A freezing rain pelted against the glass, and the sudden storm, which had blown in out of nowhere, showed little sign of relenting. Clouds hung heavy over the spires of Westminster, the swirling mists turning more leaden by the moment.

Darker still was the news staring him in the face. He lowered his gaze back to the dispatch on his desk. "The devil take it," he muttered, smoothing at the creases in the travel-worn paper. But nothing could take the edge off his anxiety.

"I would gladly return it to Lucifer if I could, sir." Major Chertwell essayed a grim smile. As the officer in charge of coordinating military intelligence with their Russian allies, he had long since learned that a sense of humor, however black, was an essential weapon for survival. "But the damn fellow seems to have gone to ground, leaving us with this hellish problem."

"Hellish indeed." Lynsley rose. He crossed the carpet and pressed his palm to the mullioned glass. A chill seeped through his skin, and despite the layers of tailored finery, he couldn't repress a shudder. "A traitor? One of our own?"

"The evidence seems incontrovertible, my lord. Only someone who moves within the highest circle of Society would have access to such information."

"Tell me again what you know."

"Our agent in Berlin has penetrated Napoleon's Eastern spy network. For nearly a year, he has been aware that highly sensitive information was coming out of the very heart of London. Sometimes it was actual government documents, sometimes a summary of troop movements, or secret meetings with England's allies. At first it was only a trickle; then the flow became truly alarming. But it wasn't until recently that he discovered how the information was being smuggled out of the country." Chertwell withdrew a small leather-bound book from his pocket and placed it beside the letter. "That our agent discovered the document hidden in here further confirms our suspicions." He ran a thumb over the gilt spine. "The volume is a rare early edition of Milton's *Paradise Lost*. My source assures me that there are but a handful of gentlemen here in Town who have the means and opportunity to lay hands on such a treasure."

"Your argument appears compelling." Lynsley let out his breath in a long sigh. "So our enemy is likely rich and titled?"

Chertwell covered the incriminating paper with a note of his own. "I have made a list of the possibilities, sir."

After a last glance at the mizzled shadows, the marquess returned to read over the names. "Bloody hell." He spent another few moments contemplating the list. "You realize the implications of investigating the private affairs of these men?"

The major looked equally grave. "Yes, sir. You have made it clear that this is an extremely delicate situation."

"And extremely dangerous. The dilemma is, we are damned if we do and damned if we don't," mused Lynsley as he perched a hip on the corner of his desk.

At first glance, he would not stand out in a crowd. Over the years he had learned a number of subtle mannerisms to appear shorter and slighter than his true height. As for his features, they were well cut, but a self-deprecating smile softened their patrician edge. His hair, just beginning to turn silver at the temples, was neither long nor short, and its mouse brown hue was echoed in the somber earth tones of his clothing. Many people thought him a bland, rather boring bureaucrat. A fact that suited him perfectly.

His official title—Minister to the Secretary of State for War—was a deliberately vague cover for his true responsibilities. Charged with countering espionage and intrigue, he dealt with the most dangerous and diabolical threats to England's sovereignty. And while he preferred to work with only a small group of trusted associates, events had unfolded in such a way that he had no choice but to take the major into his confidences.

Lynsley reluctantly went on with his explanation. "If word slips out that we have allowed such treason to take place under our nose, the resulting scandal could topple the government."

"Yes, sir. It will have to be handled with utmost discretion. Even then, it will take a miracle to pull it off without setting off a display of pyrotechnics in Parliament that would put Vauxhall to blush."

"A miracle." Lynsley drummed an urgent tattoo upon the leather blotter, as if summoning spirits from the netherworld.

"A miracle." The major's echo had an even more doleful ring. "Or a hero from Arthurian legend."

"Merlin," whispered the marquess.

Chertwell gave a halfhearted laugh. "Abracadabra. The heart of Galahad. The steel of Excalibur."

A moment later, the marquess rang for his secretary. "Collins, have my carriage brought around immediately." Tucking the list of suspects into his waistcoat, he turned for the door. "Don't just stand there, Chertwell. We haven't any time to lose."

The major cleared his throat. "W—where are we going, sir?"

For the first time that afternoon Lynsley actually smiled. "To take tea with Mrs. Merlin."

"Who the devil—"

"A little old lady who works magic."

"Damnation, this door latch still sticks like the devil."

"Language, girls! Language!" Dressed in dull shades of bark and brown, Miss Clemens, their house prefect, would have been indistinguishable from the woodwork if not for her stentorian shout. "No cursing! You know the rules. Inside these walls you will behave as refined young ladies. Now hurry along—gracefully, mind you, gracefully—and change, or you will be late for Mrs. Twining's lecture on ballroom etiquette."

Siena smiled, for in spite of the spinster's drab appearance, she was not really such a stick in the mud. Many a midnight raid on the kitchens had gone unpunished, and on occasion, the spoils of victory had been washed down with a bottle of Clemmie's excellent champagne.

"Refined my arse," muttered Shannon, much to the amusement of the others. "It would take a sledgehammer and chisel to sculpt me into any semblance of a drawing-room miss."

"Appearance is not the problem." Sofia regarded her friend's Valkyrean figure and shook her head. "Lud, I'd kill to have your bosom. It's a question of attitude. If you would put your mind to it—"

"Need I remind you again?" warned Miss Clemens. "One more infraction for tardiness, and the three of you will be mucking out the stables for a month."

"Hell, I would rather concentrate on riding and rapiers than on the proper way to curtsy to a duke," grumbled Shannon as the three of them took the stairs two at a time and raced to their room.

"As would I." Siena slipped out of her shirt and breeches. "But to be effective, we must be well schooled in the more subtle forms of warfare."

"Easy for you to say," shot back Shannon. "You seem to have a natural talent in the classroom as well as on the fencing field." She made a face. "Lud, you even excel in art history."

"I find the subject interesting, don't you?"

Shannon shook her head. "Not unless the paintings portray some of the more esoteric uniforms or weaponry of the period."

"La, Nonnie is right, Siena. You should have been to the manor born," teased Sofia. "A fine lady, with nothing better to do all day than dabble in watercolors and collect priceless paintings."

"Ha—in another moment you'll be collecting my boot

up your backside," retorted Siena. She turned quickly, using a laugh to mask the fact that the barb had struck a sensitive nerve. As she reached for her chemise, she caught a glimpse of her own reflection in the looking glass. Cheekbones sharp as sabers, lashes dark as gunpowder, gaze guarded as the Crown Jewels. Fighting had become second nature. And she was good at it.

But Shannon was right—a number of subjects seemed to come naturally to her, especially art. She liked the way it challenged her to think and to see things from a different perspective. Was it a weakness to appreciate such things? At times she wondered. But she was not about to admit it aloud. A Merlin was not meant to let down her defenses, not even for a moment.

A shadow fell across her face. Storm clouds were scudding in from the sea, obscuring the sun, and already the echo of thunder rumbled through the school courtyards. *Light and dark.* At times, she couldn't help recalling odd flashes of her life before the Academy. An old prostitute had once given her a brightly colored penny print. Oh, how she had guarded that scrap of paper.

Drawing on her yoga training, Siena took a deep breath and shrugged off such strange musings. After all, Da Rimini had drummed into her that thinking too much could be dangerous . . .

"For pity's sake, Siena, stop woolgathering," chided Sofia. "Unless you wish for us to be shoveling manure for the next few weeks."

Her friends were already dressed and sorting through their hair ribbons for the finishing touches to their toilette.

"And you know how *La Grande Dame* dislikes getting her hands dirty," drawled Shannon as she mimicked a ballroom twirl.

"*Merde!*" A crumpled kidskin glove flew across the room. "Just because I like silks as much as saddles doesn't mean I can't whip you in a match of riding skills. Just name your stakes."

Shannon speared the fuchsia missile with a hairpin and tossed it back. "Ha—a challenge? What sort of race do you have in mind?"

"Stubble the horseplay." Siena grabbed for her indigo gown. "Has anyone seen my India shawl, or has it wound its way back to Bombay?"

Her friends were too sharp to miss the slight edge to her voice. They exchanged puzzled looks.

"Is something wrong?" asked Sofia as she pulled the missing item from beneath a pair of muddied riding boots. "You seem in a strange mood."

Shannon nodded. "If I had just flattened *Il Lupino*, I'd be crowing from atop the highest chimney pot."

"I fear . . ." Her friends would likely laugh to hear what she had been thinking. "I fear I can't explain it."

"Fear?" scoffed Shannon. "Ha, you are the most fearless of us all."

Sofia said nothing but fixed her with a searching stare.

"Forget it," she muttered, suddenly feeling foolish for even hinting there might be a chink in her armor. The training of the Academy only echoed the lessons of the alleyways—never show any vulnerability.

The tread of Miss Clement's half boots suddenly interrupted the exchange. Siena swore under her breath, sure that a stern scolding was in order, along with the threatened detention.

But the prefect appeared oddly distracted. She shooed Sofia and Shannon out of the room with a vague wave. "Be off, you two. As for Siena . . ." A hesitation hung in the air. "You need not hurry. Mrs. Merlin has excused you from your next class. She wishes to see you in her office as soon as you have changed into your new emerald green ball gown. Withers will be here in a moment to dress your hair."

Siena turned, her eyes narrowing at the news. "Why?"

Miss Clemens lifted her bony shoulders. "I am not privy to that information. But I expect you will find out soon enough."

Was it her imagination, or did the words indicate that the time had come?

"York says she spotted a fancy carriage pulling up to Mrs. Merlin's private entrance not ten minutes ago," added the prefect. "Two gentlemen got out."

Dagger points danced down her spine. Her palms began to tingle. *Fear.* The friendly banter echoed in her ears. Her only real fear was that the school directors might decide she wasn't sharp enough for a real mission. The gentleman with the ice blue eyes would, as was his wont, be kindly but firm. Only the very best measured up to the Academy's stringent standards for the Master Class. Those who did not make the grade were directed into less demanding programs, ones that trained them for other useful duties. Innkeepers, lady's maids . . .

Siena's hands clenched, then her chin rose. *A challenge?* She would rise to the occasion and prove herself. She *was* one of Merlin's Maidens.

And Merlins were meant to fly.

Chapter Two

*S*treet orphans!" Chertwell choked on his tea.

"Kindly remember you are sworn to silence." Lynsley helped himself to another biscuit.

The major uttered an oath.

"Need I also remind you that a lady is present?"

Chertwell's face turned nearly as red as his regimentals. "Your pardon, madam," he said stiffly. "I meant no offense to you or your pupils, but I feel duty-bound to voice an objection to this . . . joke?"

His hopeful look was snuffed out by the headmistress's brisk reply. "Lord Lynsley is quite serious. As am I." Mrs. Merlin was a frail, feather-thin widow with a cap of dove grey curls framing her narrow face. Age had softened her features and blunted the poke of her prominent nose, but behind the oval spectacles, her silvery eyes gleamed with a hawkish intensity. "Won't you try a strawberry tart, young man? They are quite delicious."

"I don't want a damn tart! I want an explanation!" Sputtering, the major shot an accusing look at Lynsley.

"England is in imminent peril while we are sitting here having a tea party!"

"Dear me, Thomas, is the major subject to megrims?" Mrs. Merlin darted a look at Lynsley. "Shall I fetch a vial of vinaigrette?"

Chertwell's jaw dropped a touch, then snapped shut. His silence did not preclude a pronounced scowl.

"Excellent. I see we may forgo the hartshorn and apply instead a healthy dose of reason to the problem." Moving with a ruthless efficiency that belied the sweet smile, Mrs. Merlin set aside her teacup and snapped open a document case. A quick rap squared the sheaf of papers within. "But before we get down to business, perhaps you ought to finish your explanation."

"Thank you, Charlotte. As always, a meeting with you is an educational experience." Lynsley settled back against sofa pillows. The lines deepened at the corners of his eyes, turning his gaze more shadowed. "As I was saying, Chertwell, the students of Mrs. Merlin's Academy for Select Young Ladies are hand-picked from the legion of orphans who roam the stews of London. There are, I regret to say, a great many to choose from." He stared into his tea. "I select all of them myself. I look for signs of courage and cleverness. And looks. Beauty can be a weapon in itself."

"Let me get this straight." Through gritted teeth, the major managed a mutter. "You take in a ragtag rabble of female urchins and mold them into a special fighting force?"

The marquess allowed a faint smile. "England's ultimate secret weapon."

"God save the King." A stern look from the school's

headmistress caused Chertwell to swallow any further sarcasm.

Lynsley continued as if uninterrupted. "I convinced the government to give us this old estate, which had been used as cavalry pastures. I pay the operating expenses out of my own pocket, and Mrs. Merlin oversees all the day-to-day duties. The idea was inspired by a book I read on Hasan-I-Sabah, a Muslim caliph who raised a secret society of warriors at his mountain citadels. His men were known for their deadly skills and fanatic loyalty. The caliph used them only in times of dire danger to his rule. And legend has it they never failed on a mission. The very name *Hashishim*—or Assassins—was enough to strike terror in the heart of the Master's enemy."

"Assassins?" Chertwell blinked. "Surely you don't mean to imply that these girls . . ."

"Are trained to kill." Mrs. Merlin brushed a bit of powdered sugar from her lip. "But of course."

"Merlin's Maidens receive expert instruction in a number of disciplines," explained Lynsley. "Use of weapons is only part of the curriculum. They also are taught all the social graces—proper speech, proper manners, polished skills at music, art, and dancing—so that, if need be, they may move in the highest circles of Society."

"Indeed, our girls follow a course of study much the same as that at any other school for highborn young ladies of the *ton*," added Mrs. Merlin. Surrounded by cheery chintz florals and delicate Sèvres china, the elderly lady looked the very picture of prim propriety. Save for the tip of the poniard that slipped from her cuff as she consulted one of the documents. "The emphasis is on violence as a last resort."

"It sounds . . ." The major shifted his seat on the sofa.

"I would say 'absurd,' but I fear you would fillet my liver with that blade."

Mrs. Merlin smoothed the sprigged muslin over the razored steel. "I assure you, Major, our students are carefully screened, and once they are here, they are subject to rigorous training and constant testing. Those who fail to make the grade are sent off to be taught a more suitable profession." As she pushed her spectacles back to the bridge of her nose, a gleam of candlelight winked off the lenses. Under less serious circumstances, it might have been seen as a twinkle. "You see, Major, unlike in the military, wealth or rank cannot buy you a place in our Academy. Merlin's Maidens win their badge of honor by merit alone."

Chertwell thought for a moment. "Why girls?"

"An astute question." Lynsley gazed up at the painting above the mantel, a depiction of Boudicca, the ancient British Warrior Queen, in full regalia. "Because females have far more flexibility when it comes down to devising strategy and tactics. They can learn to master the martial arts as well as any man, whereas men cannot perform certain feminine disciplines. They will always find certain doors closed to them."

"Clever," conceded the major. "I can see where sex can indeed be a more effective weapon than steel." He tapped at his chin. "However, abstract theory is one thing, and practical application is quite another. Have you ever employed these Hellion Heroes in an actual mission?"

"Arthur Wellesley would not be alive today if one of the leaders of the Mahratta uprising in India had not suffered an untimely demise during a tiger hunt—an arrow to the throat, I believe . . ." Lynsley proceeded to rattle off several other names and places.

"God save the King." This time the major's murmur held a note of awe rather than sarcasm.

Mrs. Merlin moved the tea tray to one of the *chinoise* side tables. "Having reviewed your requirements, I have selected the student I think is most qualified for the job."

"Who?"

"Siena."

He steepled his fingers and appeared to be contemplating his watch chain. Several moments passed before he spoke. "An interesting choice."

"The nature of the assignment is extraordinarily complex," replied the headmistress. "The agent we choose will require a depth of character to match up against the gentlemen you wish to have investigated."

"Indeed. I agree that she is one of our best students." Lynsley twisted at one of the fobs. "Yet I confess there are parts of her that remain a mystery to me."

"Beneath the steel, there is a sensitive side of her nature—which only adds to her allure. And not only is she skilled in all forms of weaponry, but her knowledge of art will prove useful in this case." Mrs. Merlin held his gaze. "I feel confident in the choice. But no doubt the two of you will wish to conduct your own interview. Shall we call her in?"

The slide of silk was smooth, sensuous against her skin as she rose from the straight-backed chair. Siena straightened the ruched bodice, her fingers lingering on the row of seed pearls that decorated the plunging décolletage. A handful would have fed her for a year in St. Giles. But here they were insignificant baubles, tiny specks on a sea of gold-threaded emerald splendor. The gown was a sinfully expensive extravagance, cut snugly in the bosom and hips, with waves of ivory lace frothing down to the gold-fringed hem.

It was more fitting for a fairy tale princess than a penniless urchin, a fact that Siena had been quick to point out. But Mrs. Merlin had simply flashed her cat-in-the-cream-pot smile as she added the expense to the school accountings. That appearances could be deceiving was an integral lesson to learn, she had counseled.

Siena's lips quirked. The elderly headmistress was living proof of the old adage—she could still blast a hole through a guinea at thirty paces, though she needed her spectacles to do so.

As her own gaze took in the familiar details of the small waiting room, Siena couldn't help recalling her first meeting with Mrs. Merlin. She had been dressed in rags, rather than riches, and her skinny little limbs had been covered with mud and bruises. Frightened out of her wits by the strange new surroundings, she had responded to the headmistress's first gentle words with a gutter curse.

Instead of a slap or a punch, she had been offered a strawberry tart and tea. It was her first taste of true kindness. And true patience. Gaining the trust of a street-savvy urchin was no easy task. Siena had found it hard to believe that a real bed, clean clothes, and regular meals were anything other than cruel tricks, designed to soften her up for the kill.

Old habits died hard. Even now, she knew a small part of her remained wary, watchful.

"They are ready for you," whispered the secretary.

Discipline. Duty. Desire.

Marshaling her wayward thoughts, Siena gathered her skirts and glided gracefully through the doorway.

"How delightful that you could join us, my dear." Ever

the gracious hostess, Mrs. Merlin indicated her guests. "You are, I believe, acquainted with Lord Lynsley."

Siena performed a perfect curtsy and allowed the gentleman to lift her hand to his lips. "It is a great pleasure to see you again, my lord."

"The pleasure is mine, Miss Siena. I trust your studies are going well."

"Very well, thank you." Dropping her gaze in maidenly modesty, she answered with the requisite small talk. Yet beneath the flutter of her lashes, she remained alert. This was, she knew, a test of her skills. A test she was determined not to fail. "The weather, however, has been quite wretched of late, has it not?"

After exchanging a few more pleasantries on the subject, the marquess indicated his companion. "Allow me to introduce Major Chertwell, who is on leave from his posting in Prussia."

The officer was staring at her with an expression of frozen horror. Like a mouse facing a cobra, she thought. She must charm him into thinking she would not bite.

A melting look. An arch of admiration. A caress of her fan. The famed Spanish courtesan known as *La Paloma* had taught the Academy students any number of tricks for putting a gentleman at ease. "That sounds frightfully important, sir," said Siena. "Are you attached to the diplomatic corps or the army?" Not a trace of the guttersnipe was evident in her cultured tone. She could converse in French, if need be, or fall back into the rough patter of the stews.

"Er . . . neither."

"Major Chertwell serves as a liaison between the two," murmured Lynsley.

Feigning flattery was the first order of drawing-room

decorum. Followed by a subtle flirtation. Siena gave an inward sigh. She did not envy the highborn daughters of the *ton*. It took a great deal of effort to sound so egregiously silly.

And training.

Her efforts were quickly rewarded—as *La Paloma* had promised, men were very predictable. Encouraged by several more questions and sultry smiles, Chertwell relaxed enough to carry on a coherent conversation.

Mrs. Merlin allowed the interlude to go on for some minutes before suggesting some music. "I know Lord Lynsley is quite fond of the pianoforte. I am sure he would be pleased to hear you play."

Siena seated herself at the instrument. "Have you a favorite piece, my lord?"

"I leave it to you to choose."

She thought for a moment. *Ebony and ivory.* Light and dark. She must coax them into perfect harmony. Placing her fingers upon the keys, she began a difficult Mozart sonata. The notes flowed softly at first, then crested to a skilled crescendo. Without missing a beat, she played through the entire score. It was, she knew, a flawless performance.

"Bravo." The marquess's soft clap sent a trilling shiver to the tips of her fingers.

So close and yet so far. Had she been convincing? She had seen the shadow of doubt in Lord Lynsley's eyes as she entered the room. He had the most penetrating gaze she had ever encountered, like pale blue slivers of ice. Sometimes she felt he saw her more clearly than she saw herself.

Lynsley turned to his companion and arched a brow.

"Do you wish to ask Miss Siena about her other accomplishments? Dancing? Whist?"

"Er, no. She appears a paragon of propriety in the drawing room."

"In that case, run along and change into less formal attire, Siena." As her student left the room, Mrs. Merlin added, "I have asked Da Rimini to meet us in the armory. A short exhibition of fencing and shooting should serve to answer any further questions."

A half hour later, a rather white-faced Chertwell pressed a handkerchief to his perspiring brow.

"Convinced?"

"Er, yes. I shall take your word that the young lady can handle a horse with equal expertise."

Lynsley repressed a grin. "She rides like a bat flying out of hell."

"Then let us pray she can catch up to the devil in Town—"

"The Merlins will chase Lucifer to Cathay and back, if that is what is asked of us." Siena, still clad in buckskins and boots, strode into the study. Perching a hip on the corner of the headmistress's desk, she peeled off her fencing gauntlet and dropped it onto the polished oak. "Or, if you prefer, into the heart of the unknown."

"London is far enough," replied Lynsley dryly.

She decided to dare a direct challenge. "So—do I get the assignment?"

The silence seemed to stretch on forever.

"Here are your orders." Lynsley slowly withdrew an oilskin packet from his pocket. It was sealed with a black wafer bearing the sign of a soaring hawk. "You are to leave immediately and proceed to the address noted on the first page. You will find clothing, money, and several trustworthy servants waiting for you. From there . . ."

He drew a breath. "Most of the details are spelled out, and I will fill you in on the rest as I walk you out to the stables. A messenger will visit within a day or two to supply you with complete dossiers on the suspects. After that, you understand that . . ."

"That neither you nor the government can acknowledge any connection between us."

"Precisely, Siena. You will be entirely on your own."

"I know the rules, sir."

"I have had your things packed as we speak," said Mrs. Merlin. "The saddlebags are waiting outside the door, along with your weapons."

A spasm of surprise crossed Siena's face. "I—I had thought I might make a quick return to my room, to take leave of my friends."

"It's best to be off without delay." The headmistress gave her arm a gentle pat. "I shall pass on your farewell."

She quickly smoothed the disappointment from her features. It would not do to fall flat on her face in the first minute of the assignment. "Yes. Of course."

"Good luck." Chertwell hesitated before inclining a small bow. "And Godspeed."

"We are trained to depend on our own skills, sir, rather than serendipitous fortune," she replied with a show of bravado. "But it does not hurt that Luck is a Lady."

To herself she added a more solemn vow. *I will prove to Lord Lynsley that I have earned my wings.*

The moon, a shivering sliver of pale crescent light, ducked in and out of scudding clouds.

Julian Henning, the Earl of Kirtland, cocked a brow

at the stormy skies. Even the heavens have something to hide, he thought with a self-mocking shrug. Drawing to a halt, he peered into the gloom ahead. A windswept rain lashed at the trees, the swirling gusts tugging at his caped cloak and wide-brimmed hat.

It was a hellish night to be out—a sentiment echoed by his stallion's impatient whinny.

"Sorry, Hades. I take it you would prefer a dry stall and a bucket of oats." He, too, ought to be lounging before a roaring fire, a book of fine poetry in one hand, a glass of aged brandy within easy reach. But he had grown moody, restless with the creature comforts of Henning Hall, his ancestral manor house. Tomorrow at first light he would be traveling to his town house in London, and despite the foul weather he had felt a sudden need to savor the space and solitude of his estate lands. Town life was crowded, confining.

Or perhaps it was some darker inner urge that had driven him outdoors. A black humor was an all too familiar companion these days.

"We'll ride on to the bridge, then turn back." Wrapping the reins around a sodden fist, the earl urged his mount forward. The thud of hooves was muffled by the wet earth. Fog blurred the gorse and thorns into spiky shadows, their swaying forms faintly threatening in the haze.

The path narrowed as it threaded through a copse of oaks. As the last flicker of stars was swallowed in the mists, Kirtland was forced to rely on memory rather than sight to make his way among the trees.

"Bloody hell." A branch slapped at his cheek. "Only a madman would be out in this weather," he muttered. A madman or a desperate man. *Which was he?* Adding a low oath, the earl cut through the last leafy tangle and broke onto open ground.

He was neither, he assured himself. An outcast, perhaps. But he didn't give a damn for the opinion of Society. In the drawing rooms of London, rumor and innuendo swirled around his name, dark and muddled as this storm-tossed night. Obscuring the true shape of things.

A mizzle of moonlight filtered through the clouds, catching the sardonic curl of his smile. Money smoothed the rough edges. As did an august title. So, despite the whispers, there were few who dared give him a direct cut. It was his own choice to avoid the frivolous spin of the ballrooms and—

The crack was as loud as cannon fire.

"Damn." Kirtland pulled back on the reins, steadying his stallion's spooked steps. Up ahead, the ghostly outline of the bridge came into view, the remains of the snapped timber jutting up from the roiling currents. The crossing was often used as a shortcut to the London road, but now it was a treacherous trap—anyone approaching from the other side would not see the danger.

At first light, he would have his bailiff ride out to rope off the area and make the repairs.

As he turned for home, the earl caught sight of a movement on the opposite bank. Surely no one else was driven by demons to be out on a night like this. He looked again, thinking perhaps he had only imagined the black blur. But an instant later, a horse and rider came out of the mists at full gallop.

"Beware!" shouted Kirtland as they hit the first planks. "The bridge is about to collapse!"

Even as he cried out, he knew it was too late. The remaining piling sagged, then split with a shuddering snap.

The earl spurred forward to the water's edge, on the off chance the stranger survived the plunge. The odds were heavily against it, but he could at least stand ready to help him escape from the surging waters.

But to his amazement, the rider managed to control the skidding stallion, straighten its head, and urge the lathered beast into an arching leap. Hooves flying, cloak flapping, they hung for a moment in midair, a dark-winged shape silhouetted against the mist. Then suddenly they were on solid ground, fighting for balance on the steep bank.

Bloody hell. Kirtland could scarcely believe his eyes. An experienced cavalry officer, he was well aware that only a horseman of iron strength and nerve could have pulled off such a feat—

Just then, a length of the splintered timber snagged the stranger's boot, threatening to tumble horse and rider onto the rocks below. The earl reacted in a flash. Swooping dangerously close to the river's edge, he kicked the shard free. "Give me your hand!" he called, hoping to be heard above the roar of the water.

The stranger grabbed hold of Kirtland's outstretched arm, and the earl angled his stallion for higher ground. Linked together by their riders, the two horses scrabbled to firmer footing.

Aware of his own pounding heart, Kirtland ventured a sidelong glance at his companion. The oilskin hat was tilted askew, and the woolen muffler had come half-undone, but the fine-boned features betrayed nary a twitch of fear. Indeed, unless he was much mistaken, it was annoyance that blazed in the narrowed gaze.

"Let go of me!"

There was no mistaking the voice. The rider was not a man but a boy—and a downy one at that.

"Now hold on a moment, lad." Irked at the curt command, he held fast as their horses slowed to an easy trot. "Common courtesy calls for a more civil remark than that."

"To hell with courtesy. I'm in a hurry."

"A date with the devil?" he shot back. "If I hadn't happened along, you would have been crossing the River Styx rather than the River Thames—"

As the clouds parted for a moment, the brief flicker of light caught the boy full in the face. *He* was a *she*.

"I'll be damned."

The hand gripping his gave a sudden wrenching twist that nearly spilled him to the ground. Kirtland, however, knew a few tricks of his own from the brutal battlefields of Portugal. Kicking free of one stirrup, he let himself drop low, then suddenly straightened his other leg, catching the young lady off guard.

The momentum of his move yanked her from her own mount. As she fell awkwardly across her saddle onto his, the earl caught a glimpse of the brace of pistols and a Hussar's saber hanging from her horse. "What is a young lady doing out at this hour, armed to the teeth with cavalry equipment?"

Her answer was a fist aimed at his jaw. He jerked back in the nick of time. The blow glanced off his shoulder. She was now facing him, fighting for balance.

"Damnation! That is rough thanks for having saved your wretched neck." Her muffler had fallen away, and, in truth, it looked to be a rather lovely neck, smooth and creamy as alabaster.

"Consider yourself fortunate that I do not break your arm." She twisted, trying to break his grip, and her spurs grazed his stallion's flanks. Hooves kicked at the ground, setting up a swirl of fallen leaves.

"Why, you hellion."

His shout froze her for an instant, giving him just enough time to pin her arms behind her back. She had lost her hat in the first throes of the struggle, but a black silk scarf, tied in pirate fashion, still covered her hair and brow. Its midnight hue accentuated the golden glare of her eyes. She was as mad as a wet cat.

A panther, sleek and sinuous in its fury.

The earl trapped her against his chest. Still, it took all of his considerable strength to keep her from breaking his grip. "You owe me more than a slap, my little spitfire." His stallion whinnied and reared, rocking them back in the saddle. He could feel the curves of her breasts and the press of her buckskinned bottom as he pulled her astride his thighs. A strange lick of heat flared around the edges of his anger. She was all leg and lithe muscle. So unlike any female he had ever encountered before. Intrigued, he drew her closer.

"Son of a bitch—"

Kirtland drew in a sharp breath, then laughed softly. "Actually, my mother *was* a whore. But she was clever enough to coax my father into marriage."

She didn't blink. "Bastard or not, let me go." Freeing an arm, she let fly with an elbow, driving the air from his lungs.

His temper, already frayed, was now perilously close to snapping. He had risked life and limb, and by God, he was going to wring a civil thanks from the hellion. As well as an explanation for this mad escapade.

He recaptured her arm and hardened his grip. "Not so fast."

Biting back a grunt of pain, she countered with a twist that nearly cracked the bones of her wrist.

Feeling somewhat ashamed of using brute force on a female, however strong, Kirtland drew her closer, the stubbling of his whiskered jaw scraping against her cheek. "*Pax*. I mean you no harm." Fisting at damp linen and wet wool, he molded her curves to his chest. Through the layers of fabric he felt the thud of her heart pounding against his pulse.

She shivered, then drew back, her eyes unreadable in the squalling rain. "A gentleman of honor?" Her words were half-mocking.

"You have nothing to fear from me."

"Trust me, I don't fear any man."

For an instant, they both were very still, as if seized by some strange alchemy. Kirtland thought he detected a glimmer of his own grudging admiration reflected in her gaze. *Strength against strength*. Neither yielding an inch.

"Nor devils nor dragons, I imagine."

Her mouth twitched in amusement. "However, I suppose you do deserve a thanks for your heroics."

"You are welcome." Without quite knowing why, he tilted her chin and kissed her. Her lips were soft, lush, the pliant curves so at odds with the rest of her body. She tasted of jasmine and salt. Of wild honey. Of fiery desire . . .

She, too, appeared gripped by the same sensuous spell that held him in thrall. A slave to some mysterious force. Her hands, now free, slid toward his throat, but only to curl in the tangle of his rain-soaked locks.

Groaning, he deepened his embrace.

"Who the devil are you?" he rasped when finally he lifted his mouth from hers.

The breath of air broke the enchantment.

"No one you will ever see again."

Before he could respond, she twisted free. Suddenly all was a blur, with her body appearing to bend at an impossible angle as she arced into a back flip and slid down off his stallion's rump. He whipped around just in time to see her vault onto her own horse and gallop off.

A druid? A wood nymph? A figment of his own benighted thoughts?

Kirtland rubbed at his eyes, uncertain of anything save for the ethereal sweetness lingering on his lips. He continued staring into the mist until the shadowy tendrils had long since ceased to swirl. Then, shaking off the numbing chill, the earl turned for Henning Hall.

Perhaps it was best he was leaving the country for the city at first light. Isolation was definitely having an unnerving effect on his state of mind.

Chapter Three

Red brick, green door.

Siena reined in her mount. *And a brass knocker in the shape of a hawk's head.* The street was deserted, but she kept her face and weapons well under wraps as she rode around to the mews.

A soft rap, and a whispered word.

The door slid open. "You have made good time, given the storm." A hand took hold of the bridle and drew the stallion into the darkness. Behind her, an iron bar dropped back into its brackets. "You encountered no problems on the journey?"

"None to speak of." Siena swung down from the saddle.

"I am Oban. I'll be handling the duties of groom and footman." A flint struck steel, and in the first spark of light, she caught a glimpse of his profile, hard and jagged as the Scottish accent that burred his speech. The misshapen nose and scarred lips gave him the look of a man who had experienced his fair share of punches. So, too, did the fist holding the lantern. It was as huge as a ham hock, and the knuckles gave a menacing crack as they tightened on the handle. "I'll take you up to meet Rose. She will see to your personal needs."

Lord Lynsley was serious about security, thought Siena as she followed the hulking silhouette to a side stall.

"This way." Oban kicked away the straw to reveal a trapdoor. "There are several other hidden passageways out of the house. I'll show them to you first thing in the morning, along with a map of the quickest escape routes from the neighborhood."

He said nothing more, save to point out the mechanics of the latches and locks as they passed through the narrow tunnel into the town house cellar. Siena welcomed his reticence. She was in no mood to answer any further questions about her midnight journey.

Rose proved to be as quietly efficient as her compatriot. A plain, middle-aged woman with sharp features and a brusque step, she wasted no time in pleasantries. "A tour of the residence can wait until morning. No doubt you are anxious for a few hours of sleep," she said as she took Siena's sodden cloak and hung it by the cellar stairs. "Follow me."

As they passed through the paneled corridor, Siena glimpsed several of the rooms. They were small, but opulently furnished in a mix of plush velvets and jacquards. Garnet and ruby were the dominant colors, accented with a profusion of gilded decorations that reflected the current fad for all things Egyptian.

Accustomed to the spartan simplicity of the Academy, Siena found it a bit overwhelming. But as she rubbed at her eyes, she reminded herself that from now on, everything about her must be designed to draw notice.

Rose led the way up a curved staircase of polished mahogany to the third floor. Crossing the carpeted landing, she opened the far door.

A fire had taken the chill out of the bedchamber, the pillows were plumped upon the carved tester bed, and a night rail—a lacy confection befitting her new persona—lay neatly folded atop the turned-down silk sheets.

"A bath, my lady?" Wisps of steam, redolent with the lush perfume of jasmine and clove, were already rising from a tub set by the Oriental screen.

Siena nodded, suddenly aware that her fingers could scarcely keep a grip on her scabbard. But her shivering was not all on account of the wet clothing clinging to her body or the bone-deep fatigue. The stranger's touch still lingered on her cheeks, her lips . . .

"And a glass of brandy, if you please."

It took only a few minutes for the spirits and the last buckets of hot water to arrive. She waited until she was alone to strip off her sodden garments and sink into the scented suds. Lud, the liquid heat felt delicious, flowing over and inside her. But it also stirred a more wicked warmth.

A rain-lashed gentleman with eyes as dark as sin. And yet, enveloped in his arms, she had experienced a strange sense of comfort. For an instant, she had embraced his strength, melting to his kiss rather than fighting it. He had felt reassuringly solid beneath her hands. His wind-roughened mouth had been surprisingly gentle. Even his gruff growl had offered a measure of safety.

You have nothing to fear from me.

Recalling his touch, Siena skimmed her fingertips to the small hawk tattooed above her left breast. As one of Merlin's Maidens, she knew better than to let girlish imagination take flight. *A friend?* They had none, save for duty, discipline, and determination.

Siena set the glass to her lips, intent on turning her attention to a dispassionate assessment of her own performance. Yet another swallow of brandy did not quite chase the black-haired gentleman from her mind. She gave herself high marks for horsemanship—but so, too, did he deserve accolades. Indeed, he had ridden like the very devil, unswerving, unflinching in the face of the drenching darkness.

In command.

From his iron-fisted control of the reins and firm seat in the saddle, she guessed that he had some experience in the military. It would have been interesting to test her skills against him in some other equestrian maneuvers.

A sudden smile curved her lips. Lud, but there was no doubt that she had gotten the best of him with her unexpected acrobatics. She could hear *Il Lupino's* exhortation echoing in her ears. Keep the enemy off-balance. Not that she meant to think of the stranger as the enemy.

Not that she meant to think of him at all. No more distractions. It was time to put all memories of the gentleman behind her, time to think of the challenges ahead. The mission, as sketched out by Lord Lynsley, called for discretion, but most of all deception.

Slanting a look at the silky night rail, she felt a flutter of excitement at the idea of slipping out of her old skin and into a new one. Come morning, one of Merlin's hawks would appear as a bird of a different feather. The rippling water stirred the scent of honeyed florals and musky spices. Heady with hints of powerful passions, hidden dangers.

All her training had been for just such a moment. The basic instincts of survival honed of its rough edges, sharpened to a sense of purpose by the Academy. As a small child, she had battled blindly against brutal bullies. Sometimes she had won; sometimes she had lost. The harsh reality was that the law of the jungle governed the stews. Left unchecked, the strong could always dominate the weak.

But now she could truly fight back. With a purpose.

Lifting the sponge high overhead, Siena squeezed a drizzle of the water over her face. Any inner misgivings washed away with the last of the drops.

She couldn't wait to spread her wings.

The Earl of Kirtland took another brusque turn before the blazing fire. Although the library occupied an entire floor of his London town house, he couldn't help feeling caged in. Of late, he had experienced the same uncomfortable sensation each time he entered the outskirts of the city. But this time, he hoped the visit would be worth the aggravation. Since his arrival that morning in Grosvenor Square, he had been looking to confirm an intriguing rumor . . .

"Do stop pacing like a bear with a thorn in his arse." Deverill Osborne looked up from the book he was perusing. A friend since their first days at Eton, he was the only one of Kirkland's acquaintances who dared tease him in such a familiar fashion.

Kirtland reluctantly took a seat at the reading table. "Have a care with that, Dev. It's worth a bloody fortune."

Osborne casually flipped another page. "Seeing as you are richer than Croesus, you can well afford it if I spill my claret over the gold-leafed illuminations."

"But *you* could not." Kirtland quickly drew the leather-bound volume back across the velvet display cloth. "For I should slice out your lungs and liver and chop them into mincemeat."

"Come now, it's only a book."

"And the Magna Carta is only crinkled parchment and a dribble of ink," growled the earl.

"I take it you are going to tell me what makes it worth all the fuss." Grinning, his friend added another splash of wine to both of their glasses. The opposite of the earl in both looks and manner, Osborne was fair-haired and fun-loving. His breezy charm and sunny disposition made him a favorite within the highest circles of Society— especially the ladies. And yet, despite all outward differences, they were more alike than most people guessed.

"Trying to educate you on the fine points of bibliography is a waste of breath. The only pages you bother to read are those of the betting book at White's." Kirtland exaggerated a pained grimace, though he knew very well that his friend was not nearly so shallow as he pretended to be. "However," he continued, "even *you* ought to appreciate its exquisite beauty." His sarcasm softened as he looked down at the delicate brushstrokes and jewel-tone colors. "This is a rare fourteenth-century Burgundian Psaltor, illuminated by the monks of St. Sebastian Abbey. To my knowledge, there are only two other examples of their art in all of England."

"Indeed?"

"And word has it that they may both be coming up for auction in the next few months."

"Ah, so *that* is what brings you to London at the height of the Season?" Osborne eyed the earl from over the rim of his wineglass.

He nodded. "That, and the quarterly meeting of The Gilded Page Club. We have several important acquisitions to consider for our collection."

"What is it that the six of you do inside the confines of your club town house?" His friend cocked a brow. "And by the by, is that hideous golden knocker meant to be a serpent?"

Kirtland allowed a small smile. "A bookworm."

"One of you has a rather twisted sense of humor."

"Actually, we are all quite serious about scholarly pursuits. As for what we do . . ." His fingers traced over the corded leather and gold-leaf lettering. "We meet over the course of a week each quarter in order to share our research and exhibit the latest additions to our own private libraries. In addition, we review what rarities are coming up for sale, both here and abroad. Occasionally we add to the Club Collection."

"Who are the other members?"

"Dunster, Fitzwilliam, Winthrop, Leveritt, and Jadwin."

"The devil you say." Osborne made a face. "The six of you certainly make odd bedfellows. How long have you been part of the club? I don't recall you having mentioned it before."

"We are not in the habit of discussing scholarly matters," replied Kirtland dryly. "As for The Gilded Page, I was invited to join two years ago, to fill the spot left vacant by the death of Lord Woodbridge."

"The fellow probably expired from sheer boredom," quipped Osborne. "I can't quite picture how you rub together very comfortably with the others."

"One does not have to be on intimate terms with a man to enjoy discussing books and art."

"Sounds dreadfully dull." His friend toyed with the ends of his cravat. "Skip tomorrow evening's meeting and come with me to Lady Sefton's masquerade ball."

Kirtland's reply was somewhere between a snort and a snarl. "You know damn well I have no intention of appearing in Society."

"Your absence only encourages the rumors. People repeat the gossip surrounding your court-martial, and it grows more twisted with each telling. They say you betrayed a sacred trust and are a loose cannon. Just waiting for the slightest spark to explode."

"I couldn't care less what whispers are making the rounds of the drawing rooms."

Osborne lifted a brow but remained tactfully silent.

"Let them talk." He turned away from the candlelight and carefully squared the leather binding upon the velvet cloth. Wagging tongues, razored teeth. Was it any wonder that he much preferred books to people?

His friend waited for some moments before offering another comment. "Each passing word only distorts the truth."

The earl laughed harshly. "Since when has the *ton* cared for the truth? Society finds scandal far more entertaining." He gestured at his library shelves. "If you wish to find anyone interested in *that* concept, you will have to search out the writings of Plato or Aristotle."

"Have they also penned a chapter on cynicism?"

Despite the show of insouciant wit, Osborne could be quite perceptive. Sometimes too much so.

"I am in no mood for a lecture, if you don't mind."

"Still, I feel obliged to voice my concern. I would hate to see you become a hermit, bloodless and bitter. Or a monk." His friend's stare was like a knifepoint probing against a raw spot. "Speaking of which, is it true that you gave Adrianna her congé?"

Kirtland felt himself flush. "She was becoming too demanding."

"Ah. You mean she wished to see you on occasion?"

"I am not quite as bloodless as that," he replied, trying not to sound too defensive.

He thought for a moment of mentioning his encounter with the midnight Valkyrie but decided that the truth would sound stranger than fiction. Or, for that matter, more sensational than any of the gossip swirling through Society. His lips quirked on recalling that strange interlude. Never again would he accuse Mrs. Radcliffe, the famed novelist, of possessing an overwrought imagination.

"Still, you ought to leave the cozy confines of Henning Hall more often. It is important to know what is being said."

Something about his friend's tone cut short his musings. "What the devil is *that* supposed to mean?"

"A bit of friendly advice is all." Osborne rose and moved to the mantelpiece. "Since we are speaking of truth, Julian, the fact is that Lord Lynsley was asking me about you the other evening. Discreetly, of course, but the question of loyalty to King and country came up."

The earl felt his jaw go rigid. "You doubt my loyalty?"

"Not for an instant."

Kirtland slowly let out his breath. Osborne was his closest friend. Perhaps his only friend. And though he would never admit it aloud, the slightest hesitation would have cut him to the quick.

"But for all his outward affability and supposedly minor position in the ministry, I do not underestimate the marquess's influence. Or his intelligence—in every sense of the word. Is there any reason he might think you involved in some intrigue?"

"Intrigue?" Kirtland made a face. "Oh, quite right—I am conspiring with my sheep to corner the English wool market." He raked a hand through his hair. "In case it has been forgotten, I am retired from active duty. My life is not nearly so interesting as the two of you seem to imagine."

"Hmmm." Osborne's chuckle faded to a more serious sound. Looking puzzled, he paused and propped a boot on the fender. "I admit, it seems odd. And yet, I suggest you have a care as to the activities and company you mean to seek out in Town."

"Very well—no rolling barrels of gunpowder down the corridors of Parliament or taking tea with Marshal Soult."

"I'm not joking. Try not to stray from the ordinary. You already have a reputation as a dangerous man. One who lives by his own rules."

"And why shouldn't I? The rules of Polite Society are naught but a collection of pompous platitudes mouthed by hypocrites."

"Damn it, Julian." A slap to the marble mantel echoed the exasperated oath. "I am trying to help. Yet you refuse to defend yourself, your honor."

"I did nothing wrong. It was Colonel Hartland who betrayed a spineless lack of honor by refusing to speak up in support of my actions. By overriding General Darymple's orders, I saved the lives of my men, and were I to be court-martialed a hundred times over, I would make same decision every time."

"I agree that Hartland was wrong to renege on his promise of support," replied Osborne. "He should have stood up for your decision in spite of Darymple's wrath, rather than leave you at the last moment to bear the brunt of it alone. He was weak, and afraid for his own position. But the fact is, a bit of compromise on your part might have avoided the whole ugly affair."

"I am at peace with myself. That is all that matters."

"Are you?"

Kirtland turned his gaze to the crackling coals.

"Unlike the pages of your books, the world is not black-and-white, but an infinite range of greys," continued Osborne. "All I am saying is try to temper your lofty principles. It does no harm to keep some of your more outspoken opinions to yourself."

"I—I shall try."

But the earl's words had little conviction behind them. Compromise never came as easily to him as it did to others. Perhaps that was why he much preferred living alone.

"Be assured that I have learned my lesson," he muttered. "These days, I do not go looking to stir up trouble. Aside from you and the members of The Gilded Page Club, I have no intention of associating with anyone." He traced the intricate pattern of gold tooling on the leather binding. "Bloody hell. It is not as if I can get into much mischief discussing the artistic merits of incunabula with a group of book collectors."

A deft twist of the hairpin freed the last few curls of the topknot, allowing them to fall in artful disarray.

"You are very adept with your hands, Rose." Siena eyed the effect and allowed a small smile. The maidservant's fingers, though small and rather stubby, possessed a nimble grace. No doubt she was equally skilled at handling a blade or a picklock if need be.

"Thank you, milady." The woman's voice had the same clipped precision as her movements.

"I am no more a lady than you are," murmured Siena, savoring the irony of the moment along with the last sip of black coffee.

"Best we play our roles, even in private." The words betrayed no emotion. That in itself served as an oblique reminder that any personal attachments might only get in the way of performing their respective duties.

Siena nodded in understanding. The arrangement, however intimate, was purely about getting the job done.

Her gaze shifted to the schedule in her lap as Rose put the finishing touches on her toilette. A review of the escape routes with Oban at ten, Lynsley's messenger was due to deliver the ministry files at noon, a drive in Hyde Park at the fashionable hour of five . . .

She set the paper aside. "You may inform Oban I won't need him to handle the ribbons this afternoon. I will put the team through its paces myself."

"As you wish, milady."

"And ask him to have a colored whip made up. Something along the lines of a shocking pink would do nicely."

With its canary yellow lacquer set off by lime green upholstery and matching wheel spokes, the high-perch phaeton was already sure to draw attention. But the more outrageous extravagances she could add to the trappings, the better. She meant to make a lasting impression.

"As for personal preparations, a bit of powdered gold mixed with the face powder will create an exotic glow. The lip color should be a deep scarlet, with matching ostrich feathers to top off the coiffure." As Siena spoke, she made a mental note of the alterations she wished to make on her carriage dress. "Can you set a stitch, Rose?"

"Quickly and neatly," came the prompt reply. "I served a short apprenticeship with one of the most fashionable French modistes here in Town."

No doubt there was an intriguing story behind the facts, but knowing Rose was not likely to embroider any details, Siena merely murmured, "Excellent." Her brows, dark with kohl, drew together in a perfect raven-wing arch. "Here is what I have in mind . . ."

The first part of the mission, as outlined by Lord Lynsley, called for her to make a grand entrance into Society. But the details on how to accomplish such a feat had been left to her discretion.

Or, more precisely, indiscretion. Siena intended for eyes to pop when she rolled down Rotten Row for the first time. And for tongues to wag . . . She had already chosen her *nom de guerre*—the Black Dove—and Oban would make sure that it was repeated often throughout the park. By midnight all of London would be abuzz with the news that a colorful new ladybird had come to roost in Town.

From there, the next move should go smoothly . . .

Six names. The files would provide a more intimate acquaintance with the gentlemen in question. But facts were only a skeleton. To flesh out a true portrait, there was no substitute for a face-to-face meeting. More could be read in the blink of an eye, the frisson of a frown than in a ream of ministry notes. Words, however eloquent, could say only so much. The nuances of sweat, of smell, of sound turning shrill with fear were all too often lost in translation.

Yes, the sooner she saw for herself just who—and what—she was up against, the better.

Lynsley had left no doubt that time was of the essence. A terse written message had arrived at dawn from the marquess himself. A breach of his rules, to be sure, but one that he explained was unavoidable, given the gravity of the situation.

Her mission was even more important than before. A new theft had occurred. A letter—a frank appraisal of the Eastern allies from the Tsar, meant only for the eyes of Lord Castlereagh—had been stolen from the Secretary of

War's private safe. If it were made public, the Russian leader would be forced to distance himself from England, with catastrophic repercussions for the efforts to halt Napoleon's march into Prussia and Poland.

The marquess believed that the traitor still had the stolen dispatch in his possession. Siena's assignment was now not only to discover the rogue lord's identity, but also to retrieve the Imperial paper. No matter what the cost.

"Why do we bother riding in the park now, when we cannot manage more than a sedate walk," groused the earl. He had forgotten what a crush of horseflesh and humanity crowded the wide swath of bridle path known as "Rotten Row" at this time of day. The afternoon promenade was a daily ritual for the *ton*. It was as if all of fashionable Society turned out along the south edge of Hyde Park to breathe in the sooty air and latest *on dits*.

"The point of the exercise is not to fly by in a blur of sweating muscle and lathered flesh, but to be seen," replied Osborne. "As you well know."

Kirtland uttered an oath.

"And keep your damn voice down. We are trying to polish your image, a hard enough task without offending the ears of the Dowager Duchess of Roxburghe."

"I doubt she could hear a troop of swearing Hussars if they rode up her backside . . ." A quelling glance from his friend caused him to let the retort trail off.

Osborne tipped his hat to a trio of strolling ladies. "Do try to smile, Julian," he murmured out of the corner of his mouth. "The countess is bosom bows with Sally Jersey. And as her daughters are entering the Marriage Mart with modest dowries, she will be inclined to speak favorably of you to The Dragon if given the least bit of encouragement."

The observation earned yet another ungentlemanly comment, though this one Kirtland refrained from saying aloud.

"And look, there are Grafton and Stevens."

The earl gave a grudging nod to his two former army comrades as Osborne beckoned them over.

"Are you in Town for the Season, Kirtland?" inquired Colonel Stevens.

"I've not yet decided on my plans," replied the earl.

"Well, come around to Manton's one morning if you wish to knock the rust off your shooting skills."

"Hah!" Captain Grafton gave a gruff laugh. "Somehow I imagine Kirtland has kept his trigger well oiled."

Though Grafton smiled, the earl thought he detected an undertone of resentment. He knew a number of his fellow officers thought he had gone off half-cocked in his confrontation with General Dalrymple. No matter that Dalrymple—who was mockingly referred to as "The Dowager" by his troops—had been recalled to London shortly after the earl's court-martial and relieved of his command. Kirtland had defied authority, and insubordination was far more frightening than incompetence to the military mind. And far more dangerous than enemy bullets or blades.

"Thank you for the invitation, but contrary to the captain's assumption, I am out of practice in the disciplines of warfare," said the earl. "The only weapon I wield with regularity these days is a book knife."

"Which, I might add, you looked ready to use in slicing out Grafton's tongue," murmured Osborne as the officers rode off to greet another group of gentlemen.

"Someone ought to trim him down to size. He has always possessed a puffed-up sense of his own importance."

"Some might say the same of you."

Kirtland felt his lips twitch. "Touché."

"You owe me a forfeit, then—you must try not to look so bored for the rest of the ride." Straining to see through the crowd, Osborne stood in his stirrups. "I think I spy Lady Heffelin's barouche up ahead. Come on, you will actually enjoy making her acquaintance. She is sharp as a tack despite her age, and a great reader of the classics—"

A sudden commotion cut short his words. A high-pitched gasp was swallowed in a rumble of male applause.

All heads turned toward the Serpentine. The earl looked around to see a high-perch phaeton tooling down the path. It was not just the color—a blinding yellow—that arrested his attention, but the fact that the driver was a statuesque female standing, rather than sitting, atop the box. There was no mistaking her sex, seeing as a great deal of it was on prominent display. Clad in a shockingly low-cut froth of champagne-colored silk, she held the reins in one green-gloved hand while brandishing a pink whip with the other. Quite competently, he noted. The flick of the long lash was keeping the team of snow-white stallions in perfect step despite the breakneck pace.

He and Osborne were not the only ones staring. A gaggle of young bucks on horseback were vying with several of their friends in curricles for the best vantage point. In the jostling, one of the animals spooked. Rearing in its traces, it bolted forward. The driver, a cow-handed dandy, lost control of the reins. Clutching at his seat, he managed to keep from falling beneath the wheels, but his shrill curses did nothing to slow his team's wild flight.

"Bloody hell." Kirtland saw there was no way of averting disaster. The two vehicles were headed on a collision course, with no more than a hairbreadth of room for maneuvering. On one side of the graveled way was a group of children and their nannies playing at hoops. On the other was a line of close-set elm trees.

Someone screamed. A lady fainted. The earl braced himself for a crash. Splintering wheels, crushed limbs . . . But at the last second, the phaeton veered left, then sharply right, a deliberate maneuver that required an iron fist and steel nerve. Somehow, the lady remained perfectly balanced as it tipped onto one wheel and passed between the runaway curricle and the trees with scant inches to spare.

Cheers flew up from the crowd. Acknowledging the accolades with a jaunty salute, the lady righted her rig and kept on going.

"God, it looks as if she's taking another spin around the lake." Osborne began laughing. "I knew a fellow at Eton whose family motto was 'Luck favors the bold.' Perhaps the lady is a relation." He watched her fluttering gold-threaded silks disappear around a bend in the carriage path. "If I hadn't seen a female perform such a feat with my own eyes, I would dismiss all reports of this incident as utter nonsense. Or the delusions of an unstable mind."

"As would I." Kirtland shook off a strange sense of foreboding. "I, too, am reminded of an old aphorism—Lightning never strikes the same place twice."

"Meaning?"

The earl shook his head. "Never mind. The essence would most likely be lost in translation."

Chapter Four

*R*avishing."

"Exquisite. Absolutely exquisite."

The formal meeting of The Gilded Page Club had not yet been called to order, and as they waited for the others to arrive, Fitzwilliam, Dunster, and Winthrop were perusing some offerings from a Bond Street dealer in rare books.

Kirtland had come early to the club town house and was engaged in studying a seventeenth-century Spanish Bible. However, on hearing the comments, he put it away and joined the other three club members at the main display table.

"It's a handsome enough engraving," muttered the earl as he leaned in for a closer scrutiny. "But the letterform and the detailing of the decorative acanthus leaves are hardly out of the ordinary."

"And those breasts . . ." Baron Fitzwilliam paid him no heed. "Luscious as perfectly ripe melons."

Breasts? Kirtland squinted and tilted his head. Either his eyesight or his hearing was sadly askew for the shape remained naught but a simple *T.*

"Drool all you want, Fitz." The Marquess of Dunster was quick with a jeer. "I doubt you'll be offered a taste."

The earl cast a sidelong glance at the trio and suddenly realized no other eyes were focused on the printed page. "What the devil are you talking about, Dunster?"

"The newest highflyer in Town."

"Caused quite a flap on her first appearance in Hyde Park yesterday," added Fitzwilliam with a casual flutter of his hands. Unlike the others, he was dressed informally, the loose cut of his jacket reflecting the style currently in vogue with the artistic set. As if to emphasize the slightly raffish image, he wore his wavy auburn hair long and brushed straight back from his forehead.

"With feathers like that, is it any wonder?" Dunster's smirk revealed a gleam of white teeth. "I have never seen such transparent silk."

Like a wolf ready to devour some tasty morsel, thought Kirtland. Which was fitting, as the marquess had a reputation for chasing after female flesh as well as rare books. Given his wealth and his classical good looks, it was likely he did not have to break much of a sweat. With his pomaded blond hair brushed to a brilliant shine and a smooth smile that looked to be sculpted of marble, he exuded the arrogance of an Adonis.

"Silk?" Lord Winthrop leered. In contrast to Dunster, he was short and stout, with a dark, pointed beard that gave him the look of a dissolute satyr. "From where I was standing, it did not appear there was much of any fabric—transparent or otherwise—obscuring that delectable décolletage."

"Let us pray she did not take a chill."

"I would warm her up soon enough," sniggered Winthrop.

"With what? That piddling appendage you call your cock?" drawled Fitzwilliam. "While I, on the other hand—"

"Have even less to offer the likes of the Black Dove," retorted Winthrop. "From what your current mistress says, the only way to enlarge your member is to use a magnifying glass."

"If you gentlemen wish to dissect the fine points of anatomy, go attend a lecture at Royal Medical College," snapped the earl. "Otherwise, do you mind if we focus our attention on the subject of typography?"

The lewd laughter gave way to a stiff silence.

"Lud, Kirtland, one would think the only substance flowing through your veins is piss and printer's ink . . ." Winthrop bit back the rest of his retort, and as he turned from the candlelight, the earl caught a flicker of fear on his face.

His teeth set on edge. It was true that he had a rather volatile temper. But like the other facets of his character, it appeared to have been blown all out of proportion by the tattlemongers.

A second glance showed that the others were also eyeing him uncertainly. Did they think him a threat? The truth was, even after two years of belonging to the club, he knew very little about his fellow members, save that like himself, they all possessed great wealth, august pedigrees, and an interest in rare books.

Was Dunster really a rake who had bedded half the married ladies of the *ton*? There appeared to be an underlying conceit to his finely chiseled features, but the earl knew well enough that the glare of notoriety could distort the view.

And what of Fitzwilliam? A crack whipster and marksman, he was also said to pen soulful poetry. But that, too, the earl knew only from hearsay.

Winthrop, an acquaintance from university days, was not quite as much of a blank page. Kirtland had witnessed first-hand the other man's talent for historical research and archi-tectural sketching. As well as his taste for tavern wenches. Still, he could hardly claim to be friends with the fellow.

The fact was, the earl knew more about the ancient phi-losophers than he did about his contemporaries.

He looked away. Though only a few feet separated him from the others, it felt like they were worlds apart. The fault was his own. He had never found it easy to be part of the ribald camaraderie that most gentlemen favored. Drinking, gaming, ogling the latest opera dancers—all the pursuits that passed for privileged pleasure left him bored to perdition.

Still, they did share a common interest in the art of books. Recalling Osborne's oblique warning on the dan-gers of isolation, the earl decided that he ought to make more of an effort to fit in.

He forced the grim set of his lips to relax. "I still have a bit of blood running through my veins, Winthrop. How-ever, I don't quite see what all this fuss is about. There are flocks of lovely females whose favors are for sale."

"Ah, but this one is a bird of a different feather," assured Dunster. Seeing Kirtland's skeptical sneer, he hastened to add, "You ought to have seen her handle the whip and ribbons. Threaded a team of blooded stallions through the crowded park without blinking an eye."

"With a touch like that, imagine her prowess when mounted on a single steed," murmured Fitzwilliam.

"Hah!" Winthrop snorted. "Your imagination is as close as you will come to those graceful fingers and long, lithe legs."

"Never seen anything quite like her," said Dunster. "Just

ask the others when they arrive if she isn't some unique species. Decked out in those flashy baubles and bright silks, she looked like some exotic bird of paradise."

"Sent down from the heavens." The baron sighed.

"You are exaggerating her charms," muttered Kirtland. "I saw her from afar, and while there is no denying she cuts a colorful dash, there are other brazen beauties who are just as ripe for plucking."

"It's not just her stunning looks that set the Black Dove apart. It's her announcement."

The earl couldn't help himself. "What announcement?"

"How she intends to choose a protector."

"It usually works the other way around," he said dryly.

"Not in this case," replied Dunster. "She has let it be known that she will assess the gentlemen who qualify for consideration and make known a short list of finalists for her favors. The lucky devils will then be subject to a personal interview before she makes her decision."

The earl's skepticism winged to new heights. "The ladybird may be in for a rude surprise. I would be willing to wager that money is more seductive than a pair of shapely thighs."

Dunster stroked his chin. "You think she will renege on her promise and surrender to the highest bidder?"

His lips curled in a sardonic smile. "How many females do you know who value principle over greed?"

The marquess gave a bark of laughter. "Damn, but you have a point, Kirtland. Perhaps I shall make an offer— that is, unless you are planning on taking the lady under your own wing."

"I doubt she would be worth the price." On the far wall, flickering shadows danced across a painting of a reclining nude. Her voluptuous smile played hide-and-seek with his gaze, beckoning for an instant, then disappearing in a wink of darkness. As the earl's eyes slid down over the fleshy curves, ripe with the promise of pleasure, his own expression compressed to a cold, hard line. A woman who might touch more than fleeting physical need? It was naught but illusion.

"There are any number of beautiful females who can offer physical pleasure at far less cost," he finished.

Before any of the others could frame a reply, the door opened to admit the last two members of The Gilded Page Club.

"Forgive our tardiness." Viscount Leveritt, the eldest of the group, headed straight for the tray of spirits on the sideboard. A connoisseur of fine brandy as well as Dürer woodcuts, he quickly poured himself a glass. But rather than savoring it in his usual manner, he tossed it back in one gulp. "However, I assure you that the announcement we bring will more than make up for the delay."

Lord Jadwin's normally placid features were also flushed with excitement. "Indeed, indeed. Just wait until you hear the news!"

"What? Has the Dove settled on a love nest?" quipped Dunster.

Looking momentarily befuddled, the viscount smoothed at the intricate knot of his cravat. It was rare to see him with so much as a fold out of place, for he was a stylish dresser who paid meticulous attention to detail. "I don't recall any ornithological prints being on the agenda for this evening?"

"Dunster is referring to a bird in the flesh," said the earl.

"Oh—the new slut." Leveritt dismissed her with an

offhand wave. "There are plenty more where she came from."

Kirtland felt a certain smugness at hearing his own sentiments echoed aloud.

"But there are only two St. Sebastian Psalters in all of England. And we have just learned that the rumors are true! The Duke of Marquand has decided to sell them at a special private auction."

A slow, spiraling heat spread through the earl's limbs. The mention of fleshly treasures had left him cold, but he had lusted after those manuscripts for ages. Pressing his fingertips together, he could almost feel the smoothness of the ancient vellum, infinitely more enticing than any courtesan's flesh. And even the most alluring topaz eyes would pale in comparison to the jewel-bright tones of the painted colors. Yes, females would come and go, while the art inspired by eternal love and devotion endured.

Love. Thank God he had not fallen under that spell. He would save his caresses for the painted page

"You have not yet heard the best of it." Jadwin, eager to share in the announcement, edged in. "Only a very small, very select group of collectors are being permitted to bid." He paused. "But after several bottles of White's best port, the duke's representative agreed that the members of The Gilded Page are among those with the money and the knowledge to appreciate such treasures. We were able to secure an invitation for all six of us to Marquand Castle for the sale."

"There is to be a house party, a fortnight in the wilds of Devon," added Leveritt. "The duke insists on becoming acquainted with the prospective buyers, and each one will have to submit to a private interview. It seems he has become a trifle eccentric in his old age and wishes to ensure that his books are going to suitable home."

"Bloody hell, we are looking to make a business transaction, not a betrothal," grumbled Winthrop.

"What's the difference?"

Dunster's sardonic quip elicited a rumble of laughter. "Such a special opportunity calls for a toast, don't you think?" He raised his drink. Light winked off the cut crystal, yet to Kirtland the glint in his eye had the sharper intensity. "May the best man win."

"As long as that man is me." Winthrop said it lightly, yet the hard line of his jaw spoke volumes as to the strength of the sentiment.

The laughter died away quickly as the gentlemen drank.

Through the swirl of his brandy, the earl saw the others angling glances around the room. His hand tightened, the faceted glass prickling against his palm. Each member had his own reasons, his own passions for wanting to possess such a prize. They were all smiles now, but hidden in all the polish and sparkle of civility, most serious collectors had a darker side. Obsession could lead to cutthroat competition.

War. Though he gave a wry grimace as the spirits touched his tongue, Kirtland knew a battle of wits was brewing, with the strategies and tactics of actual combat likely to come into play. From now on, he could not afford to let his guard slip. Not if he wished to have any chance at victory.

"As the hour grows late, perhaps we ought to proceed with the program for this evening's meeting." It was Leveritt who moved to break the awkwardness of the moment. "I shall have Rusher bring in the folio of Raphael's engravings that my agent discovered in Florence. You are in for a real treat, gentlemen. Few people are aware of the artist's erotic work. Even fewer have seen an example."

The murmurs grew a trifle less muted as the members took their seats around the table. Rusher, the town-house butler, entered the room a few moments later, wearing his usual gold-braided livery and pompous smile. He made a show of unfolding a black velvet tablecloth and placing the leather case atop it before taking his leave with a low bow.

Kirtland closed the book on letterforms. Though he did not usually take an interest in viewing graphic sex, he was mildly curious to see how a man of Raphael's talent would handle the subject.

Leveritt untied the ribbons and slid out the first of the unbound prints. "The series depicts the Goddess Diana being ensnared by a passion for a handsome satyr. Here we have the Huntress, resplendent in—"

Without so much as a warning knock, the door swung open.

"Damnation, Rusher, you know the club rules! We are never to be interrupted in the middle of—"

This time it was shock rather than anger that cut short his words.

"Yes, it is terribly naughty of me to intrude." Limned in the light of the corridor sconces, the silhouette appeared more spectral than human. But the sultry voice was clearly female. As were the hands that sketched a sinuous salute. "But then, I have never paid much attention to rules."

Kirtland watched as the lady peeled off a pair of elbow-length black gloves and let them fall to the floor. The soft whoosh of leather was echoed by a collective intake of breath. A voluminous cloak hid her face and figure, but as she glided across the carpet, a pair of golden slippers flashed from beneath the flounced hem, leaving a trail of sparks in their wake.

"I trust you won't mind if I join you for a short interlude."

"Er . . ." Leveritt appeared to be having great difficulty in recovering his voice.

Seeing no one else capable of speech, the earl took it upon himself to assume charge of the situation. "I fear you have stumbled into the wrong gathering, madam. This is a private meeting of book collectors."

"Oh, there is no mistake, sir." She turned to face him. As if lit by an inner fire, two glittering amber orbs peered out from the hooded shadows. Her gaze held his for only an instant before moving on to the Raphael print.

There was something about that fleeting look that sparked the oddest sensation. A flash of recognition? His palms prickled as her fingers smoothed at the dark wool of her cloak. It was, of course, absurd to imagine he had seen those eyes, those hands before.

"This is The Gilded Page Club, is it not?"

Kirtland nodded.

"Then I have come to the right place." A toss of her head threw back the folds of fabric, revealing an artfully arranged tumble of raven curls, crowned with a delicate circlet of laurel leaves.

Even the earl felt the air leach from his lungs. The styling was an identical match to the engraving, lying in front of Leveritt, right down to the last hair.

"I'll be damned," murmured Dunster.

"Come, sir," said the lady. "Don't tell me you are concerned with the state of your soul when the pleasures of the flesh are at hand."

The earl was not the only one who suddenly recognized the daring driver of the phaeton.

"W—What brings the Black Dove to our town house?" asked Winthrop in a hoarse whisper.

"A proposition," she answered, loosening the strings at her neck. "A mutual love of things that glitter, shall we say." The cloak parted, showing a gold chain and a jeweled pendant shaped in the form of a stag. As in the picture, they were nestled between two perfectly shaped bare breasts.

Kirtland considered himself a connoisseur of ideal beauty. And in his experience there was usually no comparison between art and reality. Now, however, when forced to match paper against flesh, he had to admit that the lady put inspiration to blush. She was magnificent. Absolutely magnificent.

He had precious little time to admire the view. The Black Dove spun back in a blur of steps, capes flaring out from her shoulders. The trailing flounces flew up, offering a tantalizing glimpse of alabaster leg, then fell back to earth as she went perfectly still.

Someone groaned.

Silence swallowed the sound. Not a muscle twitched, not a paper stirred.

Her arms slowly spread, and with a theatrical flourish she flung the garment into the earl's lap. With the same sweeping gesture, she loosened the weapons tied at her waist.

Striking the same statuesque pose as Raphael's Diana, the Black Dove then nocked a small gilded arrow in her Cupid's bow and aimed it heavenward. The string stretched taut, wood and cording forming the outline of a heart.

The air seemed suddenly alive with a pounding pulse.

Kirtland was vaguely aware of an echo in his ears. Like cannon fire, it seemed to thunder a warning of impending doom. Yet like the others, he stood mesmerized by the sight.

The courtesan's resemblance to the engraving was uncanny. Every detail of her dress was an exact replica of the original. Slung low on her left hip, a slim quiver hung from a tasseled silk cord that was knotted at her waist. A pair of serpentine gold bracelets encircled each arm from wrist to elbow, the flashing fangs studded with tiny diamonds. Aside from the wealth of weaponry, and a silken oak leaf strategically placed between her thighs, the Black Dove was as naked as a newborn babe.

She held fast to the moment, allowing the full impact of her scandalous state to strike home. Then, arching her back, she let fly with her missile. Like a bolt of lightning, it struck a glancing blow to the chandelier before ricocheting off the ceiling rosette.

No one in the room paid the least attention to the shower of plaster and splintered glass that fell upon the table. Not even Leveritt flinched as the barbed steel came perilously close to piercing his priceless art.

She cocked a smile, looking supremely sure of her spellbinding effect on every male present. Her limbs, now relaxed in a supple splendor, glistened with sun-kissed glow. Perfumed oil highlighted the allure—jasmine and some earthier scent the earl could not identify. Not that his cognitive powers were functioning with any clarity, he thought wryly. He, too, was staring like a puerile schoolboy. And much as he wished to express a stern disapproval of such wanton debauchery, a part of him had the urge to applaud such outrageous daring. It was a rare female who possessed the courage or the cleverness . . .

His jaw tightened. *Impossible.*

He forced his eyes up from the lush swell of flesh and rouged nipples to study her face. The night had been dark, and his midnight Valkyrie's features had been obscured by a squalling storm and their tempestuous struggles. Still, he could have sworn that there was something hauntingly familiar about the pliant curves of the painted lips, the tilt of her chin.

Or perhaps he had been away from feminine company for so long that all women were beginning to look alike.

Damn. Kirtland wasn't sure whether to laugh or groan. Betrayed by his body, he fisted the folds of her cloak, fighting down a sudden, unwilling flare of desire. He would have to see about engaging a new mistress, and soon. *But not this one.* No matter that she sparked an inexplicably potent attraction.

His own conflicting feelings were overshadowed by the courtesan's next move.

"So, gentlemen, are you interested in hearing what I have to offer?"

Setting aside her bow, Siena placed a hand on her hip. The air fairly crackled with anticipation, and for an instant she understood what Mrs. Siddons felt like on the stage of the Theatre Royal. There was a powerful thrill to having an audience riveted on every nuance of expression.

A tiny twitch quivered on her lips. Though in this case, the gentlemen were looking somewhat lower than her face.

She held the pose a touch longer, using the silence to survey the surroundings. After reviewing the files, and following up on several contacts suggested in Lynsley's notes, she had learned all the details of this evening's club meeting. Rumors of the forthcoming sale of the Psalters had also reached her ears, and she had acted on instinct.

"By all means, yes." It was either Fitzwilliam or Winthrop who finally managed to croak a reply.

"I was hoping as much." With a slow, swaying step, she paraded in front of the table, giving the company a full display of her charms. Her early life on the streets had taught her not to be self-conscious or ashamed of her body—a lesson that suited the Academy's purpose quite well. "You six are accorded to be the very cream of London Society—gentlemen of title, taste, and wealth."

"Precisely." Dunster leaned a little closer to the candelabra, no doubt aware that the light gave his patrician profile a golden gleam.

"As I am determined to settle for no less in my choice of protector, I have decided to simplify the selection process. Why waste precious time looking elsewhere when all that I require is here in this room?"

"W—why, indeed?" stuttered Jadwin.

"How do you know that?" The black-haired gentleman was the only one not grinning from ear to ear. *The Earl of Kirtland.* He wore an inscrutable expression, the hard-edged planes of his face revealing little save for an aura of chiseled strength to his features. And yet, the austere aloofness was at odds with the intensity of his gaze.

"I have my sources," she replied.

His eyes narrowed.

"And quite accurate they are," Dunster was quick to offer assurance. With curling blond hair crowning the smooth symmetry of his features, he was more conventionally handsome than the dark earl. But a certain slyness to the curve of his mouth gave his smile a predatory pinch. "You won't be disappointed."

"Not at all," chorused the others. Save for one.

Siena shifted her stance, angling her hips to an even more suggestive thrust. "I have every expectation of being completely satisfied."

It was the earl who cut to the chase. "You have yet to explain how you mean to make a choice."

"It's actually quite simple. You gentlemen all mean to travel to Marquand Castle for the sale of some moldering manuscripts. Allow me to accompany you and to devise a series of private entertainments for the fortnight." She pursed her lips to a provocative pout. " Surely you will require more animated company than paper and ink to keep you amused."

"Games?" The earl made no attempt to temper his disdain.

"They shall be slightly more sophisticated than pin the tail on the donkey, milord." Siena gave a feline stretch and a cat-in-the-cream-pot smile. "As will be the prize," she purred.

Kirtland looked as if he had swallowed a mouthful of nails. "Let me hazard a guess."

The others reacted with a good deal more enthusiasm. "I am certainly up for the challenge," said Fitzwilliam. "What say you, gentlemen, to adding an extra dimension to the competition?"

"Two birds with one stone, as it were," murmured Siena.

Lusty laughter greeted her quip, the flickering of the candle flames accentuating the glint of teeth. *Hungry.* They were all smiles now, but already a look of speculative greed was beginning to shade their expressions. These were men used to having their every desire gratified. Men who didn't like to lose at anything. Driven by greed, by pride, by . . . what other powerful emotion?

It was up to her to discover the answer.

Lowering her lashes, she angled a look at Kirtland. He sat solemn, silent, watching the other members with a Sphinx-like stare. What would it take to chip away at the stony façade? To find some fissure, some crack in that unblinking composure? For even solid rock had a weakness. It was simply a matter of hitting the right spot.

He turned slightly, seeming to sense her scrutiny. Despite the warmth of the fire, goose bumps prickled the length of her spine. As if a swirl of wind, lick of rain, and brandied kiss were trailing over her flesh. Siena suddenly felt . . . more than naked under his gaze.

She covered her shiver with a slow, sauntering spin around the table. It was merely a quirk of light that made the earl seem familiar. She looked again but found it impossible to judge the true shape of his mouth, distorted as it was by a grim clench. The midnight stranger had not been so hard, so hostile.

"So, do I take it we have an agreement?" she demanded.

"No." Kirtland's growl was the lone voice of dissent.

"Afraid you are not up to the challenge, Major?" Siena countered his aggression with a bold thrust of her own. She reached for her cloak, letting her fingertips graze across the front of his trousers. "Ah, but I daresay you have nothing to be ashamed of. You may have been stripped of your commission, but it appears that your saber is as sharp as ever."

If looks could kill. Turning quickly from his daggered gaze, she silenced the lewd laughter with a wave. "Your decision, gentlemen?"

"Let us take a formal vote. Who is opposed to the idea?" asked Dunster.

The earl's lone voice had no echo.

"There is just one other thing—it must be all or nothing," she said. "If one of you chooses not to play along, I am afraid I shall have to withdraw my offer."

As she had hoped, a groan rose from the others.

"Damnation, Kirtland," said Winthrop. "I pray you don't break ranks with us now."

She held her breath, wondering if the bluff would work.

The earl hesitated, clearly reluctant to commit himself to the fray. "How do you intend to obtain an invitation to Marquand Castle? It is not quite the same as seeking admittance to the Cypriot's Ball."

"You may leave that to me, sir. As I said before, I have resources here in Town." She had no doubt that Lynsley's contact could somehow arrange things with the duke.

He glanced at his fellow members. "Very well. If you show up at the duke's auction, I shall consider it my duty to play along."

"So you concede defeat, Lord Kirtland?"

She watched the earl fold his arms across his chest, the black cloth of his coat stretching slightly from the rippling of hidden muscle. The sardonic smile curled tighter.

"Perhaps for now, madam. But according to you, the real game has yet to begin."

Chapter Five

*I*s it true?"

Kirtland nodded, not quite trusting his voice. Even though he and his friend were ensconced in the comforts of his own town-house library, the memory of the previous evening still intruded on his peace of mind.

"Art imitating life—or is it the other way around?" Osborne chuckled. "A singular performance." He loosened his cravat and propped his feet on a bookstand. "Damn, whatever the price of admission, it would have been worth the show."

The earl grimaced. "She will exact far more than money from any man who plays her game."

"Don't be so melodramatic," chided his friend.

"*Me?*" retorted Kirtland. "It was the lady who stripped off every last stitch of clothing and sent an arrow quivering into the Adam ceiling." He sipped at his brandy. "We ought to send her a bill for the damage. The plasterwork will likely never be the same."

His friend coughed. "Every last stitch?"

"Not quite literally—there was silk cord around her hips and a bit of fabric cut in the shape of an oak leaf."

"*And?*"

"And not much else," admitted the earl. "Save for the tattoo of a bird above her left breast."

"A tattoo?" Osborne pursed his lips. "How odd. I once heard a rumor about a cadre of women . . ."

"What of it?" urged the earl as his friend lapsed into silence.

"Never mind. It's too absurd for words." After a moment, Osborne resumed his teasing tone. "It appears that a library is a far more fascinating place than I ever thought. Had I known that reading could give rise to such pleasure, I would have listened to your lectures on books and art more carefully."

"I'm glad you find the situation so bloody amusing."

"Come, you are usually the first to appreciate life's little absurdities. Where is your sense of humor?"

"Filed on the bookshelf next to *As You Like It* and *The Merry Wives of Windsor*," he snapped. "It's not funny Dev; it's . . . unsettling." Though articulating why was proving devilishly difficult. Like the lady herself, the right words seemed elusive—vague blurs hovering at the edge of his consciousness, tantalizingly out of reach. "She is unlike other females—"

"That's for certain," interrupted Osborne with another wry laugh. "How many other women would have the ballocks to do what she did?"

Kirtland swore a warning through gritted teeth.

His friend eyed him askance. "Lud, again you are acting like a bear with a thorn in his arse. If I were you, I would not be growling over the fact that London's most alluring courtesan is singling out the six members of The Gilded Page Club as the finalists for her favors."

"But *why?*" persisted the earl. "I swear, there is more to this than meets the eye."

"Not a great deal more, from what you have described."

The earl could not help but surrender to a bark of laughter. Perhaps his friend was right, and he was over-reacting to the situation. Perhaps the lady was just what she appeared to be—a sensuous sylph willing to sell her services to the highest bidder.

Osborne settled himself a bit more comfortably in the arm chair. "Speaking of arses, was she . . ."

"A work of art." He sighed. "Not the softly rounded voluptuousness of Rubens or Titian, but a litheness of curves that was infinitely more intriguing in its vitality. The tautness of muscle only accentuated the more feminine forms. The effect was extremely . . ."

"Potent."

Potent. The brandy on his tongue took on a hotter burn. Like a lick of fire. Rising, Kirtland topped off their glasses before perching a hip on the edge of his desk. "I suppose you could say that."

"Then you should be giddy with delight at the prospect of her presence at Marquand Castle. It will provide a most welcome distraction from the musty manuscripts and prosy peers."

"Precisely." A distraction was the last thing Kirtland wanted. Especially one as provocative as the Black Dove. On returning from the battlefields of the Peninsula, he had decided that books were far better company than people, save for the rare exception like Osborne. Despite his show of outward indifference, the betrayal of friendship by his fellow army officers had been wounding. He did not mean to make himself vulnerable again.

Which made the strange sensations she stirred within him even more inexplicable. *Fire and ice.* Desire dueling with reason.

No wonder he was on edge. "I cannot help but think it is no coincidence that she has chosen us as her quarry."

"Hmmm. The dove turning into a hunter?" mused his friend.

"Or being staked out as bait."

There was a moment of silence. "You believe a competitor has arranged for her to serve as a diversion?" Osborne's voice lost a bit of its teasing tone.

"Possibly."

"That would require a great deal of quick planning and a great deal of ready blunt, wouldn't it?"

"Indeed." The candlelight turned to spun gold in the slow swirl of the earl's brandy. Lifting his glass, he watched its faint reflections cast hide-and-seek patterns across the wood paneling. "But to a certain group of people, the reward would be well worth it."

Intent on his own observations, his friend steepled his fingers and regarded the flickers of amber. "That throws a different light on things, I suppose. But forewarned is forearmed. No reason not to enjoy the game, as long as you play with your eyes wide open."

"Don't worry. I have no intention of losing my focus. Or the St. Sebastian Psalters."

"God help the enemy. Not for all the painted prayer books in Christendom would I want to be the one standing in your way when you get that look on your phiz."

*   *   *

Dunster, Fitzwilliam, Jadwin, Leveritt, Winthrop. The files lay aligned in alphabetical order on the table of her town-house study.

And Kirtland.

Siena hesitated, then placed his packet slightly apart from the others. She would leave the earl for last.

Stepping back, she shifted the candles, pooling the papers in a circle of bright light. The rest of the room was dark and silent, save for the feathery brush of her bare feet on the carpet. And even that faint sound stopped as she paused beside her chair and fixed the files with a focused stare.

Recalling the lessons of the Indian fakir, Siena held her breath and tried to sharpen her sixth sense. Lurking within the ink and foolscap was a hidden text, one that would reveal the enemy, if only she could decipher the unwritten message.

Whether it be mystical meditation or mere intuition, could she trust in feelings as well as facts? Her lips compressed to a thin line. She could certainly use some occult magic—or perhaps her friend Sofia's uncanny skill with the tarot cards—to interpret the truth. So far, the notes on each man had not been overly revealing.

She reopened Dunster's file and read over the first few pages. On the surface, he appeared an unlikely suspect for high treason. Heir to one of the oldest titles in the land, he was a scion of wealth and privilege. Lynsley's agents had uncovered no ruinous gambling debts, no family skeletons in the closet that might make a man desperate or vulnerable to blackmail. And if his penchant for cuckolding his fellow peers showed a certain taste for betrayal, it was of the sort that was accepted—even lauded—by Society.

The material on Fitzwilliam yielded even less to go on.

He looked to be the very pattern card of a proper lord. A prosperous estate in Oxfordshire, an imposing town house on Grosvenor Square, a well-matched marriage allying two noble names. A discreet mistress tucked away in a quiet part of Town. Why, the damn fellow even penned poetry.

Thumbing through several samples, Siena had to admit that they weren't half-bad. Lynsley's cover note dismissed them as derivative of Wordsworth's style, but to her, the stanzas showed a certain talent for rhyme and meter.

But then, all six suspects were connoisseurs of literature and art. No doubt they would be diabolically clever at manipulating words.

One by one she worked her way through the rest of the files, her growing frustration echoed by the crackle of each turning paper. *What was she missing?* Surely among all the detailed data on finances, family, and personal habits was the telling clue.

If only her intellect would prove as sharp as her sword.

Winthrop's folder fell closed with a thump. Nothing out of the ordinary there that she could see, aside from the fact that he took his sexual pleasure with tavern wenches rather than expensive whores. A sigh escaped her lips. Going by the book, none of the gentlemen seemed remotely sinister.

Her eyes strayed to where the candlelight edged up to shadow. The Earl of Kirtland was a different story.

Standing alone before his bedchamber hearth, Kirtland was not feeling quite so sanguine as he had earlier in the evening. Osborne's sardonic humor had mellowed his own misgivings for a time. But now, with the effects of the easy camaraderie and aged brandy wearing off, a sense of uneasiness had once again enveloped him in a black humor.

Black as midnight lashed with a sudden storm. Black as pirate silk pulled low over amber eyes.

A chill teased at his limbs, despite the roaring fire. Why was it that the unknown Valkyrie had plundered his peace of mind? As she had said, she was no one he would ever encounter again.

And yet . . .

The cold turned to a slow, curling heat. But as the earl stared at the dancing flames, he told himself he was only seeing shadows—strange, sinuous shapes of his own desire.

Women. He had never felt vulnerable to such flights of imagination before. Maybe Osborne was right about the dangers of self-imposed solitude. Living alone, with only his own thoughts for company, could give rise to bizarre ideas.

Kirtland tightened the sash of his dressing gown, hoping to throttle any further fancies. He turned for his bed but realized he was far too restless for sleep. Veering around the canopied posts, he began to pace. Only to discover that physical agitation was a mistake. The swoosh of silk against his bare skin a far too physical reminder of the Black Dove's brazen touch.

And her taunting challenge. She thought herself capable of besting him in any sort of competition? Even as he dismissed the notion as ridiculous, he felt himself growing aroused.

Damn.

It was lust, pure and simple, that had him so out of sorts. It had been an unnaturally long time since he had bedded a woman. In Spain, he had enjoyed more than his share of sultry señoras, but since returning to England with a cloud hanging over his honor, he had spent much of his time brooding in the solitary splendor of his estate. He had his beloved books for company. What more did he need?

Yet contrary to Osborne's needling, he was not a monk, shriven of all normal, masculine urges. If there had been any doubts of that, the encounter with the midnight Valkyrie had put them firmly to rest. As for his reaction to the Black Dove and her golden arrows . . .

Strangely enough, both women wielded weapons that had found a chink in his armor.

The earl gave a baleful glance down at his own stiffening sword, then to the ormolu clock on the mantel. He had heard that his former mistress had not yet chosen a new protector. He did not doubt that Adrianna would welcome his person—and his purse—back into her boudoir for a night.

He dressed quickly and called for his carriage to be brought around. But at the last minute he added a detour to the familiar directions. He, too, had sources, and the information had not been all that difficult to discover. As the cobbles grew rougher under the wheels, Kirtland looked out the paned glass and spied the small brick town house on Hadlow Street.

As ordered, his coachman drew to a halt in the middle of the block. The house, separated from its neighbors by an alleyway on each side, was dark, save for a sliver of light showing through the draperies on the third floor. *The lady's aerie?* he wondered. For despite her chosen moniker, the earl thought of her more as a hawk than a dove. A lithe raptor, beautiful but dangerous.

Forcing his attention back to earth, he saw that the entrance was faced in white Portland stone, with two simple columns framing the door. The front gate, a tall scrolling of iron, was shut tightly . . .

Kirtland frowned.

A moment later, he was on the street, moving quietly across the stones. Just as he thought, a closer inspection revealed that the lock was a model made by a small Bavarian firm renowned for its complicated mechanisms. He had seen several of them before—the embassy in Lisbon, a munitions warehouse in Oporto. But never one on a private residence.

Crouching, he traced a finger along the distinctive brass handle, making note of the special dead bolts that fit perfectly into a reinforced steel plate. The complex system of wheels and levers looked to be fashioned with the same precision. No picklock or probe would defeat such troops.

With his cheek pressed up against the bars, he spotted a tiny trip wire running from the base of the hinges to an underground pipe. Even if by some miracle the lock was forced, the slightest opening of the gate—an inch, maybe two—would likely trigger a warning bell in the cellar.

Why the devil did a courtesan have need of such elaborate security?

Not to guard her virginity.

Dusting his palms on his trousers, Kirtland rose and stepped into the shadows of a linden tree. The cloud of mystery surrounding the Black Dove seemed to be taking on a darker, deeper hue. He hesitated, feeling uncertain of which way to turn.

This was unfamiliar ground—a man used to taking decisive action, he was suddenly gripped by indecision. Reason said to walk away and forget about what he had seen. And yet, a reckless desire urged him to break through all the carefully constructed defenses and confront her.

Ha, he would like to see just how *she* reacted to having her inner sanctorum invaded!

Stirred by a sudden prickling at the back of his neck, Kirtland looked up at the darkened windows and thought he caught a flutter of the draperies.

Was it his imagination, or was someone watching him? A rustling in the alleyway seemed amplified by the sooty brick. Four-footed scavengers? Or an even stealthier threat? He strained to see what might be prowling in its depths, but the opaque shadows masked any movement.

In Spain, his inner alarm bell had saved his life on more than one occasion. Tonight, however, he wondered whether the warning was merely the jangle of over-wrought nerves.

After one last look around, the earl retreated to his carriage and headed off into the night.

If ever a man had reason to feel resentment, it was the Earl of Kirtland.

Siena paged through his military record and could not help feeling a reluctant respect. He had won a fistful of medals for valor in battle, along with glowing citations from Wellesley for his work with the partisans behind enemy lines. Staff commendations and military correspondence showed that he had also earned the respect of his fellow officers, even though his aloof demeanor had set him apart as a bit of a loner.

No one questioned the earl's bravery. Merely his penchant for ignoring the chain of command.

It was not that he was undisciplined. Quite the opposite. He had drilled his troops into a fighting force of iron-willed order and lethal precision. And to a man, his soldiers were intensely loyal, looking up to him as a leader who did not hesitate to put his own life on the line. The word was that they would follow him to hell and back if so ordered.

Taking up her penknife, Siena spun it in her fingers. The familiar feel of steel, however short and slender, was reassuring. Something she could get a grip on, while the earl's true character was still elusive, out of reach. But one thing was easy enough to grasp.

Julian Henning did not suffer fools gladly.

A fact that was brought to a head by one explosive incident. A war of words that had cost the earl his rank. And his honor in the eyes of Society. Though some of his fellow officers had remained loyal to him, the majority viewed him as . . . dangerous.

Though she had read over all the documents several times before, Siena took her time in reviewing the facts of the case again.

Despite overwhelming evidence that the British forces were being lured into an ambush, General Dalrymple had insisted on sending his lead battalions in pursuit of a French cavalry squadron. Instructed to march his men through a treacherous mountain defile, Kirtland had shredded the dispatch and kept his troops in place, choosing instead to go on alone, in direct defiance of the written orders. A daring feint had drawn out the enemy fire, single-handedly saving a number of soldiers from senseless slaughter.

His actions did not win him any gratitude from the general. Furious over the questioning of his authority, Dalrymple had threatened to court-martial Kirtland for dereliction of duty. The rules and regulations were lined up in the general's favor, no matter that common sense sided with the earl.

Siena frowned as she went over the confidential transcript of the disciplinary hearing. At the last moment, Kirtland's direct superior had wavered in a promise to support the earl's decision, which added to the gravity of the situation. The army high command had been caught in an embarrassing dilemma. Though they were reluctant to lose Kirtland's services, they feared if he went unpunished, it would set a dangerous precedent. After much discussion, they had come up with compromise—a reprimand and reduction in rank, with the private promise of its being restored rather quickly.

A slap on the wrist.

Disgusted with the hypocrisy and the betrayal of trust, Kirtland had refused to go along with the deal. The military had been left with no choice but to demand him sell out his commission and return to England. As no official reason had ever been announced, rumors had run rampant over the true nature of the earl's disgrace.

A part of her applauded his rebellion. That was true courage, to risk himself and his reputation rather than his men. Perhaps Kirtland's standards were impossibly high, but he appeared a man of principle, demanding no more of others than he did of himself.

Closing her eyes for a moment, Siena now viewed his unyielding austerity in a different light, the facts softening the harsh planes of his face. In the past, she, too, had sometimes stood her ground against impossible odds, even though retreat might have been a wiser choice.

Her grip tightened on the knife. She could not allow herself to see things in aught but black-and-white. There was no room for subtlety, for sympathy. The earl had disobeyed a direct order and paid a dear price.

Ruined, resentful—was he now demanding repayment?

She stood and stretched, her loose Turkish trousers and linen shirt affording a sinuous ease of movement. Hands clasped high overhead, she held the position, standing still as a statue, though her thoughts were spinning like whirling dervishes. Releasing her breath in a long, low whoosh, she bent low and grasped an ankle. As she rose, she set the ball of her foot on her hip bone.

Lud, if the guttersnipes from St. Giles could see her now, they would fall down on their arses laughing.

Yoga. It was an odd name for an odd—but highly effective—discipline of body and mind. *Balance. Focus. Free the mind of distractions.* She tried to picture a single searing light, but the flame kept flickering, as if caught in a gusting wind—

Oban's sudden appearance in the doorway took her by surprise. Though their acquaintance was short, it was already clear that he wasted no words on small talk. "Is something amiss?" she asked, feeling for the knife strapped to her leg.

"Perhaps. The Earl of Kirtland just paid us a visit. And he seemed particularly interested in the gate lock."

She frowned. "How did he learn where I live?"

"He is a former military man, is he not?"

Siena wondered how much the taciturn Scot knew of her mission.

He seemed to sense her query and went on. "His name was in all the newspapers for a time last year. Something to do with a conflict with his commanding officer. The details were hushed up, but it was no secret that he was forced to resign his commission. Came home in disgrace, he did."

So, his humiliation by the government had been very public. Siena shifted her stance. A man with any pride would feel cut to the quick. Would such a wound fester enough to turn poisonous?

Siena wasn't quite sure how she would feel in his place. But she might very well wish to strike back. With a vengeance.

Setting aside such musings for later, she turned her thoughts back to the matter at hand. "You are right about the earl. He is no stranger to surveillance tactics. And it isn't exactly a secret where the Black Dove keeps her nest. I made no effort to hide my comings and goings."

Oban nodded but made no move to leave. "The earl was not the only one prowling."

Siena looked around sharply. "Who else?"

"I regret to say that I saw only a silhouette of the intruder as he climbed over the garden wall. He was tall, broad-shouldered, and moved quicker than a cat."

The description did not seem to fit any of the other members of The Gilded Page Club.

"I will keep better watch in the coming nights."

As will I, she promised herself. But for now, her talons would stay hidden. She slipped the knife back into its sheath. "Anything else?"

"Aye." Oban took a small packet from his pocket. "Whoever it was left this."

Chapter Six

*T*he trilling melody of a country gavotte drifted out from the ballroom, accompanied by the clink of crystal and a lady's high-pitched laugh.

But the Marquess of Lynsley was not drawn to the dancing. Instead, he shifted a step deeper into the alcove of the cardroom, intent on watching one of the games unfold. To his ear, the shuffle of pasteboard struck a slightly discordant note to the gaiety of Lady Haviland's soiree. As of yet, it was nothing he could put a finger on. However, ever since the fair-haired stranger had joined the near table, it seemed that play had taken a more serious turn.

"The deuce take it. I believe you have won again," Lord Henniger, an octogenarian who hated to be parted from so much as a farthing, slapped down his hand.

"Luck appears to be running in my favor tonight."

Lynsley did not recognize the gentleman who spoke, which in itself was odd. He made it his business to know the faces of even the most marginal members of the *ton*.

A half turn allowed him to make a closer scrutiny of

the stranger's countenance. There was something exotic about the man's looks—high, slanting cheekbones, an aquiline nose, lips that were almost feminine in their full contours. His eyes were an unusual shade of arctic blue, with a glacial glitter that seemed at odds with the overheated cardroom. *Cold, calculating.* The impression was accentuated by a mane of pale blond hair. Pulled back from his face in a severe style, it was tied in a queue with a black velvet ribbon.

"Shall we play another hand, gentlemen?" continued the stranger. Like his looks, his speech had a hint of foreignness to its tone. "After all, Fortune is a fickle mistress."

"I wouldn't waste my blunt if I were Henniger," murmured Major Chertwell as he joined the marquess in the shadows. "Alexandr Orlov rarely loses at cards."

Lynsley did not look around. "You know the fellow?"

"I've met him on several occasions. A strange breed. His mother is English, from a gentry family in northern Yorkshire, and his father is a Russian of questionable lineage who clings to the fringes of the upper class." The major's return to Prussia had been delayed by the latest theft of government secrets. In the meantime, he had, like Lynsley, been making the rounds of the clubs and balls, seeing what gossip might prove useful. "Orlov himself was raised in St. Petersburg and runs tame among a set of young noblemen from the Tsar's Imperial Guards. A wild bunch, known for their heavy carousing, but from what I gather, Orlov is a bit of a lone wolf."

"Is he an officer as well?"

"Nobody seems to know quite what he is."

"I wonder what brings him to London," said the marquess softly, his eyes never leaving the foreigner's face.

"Business." Chertwell's tone tightened. "Word has it Mr. Orlov has been hired to represent the interests of a reclusive collector at a forthcoming sale of rare *objets d'art*."

"Would those objects happen to be a collection of fourteenth-century illuminated Psalters?"

"By coincidence, yes."

"Coincidence, indeed." Lynsley took care to keep his face expressionless as he watched the flutter of cards fall to the table. "So, Mr. Orlov will be attending the auction at Marquand Castle."

"So it seems." Chertwell watched the Russian take a card from the deck. "Another rumor I've heard says that the fellow may in fact be working for himself, amassing a collection of valuable items for his own personal gain—without having to pay for them."

"A thief?"

"A very high-class one. By virtue of his position in society, he is invited to a great many fancy parties. My informants in Prussia mentioned that he has been present at a number of houses where expensive art or jewelry has gone missing."

As Orlov reached out to rake in his hand, the marquess allowed an inward smile. Showing beneath the Russian's starched shirtsleeve were several fresh scrapes on his wrist. Lynsley's trained eye also spotted telltale smudges of brick dust clinging to the cuffs of his trousers. An amorous assignation? Or had the Russian been looking for more than a quick tumble in bed?

"The plot thickens," he murmured. "Though whether Mr. Orlov has anything to do with our story remains to be seen."

Chertwell signaled for a passing footman to refill his

glass. "As if we need any new complications. My superiors are demanding to know when we will shut the book on this case."

"As are mine. But seeing as we all wish for a happy ending, we cannot afford to rush. A mistake at this point would be difficult to erase."

"I don't suppose there is any way to send . . . an alert on this new development."

Lynsley didn't blink. "Let us wait and see before making a decision. If it proves necessary, I can pass on a message."

"Beggared again." From the table came a loud snort as Henniger threw down his cards in disgust. "Come Redmond, come Willis, let us seek out the supper room and wash away the taste of defeat with some champagne and lobster patties."

"Anyone else care for a game?" As if sensing the scrutiny, Orlov looked around to the alcove. "Ah, Major Chertwell. What an unexpected pleasure to see you again. Might I tempt you to join me in a hand or two?"

Chertwell shook his head. "Unfortunately, I am promised to a friend's sister for the upcoming set of dances."

"A pity." The Russian angled his ice blue eyes to Lynsley. "Perhaps your companion . . ."

The major had no choice but to make the introductions before heading off to the ballroom.

"I am honored to make your acquaintance, Lord Lynsley." It might only have been the accent that added an edge of irony to Orlov's words. "Indeed, I had been hoping for some time that the opportunity would present itself."

The marquess shrugged. "I cannot imagine the reason."

"You are being far too modest. Your reputation precedes you."

"As what?" he asked quickly, hoping to catch the other man off guard.

"Why, as a scholar, sir. I have heard that you have quite an interest in books."

A game of cat and mouse rather than *vingt et un?* The marquess decided to play along for the moment. "That depends on the subject matter. What of you, Mr. Orlov? Are you interested in literature?"

The Russian smiled, revealing teeth white as winter snow. "I am interested in anything that promises to make me a handsome profit."

"Pragmatism over poetry?"

"Art is a luxury reserved for the indolent rich." As he spoke, Orlov shuffled the deck with practiced precision and laid a row of cards facedown on the table. "Those of us who must work for a living are often forced to choose between idealism and reality." With a quick sleight of hand, he rearranged them into a half circle.

The marquess remained silent.

"Speaking of choices, Lord Lynsley, would you care to pick a card?" continued Orlov. "In Russia, we have a little game we call 'St. Peter's Pistol.' You get one shot at victory—the highest card wins all."

Lynsley regarded the scattering of silver upon the table. Ballroom betting was rarely for more than pin money. "What wager do you have in mind?"

"Something other than mere shillings. The higher the stakes, the more compelling the game."

"Only if you like taking risks," replied the marquess.

"Don't you?"

"I am really not much of a gambler. I dislike leaving things to chance."

"So, you prefer to watch?" Orlov swept up the cards and returned them to the top of the deck. "I see my friends were right—you are a very cautious gentleman, ruled by logic and not emotion."

"Or perhaps I simply lack the imagination to do aught but perform my clerical duties."

For an instant, a spark of amusement warmed the ice from the other man's gaze. "Somehow I doubt that." He rose and tucked his winnings into his waistcoat pocket. "I have enjoyed our conversation immensely, milord. Perhaps we will have opportunity to meet again during my stay in England."

Lynsley watched the Russian saunter away, the black velvet ribbon of his tied-back locks waving a last mocking salute.

"You may bet on it, Mr. Orlov," he said softly.

Siena regarded the package left by the intruder for a moment longer before lifting it from Oban's palm. It was a small, roughly stitched leather purse, wrapped in a length of twine. Loosening the knots, she emptied the contents into her hand.

A gleaming gold coin and a folded piece of vellum.

Moving to the table, she saw that the money was French. One side bore a portrait of the Emperor, while the other was emblazoned with three words. *Liberté. Egalité. Fraternité.*

Setting it aside, she smoothed open the sheet. It looked to be the frontispiece from an old book. Aside from the elegant italic title, there was no other printing on the page. Pasted in the blank space was an ornate bookplate depicting a family crest. A scrolled banner beneath the shield provided room for a name to be entered.

Julian Henning. The script was written in a bold, slanting hand.

Siena studied the fierce eagle rampant, its gold talons and menacing beak standing in sharp relief against a crimson background. A solitary nature and snappish temper appeared to run in the Kirtland blood.

And now, someone was implying that the current earl was tainted by treason.

The accusation could not have been writ plainer, but it paled against the far more subtle message—despite every precaution, someone knew of her mission. Or at least suspected she was not just a soiled dove.

Should she send word to Lord Lynsley and inform him of the disquieting development? It would, of course, be tantamount to conceding defeat.

"Any problem?" asked Oban.

"No." Siena decided not to share the contents of the purse with him. It wasn't that she didn't trust him. She didn't trust anyone.

Had she made some tiny slip, some subtle gesture that had betrayed her charade? Her hands, now empty, fisted, and, as she turned abruptly from the table, Da Rimini's favorite exhortation echoed in her head.

The most dangerous enemy is often yourself, Volpina.

For all his lecherous leering, the wily old wolf understood the art of war. Siena forced the knotted tension from her muscles and mind. There was no need to overreact to the first attack. Go slowly, feel out the enemy's strengths and weaknesses before taking the offensive.

"I doubt we will have any more nocturnal visitors," she

went on. "Come morning, we shall go over any other precautions to take for the next few days."

Oban nodded and departed just as silently as he had arrived.

Left alone, Siena slowly cut a riposte through the air, pausing, perfectly balanced, on the balls of her feet. Time was running out, and not even the considerable magic of Mrs. Merlin and the marquess could conjure up a new plan to trap the traitor. She would wait before sending any message to Lynsley.

A spinning leap and she landed light as a feather atop the window ledge. Peering out through a gap in the draperies, she smiled. Her shadowy opponent had been clever, attacking from an unexpected angle. But having been taught by a master of Machiavellian deception, she, too, had a few tricks up her sleeve. Come tomorrow night, she would wing into action.

The rope slithered across the slates, the looped end falling into place around the chimney pot. A quick tug tightened the knots. Satisfied with its hold, Siena slipped the hood down over her face and donned a pair of whisper-thin leather gloves. Like her slim-cut trousers and shirt, they were black as the shadows shrouding the walled garden. Each of the six members of The Gilded Page Club would have an unannounced visitor over the next two nights, starting with the Earl of Kirtland.

Her feet left the earth, and she rose quickly, as if on silent wings, to the narrow ledge of the second floor. Centered in an arch of Portland stone, a bank of leaded windows overlooked the neatly pruned hedges and ornamental plantings. *The library.* It would be a pleasant spot to linger in the afternoons, she noted as she edged closer.

The angled light would fill the room with a golden glow, mellowing the brass fixtures and oak paneling to the color of aged sherry.

She froze, ready to fly for cover, as a sudden rasp of metal rattled the glass. The window opened a crack to the cool evening air, but after a moment she heard steps moving away from the casement. They were followed by the clink of crystal and a splash of liquid.

Flattening herself against the wall, Siena slipped closer and ventured a sidelong peek into the room.

Brandy in hand, Kirtland had taken a seat in the leather chair by the hearth. A book lay open upon the side table, and as he stretched his long legs out toward the fire, he resumed his reading.

She could not help but note that he had shed any semblance of lordly formality. His feet were shod in naught but stockings, and he wore no coat or waistcoat. His linen shirt was open at the throat, revealing a glimpse of tanned flesh and dark curls. The rolled sleeves bared his forearms as well, the light from the brace of candles limning the cording of muscle. As he raised his glass to his lips, Siena saw that several deep scars cut across sinew and bone—a stark reminder that Kirtland was a battle-hardened soldier. She must never lose sight of that fact.

But as he stirred and turned the page, he was hardly the picture of a perfidious traitor. His hair fell in tousled disarray across his brow, the silky black strands curling around his ears and collar, softening the angled planes of his cheek and jaw. The fringe of sable lashes deepened the color of his eyes to a swirl of smoky green. Or molten jade, for despite the blinking shadows, she could see flecks of fire in their depth.

He smiled—a mere quirk of his lips—and the breath

caught in her throat. Steadying herself against the stone, Siena was suddenly sure she recalled the full, sensuous contours of that mouth. The taste of brandy and a male essence far more potent than spirits.

She bit back an oath. The similarities were striking, but the notion was . . . insane. Kirtland could *not* be her midnight stranger.

And yet, for an instant, she could not help imagining what it would be like to kiss him. To find herself in his lap, soft leather beneath them rather than sodden saddles and bucking horseflesh.

Siena quickly reined in such seductive thoughts. No question the earl was a sinfully handsome man, but he might also be the devil—

"Hell's bells."

Out of the corner of her eye, Siena saw a blur of black fur land on Kirtland's shoulder. "Move away, Lucifer," he muttered.

A tail twitched, and with an arrogant arch of its back, the cat reached out a paw and swatted at the page.

"Ah. Do I take it you would prefer William Blake's poetry to that of Southey? *Tyger, tyger, burning bright . . .*"

The cat cocked its head, its fire gold eyes fixing Kirtland with an unblinking stare.

The earl raised a brow. "Paradise Lost, perhaps?"

Lucifer did not appear as amused as his master. With a low growl, the animal turned its claws on the flap of Kirtland's collar.

"Ouch—I appear to have fallen from grace," exclaimed the earl as he rubbed at his neck. His fingers curled into the cat's fur and began a slow tickling.

Lucifer's rumblings settled into a steady purr. Inch by

inch he slipped down the front of Kirtland's shirt, landing with a tumbling somersault smack atop the book.

Laughing, the earl extracted the pages from under the ball of fur. "Imp of Satan, look what you have done! The pages are dog-eared."

The cat answered with a feline smirk.

From the doorway came a low *woof*.

"No offense, Mephisto," he murmured as a huge hound shambled into the room. Its shaggy fur was the color of Toledo steel, save for around its massive jaws, where the wiry whiskers had gone white with age.

Woof. The hound plunked its head in Kirtland's lap, cheek by jowl with the cat. The earl dutifully scratched behind one ear, while Lucifer bit at the other. A look of blissful contentment on his bearded face, Mephisto gave a loud snuffle and licked at his master's fingers.

"Right. Us old dogs must stick together."

The hound thumped his tail on the carpet.

"Go warm your ancient bones by the fire." It was only then that Siena saw the scruffy blanket folded close by the carved-marble hearth. "I shall leave orders with Givens that the logs be lit while I am away."

Both animals looked up sharply.

"It will only be for a fortnight or so." He looked rather guilty as he tickled under the upturned noses. "Besides, you know damn well that Cook is far more generous with tidbits of chicken than I am."

A man who loved animals? It was hard to see him as a villain.

Siena had not really expected her spying to catch the earl in the act of treason. She had simply wished to take a measure of the man in an unguarded moment. According to Da Rimini, knowing the enemy was a weapon in itself.

But never in her wildest dreams had she imagined she might find this cozy domestic scene. In their first encounter at The Gilded Page Club, Kirtland had been a forbidding presence, so stern, so solemn in his unrelenting black evening clothes. Disapproval had pinched his features, thinned his mouth.

Watching him with his cat and dog made him appear very human. The man by the fire looked younger, more carefree. Here, among his books and pets, he did not seem a man embittered by the unfairness of war but a man at peace with himself.

The hound circled the blanket and lay down, tucking his nose under his tail. A moment later, the cat jumped from the earl's lap and sauntered over to take up a new perch atop the canine rump.

"Fickle beast." Kirtland set aside his much-abused book and rose. "I, too, think I shall retire for the night." He extinguished all the lights, save for a single candle, and quietly closed the door.

Siena had seen enough.

And yet, it was not enough. She hesitated, then looped the rope around her arm and climbed to the next ledge. Oban's sources had indicated that the earl's bedchamber was also located at the rear of the town house, directly above the library. Siena crept close to the casement and waited for a flicker of light to appear.

The earl entered, unaccompanied by any valet to minister to his preparations for bed. A self-reliant man. And one of simple tastes, she noted as he lit the brace of candles on his bureau. The furnishings were dark mahogany, with a palette of deep green and burgundy complementing the discreet accents of brass and leather. No expensive silver grooming implements or bottles of fancy cologne and pomade cluttered the dressing table. A set of well-worn wooden brushes, a looking glass, and a plain vial of bay rum. Spartan, as befitting a decorated war veteran. They exuded an essence of masculinity.

An aura accentuated as Kirtland undid the fastenings of his shirt and tugged it over his head.

His sculpted shoulders looked even broader without the tailored encumbrance of clothing. The candles cast the chiseling of muscle and sinew in sharp relief, light and shadow cutting a clear picture of every nuanced contour. Smooth as marble, hard as granite. The symmetry of corded flesh and angled shoulder bones was marred by a single sword scar near his neck, its puckered red color a harsh contrast to the sun-bronzed splendor of the rest of him.

Santo Cielo. Siena had seen Da Rimini and his fellow instructors at the Academy stripped to the waist, but never a man as magnificently masculine as Kirtland. The scar only added to his allure. Only *putti*—pudgy little angels—were unflawed. The earl was certainly no angel. He was . . .

A Greek god?

He turned, and as he performed his ablutions at the washstand, she caught a first glimpse of his bared chest. Sable curls dusted his tanned flesh, their silky texture a tantalizing counterpoint to the hard, slabbed planes of his collarbones. Beneath the dark, flat nipples, muscles rippled over his ribs, the ringlets running down the center of his abdomen in a teasing trail, drawing her eye ever lower.

Siena felt a strange lick of heat as she watched a splash of water trickle down through the wisps of hair and disappear beneath his trousers. The earl's shoulders accentuated the sharp taper to a narrow waist and sword-straight hips. At this angle, the flames cast a reddish glow over his torso. Poised on powerful thighs, he looked like Apollo in all his bellicose beauty.

A warrior deity.

Kirtland toweled off, a shake of his head sending a shower of golden drops through the air. He threaded his fingers through the tangled locks, pushing them back from his brow. Damp strands clung to the curve of his neck, the curling ends grazing the ridge of his shoulders.

Her mouth went dry as his hands moved to the flap of his trousers. As the buttons slipped open, the melton wool hung for an instant on his hip bones before falling around his feet in a pool of dark folds. He picked the garment up from the carpet and carefully smoothed out the creases before draping it over a chair.

A man who paid meticulous attention to detail, noted Siena, trying to avert her gaze from the thin cotton drawers that served as the earl's fig leaf. Given his current position in front of the flickering flames and the transparency of the fabric, a bit of greenery would have provided far more cover. As it was, little was left to the imagination . . .

None was needed after a quick tug to the drawstring sent the undergarment fluttering to the floor.

Siena suddenly experienced the oddest sensation inside her chest—like a bird was beating its wings against her rib cage. It took her a moment to master its wild thrashings and regain control of her thudding heart.

It wasn't that she hadn't seen a man naked before. Given the nature of the missions assigned to Merlin's Maidens, the Academy had considered it an integral part of their education to be intimately familiar with the physical makeup of men. Science lectures had presented a dispassionate view of anatomy and biological functions, while art classes had drawn on nude models to illustrate the mysteries of the male form. Giovanni Musto, the assistant equestrian instructor, had provided a particularly well-endowed example of what to expect. The young man was, as Shannon had once quipped, as well hung as a stallion.

Being Italian, Giovanni had a rather more lyrical way of referring to his private parts—*gioielli di famiglia.*

The family jewels.

No wonder the Earl of Kirtland was counted among the wealthiest men in all of England.

Set against the marble whiteness of his thighs, the thatch of raven-dark curls formed a dramatic crown for his maleness. Siena had seen a number of classical dieties presented in all their erect glory, but even in repose, the earl's embarrassment of riches put the whole of Mount Olympus to blush.

Siena felt a naughty rush of heat stealing over her cheeks. All she knew of Kirtland painted a portrait of a man of rigid discipline, of demanding self-control. Yet she couldn't help wonder what he would be like in the throes of unbridled passion, limbs taut, flesh on fire, that deep baritone voice smoky with need.

Not that she had actually experienced the intimate coupling of flesh. She had seen it often enough in the alleyways of St. Giles. Girls growing up in the slums learned far more about the realities of life than highborn females. And the lessons were often harsh. Her hands clenched for an instant. She had never been forced to submit to a man, but she had seen what happened to others who were not as quick or as tough as she was.

Still, seduction was part of every student's basic training. Siena knew what was expected from her, if necessary. And she accepted that a mission might require her to sleep with a man—though she hoped it might be with someone she could respect.

A cynical smile quickly tugged at her lips. Given the nature of her assignments, that seemed unlikely. At least let the man be physically attractive, she thought. There was no doubt that the earl was sinfully—

"Damn." The earl's voice cut through the shadows.

Snapping out of her reverie, Siena realized that he had moved a step closer to the windows. Her grip tightened on the rope. Had she made some sound, some slip that had given away her presence?

Kirtland reached down to retrieve his pocket watch from the carpet. He placed it atop the dresser, then turned and walked back toward his bed, the flexing curves of his buttocks and long legs radiating a primal grace. A man at ease in his own skin.

And just what skin was that? Soldier? Hero? Lover? Traitor?

Siena drew in a deep breath. She had come seeking to sharpen her perception of the earl, but what she had seen had only given rise to more questions than answers. The only thing she had learned for sure was that he was kind to animals. And that he slept in the nude.

From the bookshelf by his bed, the earl picked a volume from the leather-bound set of Shakespeare's works, plumped the pillows, and settled between the sheets to read.

The candlelight caught the gleam of the gilt title. *Hamlet.*

Good night, sweet prince.

She cocked a silent salute before taking the rope in

hand and dropping down into the darkness. And yet, she could not quite slip away from the strange soliloquy taking voice in her own head. *To be or not to be ... distracted by unaccountable emotions.* She had been trained to keep a distance from the suspected enemy. *You may fight with your heart, Volpina, but never allow it to gain the upper hand over your head*—Da Rimini's exhortations chorused a steely echo to her own whispered warnings.

She should not be at all drawn to Julian Henning. He might be a traitor, a man who would crush all the ideals she held dear. However, it was hard not to feel a grudging admiration for him. Even in the privacy of his own home, the earl seemed to radiate a certain strength of character that belied the notion of duplicity and deception.

But as her feet hit lightly upon the ground, she steadied her resolve. She would *not* be seduced into thinking his principles were as finely honed as his body.

Such a mistake could be fatal.

Chapter Seven

"When do you leave for Marquand Castle?"

"On the morrow," growled the earl. Osborne's suggestion of a rousing gallop in the park had seemed like a good idea an hour earlier. But rather than clear his thoughts, the vigorous exercise had only exacerbated his foul mood.

"You do not sound like a man about to set off in quest of his eternal *amour*." Osborne slowed his mount to a walk. "I would have expected a little more enthusiasm. After all, the journey has all the makings of an epic adventure—trial by combat, romance—"

Kirtland silenced him with an oath. He had not slept well at all, and his head felt as if a blade were boring into his skull. "Stubble the sarcasm if you don't mind. I am no knight-errant, playing a part in some medieval *chanson de geste*."

"You *are* storming a castle. And while there may be no fire-breathing dragon guarding its walls, you will be facing off against a shadowy foreigner who seems equally intent on winning the prize."

The earl jerked back on his reins. "What the devil do you mean?"

His friend gave a long-suffering sigh. "If you would show your phiz at White's on occasion, you would discover that books are not the only sources of valuable information. Last night I happened to hear that a Russian has recently arrived in Town, and he has made no secret of the fact that he has been sent by a private collector to bid for your precious Psalters."

"Who?"

Osborne shrugged. "Haven't a clue as to the identity of the collector. But the agent is a gentleman by the name of Alexandr Orlov. Or at least he claims to be a gentleman. No one in Town knows much about him, save that his mother is rumored to be English and his father a minor member of the Russian gentry. Orlov himself is said to spend most of his time carousing with a rakehell crowd of officers from the Tsar's Imperial Guards."

Kirtland frowned, the curl of his lip turning into a wince as his stallion shied away from the snap of a lady's parasol. "There is something damn peculiar about this auction," he muttered. "Something . . ." He let his voice trail off, unsure of the exact word he wished to choose.

"Sinister?" suggested Osborne with a slight chuckle. "Really now, you—" His brow arched as the scudding sun hit the earl full in the face, bringing to light the deep shadows beneath his eyes and the tautness etched at the corners of his mouth. "You look like hell."

"I had a fitful night," he replied. "Strange dreams." He did not elaborate on the subject, knowing his friend would laugh even harder at the weird stirrings of his imagination. The sensation of being observed by unseen eyes had been unsettling, to say the least. The breeze from the open windows had crept in like a cool caress, raising a prickling of goose bumps along his flesh.

"Dreams?" His friend's expression took a more quizzical cant as they fell into the shadows of the stately linden trees lining one side of the bridle path. "It's not like you to fall prey to flights of fancy. Next you are going to say you saw evil spirits lurking . . . speak of the devil."

The earl followed Osborne's gaze to the swath of turf bordering the Serpentine. A lone rider spurred to a canter as he rounded the stone embankment, his fluid movements matching the stallion's powerful stride. His azure coat and buff breeches seemed purposely chosen to set off the mane of golden hair tied back from his face. Contrary to fashion, he was hatless, with only the thick, sky-blue velvet ribbon as a concession to propriety.

"That's Orlov," murmured Osborne. "Flashy cove, isn't he?"

Kirtland didn't answer until the Russian was lost to sight among the snaking turns of the shimmering waters. "Sometimes where there is flash, there is fire. He rides like a man with experience in the saddle."

"You judge him to be more than a mere popinjay?"

"Only a fool underestimates the enemy before taking full measure of his strengths and weaknesses."

"A wise strategy." A gust of wind tugged at the crown of Osborne's high crown beaver hat, and for a moment, the ruffling of fair hair obscured his profile. "I trust you will display equal intelligence in regard to Lord Lynsley. I have been thinking . . . we must come up with a discreet way to let him know there is no need to poke around in your affairs—"

"To hell with Lynsley," muttered the earl. "He can poke his head up his arse for all I care."

"Is there a particular reason you are in such a black humor?"

"Aside from you and your insufferable chatter?" he shot back. "Let us drop this absurd discussion of castles and dragons."

Osborne's expression clouded. "I have only been trying to tease you out of a sulk. Not to speak of doing my best to keep you out of trouble." His spine stiffened, and, moving without his usual grace, he turned his horse toward the South Gate. "Damn it, Julian. I am your friend, so stop treating me like the enemy. I'm just trying to help. God knows, you have pulled my irons out of the fire on countless occasions in the past."

Kirtland felt a sudden stab of guilt. The *ton* did not always give Osborne the credit he deserved for the courage of his convictions. It was easy to mistake the breezy banter for a lack of real substance. But he, of all people, should know better. Their very first encounter at Eton had come when Osborne—the smallest of all the other new boys—had been the only one brave enough to join him in standing up to a bullying prefect. They had both suffered a beating. But while the bruises were soon gone, the bond forged in battle remained a lasting one. Since then, the two of them had weathered countless school pranks and grueling military campaigns together.

And when he had suffered through the darkest moments in his life, Osborne had stood by him, heedless of the cost to his own reputation in Society.

"My apologies, Dev," he said softly. "I have been acting like an ass."

Osborne relaxed in the saddle and grinned. "Yes, you have. But you are forgiven."

They rode for a few minutes in silence, and Kirtland

was grateful for the unspoken understanding between them that required no further words.

"I appreciate your concern," he went on once they had passed by an abigail walking a pair of yapping pugs. "Truly I do. But it's hard to view Lynsley as a threat. He sits in some cubbyhole in Whitehall and files meaningless reports. Besides, I have done nothing to warrant his attention. Let him ask questions and write up some prosy document." The earl frowned. "I'm more concerned about this fellow Orlov."

"Heed your own words about jumping to conclusions, Julian. Lynsley is no mere bureaucrat, whose skills are confined to shuffling papers. His official title is deceptively boring. As is his outward affability and unruffled demeanor. But I have heard stories from a reliable source that would make your hair stand on end."

A foreboding needled at the nape of Kirtland's neck.

"You remember Nelson's bombardment of Copenhagen in '01, and how the leading ships were in peril until the Trekroner battery was silenced?" Osborne spurred forward to a more private spot on the bridle trail. "Well, Lynsley was serving a temporary post as embassy secretary at the time. And though he was a member of Lord Gervin's diplomatic mission to Sicily three years later, he did not return to England with the rest of the group. It wasn't until the official announcement of the prince's assassination— and Sir John Moreton's murder—was made public that he reappeared in London. Word from my source is that Lynsley was also left for dead in the back alleys of Naples but somehow managed to survive."

"Well, well." Kirtland wasn't sure what to make of the revelations. "It appears the marquess is more interesting than he looks."

"Quite. And it's not just his past that makes one curious. His current doings are all very hugger-mugger."

"For someone who seems to spend most of his time in ballrooms and boudoirs of Mayfair, you appear remarkably well-informed on confidential government matters."

"I am not quite such an indolent idler as that." Osborne gave a flick of his crop. "Although I, like you, have sold out my army commission. I spend some hours each week reading over reports from abroad for a friend on Burrand's general staff."

The unexpected announcement caught the earl off guard. "I am glad to hear you are using your head as more than a target for Gentleman Jackson's fists," he replied, though the news also struck a raw nerve. Knowing that the situation in Eastern Europe was a powder keg ready to explode, he, too, would have liked to offer his services to military intelligence.

But the chances of that ever happening were as likely as St. Peter inviting Lucifer inside the Pearly Gates to take tea, he reminded himself.

"Seeing as you are privy to state secrets, any further idea of why Lynsley was asking about me?"

"Not yet, but I am working on it. In the meantime, try not to do anything that might antagonize the marquess."

"*I* did not go out of my way to draw his attention in the first place," he said stiffly.

Osborne rolled his eyes. "Perhaps it's a good thing you are leaving Town for a time. Out of sight, out of mind."

A heavy mist swirled through the moors surrounding Marquand Castle, muddling the nascent greens and yellows to hazy shades of grey. Stark, forbidding, despite the tantalizing hint of spring. Rather like the Earl of Kirtland . . .

Stop thinking of the man. As Siena looked out the window of her quarters, she warned herself not to concentrate her attention on Julian Henning. There were the other suspects to consider, though the nocturnal visit to each of their residences had left her as much in the dark as before. Indeed, even after a last, meticulous review of the information before consigning the files to the fire, she felt no closer to finding a telling clue.

The traitor had eluded the snare of pen and ink. She would have to catch him in the flesh.

Mindful that every moment mattered, Siena moved away from the casement and unlocked her personal traveling case. Rose had hung up the gowns and unpacked the other clothing, but as there were still several hours until the formalities commenced in the drawing room, she had retreated to the attic quarters assigned to the visiting maids. No doubt she would be mapping out an exit route and inquiring about the routines of the castle—the number of servants, the time of the meals, the location of the guest rooms. Anything that might prove useful in planning the next move.

Rose herself was proving not only useful but also invaluable. Her skills with a needle and curling iron were matched by a sharp eye and an unflappable demeanor. Steady as a rock was Rose, with a precise efficiency that ran like clockwork. If she offered little in the way of casual conversation, her pragmatism was reassuring if anything went wrong.

Not that Siena meant to rely on anyone else in a pinch. Unfolding the cloth from around her private arsenal, she ran an oiled rag over her sword blade, checking that the arduous carriage ride had left no nicks on the steel. The case would remain locked to the prying eyes of the duke's servants. Lud, what a gabble of gossip the sight of the assorted weapons would provoke, for along with knives and pistols, she had included a few more exotic implements. They would only appear under extreme circumstances, but as an everyday precaution, she would go nowhere without a small knife strapped to her leg.

The case also held other tricks of the trade. Colorful Italian tarot cards, sleeping potions, painted masks—all the things she would need to play her deadly games with the gentlemen of The Gilded Page Club. There were also a few more lethal concoctions, enclosed in a smaller box. The thought of using them made her skin crawl. It was one thing to kill an enemy with a straightforward sword thrust or shot. But to tip a powdered poison into a drink . . .

However, orders were orders. If it came to that, she wouldn't spill a grain.

Lynsley's contact had proved highly efficient in finding the supplies. He had also taken care of arranging the invitation to the auction. She imagined it had taken some skillful maneuvering, but the name of "Lady Blackdove" now graced the ducal guest list.

A lady. Siena nearly laughed at the irony of an urchin from the slums impersonating a refined female of noble birth. Her training would allow her to play the role faultlessly. But at the same time, she was keenly aware of being an imposter. *Who was she?* She knew nothing of her past, her parents.

You are what you make of yourself, Volpina.

Da Rimini had often challenged her with such taunts when she had thought herself too exhausted to lift her sword. There was some wisdom to his words. The past was the past—she must focus on the present.

Satisfied that all was in perfect readiness, Siena hid

the key in the sheath of her knife. Like Rose, she meant to make a preliminary reconnaissance of Marquand Castle before the formal welcoming ceremony that evening. They had timed their travels to be among the earliest arrivals at the duke's estate. And from all outward appearances, eccentricity must run in the family.

The rambling structure looked to be an architectural oddity, with elements that reflected a hodgepodge of centuries and sensibilities. A central tower of weathered stone rose to a crenellated crown—no doubt the remnants of an ancient fortress that had inspired the original name. Attached to each side was an L-shaped wing, with blackened Tudor timbers and whitewashed stucco becoming a sprawl of Georgian brick as it turned the corner. The longer length of each side faced an interior maze of terraced gardens. At the far end of the greenery was a massive conservatory, an improbable pagoda of turreted glass that connected the two wings.

A flight of fancy if ever there was one, reflected Siena. She had made a rough sketch based on the first, fleeting view. But the sooner the details were added, the better.

She sat at the desk and began making a few notes on her own situation. The butler had, after hushed consultation with an elderly majordomo, assigned her to quarters on the second floor of the East Wing, overlooking the winding gravel drive. The rest of the rooms along her corridor looked to be deserted.

Was her isolation designed to protect her from the advances of the men, or the other way around? Her lips pursed. In either case, the privacy suited her purposes quite well. She planned to be moving about during the night and wished to avoid any awkward encounters with amorous guests. And while she would have preferred windows looking out over the gardens . . .

The thud of hooves drew her eye from the paper. Siena rose from her chair, angling for a clearer view of the oncoming rider. Who, she wondered, had chosen to forgo the relative comforts of a closed carriage in order to gallop across the wild moors?

An answer was not long in taking shape. Cutting through a row of ghostly apple trees, a hard-charging stallion suddenly broke free of the fog. Flanks glistening, mane whipping in the wind, the black beast cleared the orchard fence without breaking stride and crossed the back lawns at a pounding pace.

Had the magic of Devon's druids conjured up a mythical centaur from the swirling vapor? Nose pressed to the windowpane, Siena stood mesmerized by the animal grace of the apparition. So matched were the movements of horse and rider that it took her a moment to distinguish between the two.

"Bloody, *bloody* hell." The glass was like ice against her flesh. And then like fire.

It was some darker, devilish alchemy at play. For as the figure came into focus, all her previous doubts were put to flight. There was no mistaking the magnificent mount or the powerful thighs astride the hard saddle. No denying the terrible truth.

Her midnight stranger and the Earl of Kirtland were one and the same gentleman.

With a flick of his gloved hands, Kirtland slowed the stallion to a walk. His breath formed fine clouds, pale against the stubbling that shadowed his jaw, and the flapping shoulder capes of his oilskin cloak further obscured his face. Not that she needed any nuance of expression to identify the earl. The arrogant tilt of his nose, the supreme sensuality of his mouth, the chiseled contours of his body were already branded upon her consciousness.

He looked up, raindrops clinging to his dark lashes. But nothing could water down the intensity of that hooded gaze. Like an eagle.

Siena spun away from the window, hoping he hadn't seen her staring. Recalling the earl's family crest, she rubbed at her own indelible marking. Two birds of a feather? Solitary raptors circling in wary speculation, wondering if the other was fair game.

The hunt would begin in earnest this evening, when all the guests were expected to gather in the drawing room at the stroke of seven. Along with her suspects, ten other gentlemen had been invited to bid for the Psalters. She had no reason to view any of them as a threat. Indeed, they might even prove unwitting allies in flushing out her prey, for the man she sought was governed by primal passions— whether they be anger, revenge, greed. Or jealousy.

Adding herself and various Marquand family members present, the assembled group would number an even two dozen.

Following a formal welcome from the duke himself, his secretaries were to pass out a detailed schedule for the days preceding the auction. A variety of amusements had been planned. Somewhere between the lines of the riding and shooting, the eating and drinking, the betting and bluffing, she would have to pencil in trapping a dangerous traitor.

The odds were still stacked against her, but the game was only just heating up.

Chapter Eight

*T*his promises to be a memorable interlude, does it not, gentlemen?" Smoothing a last preening touch to his hair, Dunster paused at the threshold of the drawing room and turned to the other club members. "Shall we go in?"

The six of them had agreed to meet upstairs and come down together. Though Kirtland would have preferred to make his own plans, he considered himself pledged to be part of the group.

Taking the lead, Dunster chose a spot by the arched windows, which afforded an excellent view of all the formalities. A footman brought champagne, and the marquess, resplendent in a claret-colored evening jacket and gold-threaded waistcoat, quickly proposed a toast. "To the coming competition." He smiled, the flash of teeth mirroring the hard-edged glint of his glass. "Those who think that the appreciation of art is a dull subject have never experienced the thrill of having their fingers a hairbreadth away from possessing perfection."

An air of anticipation, heady as the scent of the magnificent hothouse roses, swirled through the duke's drawing room as the other guests began to make their entrance. To the earl, it appeared to sharpen the shimmering light from the crystal chandeliers and deepen the jewel-tone colors of the rich furnishings. Even the gilt frames of the paintings seemed to reflect the glitter of each individual's desire.

"Aye, it's anything but academic," agreed Leveritt after a long sip of the sparkling wine. Unlike Dunster, the viscount had dressed in muted shades of grey for the occasion, relying on subtle touches, like the unusual knot of his cravat and the cut of his lapels, to distinguish himself from the others.

Kirtland repressed a sardonic smile. In a competition of style, Leveritt's understated elegance won hands down.

Jadwin, who was standing in the viscount's shadow, surveyed the surroundings. "Speaking of academics, I see that Lord Brewster has come down from Oxford. Given his fortune and his scholarship, he must be considered a serious contender."

The marquess dismissed the idea with a brusque wave. "I assure you, he is no match for me."

"Don't let your palms get too itchy, Dunster. You are not the only one imagining your hands caressing a sublime beauty." Fitzwilliam had his gaze locked on the entrance to the drawing room, watching like a hawk for the first flutter of the Dove. "By the by, does anyone know whether our luscious ladybird has arrived?"

The earl wrenched his eyes away from the doorway, unwilling to be seen staring. Swearing silently, he edged a step away from the other club members, trying to distance himself from the lewd talk of her charms. But the subject seemed to take on a life of its own.

"Yes, she has. Just after nuncheon," offered Winthrop. His thick fingers, which rarely seemed still, twitched his beard to a sharper point. "According to my valet, the footmen have been speaking of nothing else all afternoon. Had them tripping over their boots to show her the way around the East Wing, and the most direct route to the conservatory at the far end of the gardens."

"Where the duke's nephew invited her to pick her choice of flowers for her evening coiffure."

"That's gilding the lily," quipped Fitzwilliam. "She needs no adornment to accentuate her charms."

"Indeed. I, for one, would say she looks better plucked than decked out in all her fancy feathers." Dunster's teeth seemed to have a predatory gleam. For some unaccountable reason, Kirtland felt the urge to knock them down the marquess's throat.

"Those rose-tipped nipples, those silky black curls," continued the marquess. "Just aching for a man's caress."

"It's your own length of flesh that is throbbing for release, Dunster," replied Fitzwilliam.

"No doubt he's hard up for a female's touch." Winthrop ran his thumb along the lip of his wineglass. "Not that I wouldn't mind finding my cock in her velvety grasp."

"Or buried deep within her petals . . ."

"Are you gentlemen talking of flora and fauna rather than parchment and pigment?" From behind them, a stranger's voice interrupted the conversation. "I cannot say I am sorry to see my fellow competitors so easily distracted."

The earl turned and immediately recognized Orlov. Despite the other man's slight smirk, he found himself welcoming the intrusion.

"Might I be so bold as to introduce myself?" The Russian bowed to the group with a low, sweeping flourish. The gesture seemed deliberately flashy—like his attire. Tonight he was dressed in an azure blue velvet evening coat, matched with buff pantaloons and a wide-striped silk waistcoat of ivory and jonquil. To top it off, he had knotted a length of gauzy paisley silk at his collar instead of a starched cravat. "I have heard much about the gentlemen of The Gilded Page Club."

"Who the devil is this jackanapes?" muttered Dunster under his breath.

The Russian's smile stretched a touch wider. "I am Alexandr Orlov, visiting from St. Petersburg."

Kirtland and the other club members had no choice but to respond. However, both Leveritt and Jadwin ignored the Russian's outstretched hand.

"I take it you are interested in rare books, Mr. Orlov." Winthrop was the first to break the cool silence that followed the individual introductions.

"Not really. I am merely representing the interests of, shall we say, a friend." The Russian flicked a mote of dust from his sleeve. "My duty is simply to ensure that the Psalters do not fall into the wrong hands."

"You are not the only one intent on taking home the prize," said Dunster.

"I imagined as much." Orlov's hair was loose tonight, and a toss of his head set the golden locks to dancing along the ridge of his shoulders. "We wouldn't all be here if the prize were not worth fighting for." Kirtland caught a slight narrowing of the Russian's eyes as the man turned to him. Like slivers of arctic ice. The look—at odds with the oiled charm—melted in an instant. "Wouldn't you agree, Lord Kirtland?" he asked with exaggerated innocence. "As a former military man, you are the most experienced among us in the art—and the betrayals—of war."

The earl saw his fellow club members stiffen at the allusion to his disgrace, but his own reaction was one of mild amusement. If the Russian's tactics were to get under his skin, the fellow would have to employ a less cack-handed attack. "I may no longer hold any army rank, but I trust that my battle skills have not grown too dull from disuse."

Orlov acknowledged the riposte with an ironic salute. "A bit of friendly competition always serves to sharpen the senses. I look forward to a spirited duel of wits."

"Damned impertinent fellow," muttered Winthrop as the Russian moved off to fetch a fresh glass of champagne. "I wonder that Marquand's man of affairs allowed him to join our company."

"His friend must be someone of great influence, to have garnered an invitation for a surrogate to be part of the proceedings." Leveritt frowned. "At least the coxcomb's English seems polished enough, even if the same cannot be said for his manners."

"His mother is from Yorkshire." Kirtland saw no reason not to share what little he knew of the man.

"You know him?" asked Dunster, his look of irritation suddenly giving way to an air of alertness.

"Only by reputation. I heard a few things about him before I left Town."

"So did I." Jadwin looked a bit smug. "And even if what they say is only half-true, Dunster, you may find yourself with a rival for the title of Master of the Mayfair Boudoirs."

The marquess did not join in the laughter.

Kirtland noted the tautness around Dunster's mouth.

Something had put the man on edge, whether it was the Russian's deliberate insouciance or Jadwin's veiled barb. It was not the first time that the earl had sensed a friction between the two club members. One that went deeper than friendly bantering. As for Orlov, he himself was undecided on whether to think of the Russian as a puffed-up jackanapes or someone more subtly sinister.

But further musings on the other gentlemen present were suddenly overshadowed by the entrance of the Black Dove.

She had chosen a crimson gown, a sleek, high-waisted Grecian design that was cut to accentuate her willowy height. In concession to ducal propriety, the bodice was less scandalously revealing than her usual garb. Yet there was no question that every male eye in the room was on her magnificent bosom, whose alabaster curves were teasingly evident above the pleated ruffles of red.

Including his own.

She moved through the crowd of gentlemen, a tongue of fire licking up around coal black embers. Much as he wished to ignore her, his gaze was drawn to her incendiary presence. Like a moth to a flame.

Turning on his heel, Kirtland sought to douse his growing heat with a sip of the sparkling wine. And yet, even then he could not seem to escape her allure. He heard the soft rustle of silk, and a moment later a cloud of ethereal scent enveloped his senses. A lemony verbena spiced with lusher hints of cinnamon and cloves. *Light and dark.* Unlike the cloying scents usually favored by women of her profession, it was a mysterious blend. One that left much to the imagination.

Damn. He forced himself to think of the smoothness of flesh-colored vellum, the scent of rich leather, the feel of corded spines, and the soft sheen of gilded letters. Books should be far more seductive than a fancy trollop.

"Damn." It was Dunster who uttered the oath aloud. "It looks as though that bastard Orlov is introducing himself to the Dove. He may have *carte blanche* to bid on our books, but I've no intention of allowing him to insinuate himself into our own private competition."

"It is the ladybird who has the last word on that." The earl did not bother to watch the performance.

"Her proposal included only us."

"It was not exactly a binding legal contract," sneered Leveritt. "What do you plan to do—sue her for breach of promise?"

"There are other ways of making her pay," muttered the marquess darkly.

By deliberate design, Siena did not approach the members of The Gilded Page Club directly. It had been a week since she had appeared at their meeting. Let them watch her flirt a bit, she thought. Hovering just out of reach would rekindle the flames of desire.

And so, she did not object when the tall, golden-haired gentleman boldly moved in to block her path.

"You must be the magnificent Lady Blackdove that everyone is talking about. Allow me the liberty of introducing myself—Alexandr Orlov."

As he murmured his name, the Russian turned her gloved hand palm up and placed a kiss on her bare wrist. Siena repressed a shiver. His lips, though full and firm, were cold. As were his eyes.

"This is, to be sure, an exciting moment," he finished.

She had been taught about men like Alexandr Orlov. They were the sort who looked to turn any situation to their advantage. "Good evening, sir," she replied coolly. "Indeed, it is, for we are about to hear the duke explain the details of the coming auction."

"You already have an unfair advantage, milady. I fear I shall have trouble concentrating on mere words," he murmured.

"I advise you to pay close attention. Otherwise, you might risk your chance of winning the Psalters."

Orlov placed a hand on his heart. "Until now, I would have said that the prayer books were the finest treasures in Marquand Castle. However . . ." His voice trailed off in a sigh.

Did he hope to charm his way into her bed? If so, he faced an impossible climb.

"However," he repeated, "I may have to revise my thinking." His fingers caught the tassels of her fan and slowly smoothed the fringed silk.

Slanting a sidelong glance at the members of The Gilded Page Club, Siena saw a stirring of impatience within their ranks. It was time to move on.

"Thank you, Mr. Orlov." Siena brusquely put an end to his attentions. "No matter how often we hear a compliment, those of our sex always appreciate being noticed. But now, if you will excuse me, I see some acquaintances I must greet."

The Russian accepted the set-down with a show of good grace. "What fortunate gentlemen. Perhaps we will have an opportunity to get to know each other better during the coming days."

"Are you a wealthy man, sir?"

"Alas, unlike you, Lady Blackdove, I haven't a feather to fly with."

"Then let us be frank, sir." She dropped her voice to a

discreet whisper. "We will not be forming a more intimate acquaintance."

He cocked a sardonic smile. "Is money all that matters to you?"

"But of course."

"And yet, it is said that money is the root of all evil."

"And you are implying that *your* root will do me some good?" She tapped her fan to his cheek. "I think not, sir."

He laughed softly.

"As for those who malign the power of money, they are the ones who have never gone without it."

Orlov stepped aside, but not before leaving her with a parting shot. "There are some things in life even more powerful than greed, madam."

Like lust?

Surrounded by hungry eyes and wolfish smiles, she was inclined to agree.

Leaving the Russian behind, Siena moved on to where The Gilded Page Club had gathered. "Good evening, gentlemen." With a silky whisper of her skirts, she glided to a position in the center of their circle. "I am gratified to see that no last-moment obstacle prevented any of us from making the journey."

Kirtland edged back, his face falling into the shadows of a decorative urn.

"As we did not meet each other formally during our initial encounter, shall we begin this evening on a more proper note?" She fluttered her lashes, fanning the recollection of her wanton nakedness. "For this fortnight, you may call me Lady Blackdove. The winner of our private competition will naturally be granted the use of a more intimate name."

One by one, the gentlemen introduced themselves.

Fitzwilliam . . . Jadwin . . . Leveritt. Each file began to take life as a face, a touch.

"Thou that art now the world's fresh ornament . . ." Baron Fitzwilliam had brushed his long, curling hair to the gleam of burnished copper. His way with words was equally polished as he flashed an easy smile. "Shakespeare would have waxed even more poetic had he witnessed your entrance. Your gown is stunning." He paused just a fraction. "Though its beauty cannot quite measure up to your own natural splendors."

Siena acknowledged the compliment with a coy flutter of her fan before moving on. The gentleman had a clever tongue. But did the outward charm disguise an inner anger?

Leveritt and Jadwin murmured no more than their names, unwilling—or unable—to match the baron's way with words.

"The gown is indeed ravishing." When it came to his turn, the Marquess of Dunster held her hand a touch too long after raising it to his lips. "I saw that mongrel Orlov sniffing around your skirts. I should be happy to kick some manners into him."

"La, I am sure that violence won't be necessary." Siena gave a mock shudder. "You gentlemen seem to find blood sports appealing, but I can think of far more enjoyable activities to satisfy such primal urges."

"As can I." Winthrop took hold of the opportunity to make his own obeisances. After bowing low over her glove, he wasted no time in asking, "When will we learn more of the games you have planned for the coming days?"

Speaking of dogs, thought Siena. For all their tailored elegance, the members of The Gilded Page Club reminded her of a pack of curs fighting over a bone. All save Kirtland. The earl did not allow his lips to stray anywhere near her.

"I shall hand out the first of the challenges tomorrow morning at breakfast. At which time I shall explain in more detail how the competition will be conducted," she answered. "Shall we meet at ten?"

Dunster licked his chops. "I can't think of a more delectable way to start the day."

The others chimed in with equal enthusiasm. Siena kept up a flirtatious banter, trying not to sneak a look at the earl. She already knew his expression was black and brooding as a midnight storm. She could guess at the surface reasons, but she could not yet fathom the full depth of his character. What secrets lay hidden inside that forbidding figure? He was a conundrum, a contradiction. The papers had revealed one side of the man while his fleeting kiss had revealed quite another.

Was Julian Henning capable of betrayal? Or was it her own heart that was playing her false?

The quickening beat in her chest seemed to drum a warning not to let her attention tarry on Kirtland. There were five other men whose most intimate thoughts she must strip bare.

The florid flatteries told her nothing useful. As they all paused to accept another round of drinks, Siena adroitly changed the subject.

"In addition to the first game in the morning, I would like to schedule a short, private meeting with each of you in the afternoon." It was, she knew, an aggressive gambit to try an early attack from two angles. But she had learned from *Il Lupino* that a quick start could often put an opponent enough off-balance to reveal a telling weakness. "As you are all accorded to be discerning connoisseurs of art as well as flesh, I should like for each of you to acquaint me with some specific treasure of Marquand Castle. Count on a half hour each. It will give us a chance to converse on a more intimate footing."

"An excellent idea." Looking smug, Jadwin took the lead and was quick to rattle off a brief history of the house. "The conservatory was designed by the same man who created Prinny's Pavilion in Brighton. The height and circumference of the glass cupolas are an engineering marvel," he added. "I should be delighted to show you around the structure and point out its most salient features."

Siena smiled. "Excellent. Shall we meet at three?"

Leveritt invited her to view the portrait gallery, and Winthrop offered his expertise on the medieval tapestries. Dunster chose the collection of Rembrandt etchings while Fitzwilliam suggested a tour of the formal gardens designed by Capability Brown.

Feeling rather flushed with the success of her first thrust and a second glass of the duke's excellent champagne—Siena was emboldened to confront the earl. He alone had made no offer.

"Have you no field of knowledge you wish to share, Lord Kirtland? No passionate interest?"

"You appear to be having no trouble in keeping yourself occupied while you are here, madam."

"But I should like to hear your opinion on some facet of art."

His brow arched upward. "Why?"

His question took her by surprise, but she quickly regained her balance and replied coolly, "Because I wish to get to know those who are in the running for my favors."

"I will not be breaking into a sweat anytime soon. I don't run. Nor do I jump through hoops."

"That is hardly a gentlemanly reply."

His sardonic sneer—a look she was beginning to recognize all too well—curled to new heights. "Seeing as your sources seem quite well-informed as to our personal peccadilloes, that should not come as any shock."

Did the man ever smile at people? Or was it just his animals that were favored with a flash of real warmth. Siena stared at the hardness of his mouth before countering, "What is surprising is your reluctance to accept a challenge from a female. What are you afraid of?"

His face remained absolutely impassive, but a strange spark of light turned his emerald eyes to pools of molten jade.

The earl did not lack passion—she knew that already. He merely kept it well hidden. Along with what else? That was her job to discover. "Your Spanish allies would call it *mano a mano*."

"My Spanish allies would also say you possessed iron *cojones,* madam. I would agree with them, save for that I have seen evidence to the contrary."

A soft laugh slipped from her lips. "Touché, sir."

For an instant, the earl's expression betrayed a twitch of amusement. It was quickly obscured by the wink of cut crystal as he raised his glass in mock salute. "As you see, madam, a match between us would hardly be fair." With that, he turned on his heel and walked off.

Siena had little time to contemplate the skirmish, for a bell chimed, announcing that the Duke of Marquand had entered the room.

"Welcome." Age and arthritic joints now confined him to a bath chair, and his voice seemed a bit fragile as well.

"I am pleased that you all accepted the rigors of a journey to the Devonshire moors." He waited for his servants to roll him up onto a low dais discreetly disguised with garlands of ivy before going on. "Unfortunately, my condition makes it difficult for me to travel these days. I do hope you will think the discomfort worthwhile."

Polite laughter greeted the self-deprecating remarks. Someone lifted a glass in toast. "Hear, hear."

The duke cleared his throat. "I am sure you are all eager to hear more concerning the auction of my Psalters. First and foremost, I imagine you are wondering why I have invited you here for a fortnight." He paused, a slight twinkle coming to his crinkled eyes. "A prerogative of age. I like a party, and so few of my friends are still alive . . ." Once the chuckles had died down, he continued. "On a more serious note, my books have been a great love of my life. But as my heir does not share my feelings, I have, with his blessings, decided to see that a select group of my treasures goes to a collector who will appreciate their beauty."

Siena watched as a solemn, middle-aged man dressed in black helped Marquand lift a glass of water to his lips. It appeared as if his physical infirmities did not allow his body to keep pace with his lively mind. Still, it was evident why the duke was renowned as the most erudite art connoisseur in the realm. No wonder other collectors saw this auction as a golden opportunity.

"Call it the whim of a foolish old man, but a dukedom does allow me the privilege of eccentricity. So, the two weeks afford me the chance to conduct a private interview with each prospective buyer in order to ensure that all are worthy candidates to possess my Psalters. A younger man would no doubt accomplish the task in a far shorter time, but be that as it may. Be advised—some of you may find yourselves excluded from the actual bidding."

A fit of coughing forced him to interrupt his explanation. "Forgive me, my strength seems to be waning. I shall leave it to Stoneleigh, my personal secretary, to finish the rest of the explanations. As you all shall have a good deal of leisure time, I have asked him to arrange a number of daily activities and excursions for your pleasure. You are, of course, free to do exactly as you choose. I should like for you to treat the castle as if it were your own home for the coming fortnight. Should you have any specific wishes, you have only to ask him to make the arrangements."

After accepting another drink of water from his secretary, the duke signaled for the liveried footman to roll his chair toward the door.

Stoneleigh took his place, speaking in a clipped tone about the dining hours and the variety of daily activities that would be available. A schedule, he explained, would be posted each morning in the breakfast room. His little speech ended with a shake of the silver bell, summoning them to the welcoming banquet.

Fitzwilliam was quick to offer Siena his escort to the dining room, a move that drew scowls from some of the other club members. "Are you, perchance, an early riser, madam?" he inquired.

"I am quite flexible when it comes to bedtime habits," replied Siena with a flutter of her fan. "Why?"

"Instead of viewing the gardens in midafternoon, I thought you might like to see them before breakfast, when the light is still pale and pure as a virgin's breast."

"Is that a line from one of your sonnets, sir?"

"Not yet. But I am sure you will inspire me to write an ode."

"Not to virginity," she said dryly. "Very well. I shall meet you at nine on the upper terrace." *So far, so good,* she thought as they separated to take their assigned places at the banquet table. Now that she had the gentlemen all under one roof, it was time for the games to begin in earnest.

A banked fire glowed in the hearth, and the soft crackling of its coals was a welcome respite from all the clinking crystal and male laughter.

Kirtland paused on the threshold and pressed his fingertips to his temples as he surveyed the study. It was one of a number of Tower rooms that displayed the duke's vast collection of artistic treasures, and its quiet splendor offered a refuge from the smoky revelries of his fellow collectors. The banquet had stretched on interminably, serving up course after course of rich foods and banal conversation. The combination had left a bad taste in his mouth, and when finally the few ladies present had withdrawn, leaving the men to their port and cheroots, he had excused himself as well.

Was he, as Osborne had hinted, in danger of becoming a hermit? The earl admitted that he did not suffer fools gladly, and the trouble was, so few people were truly interesting. Most cared for naught but feasting on the latest gossip. He caught a number of furtive glances directed his way during the meal. No doubt his presence—and past scandal—were providing a juicy tidbit to gnaw on.

Swearing silently, he looked to the sideboard, where the candles spilled a mellow light over a tray of decanters—ruby ports, tawny sherries, fiery brandies. Deciding he needed a drink, he was halfway across the carpet before he realized he was not alone.

Though the alcove was deep in shadow, Kirtland had no trouble recognizing who was studying the set of engravings hung on the wall. *Bloody hell.* He had assumed that the Black Dove had retreated to her own chambers for the evening.

But apparently not.

He thought for a moment about backing off and finding another room in which to seek sanctuary, but pride pushed him on. He would be damned if he let the woman force him to retreat.

As he approached, the earl saw that the plates were from an Italian Renaissance manual of fencing. "Have you an interest in swordplay? I was under the impression that females couldn't care less about the martial arts."

She turned, but in the flickering light her expression was unreadable. "I know a thing or two about the subject. I have often observed some friends exercising their skills."

Tired and irritated at having his interlude of solitude spoiled, Kirtland replied with an edge of sarcasm. "There is a big difference between observation and actual practice."

Her bare shoulders lifted in a careless shrug as she turned back to the prints. "Perhaps. But anyone with an elementary knowledge of the discipline can see that the artist has the grip wrong in the first figure."

The earl laughed—then looked a bit closer. She was right, but in his present mood he was loath to admit it. A pair of ancient rapiers framed the row of prints. On impulse, he took one down and offered her the hilt. "Care to show me the correct way?"

Her gloved hand closed unerringly around the chaised silver, the lead finger wrapping around the quillons and ricasso in a style that ensured superb control of the blade. Without hesitation, she cut a perfect *arrebatar* through the air, ending with a flourish.

He took down the other weapon and crossed swords with her. The blades kissed with a soft *snick*.

"*En garde,*" he murmured. "Let us see how well you move through a *botta dritta.*"

The Black Dove flashed a smile. "Whenever you are ready."

The slivers of steel danced through the shadows as she matched him stroke for stroke, parrying each angle of attack with deft precision.

"*Punta sopramano,*" she countered.

Their positions reversed, with Kirtland performing the defensive maneuvers. They moved noiselessly across the carpet, at times so close his thigh brushed hers. He was intimately aware of the strength in her wrist, the lithe curve of muscle running up her bare arm.

"Your friend must be an excellent teacher." He angled a slow lunge. She deflected it past her cheek. Their faces were now mere inches apart. Kirtland saw that her eyes were even more luminous than he had imagined—a rich amber gold that once again sent a stab of recognition through him.

No. It was the surfeit of champagne playing tricks with his mind. Distracted, he nearly allowed her weapon to slip under his guard.

"He is . . . very good." Siena spun at half speed through a flawless *sopra il braccio.*

"But not as good as you?"

Was it merely a quirk of light, or did she flash a challenging wink along with a *stocatta lunga*. "Not many men are."

"A pity this is not the place to question such a bold assertion," he whispered. "I should like to test your true mettle."

Their gazes locked, like steel on steel.

"Indeed, there is not the proper space for a full range of maneuvers."

He suddenly spun a step closer. *Those cheekbones, that mouth.*

Her lips parted in a sliver of a smile.

There was no mistaking the truth now. "You!"

She cut a quick salute. "Yes, our paths cross once again."

"Who the devil are you?" he rasped. "And this time I demand more than a show of acrobatics for an answer."

Her blade blocked his path. "I don't answer to you, Lord Kirtland, or to anyone here, save myself."

"You—"

The sound of footsteps, punctuated by shouts of drunken laughter, echoed in the corridor. In a few minutes they would no longer be alone.

"You haven't heard the last word on this, madam." Unwilling to be caught up in a fresh round of gossip, the earl broke away and hung the rapier back on the wall. "The duel is not yet done," he warned, pausing in the doorway. "And next time don't count on the rules of engagement being skewed in your favor."

Chapter Nine

*H*ad she made a reckless mistake?

Tightening the sash of her wrapper, Siena moved to her bedchamber window and stared out at the sloping lawns and topiary trees. The scudding moonlight cut like quicksilver blades through the budding branches, a sharp reminder that this hide-and-seek charade was a dangerous game to play.

Too on edge to return to her quarters after the banquet, she had sought one of the smaller display rooms, curious to see some of the duke's treasured books and prints. The appeal of having such beauty and knowledge at one's fingertips was so alluring that she had been tempted to reach out and touch the copperplate engravings when the earl had entered the room. Fencing had been the last thing on her mind, but as *Il Lupino* had often said, sometimes it was necessary to improvise.

Hilt in hand, she felt confident of her abilities. But in the heat of battle, had she gone too far?

Revealing her identity to Kirtland this early in the game

was a bold gambit. Perhaps too bold. Given the way he shunned her presence, he might not have made the connection on his own.

On the other hand, she reasoned, it had been necessary to do *something* striking to keep him from staying at arm's length. She needed to be close to him—and to all of the suspects—if she had any hope of learning their secrets.

Well, there was no question she had gotten Kirtland's attention.

Her palms prickled, recalling the sweet smoothness of steel in her hand and the matching grace of his movements. Elegant, effortless. The man was a master of the sword as well as the saddle. Clashing at quarter speed, their skills were equal. In a real duel, she wondered who would come out on top.

As for their war of words . . .

So far their encounters had all been marked by conflict, with neither of them giving ground. Siena thought for a moment. One of Da Rimini's rules was to keep the enemy off-balance. So perhaps it was time to switch tactics. Could Kirtland be seduced into lowering his guard? She sensed that he was not impervious to desire. His kiss, however fleeting, had revealed an unexpected passion. An oddly vulnerable need.

A tiny spark flared as she ran a fingertip over her lip, but she quickly extinguished it with a low oath. Her decision was based purely on pragmatism, not on her own strange reaction to his intimate touch. Given his military background and experience in clandestine intelligence, the earl was the most obvious suspect. It would test all of her cunning and cleverness to cut through his defenses.

However intriguing that individual challenge, she

pushed it aside for the moment. She had another, more immediate test looming.

Seating herself at the escritoire, Siena slid a fresh sheet of foolscap upon the blotter and uncapped the inkpot. The slim shaft of ebony did not feel quite so solid in her hand as a length of steel, despite the old adage that Mrs. Merlin was so fond of repeating. *The pen is mightier than the sword.* These gentlemen had lived all their lives in a world of nuanced language and oblique meanings. A world where a word, a phrase, could shift the balance of power as surely as armies. It was, after all, a letter that had set all these forces in motion.

Including herself.

In contrast, her own early lessons in life had been grounded in the fact that physical force dominated all else. At an early age, she had quickly realized that the only way to beat brute strength was through quickness, cunning, and an absolute refusal to knuckle under to fear, no matter how scared she was inside. She suffered her share of blows, yet had somehow managed to best the bullies who would have sold her services to a tavern or brothel. But was an orphan—a street urchin with no family, no erudite education, no fancy home like Marquand Castle—a match for these highborn scions of privilege?

For the first dozen years of her life, her bed had been the dirt floor of a gin shop cellar, shared with a pack of other children, and her food had been scraps scavenged from the alleys. The Academy had polished her perception of the world outside the slums of St. Giles.

But now that understanding would be put to the test.

The nib hovered over the pristine white paper. The Gilded Page Club members were primed for the first game to be handed out in the morning. It must be a provocative one, a task that would appeal to their own desires while revealing more than they might realize.

The candles guttered as the night breeze found the cracks in the casement, and with it came the reminder of a recent evening, a fire blazing in the hearth, a gentleman reading, a dog-eared page . . .

Strangely enough, it was the earl who served as inspiration for the first test of wits.

Smiling, Siena began to write.

The next day dawned cloudless and surprisingly mild. Draping a silk shawl over her shoulders, Siena passed through the French doors of the Music Room and let herself out onto the upper terrace. Its slate tiles, still damp with the morning dew, glistened like ebony as she moved to the far railing. None of the other guests appeared to be stirring yet. The *ton,* she knew, rarely rose before noon—another reason she had chosen an early hour for the first challenge. Fatigue often fostered a mental mistake.

Fitzwilliam, however, showed no outward signs of overindulgence. His step was brisk as he came to greet her, his eyes unclouded. He cocked a look at the skies and the graveled path leading down through the ornamental shrubbery. "As the weather looks agreeable, shall we take a tour of the Conservatory grounds? From there, you shall get a good overview of Brown's genius."

"I am in your capable hands." She smiled, settling his glove a touch more intimately on her arm.

"I shall try not to disappoint," he replied with a twitch of his own mouth. "Launcelot Brown earned the moniker 'Capability' on account of his fondness for speaking of a county estate as having a great capability for improvement. He saw himself as a place maker, not a gardener, and his style of smooth, undulating grasses and serpentine lakes . . ."

As Fitzwilliam explained the basic theory of Brown's landscape design, Siena surreptitiously watched his face rather than the examples he pointed out. Like his voice, his countenance had a good-humored cant to it, affable rather than arrogant. Indeed, on recounting an anecdote from a past garden party, he showed himself capable of laughing at his own gaffes.

"You have quite a marvelous way with words, sir," she said as they paused to admire the view. "Are you equally poetic in other performances?"

Fitzwilliam laughed softly as he gave a toss of his coppery hair. "My audience has always seemed satisfied."

A subtle answer, revealing a certain self-deprecating wit.

Feeling she was learning a great deal about his character, Siena decided to sharpen her banter and probe for information about the others. "So the six of you do not fear that the competition will spoil your close friendship?"

He shrugged. "In truth, aside from a passion for rare books, we have few interests in common. Outside of the club, all of us move in different social circles. Dunster spends his leisure time with the Carlton set, while I prefer a less flamboyant crowd." He thought for a moment. "Come to think of it, Leveritt and Jadwin are the only ones who have a friendship that goes beyond the occasional meetings of The Gilded Page. They share other artistic interests, and I believe they belong to several of the same Societies."

Leveritt certainly looked the very picture of refinement, she mused. The oldest member of the Club, he dressed with an understated elegance—from his close-cropped locks, now going a touch grey at the temples, to the exquisite cut and subtle colorings of his clothing, not a hair ever seemed out of place.

As for Jadwin, she had noticed that he not only emulated the viscount's sartorial style but also copied some of his little mannerisms. It seemed likely that he looked up to the viscount as a mentor of sorts. According to Lynsley's files, both men were bachelors who were quite active in the social swirl of Mayfair.

"Indeed, they are cofounders of the Doric Club, which specializes in the study of Greek antiquities," added Fitzwilliam.

It was little details such as these that might prove useful. But not wishing to seem too curious about the others, Siena turned the talk back to Fitzwilliam and his poetry. They circled around through the topiary trees as they chatted and were about to enter the West Wing when another guest came striding up from the stables.

"Putting a filly through her paces before breakfast, eh, Fitzwilliam?"

Siena recognized the gentleman in riding dress as the Irish earl, Lord Bantrock.

"Rather the other way around," said Fitzwilliam lightly. "The lady asked for an explanation of the duke's landscape design."

Ignoring the baron's pleasantries, Bantrock took her hand and made a show of kissing her fingers. "Should you need an expert to show you around the interior of the castle, feel free to ask me."

"You consider yourself an expert on architecture, milord?" she asked coyly.

"Oh yes, I am quite an authority on boudoirs," he said with a leer.

His hand still held hers, and she gave it a playful squeeze. "Do remind me to ask your opinion of the four-poster bedstead in my room. By its size and shape, it appears to be Elizabethan, a style I find attractive." She gave a husky little laugh. "But then, I do tend to favor things that are large and well built."

Bantrock grinned. "Be assured, I shall do so at the first available opportunity. Until then, madam." Flashing a wolfish wink, he walked off.

Fitzwilliam seemed unperturbed by her amorous exchange with another man. Deciding to take the bull by the horns, she remarked, "Quite frankly, I am surprised that you do not appear more aggrieved at having another man tread on your toes, so to speak. Is it not a challenge to your pride, as well as your ego?"

He shrugged. "Your charms are very alluring, madam, and these little games quite amusing. I would gladly pay a great deal to bed you. But should I fail to win your favor, I shall not fall on my sword."

A man of moderate temperament. Siena was growing more and more sure that Fitzwilliam had not the passion to be the enemy she sought.

"However, Dunster, for one, won't like the idea of additional competition," he added.

"Indeed?"

"He was not at all happy to see the Russian hanging on your arm."

"Ah, yes, I do recall his offer to kick some manners into the man." She let the words hang for an instant. "Does he have a temper?"

"I suppose you could say so," answered the baron. They crossed the marble foyer and passed through the Tower archway. "Or rather, he grows irritated when he is not the center of attention. By virtue of his rank and his looks, he is used to being fawned over."

"And the earl?"

"Kirtland?" There was a fraction of a pause. "The earl is more of an enigma."

So even his acquaintances found him hard to read. Siena hesitated, then decided a show of curiosity would not seem unnatural, given her intention of choosing a protector. "Yet I have heard of his hair-trigger temper. Is he easy to anger?"

"Not that I have seen."

It was a very fair response, given that Kirtland was a fellow competitor.

As they came to the main stairs, Siena gracefully took her leave. "I thank you for a most engaging interlude, sir, but now I must ready myself for breakfast." She bestowed a quick caress to his cheek. "It was extremely interesting." And informative. "I give your first performance high marks."

"My pleasure," he said politely.

Siena hid a smile. The pleasure had, in truth, been all hers.

The curve of the cheek, the luster of the hair, the delicacy of the fine-boned features—her beauty was breathtaking.

Mother of God. Kirtland leaned closer to the glass case. It was just this morning that the duke had unveiled the St. Sebastian Psalters. For the next fortnight they would be on display in a special room of their own—guarded, he noted, by two burly footmen who stood just outside the doorway.

Unable to resist, the earl had stopped by on his way to the breakfast room for a first peek. Their exquisite artistry had not been exaggerated. The Madonna on the sample page was enough to make a man forget flesh-and-blood females, no matter how alluring.

"Sublime, aren't they?"

The earl looked up. Apparently he was not the only bidder interested in getting an early look. Alexandr Orlov, accompanied by Lord Bantrock, sauntered over to the display case.

"One would kill to possess such treasures," added the Russian.

"If you had ever experienced the carnage on a battlefield, you might not be so glib, Mr. Orlov," replied the earl.

"Forgive me, Lord Kirtland. Given your reputation . . ." The pause was pronounced enough to be noticeable. ". . . as a collector, I should have realized that a seasoned soldier would also have a sensitive side to his nature. So I take it art is not worth dying for?"

Kirtland wondered why the Russian seemed so intent on instigating a fight. Perhaps he hoped to goad an explosion of temper that would result in the earl's being sent home in disgrace. *One less opponent is always an advantage.* The other man might have read the legendary Sun Tzu's manual on the art of war. However, he would have to be far more clever to win outright victory with this preliminary skirmish.

"I have never thought of staking my life on it, Mr. Orlov," he answered politely. "Have you?"

"Good heavens, no." The Russian laughed and turned to his companion. The Irish lord, a noted collector from Dublin, looked as if he had just come in from riding. "As I was just telling Bantrock, I know precious little about the subtleties that you real connoisseurs hold so dear. I am merely acting on the desires of another."

"You play the part well," replied the earl. "But as the drama unfolds, the role may become more of a challenge. Have a care not to trip on your lines."

"You are saying I should watch my step?"

"Whether maneuvering on the bloody battlefields of Spain or the polished parquet of a ducal estate, there are always pitfalls, Mr. Orlov. A prudent person takes care to avoid them."

The Irishman touched the glass, his gaze reverential as he regarded the open Psalters. "Yet there is no getting around the fact that the competition to acquire these books will be very fierce." His deep brogue did not disguise the force of his own desire.

"Quite right, my dear Bantrock. However, unlike us uncouth Celts and Slavs, the English will conduct themselves with the utmost civility." Orlov quirked an inquiring brow. "At least, I believe that is the translation of Lord Kirtland's message."

The earl read a brief Latin passage from the Psalters aloud. "That is the beauty of language. It is always open to interpretation."

Stepping back, he invited the others to take his place at the center of the case. A quick glance showed that his retort had squeezed some of the smugness from Orlov's smile.

The Russian's eyes narrowed as well—to razored slits that once again had Kirtland wondering why the other man looked, for all his gregarious charm, ready to cut his throat.

"Enjoy your study of this exquisite art, gentlemen." He

couldn't resist adding a parting jab. "For all but one of us, the opportunity shall be short-lived."

"Here you are, gentlemen." Siena passed five folded missives across the table. The sixth she kept in hand. No point in putting it on an empty plate. The question was, would the earl renew hostilities by failing to show up for the first challenge? That would demand a quick shift in strategy . . .

Murmurs rose from the far end of the breakfast room as several of the other guests entered. She heard her name whispered and felt the heat of a few ogling stares. Reminded that all eyes were upon her, Siena made herself concentrate on the matter at hand.

She had no doubt that the real reason for her presence here was known to most of the other male guests. Gentlemen were as eager for gossip as ladies. And while the reclusive duke and his family might not be aware that a notorious courtesan was sitting down with the respectable guests, the members of The Gilded Page Club had no doubt trumpeted their enviable status in another, more private competition to their fellow collectors.

The charade of being Lady Blackdove, a wealthy widow dedicated to continuing her late husband's passion for acquiring medieval manuscripts, was likely as transparent as the lace fichu at her bodice. In particular, Lord Bantrock and the nabob from Brighton had been eyeing her with undisguised lust since the previous evening. And they had the air of being men who were used to getting what they wanted, whether it be art or sex.

"What the devil is this?" Leveritt's mutter mingled with the crackle of the foolscap as he unfolded the note.

Siena looked up from her momentary musings and forced a smile.

"Desire." Winthrop read aloud the single word printed at the top of each of their papers.

"Yes, desire," repeated Siena, surveying the five faces. The reactions ranged from surprise to bemusement to utter blankness. "The first task is to compose a sonnet on the subject of desire . . ."

The door opened and without a word of greeting, Kirtland took his place at the table.

She wasn't sure whether to feel relieved or disappointed at the earl's appearance. True to his word, he had evidently decided to take part in the group games, despite his personal objections.

"The first challenge, sir," she said, placing the last sheet of paper square on his plate.

With nary a glance at its contents, Kirtland signaled to one of the footmen for some coffee.

"What has such a tedious task to do with proving which of us can offer you the most satisfying terms?" demanded Jadwin.

"I wish to ensure that the gentleman I choose is . . . creative." Siena tilted her head, taking full advantage of the honey-colored light flowing in through the windows. She had chosen a gown of apricot silk with a full overskirt of sarcenet lace. A lacing of gold accentuated the snugness of the ruched bodice. The slanting sun would, she knew, ripen the color and the curves of her throat to a luscious hue.

"However," she went on, placing a hand on her hip, "if you feel your performance won't measure up, you can always turn in a blank sheet, though such action would leave you at a distinct disadvantage in the long run."

A snigger from Winthrop was quick to follow her words. "Jaddie does have a spot of trouble in keeping up with his friends."

"But Fitzwilliam has an unfair advantage over the rest of us," grumbled Jadwin, once the guffaws had died down. "He is well versed in penning soulful rhyme."

"You will all have a chance to display your particular strengths," she replied. "Indeed, I shall now take a moment to explain in more detail the rules of the coming fortnight."

The snick of silverware stilled.

"There will be six challenges, each designed to test a different skill. They will take place every other day, which shall suit the main schedule nicely, and they will . . ." She paused for effect. ". . . climax on the evening before the duke's auction."

A throaty laugh sounded from Dunster.

"The winner of each one will receive a special prize. In this case, I will treat the gentleman who comes out on top to a private poetry reading in the duke's Persian Room. I have in my possession a translation of some Arabic bedtime sonnets that I daresay will prove most provocative."

Winthrop drew in a deep breath, then echoed Jadwin's sentiment. "Still, it seems Fitz is guaranteed to win."

"Be assured, I shall not be grading the results with a schoolmaster's eye. You may take liberties with the art form. I am looking for something original, unexpected. Indeed, I require it."

"If you wish to experience poetry in motion, I should be happy to give you a private performance." Dunster stood up, looking supremely self-confident as he tucked the challenge in his coat pocket. He gave a suggestive waggle. "Now, if you wish?"

Leveritt and Jadwin both rolled their eyes, but Winthrop clapped in appreciative applause. "I didn't realize you had such a way with words, Dun," he exclaimed. "What other talents are you keeping hidden?"

"I fear Dunster is poised to steal a march on us," added Fitzwilliam. "We had better sharpen our quills if we hope to have any chance of winning this part of the competition."

"Speaking of winning and losing, you have yet to spell out the stipulations of this game, madam," said Jadwin. "I assume there are some."

"Only two, and simple ones at that. It must be written in your own hand on a single sheet of paper. And it must be delivered to me no later than the stroke of noon. I shall be awaiting the finished results in the Tudor Library, which can be found in the West Wing of the castle." Siena passed by Dunster, close enough that her skirts brushed his boots. A sidelong glance showed his mouth still curved in a scimitar smile. Hard, sharp, unyielding despite its rounded bend. The marquess was used to mowing through women like so many stalks of wheat.

Or perhaps plowing through them was a more apt metaphor, she decide as he cocked a hip and assumed an arrogant stance.

"I should think you would find it rather dull to be sequestered in a room with only books for company, my dear Dove," he murmured.

"The duke is accorded to have some fascinating treasures tucked away in the smaller library rooms through the manor house. No doubt I shall find something there to keep me amused."

The marquess did not waste any time in looking to show up his rivals. Acting as if his conquest was all but assured, he gave a casual glance at his pocket watch. "Ah, just enough time for a nap . . . to rest up for the rigors of the competition."

Fitzwilliam's earlier comments seemed to imply that victory came easily to Dunster in affairs of the flesh. Siena studied his finely chiseled features and crown of blond curls a moment longer before lowering her gaze. Given his golden looks, she imagined that was true. Could such luck weaken a man's character, spoil him into thinking he deserved special favors by virtue of his face alone?

"Any other questions, gentlemen?" she asked.

"Might you pass the strawberry jam, Winthrop?" murmured Kirtland.

"Until noon, then." With a deliberate swirl of her skirts, Siena left the men to their eggs and gammon. Dunster was not the only man whose real motives provoked a multitude of questions. But at last she was on the way to discovering some answers.

Chapter Ten

$\mathcal{T}$he sonorous clock chimes were just fading when a flutter of paper tickled the nape of her neck.

Looking up from a display of Elizabethan jewelry, Siena accepted the last of the sonnets and tucked it into the folds of her gown. "That was cutting it rather close, Lord Dunster." He had made no move to back away, and as she regarded his artfully arranged curls and smoothly shaven jaw, she was aware of the overpowering scent of his cologne. "A forfeit could have put you far back in the running for the ultimate prize."

"I have no fears on that score. I'm very good at games—and I never lose."

"A bold statement." Siena teased at the tail of his cravat. "I have yet to meet a man who is immune to the vagaries of Fortune."

His laugh possessed a cold conceit that grated on her ear. "Luck is said to be a lady. And ladies find me irresistible."

She answered with a coy smile.

"Where are the others?" he asked, slanting a quick look around the deserted room.

"Fitzwilliam accepted an invitation to join Jadwin and Leveritt in a ride to the village, while Kirtland and Winthrop went off to view some of the other ducal collections."

"And left a lady alone, without escort or entertainment? For shame. But then, they have always been rather rag-mannered when it comes to the opposite sex." Dunster's hand came to rest on the small of her back. "Why don't we take advantage of the opportunity to begin our afternoon rendezvous a touch early? I am sure you will find the Tudor treasures here more to your taste than the Rembrandt etchings." His fingers slid beneath her sash in a whisper-soft rustle of silk. "Some of the more intriguing items are hidden in the far corners of the room."

Siena let herself be led past the curio cabinets and bookcases. The shadows deepened as they turned into one of the alcoves, the dark oak and aged leather lightened only by a single leaded window centered in a narrow arch.

"Yes, I see there are some lovely books to behold." She paused and stood on tiptoe to take down a gold-tooled binding, aware that the stretch would slide the curves of her buttocks beneath his touch.

In the confined space, the echo of his quickening breath grew louder.

"I have something far more interesting to show you than a folio of flowers," he murmured, his palm pressing harder against her flesh. Hot, heavy, it felt unpleasantly damp through the scrim of silk.

"Indeed?" Siena turned, angling her hips in a provocative tilt as she placed the book back on the shelf. The air had grown heavier as well, the sharp scent of masculine arousal overpowering the more subtle smells of old parchment and paper.

Without warning, Dunster thrust himself upon her and captured her mouth in a bruising kiss. Though his lips were harsh and hard, she kissed him back, curious to see just how far he meant to go.

Emboldened, the marquess forced her back against the carved acanthus moldings, his hands roving over her breasts. "Leave your door unlocked tonight," he growled when finally he released her. "I'll come to you later, when everyone else has retired."

Siena pulled back, her lips roughened and raw from the force of his embrace. "La, that would be against the rules I have set out, milord," she said, though she kept on teasing her thigh against his groin. It was, after all, her intention to drive all of the six club members to distraction when the opportunity arose. In the heat of the moment, they might be coaxed into making a telling mistake. "Or don't you believe in playing fair?"

He groaned, a low, feral sound. "I believe in taking what I want." Hot, hungry, his mouth pressed to the hollow of her throat. "And right now I want you, naked and writhing beneath me. Be damned with all this foolish child's play. I'm the best man by far to satisfy your needs."

So, the marquess believed in taking what he wanted. How would he react to having his desire thwarted? She decided to find out.

Twisting her skirts free from his grasp, Siena slipped out of his arms. "Like the others, you shall have to prove it."

His cheeks darkened to a bloodred flush. "You may think to jerk the others around like puppets on a string, but don't toy with me, my dear little Dove. I do not take kindly to being manipulated."

How interesting. The Marquess of Dunster had a volatile temper to match his overweening pride.

"Oh, come now, sir," she chided, deciding to match fire with fire. "Don't act the aggrieved innocent with me. In both your world and mine, it all comes down to manipulating others for the best advantage." She smoothed the lace fichu back in place above her breasts. "You can hardly blame me for emulating the duke, who is dangling his precious books before all of your noses, waiting to see who will jump the highest."

Dunster's anger seemed to fade somewhat, though she doubted the flash of teeth was meant as a smile. "A clever little slut, aren't you. Very well, how much do you want for a night in your bed?"

"I'd be a fool to make a deal before all the bids are in."

"Bids?" Winthrop suddenly strolled into the alcove. To her surprise, the figure by his side was Kirtland. "Is there yet another treasure for sale that the rest of us have not heard about?"

"The marquess and I were merely discussing the theoretical fine points of an auction," she answered. "It is fascinating to become acquainted with all the dealings that go on behind the scenes."

"The action can sometimes turn ugly," replied Winthrop. "You have only to attend a sale of prime horses at Tattersall's to witness the sort of cutthroat tactics that would put a Barbary pirate to blush."

"I doubt I would be shocked, sir." She moved away from Dunster, her skirts kicking up a froth of lace around her ankles. "After all, I am quite familiar with the sale of flesh."

"Unlike some places, the mounts at Tat's are of prime quality, and trained to obey their masters," said the marquess, his voice still roughened with displeasure. "There, at least, you can count on buying biddable beasts, who are easily controlled with whip and spurs."

"An experienced rider ought not have to resort to such measures," said Kirtland slowly, his gaze flicking from the marquess to her and back again. "Trust is far more effective than fear."

Sharp as a faceted emerald, his green gaze did not miss much. Siena swore a silent oath. She must take greater care to keep even the smallest hint of emotion from her face.

"Perhaps you ought to inform Wellesley and his staff of that platitude," snarled Dunster. "Coming from you, any talk of trust would surely make quite an impression."

The earl's only reaction was an unblinking stare.

"Now, now, Dun, let us not have any misunderstandings arise." Winthrop gave a nervous laugh as he tugged at his watch chain. "We—"

"Oh, never fear, the marquess and I understand each other quite well," said Kirtland in a perfectly pleasant voice.

But Siena saw that the earl's eyes had lost all hint of color in the shifting shadows, and now appeared as two points of tempered steel, capable of cutting through solid bone and bravado.

Dunster must have sensed the same, for despite his sneer, he shifted back a step.

The earl flashed a glance at Winthrop. "Don't feel compelled to step into the line of fire again. I don't need any help in fighting my battles."

"Er, yes, well . . ." Clearly flustered by the unexpected confrontation, Winthrop was slow in forming a reply. "All I meant was, we are all a bit on edge. Naturally, each of us wants those Psalters badly, but no need to let the rivalry stir up bad blood between us." He blew out a breath.

"Come, let us go cool our heads and tongues with a glass of the duke's excellent claret."

Dunster followed, not without a last, murderous scowl at the earl. Kirtland ignored the invitation, waiting until the two men had left the room before turning for the door.

As he walked off without a word, Siena swore again. She had already sensed a subtle friction between Dunster and Jadwin. Were there other hidden hostilities? Beneath the show of masculine camaraderie, were all the club members at each other's throats? She, too, took a tight-lipped leave of the library. What she needed was answers, not more disquieting questions.

To her dismay, Orlov appeared, seemingly out of no-where, and fell in step beside her. "A damsel in distress?"

"Thank you," she said tartly, hoping to brush him off. "But I am not in need of St. Georgi to slay any dragons."

"*Nyet?*" He exaggerated a grimace. "It seems to me that one of those gentlemen leaving the library was breathing fire."

She repressed a smile. Unlike most Russians, whose temperament tended toward melancholy brooding, he appeared to have an impish sense of humor. "The smoke and flames are directed at each other."

"I wonder what has stirred such passion?"

"Books," she said blandly.

"I never cease to be amazed at what people are willing to fight over," he remarked. "A bit of paper hardly seems worth the spilling of blood."

"A strange sentiment coming from you, Mr. Orlov. Aren't you in the thick of the bidding?"

"Only at someone else's behest. If I had my choice, I should be putting my talents to other, more pleasurable use."

She could not help but laugh. "Give it up, sir. You are wasting your time—and your charm—on me."

He winked as they came to the end of the corridor. "You are not the only one who feels compelled to give fair warning, *golub*. I do not surrender so easily."

"Nor do I." She turned, to find Kirtland watching them from the shadowed recess of the arched entryway. "Good day, sir."

Having no appetite to join the evening festivities, the earl had ordered a cold supper brought up to his quarters. He had intended to pass the evening reading a book on Burgundian art that he had borrowed from the duke's collection. But somehow his mind was too restless to concentrate on scholarship. After a short time he found himself putting it aside and taking up a different page.

However, the guest list sparked no sudden flash of insight.

Damn. Kirtland grimaced. Had his intelligence skills grown as rusty as his cavalry spurs? Tossing the paper aside, he began to pace the perimeter of his bedchamber.

Like the other members of The Gilded Page Club, he had been given rooms on the third floor of the castle's East Wing, overlooking the interior gardens. Across the corridor, another eight competitors were housed in the frayed opulence of Restoration furniture and Georgian brocades. Several of the octogenarian guests were quartered in the Central Tower in deference to their aged bones.

While below him, in all her solitary splendor, resided the Black Dove.

A lady as mysterious as her moniker. A contrast, a contradiction. A conundrum. She had adopted the name of a fluttering, defenseless bit of fluff, and yet she sported the tattoo of a hawk in flight. Wings arced, talons poised. She was anything but helpless.

Hawks were hunters—what was her prey?

The question had been an unpleasant echo inside his head throughout the day. *Someone had sent her.* His wits were not so far gone that he thought her targeting of The Gilded Page Club was just serendipitous coincidence. But why? As a distraction?

If that was her mission, she was doing a damn good job of it.

He paused to press his forehead against one of the window-panes. The coolness of the night air was a welcome relief to his own heated imagination. Not that the sight before his eyes was designed to quell any flights of fancy. Limned in the moonlight, the ghostly glass spires of the conservatory looked even more dreamlike as they rose from the mists.

Exotic. Like the specimen plantings blooming within its earthy warmth. Like the sinuous stretch of a shapely leg.

The earl turned away, but not before catching a wink-ing of light moving inside the structure. A reflection of the stars, he told himself. Or was it yet another strange quirk of his own fevered brain?

He swore again. What perverse spell had taken hold of his senses since that midnight storm, that hellfire kiss? He ought to be consumed with planning his strategy for acquiring the illuminated books. Yet his thoughts kept straying to the raven-haired Dove and her pliant curves, her unbending steel.

A female as unique as the Psalters.

If his hunch was correct, and she had been hired as a distraction, the rakish Russian seemed her most likely ally. There was something similar in their styles. A boldness tempered by a wary watchfulness. Velvet smiles masking iron wills. The taunt of hidden secrets. They made a formidable pair, if indeed they were in league. *Fire and ice.* Kirtland felt a slow burn seep through his veins at the thought of them together, limbs entwined, golden hair tangled with raven curls upon the snowy sheets.

He drew in a deep breath, trying to cool the strange heat. He had withdrawn from Society for the very reason of avoiding the machinations of such men. And the wiles of such women. He had had enough of betrayal in all its guises. Those seeking power, prestige, or personal gain cared for naught but their own selfish desires. It was all a game to them.

A casual word, a vicious rumor—self-interest was at the heart of how things played out. A fact he knew all too well.

And though he had claimed not to give a damn about the cuts to his character, perhaps the wounds were deeper than he cared to admit. Osborne had intimated that he ought to fight back against bitterness rather than retreat any deeper into a brooding blackness.

Was detachment from life an acknowledgment of defeat?

Of late, he had begun to wonder. The truth was, his self-imposed isolation was growing a bit boring—a vague unrest exacerbated by the revelation of how Osborne was putting his army experience to good use. Perhaps his friend's teasing about being an idealist was not so far off the mark. He still felt that books were better companions than people, but he missed his military responsibilities, the sense of purpose, the challenge of outwitting a clever enemy.

Kirtland thought for an instant of firegold eyes and a rainswept kiss . . .

The Black Dove was clever indeed to create such a

powerful diversion. His lips quirked in a grudging smile. Oh, she was good. Very good.

If he could not put his talents to any official use, he could at least use them in his own personal battle to beat a scheming rival at his own game. He would not let the treasures within Marquand Castle slip so easily through his fingers. If the Russian—and his lovely accomplice—thought he might steal them away without a fight, he was in for a rude awakening.

And yet, as he glanced at the crumpled paper on the carpet, Kirtland reminded himself that at the moment he was only sparring with shadows. He could not overlook the possibility that his real opponent in this war of distraction was one of the other guests. Rubbing his jaw, he picked up the list and read over the names once again.

Who, aside from the Russian, might have hired the Black Dove?

It seemed safe to cross off the two elderly gentlemen from Edinburgh. One was, like the duke, confined to a bath chair, and the other seemed prone to mental wandering. The nabob from Brighton? As he had only recently returned from years in India, the chances seemed remote. Lord Bantrock, the stocky Irish lord, seemed a more likely suspect. He appeared to have both the money and the Machiavellian intelligence to come up with such a plan.

As for the other members of The Gilded Page Club, he could surely write them off.

Or could he?

Every man had his passion. And a price he was willing to pay to make it his own.

Which brought his thoughts back to the Black Dove.

Much as he wished to concentrate on books, on art, the mysterious beauty cut against his peace of mind like a razored blade. It angered him that he could not dull its edge. Or ignore the arousal of primal pride. *She dared challenge him?* He would show her that he had not lost his touch. Two could play at seduction . . .

His lips slowly stretched to a smile. An experienced soldier, he knew one of the keys to victory was keeping the enemy off-balance. So far, direct confrontation had only resulted in a stalemate.

It was time to change tactics.

Chapter Eleven

$\mathcal{T}$he first test had gone quite well, thought Siena as she sat down at her dressing table the following morning. She had made several important discoveries. After studying the sonnets, she had definitely ruled out Fitzwilliam as the man she was seeking. Letterforms could of course be disguised, but the men didn't know she had a sample of the traitor's handwriting. The baron was left-handed, and as such could not have penned the traitorous letter uncovered by Chertwell's men.

After careful consideration, she had chosen Winthrop as the winner of the first challenge. The files had suggested that he was the most dull-witted of the group, so she decided he would be the easiest of the remaining members to eliminate as a suspect. Crossing another name off her list this early in the game would be a great advantage.

So far, luck was running in her favor. As his reward, she had arranged to meet him in the Persian Room for a private reading of erotic poetry. During their hour together, Winthrop revealed his imagination to be just as unimpressive as his appearance. Though he had made a show of ogling her breasts and bragging of his amorous conquests, most of his attention had been focused on polishing off a bottle of the duke's aged brandy. Along with one of port.

The minutes had ticked by with excruciating slowness, but by the time he staggered away, she was even more certain that her first instincts about him were correct. And this morning, she had a chance to confirm those impressions. Winthrop was one of the first bidders scheduled for the requisite private interview with the duke. His secretary had warned them all that the meeting would last over an hour . . .

An hour should be more than enough time to search through his personal belongings.

Lifting her skirts, Siena strapped her knife in place, then stepped out into the deserted corridor. Rose had discovered the door to a back stairway hidden in the heavy paneling. It led down to the floor below, where the gentlemen of The Gilded Page Club were quartered. Since Stoneleigh had arranged a special showing of the duke's gun collection for the other men, it should prove easy enough to slip unseen into Winthrop's rooms. Even if she were spotted by one of the servants, the presence of a wealthy widow dallying near the male guests would only provoke a few ribald chuckles.

Her decorative hairpin, a special design forged of stiff steel, made quick work of the ancient lock. Noiselessly sliding the bolt back in place, she turned and moved to the dressing room first, deciding on a quick search through the gentleman's clothing before tackling the desk. Riffling through his waistcoats, she found nothing. The coat pockets yielded only a rather hefty bill from a wineshop on Jermyn Street. After feeling through his trousers and finding no hidden pockets or papers, she returned to the bedchamber.

The contents of Winthrop's valise were equally innocuous. But on opening his letter case, Siena hit upon a more interesting discovery. Tucked under a letter from his sister were several beribboned condoms, a recipe for a poultice guaranteed to enlarge a man's cock, and a pamphlet on sexual positions. She allowed a small smile. So far the only thing suspect about Winthrop was the working order of his male member. The last sheet of paper was further evidence as to its precarious position. It was a detailed receipt for a stay at Dr. Erector's Health Spa for Discerning Gentlemen, located near York.

But it was not the treatments listed that drew Siena's eye. It was the dates—they matched the time when the third of the government documents had been stolen. Lynsley's agents had also been able to pin down the week in which the rare copy of *Paradise Lost* had gone missing from The Gilded Page Club town house.

She carefully replaced the items and closed the case. Winthrop was not her man. That left four. Checking to make sure she had left no sign of her visit, she slipped out of his room and jingled the lock back in place.

"Well, well, what have we here?"

For a big man, Bantrock moved with surprising stealth.

"My dear Lady Blackdove, you seem to have strayed from your nest."

"Indeed." Siena toyed with the topknot of her curls, casually sliding the hairpin into the twist of ribbon. "I had a question for Lord Winthrop and thought I might find him here before nuncheon. But he does not appear to be in."

"I am sure I can satisfy any demand you have." The Irish lord caught hold of her wrist. "Why not step inside my room and let me display my expertise."

"Maybe later, sir. At the moment, my first order of business lies with Lord Winthrop."

His grip tightened. "I'll make it worth your while."

"A tempting offer, but—"

A rumble of laughter punctuated the sound of steps approaching.

Taking advantage of Bantrock's momentary distraction, she pulled free and hurried through the double doors of the connecting corridor before he could follow.

Slowing to a more leisurely pace, Siena found herself in the section of the castle that housed the main display rooms. Not wishing to risk another encounter with the Irish lord by returning to her room, she decided to linger a bit and explore. Each portal was marked with an ornate brass plate proclaiming the treasures within. The New World Room held brightly painted Aztec pottery . . . the Calligraphy Room held intricate Arabic manuscripts . . . The Renaissance Room held masterpieces from Florence and Siena . . .

On impulse, she stepped inside and was immediately enveloped in a pale, pearlescent light, despite the overcast skies. Looking up, she saw its source. An expanse of Palladian windows, arcing to cathedral heights, filled the far wall, their graceful proportions aligned to a northern exposure. The perfect artist's light, she recalled from her reading. Cool and pure.

Her gaze returned to the row of gilded frames hung above the glass front cabinets. *Michelangelo, Botticelli, Da Vinci.* She was familiar with all the famous names of the period from her art classes at the Academy, but the opportunities to view actual examples of their work had been very rare.

Recalling the erotic engravings of Raphael, she allowed an ironic smile. Oddly enough, he was one of her favorites. According to her lessons, he was reputed to be quite a lady's man. Sensual, as well as sensitive, reveling in feminine beauty, whether it be a Madonna, a pagan deity, or a lover. His drawings certainly showed a masterly touch for the female form.

But no black-and-white line work could match the power of the colors that now met her eye. She never ceased to be amazed at how such mundane materials— pigment, linseed oil, turpentine—could be so magically transformed. Powdered clays and finely ground semiprecious stones had no emotion of their own. It was the artist's hand that gave them spirit, laughter, love.

Life.

Her breath caught in her throat. She was well schooled in the art of war, a skilled practitioner of darkness, of death. Perhaps that was why she found the world of light and color so wondrously intriguing.

Seeing a copy of Vasari's *Lives of the Artists* on one of the bookstands, Siena opened it to the chapter on Raphael and began reading.

"A connoisseur of *quattrocentro* art?" Kirtland's voice suddenly cut through her reveries. His shadow fell across the page as he leaned a shoulder to the molding. "Another skill in your arsenal of talents?" Strangely enough, his tone was more teasing than taunting, and his mouth was curled up at the corners.

Siena smiled in return. "An appreciation of beauty is not reserved for the sole pleasure of the privileged few who possess wealth and rank." As she spoke, she couldn't help admiring his muscular frame. His aura of masculine vitality was undeniable—Raphael's handsome archangels suddenly paled in comparison.

He moved closer and waggled a brow, as if daring her to go on.

"Indeed, many of the greatest works of art were meant for the masses," she said slowly, trying to ignore the sinuous curling of his long hair or the sculpted lines of his broad shoulders. "Churches commissioned frescoes or altar screens to inspire and to teach. The vast majority of people could not read, and such pictures were how they learned the stories of the Bible."

"So, you *have* studied art, as well as fencing." As the earl gave a slight bow, his coat brushed against her skirts.

Oddly enough, the fleeting touch aroused a lick of heat along her spine. Her nerves must still be on edge from her encounter with Bantrock. How else to explain being so acutely aware of his closeness?

"And you appear well taught," he finished.

"I know a little. But I am no match for you in *that* subject, I am sure," replied Siena. Kirtland's skills with a sword were clear enough. Here was a chance to probe into a different facet of his character. She must not allow herself to be distracted. "As a matter of fact, I was just puzzling over a term in this book that I don't understand. Might you explain what 'chiaroscuro' means?"

"It is a term for light and dark. A style of accentuating contrast for dramatic effect." The earl took her hand and set it in the crook of his arm. "Come, let me show you."

Was it her imagination, or did he deliberately draw out the intimacy of the moment? Siena shook off yet another strange little shiver.

He turned and led her to a small portrait of a young woman. "Do you see how Da Vinci has chosen an angle of light to create strong highlights and shadows?"

She studied the face, half in sun, half in shade. "It adds an emotional depth, does it not?"

He gave an encouraging nod. "Yes. Well said."

Was Kirtland actually going out of his way to be engaging? Siena took a moment to steady her breath before going on. "So an artist doesn't just paint what he sees. He uses his mind's eye to envision an idea, then draws on his physical skills to create it on canvas."

A playful expression tugged at his lips. "Artists, like swordsmen, have a great many tricks of the trade. For example, the use of perspective was one of the revolutionary innovations of the Renaissance." He gestured to a Madonna and Child, with a trio of adoring Magi in the foreground. "As was composition. A triangular design was a favorite device in guiding the viewer's eye to the focal point."

Intrigued, she put aside her musing on the earl long enough to study the design. "I never realized how many subtle elements came into play."

As the earl warmed to the subject, his features softened. Tracing over the painted folds of ivory linen, his touch was gentle as a caress. She wondered how she had ever thought him a hard, forbidding man.

"A great many subtleties are involved," he explained. "As the finest pigments came from Tuscan soil, the painters of Florence and Siena were especially skilled in capturing the nuances of color."

A flutter of longing stirred inside her. What inexplicable yearning had taken hold of her senses? It was bad enough to be thinking about how the earl's hands would feel on her face, but now she was suddenly imagining what it would be like to experience the beauty of her namesake city. To learn more about art, poetry, and the splendor of sunlight.

"Have you ever been there," she asked. "To Siena, I mean?"

"Yes, as a young man I traveled through all of Italy."

"What is it like?" she asked. It was, after all, her duty to learn more about the earl's love of art.

Kirtland hesitated, and in that instant she saw her own longing reflected in his eyes. "It is, in a word, magical. Its treasures are perhaps overshadowed by the brilliance of Florentine art," he began. "Yet there is a raw energy to Siena that is unique."

It was the first time the earl had ever spoken so freely to her. She found herself hoping he would go on.

"Set on three hills, the city rises out of the surrounding olive groves and vineyards. Inside its walls, the cobbled streets are steep and narrow. The Piazza del Campo lies at its heart, while other landmarks include the Duomo, a magnificent cathedral of green-and-white marble, with works of art by Donatello and Pisana."

Green-and-white—like his eyes. Alight with a passion for his subject, they held her gaze.

"And of course there is the annual *Palio delle Contrade,* a wild horse race dating from medieval times that runs through the twisting byways of the city. Slashing hooves, flying elbows, daredevil riders jockeying for victory as the bells of Torre del Mangia ring out, and the crowds scream for blood." His smile revealed that beneath the usual sardonic set of his features was a dry sense of humor. "You would be quite at home there."

As his fingertips drummed lightly against her wrist,

Siena felt her heart begin to gallop. Reminded that she was dangerously close to forgetting her mission, she forced her thoughts back to the job of seducing the earl into wanting a more intimate acquaintance. "You describe it very well, sir."

"Words do not do it justice."

"On the contrary. You are an excellent teacher. Perhaps you would consent to another lesson sometime soon."

"Speaking of which, where did you study?"

"A small academy for girls. You would not have heard of it."

"Was it near London, or in some distant shire?" pressed Kirtland.

She looked away. "I cannot imagine that where a courtesan received her training would be of any real interest to you."

"I can't help but be curious." He leaned back against the display case, and suddenly his shoulder was touching hers.

Damn the man. He had no idea how the feel of his body against hers was affecting her equilibrium. Or did he?

"By your cultured tone," he went on, "I would guess you were not bred for your current profession."

A laugh escaped from her lips. "No, I was not."

"A family misfortune?" His voice was even, but his brow betrayed a furrow.

Thrust and parry. Seeing she had piqued his interest, Siena decided it was time to withdraw. Da Rimini believed that the first round of a fencing match should combine advances and retreats, especially against a skilled opponent. The earl had caught her off guard with his unexpected moves, but she must now get a grip on her emotions and shift the balance back in her favor.

Before Kirtland could ask any more questions, she turned quickly and moved for the door. "If you will excuse me now, I must go change for nuncheon."

Kirtland watched the provocative sway of her hips. With her willowy height and sinuous grace, she reminded him of a rapier forged of the finest Toledo steel. *Beautiful but deadly.* He could not help thinking of her in terms of martial metaphors, even though this last exchange had signaled a truce of sorts.

In truth, it had been awfully easy to put his new strategy into play. *Too easy.* The Black Dove's sharp intelligence—a beguiling counterpoint to her expert sword skills—made her infinitely intriguing. Beneath the cynical smiles and gaudy gowns there seemed to be more than a scheming courtesan.

The earl found himself conflicted. He wished to think of her in terms of black-and-white, but the Dove defied such simple outlines. As this interlude had illustrated, she was far too complex, a contradiction in character. His gaze moved from the Botticelli Madonna to the Raphael portrait of Imperia, the most famous Roman courtesan of her day.

Innocence and experience.

Heaven and hell.

Kirtland caught a glimpse of his own reflection in the gilded wall sconce. Was there a devilish flickering of desire?

He turned away quickly, reminding himself that he had come to Marquand Castle seeking a treasure crafted of vellum and ink, not some chimerical Valkyrie, capable of stirring flesh-and-blood longings. He must have a care that a more intimate acquaintance with her did not become a two-edged sword. Her body was a powerful weapon in itself. Even now he could feel the heat of her lovely flesh imprinted on his hands. Somehow the slow burn had seeped to the rest of his limbs, leaving a trail of singed nerves. Which was even more reason why he must discover for whom she was fighting.

"Stealing a march on the rest of us?"

Kirtland met Leveritt's slitted gaze with a grimace. "I assure you, I did not go out of my way to encounter the Black Dove."

The other man perched a hip on the edge of the book-stand. "So you have not changed your mind about playing the lady's game in earnest?"

"I have come here to compete for far higher stakes than her favors," he replied.

Leveritt gave a bark of laughter. "In that we are agreed, Kirtland. The ladybird is the least of the prizes here at Marquand Castle."

"Yet you seemed equally as enthusiastic as the others in accepting her challenge."

Leveritt carefully pinched the crease of his trousers to a knife-sharp edge. He was dressed with his usual sartorial elegance, but still took a moment to fuss with his waistcoat buttons and gold watch chain before murmuring, "As she said at our very first encounter, her presence here provides a provocative distraction."

Hearing his own sentiments repeated aloud gave the earl pause for thought. He had never considered Leveritt the sharpest of the club members. Perhaps he ought to reconsider his assessment. In answer, however, he merely gave a noncommittal shrug.

Shifting his stance, Kirtland saw that Jadwin had entered the room and was watching them with a wariness that seemed a touch too intense.

Bloody hell, he thought in some exasperation. The Gilded Page Club members had become like squabbling schoolboys, each worrying that the others might be conspiring with one another to keep some sweetmeat all to themselves.

"A game of billiards?" suggested Jadwin as he ran a finger along a row of leather-bound folios. Beneath his smile he looked somewhat sullen. "Unless, of course, I am interrupting a private conversation."

The earl quickly agreed, wishing to placate any suspicions. Leveritt, too, accepted the invitation.

The three of them found the table deserted.

"Shall I break?" Jadwin set the ivory balls in place upon the felt and chalked his cue.

Ironically, Kirtland found his gaze locked on the perfect triangle, a colorful reminder of his recent conversation. Then, with a sudden crack, sharp as a gunshot, the balls scattered, a kaleidoscope blur of skittering colors and random angles. He had always scoffed at the idea of omens, yet the sight had a strangely unsettling effect on him.

Everything about the cursed trip to Marquand Castle seemed to be taking on a strange spin.

From high atop the crenellated battlements, Siena could see out over the rolling parkland to the Greek folly on the far side of the lake. On either side, the moors rose steeply from its shores, prickly with gorse and thorn. She shaded her eyes to the slanting sun, trying to make out any trail through the rocky outcroppings and windblown trees, but the tangle looked impenetrable. A ride out would allow for a more careful survey of the surroundings.

For now, however, she was looking to map out a detailed diagram of the castle and its bewildering maze of twists and turns for one of her future challenges. The scheduled activities for the afternoon had provided a perfect opportunity. The gentlemen were all out hunting, while the four ladies of the duke's family and Count Sundstrom's wife, the only other female guest, had taken a trip into the neighboring town. Siena had declined the invitation, leaving her free to roam as she pleased.

After the challenges of the morning, she was looking forward to an interlude of solitude.

She and Rose had already studied the layout of the East Wing, but she had not yet had a chance to explore the Central Tower. The dark, spiral staircase that had brought her to the heights of the structure also appeared to descend into the bowels of the cellars. It would be worth a look around its depths for any secret chambers or hidden passageways. One never knew when such knowledge might come in handy.

Still, Siena tarried for a moment, watching the circling of a lone hawk. *So near and yet so far.* She was making headway, but that was not good enough. Time was of the essence. She had to find a way to intensify her efforts.

But impatient as she was, she knew that the tedious task of reconnoitering the castle was important. Rose had noted the details of the kitchens and servant quarters, while Oban had reported on the layout of the stables and paddocks. She meant to leave nothing to chance.

A last tilt of her cheeks to the warmth of the sun, then it was back to duty. Drawing the door closed behind her, Siena refastened the bolts and started down the steps, making a mental note of the number between each floor. She was nearly back down to ground level when from out of the shadows loomed a figure, dark save for a crowning flicker of flaming-red hair.

Bantrock?

"Ah, once again I find the lovely Lady Blackdove hovering where she should not be."

Damn. What the devil was he doing here?

"Or should I say, Black Dove," he went on, drawing out the pause between the two words. "We both know you are no lady."

"The Tower is not barred to guests." Siena ignored the innuendo. "However, I confess that I am surprised to see you here. I thought all the gentlemen had been invited to hunt on the duke's private moor."

"I'm not interested in grouse."

"Really?" she replied coolly. "Then I fear you shall be deprived of any sport. There are no other birds in season."

"The English have such quaint rules. I am not averse to doing a little poaching."

She tried to step around him, but his hand shot out to snare her arm. "Not so fast. You flew away this morning before I had a chance to test my weapon."

"Please let me go," she said. "You are hurting me."

The demand only seemed to make Bantrock squeeze tighter. His smile thinned to an ugly pinch, distorting the handsome features with anger and a far more primal passion.

"I shall scream—"

He slapped a hand over her mouth. "No, you won't." The weight of his body pinned her up against the stone. His hands were at her skirts.

Siena did not wish to betray her fighting skills. Twisting beneath his pawing attack, she used a few of the subtle moves she had learned from the Indian fakir to fend off his groping. If she could edge to the doorway, perhaps she could appear to effect a lucky escape. But her deft parries only seemed to goad him into a greater fury. Silk ripped, its jagged echo slurred against the rock and mortar. His hips slammed hard in a grinding thrust.

Left with no choice, she let fly a chop with the flat of her hand that caught him on the throat. His scream was cut short by a kick that knocked his legs out from under him.

Stunned, he took several moments to push up from the landing. "Bitch," he panted, once the string of other profanities had run out. "I swear, you will be begging for mercy before I am done with you."

"Don't count on it, sir. Given my profession, I have taken great pains to learn how to defend myself."

Bantrock spat out another curse. "As if a trollop is trained for aught but spreading her legs." Arms outstretched, he launched himself at her neck.

She sidestepped the onslaught, and with a jab of her elbow sent him careening into the sidewall. "You have fair warning, sir. Leave now or my next blow will break a bone."

The Irishman fixed her with a murderous look. "We shall see who does the battering, you poxy slut."

For all his broad bulk, he was lighter on his feet than she anticipated. Pushing off from the wall, he catapulted forward, and the force of his momentum trapped her again, pinning her hands between her body and his. She ducked a slap and managed to regain a foothold on the smooth granite.

He hit her again, a hard blow to the side of the head.

Siena made a split-second decision—she could no lon-ger afford to be subtle. Bruises to her face would raise too many questions. Spinning into action, she jerked on his arm, using his own weight to overbalance his stance. An instant later, she pivoted back, and with a quick twist smashed his face into the mortared stone. Blood spurted from Bantrock's broken nose, a slash of ugly crimson against the pale granite.

Dazed, the Irishman staggered back a step, clutching at his lacerated cheek.

Catching his wrist, she ducked low, then lifted her hip, the angle and momentum of her move forcing him head over heels. The snap of sinew separating from bone was overpowered by a howl of anguish. Then, as his head cracked on the landing, there was dead silence.

After a few moments, Bantrock began to moan softly. His legs twitched, but his arm lay limp by his side. "Sweet Jesus, I'm dying," he whimpered.

"No, you're not. Trust me, if I wanted you dead, you would be a corpse by now." Lifting her ripped skirts, she prodded him with her slipper. "Get up, before I change my mind. And get out of my sight." Given his character, the Irishman's continued presence at Marquand Castle posed too great a risk to her mission. "If you aren't gone for good by the morrow, there will be further hell to pay."

Still moaning, Bantrock crawled to his knees.

"One last bit of advice," she continued. "I suggest you keep quiet about this little encounter. Make up an excuse—something about the steep steps being treacher-ous would be in order." In this instance, masculine hubris would work in her favor. "Unless you care to be the laughingstock of the other gentlemen for allowing a woman to thrash you to a bloody pulp."

The Irishman managed to get to his feet and slink away through the archway.

Siena let out a deep breath, suddenly aware of her own aching muscles and disheveled dress. Leaning back against the wall, she closed her eyes. She could taste blood from a cut on her lip.

"A bravura performance of hand-to-hand combat."

Her lids flew open in time to catch Kirtland stepping out from the shadows, handkerchief in hand. He approached and pressed it lightly to the corner of her mouth. "I suppose I should count myself fortunate that all my limbs are still in one piece."

"What are *you* doing here?"

Instead of answering, he took her hand and slowly wiped off Bantrock's blood. Before she could pull away, he slowly traced his fingers over her knuckles, her palm. In contrast to the Irish lord, his touch was gentle as the brush of a feather.

"A courtesan's usual activities do not give rise to calluses such as these. But then, from our first encounter, it has been quite obvious that you are no ordinary madam of the *demimonde*."

The heat of him sent a tingle through her limbs. A warning, perhaps, of her precarious position? She had let herself be trapped between the unyielding stone and his broad bulk. Even more dangerous was the strength of his suspicions. He could destroy her cover and her mission if he made a public announcement of what he knew about her fighting skills.

"Who the devil are you?" he whispered.

Siena knew she would not escape this time without

giving some sort of answer. She thought fast. Lynsley's files had implied that the earl had his own rigid notion of honor—a fact confirmed by their midnight encounter. An appeal to such higher principle might do the trick.

"Someone seeking to right a wrong." As she answered, she watched his face very carefully. "A betrayal."

The only show of emotion was a tic of his jaw. "One of the men here has hurt you in the past? Is that the reason you sought out The Gilded Page Club?"

She must move with unerring steps. A slip here and her chances of catching Lynsley's traitor would be cut to shreds. "Yes. I used your club to gain invitation here," she lied. "The villain is not necessarily one of your fellow members. He hurt . . . a friend. But I am the only one in a position to make him pay for it."

"Which one of them?" he demanded.

She shook her head. "I cannot say."

"Cannot or will not?"

Her silence deflected the question. Rather than press the offensive, he fixed her with a searching look.

Siena felt herself color under its emerald intensity. *Damn.* She must *not* let her body disobey her mind.

"No matter your considerable skills, what you propose is dangerous," he said softly. "Perhaps I could help you in some way."

"No." The offer took her by surprise. It took an instant to steady her voice. "That is, this is a matter I must handle on my own."

The earl was still holding her hand. His cravat had loosened, and she could see the throb of a pulse at his throat, hear the slight quickening of his breathing. "Is there a reason?" he asked.

Not one that she could reveal.

Drawing on all her years of discipline, she quickly sought to turn the talk from her actions to his own. "I, too, have some questions, Lord Kirtland." Siena forced her attention back to duty. "Again I ask, what are you doing here?"

"I saw you on the battlements. And when I caught a glimpse of Bantrock sneaking into the Tower, I thought there might be trouble."

The irony of it drew a rueful smile. "So once again Fate intervenes, and you ride to my rescue. Like a knight-errant of old."

"Mere chance." He gave a cynical shrug. "You have studied all the members of the club well enough to know I am no storybook hero."

"So I have. Yet how else to explain your chivalrous actions?"

"I don't like it when a man misuses his strength."

She saw the fine lines at the corner of his mouth stretch tauter. He, too, had secrets.

"Even on a whore?" she asked.

Pain seemed to pool in his eyes, and she felt his fist clench at his side.

It was then that Siena suddenly recalled his words from their wild ride. *My mother was a whore.* She touched his cheek. He flinched but did not pull away. The truth was etched there on his face. His words had not been a casual quip, a glib jest. "So you meant what you said in our first encounter."

"Yes—my mother was a whore. Or so my father said. He never tired of screaming such an epithet at her." There was a rasp to his voice. "But that was long ago. It doesn't matter now."

She, of all people, knew the past was not so easy to forget.

"How did you come to choose a courtesan's life?" he asked abruptly.

"I was luckier than many girls who find themselves on the street. A kindly gentleman took me under his wing, so to speak. He saw I received a proper education."

"I doubt it was all out of the charity of his heart." The sardonic set was back on Kirtland's face. "What did he ask for in return?"

Siena shrugged. "Services rendered."

His expression seemed to grow even grimmer. "Do you enjoy what he requires of you?"

The question was so unexpected, she could not repress a laugh. "Some aspects of it."

He looked about to speak again but instead leaned down to pick up the ribbon that had been ripped from her hair. The coil of blue looked achingly delicate against his palm.

"Thank you."

Kirtland took off his coat and draped it over her shoulders. It was only then that she noticed the torn silk had slipped low enough to show the small tattoo above her left breast.

His fingertips grazed her bare skin. "Was that his idea or yours?"

Siena did not trust herself to answer. The air around them was growing dangerously charged. Like lightning hidden in storm clouds, it threatened to explode at any moment.

"A lone peregrine, who journeys far and wide?" asked the earl. He slanted a sharper look. "No—it looks to be a merlin."

"W—what makes you say that?"

"I have an eye for detail. And for art. Whoever wielded the needle got the shape of the wings just right." He stared a moment longer. "The merlin was the mark of England's ancient wizard," he mused. "Perhaps that explains why it feels as if some mysterious magic is at play here. Some spell that defies rational explanation."

So he sensed it, too? For a moment, the crackling of heat was almost audible. Siena wished to deny the inexplicable attraction, but her words rang oddly hollow. "There is nothing magical about me, sir."

"Then how do you explain this strange alchemy that seems to draw us together?"

"Would that I had the answer." She drew the remnants of her bodice up over the black bird, determined to smother the urge to touch his face, taste his mouth. "It seems to me that we are more like steel and flint than the elements of any wizard's brew." Her mouth quirked. "Sparks seem to fly when we rub together."

An odd light flared in his eyes, and for an instant Siena was sure he was going to kiss her. Then he pulled back abruptly, leaving her to wonder whether she had merely imagined it.

"Let us have a care we don't get burned." Kirtland stepped aside, once again dropping into shadow. "If you turn to the right and ascend the first set of stairs, you should make it to your quarters without being seen."

Chapter Twelve

*S*he was hiding something.

Kirtland was sure of it. He raised the brandy to his lips and threw it back in one gulp, ignoring the singe of its liquid fire.

Everyone had secrets, including himself. He had never spoken to anyone, not even Osborne, about the terrible conflict of his childhood years. Yet somehow she had sensed his pain. A high-strung mother, an abusive father, a wild punch that had finally put an end to the fighting. Her fall down the stairs had been ruled an accident, brought on by too much wine, but he knew the truth. He had avoided any contact with his father after that. When the old earl died a few years later, he had not grieved.

His jaw clenched. In at least one thing, the lady had lied—she *was* a merlin, a mystical magician with the power to draw the darkest secrets from a man's heart.

Had she told him the truth about her reasons for being at Marquand Castle? Unless his intuition had entirely deserted him, he felt he could believe at least part of her tale. But maybe it was his body and not his brain that wished to think her innocent of mercenary intentions. A heroine out of a *chanson de geste* rather than an accomplice in a scheme for profit? The thought of her being here to avenge a wrong was rather . . . romantic.

Bloody hell. On recalling Osborne's teasing about being a knight in shining armor, he chided himself for a fool. And yet, he couldn't help feeling a little bit protective. The Black Dove was clearly a hardened woman, unafraid of any man. So why did he sense that beneath all her armor there was something other than steely self interest? Was it mere illusion to think that they might be . . . kindred spirits?

Cursing again, Kirtland took up the decanter and refilled his glass. That, too, he downed in a single swallow. Then followed it with another.

He rarely drank to excess. But the explosive encounter with the Black Dove had left him in a strange mood. He had not lingered over the after-supper port and cigars with the other gentlemen but had retreated to his bedchamber to brood over his brandy in solitude.

Lies. Lust. Fraternizing with this particular enemy was fraught with perils. He better have a care that he was not seduced by his own shift in strategy.

There was only a drop or two left of the spirits. He could either seek oblivion in a fresh bottle or clear his head with a midnight ride through the moors. His mouth twitched in a tight-lipped smile as he savored the irony of the idea. Perhaps he would encounter one of Devon's legendary druids—a magician who might conjure up a counterspell to release him from the merlin's talons.

"Have you any idea why?"

"No, milady." Rose shook her head. "But Oban asked

that you meet him in the stables at midnight. Go around the granary. He will leave the third door on the left unlocked."

Siena glanced at the clock on the mantel. "I had better change into a dark shirt and breeches," she said, allowing Rose to help her out of the ruffled gown. "I won't need the sword." The walk was only a short one. "My knife should suffice."

Seating herself before the looking glass, she combed out the elaborate coiling of her hair and tied it back in a simple knot. A tendril of unease remained. *More trouble?* It was proving hard enough to fend off the unexpected challenges that had arisen. Like blades flashing from all angles, they had her scrambling to keep a step ahead of the cutting edge.

She could use a trusted ally to watch her back. Like the earl, who kept riding to the rescue. A knight in shining armor? She made a face, mocking her own girlish notions, her own dangerous longings. Just because he had shown glimpses of a different face beneath his mask of hard-edged cynicism, she must not think of him as a romantic at heart. Kirtland a hero? He could just as easily be the traitor she sought.

The reflection of Rose, hazy in the half-light, reminded her that she could not look for help elsewhere. She was on her own.

"Your cloak, milady?"

Siena shook her head. "I won't be gone long enough to catch a chill."

It took little time to traverse the graveled path leading down to the stables. All was dark, and the only sounds as she approached were the soft nickering of the horses. Following her maid's direction, she eased the door open.

"Over here," came a whisper from an empty stall. Oban left the lantern unlit. "I have a message from Town."

"Yes?"

"Keep an eye on the Russian."

A shiver, cold as ice, skated down her spine.

"His presence is cause for concern," continued Oban. "It is not yet known who he is working for. The art collector is proving difficult to track down. And so are any facts about Orlov's background. Some rumors say that he is a clever thief, who uses his entrée into the highest circles of Society for personal gain. Others hint that his services have been hired on occasion by a foreign government."

"That is all?" she finally asked when it became evident he had nothing more to say. "No other details?"

"Not at the moment." Oban spun around at a crackling in the straw, but it was only a cat, black as the witching hour, emerging with a mouse in its jaws.

Her mouth twitched. A good thing she did not believe in omens. Still, the sight of predator and prey was another chilling reminder of the dangers lurking in every corner.

"Communication is a tricky matter," he went on. "Perhaps I will receive further word soon."

"I understand," replied Siena, though inwardly she wished that Lynsley had been able to pass on more of a hint as to why Orlov's presence was worth a warning. She was more in the dark than ever. After a pause, she moved on to other surveillance matters. "Have you searched through the saddlebags of The Gilded Page Club members?"

"Yes. And as you ordered, I soaked every scrap of paper that I found in gallotanic acid. All came up blank."

She hadn't really expected to find evidence of invisible ink, but it was worth a try. "Any other news to report?"

"I've seen nothing out of the ordinary. Nor heard anything from the servants that might be of interest. But I'll continue to keep my eyes and ears open."

Siena did not doubt his vigilance. A pity she could not put his formidable fists and granite resolve to better use.

"Best we not be caught in clandestine conversation," he added, already checking that it was safe to leave their hiding place.

Glad that the darkness covered her flush, Siena followed his signal and slipped from the stall. It should have been her own voice murmuring the warning. No matter the distractions, she must stay alert to the dangers around her. Like the cat, they could pounce at any moment and she must be ready.

Her boots moved noiselessly over the damp grass. She had, at least, taken care to plan her route to and from the stables. The conservatory, its milky glass serene in the scudding moonlight, was only a short distance from the stables, and the boxwood hedges provided ample cover.

She pressed a hand to the door latch. Removing several screws from the locking mechanism ensured that it opened without a hitch. Inside, the warmth of the day still hung heavy in the air, muffling the brief stirring of the outside breeze to a muted whisper.

Her movements blended in as well, matching the swaying shadows of the potted palms. From her previous reconnoitering, Siena knew that the cavernous structure was always deserted at night. An oasis of calm.

Keeping to the grass borders, she turned down one of the narrow walkways, still puzzling over Lynsley's cryptic warning. The Russian's harmless flirtations now took on a more ominous shape. Like the row of bromeliads to her right, whose whimsical forms were distorted by the silvery light into monstrous jaws, agape with jagged teeth.

Or so it seemed. Her imagination was on edge.

"What's the hurry, Madame Dove?"

Siena whipped around, grabbing up a thin bamboo shaft from the sheaf of plant stakes by her side.

"I thought it was only barn owls that flew about at night." Kirtland's steps were as light as her own upon the mossy brick.

"When and where I choose to spread my wings is none of your concern, sir," she replied. "What are you doing out?"

He set a fist on his hip. "You are aware of my penchant for midnight rides. I was feeling in need of clearing the port and cheroot smoke from my head, and was on my way to the stables when I saw a shape skulking through the bushes." It appeared that he had imbibed his fair share of the spirits. His words were slightly slurred, and the spice of the wine and tobacco clung to his clothing. "I decided to follow, in order to make sure it was not a thief who was entering the castle."

"I, too, was merely seeking a breath of fresh air."

The arch of his raven brows was eloquent in its skepticism as he regarded her dark breeches and boots. "Dressed as a Death's Head Hussar?"

With his hair curling around his collar and his emerald eyes catching the glint of the stars, Kirtland radiated the raw masculine magnetism that men like Dunster would kill to possess. Despite all her resolve, a spark of physical awareness flared back to life. "One never knows when trouble will strike, sir."

"True." He, too, picked up one of the wooden rods and tested its flex. "You've spun a fine tale of loyalty and revenge. But how do I know that your real intention in coming to Marquand Castle is not to purloin the St. Sebastian Psalters?"

"And how do I know that *you* do not have the manuscripts secreted on your person?" She flicked the point of her stick at his caped coat and Hessians. "Perhaps you are about to gallop hell-for-leather to the coast, where a ship is waiting to whisk you off to the Continent with your stolen treasures."

Kirtland stripped off his coat and dropped it on a swath of sod. "See for yourself," he replied with a mocking bow. Like her, he was clad in naught but breeches and a shirt. The collar was open, revealing a peppering of dark curls against his tanned flesh.

With all that had happened throughout the day, she was not sure if she was sharp enough to engage in a duel of this sort. And when in doubt, the prudent move was a strategic retreat. "I concede that the books do not appear to be stuffed inside your clothing."

A flash of unholy amusement lit in his eyes. Damn the man for looking so devilishly attractive when he chose to smile. "While I, in turn, am not so sure." Quick as a cat, he slipped around the potting bench and stood in her path. "Your shirt looks suspiciously full in certain parts." His stick cut a swoosh through the air. "Perhaps I ought to demand a search."

"I am in no mood for games, sir."

"A strange comment coming from you, madam. I was under the impression that you are inordinately fond of games."

"Step aside," she muttered.

His stick came up to block her. Despite his uneven speech, his movements were sharp. "Care to make me?

I seem to recall that we still have a challenge left to settle."

Among other things.

"You seem quite sure of yourself in a *mano a mano* match of skills. Shall we put such confidence to the test?"

The opportunity was too tempting. He was offering an opening, a chance to attack when his guard was weakened by brandy. Fatigue was forgotten as she changed her mind about standing her ground. *He wished to provoke a match of skills?* The challenge of seducing him into a slip was suddenly irresistible.

Her own wooden weapon come up to cross with his. "Very well—*en garde*."

"What rules do you desire?" he asked, parrying a *girata*.

"Name them."

"What say you to a forfeit for every touch allowed?"

"Agreed."

Kirtland ventured a lunge, which she easily blocked. Dropping low, she sought to catch him off guard with an upward thrust, but he moved back with deceptive quickness, his booted feet light with a lethal grace.

"I doubt either of us will fall victim to such elementary moves," he remarked, testing her reactions with a series of slow slashes.

She, too, took her time in probing for any weakness. They circled the bench and moved to a narrow strip of greensward bordering the walkway. "Perhaps not, but I do hold a distinct advantage, sir."

"Indeed?"

"I am clearheaded, while you are clearly foxed."

"On the Peninsula, one gains a great deal of experience

in riding straight into battle after a night of carousing. The first clash of steel is a sobering sound."

"I am curious, Lord Kirtland . . ." Thinking a pique to his pride might cause a more obvious opening, Siena pressed on. She was testing his temper as well, on the chance that he would make a verbal slip. "Were you drunk or sober when you disobeyed a direct order from your superior?"

He laughed softly. "What do you think?"

Siena didn't answer.

"Have you ever faced death, madam?" he went on, evading her *controcavione* with maddening ease. "Ever taken your fencing skills from the practice yard to a field slippery with blood? Ever tested your precision with the screams of the dying echoing in your ears and the acrid smell of smoke and gunpowder choking your lungs?"

Damn. How had he contrived to turn her own weapon against her?

"I've trained—"

His make-believe blade was suddenly naught but a dizzying blur. "All the training in the world would not save you now." Its tip pressed hard against her breast. "Touché."

She knocked it away with the back of her hand. "It won't happen again."

"You wish another try?" He sketched a mocking salute. "I shall be happy to oblige you, but first you must give over your forfeit."

Her cheeks, already flushed, flamed to a hotter shade of red. In her haste to take up the challenge, she had neglected to ask the terms. "Very well," she snapped, resting a fist on her hip. "What is it you demand?"

A deadly grin glinted in the silvery light. "An item of

clothing." His weapon teased at the collar of her shirt. "I shall be a gentleman and leave it for you to choose."

Siena drew in a breath to protest, then suddenly smiled.

"Or, you may simply concede defeat and leave the field of battle with your dress, if not your pride, intact."

"The devil I will." She tugged off a boot. A moment later the other one hit the turf. Her balance would be better with both feet unshod. "Here, I shall award you a bonus for scoring the first hit. It shall be your last."

Kirtland flipped the rod to his left hand. "Far be it for me to take advantage of a lady."

A taunt. And she was reacting like an unfledged chick rather than a trained Merlin. Da Rimini would be tearing his hair in despair. *Non, non, non—you must slide to the left, then counter with a* punta sopramano.

"Gentlemanly indeed," she replied evenly. "However, the rules of engagement were that we fight on equal terms." She, too, shifted the grip on her weapon. "If you wish to fight *a sinistre,* I shall do the same."

He cocked his wrist. "The choice is yours."

The rods crossed for an instant; then she spun to the side, angling a slash at his ribs. He blocked it, but only barely. Her bare feet flew over the damp turf. Over, under, over, under—her blade beat a methodical attack, forcing him to retreat to the edge of the grass. His gaze flicked to the right, just for an instant. When he moved, she was ready.

Her rod caught his arm with a satisfying *thwack.*

"Tit for tat," she murmured.

"I wouldn't crow just yet, my Midnight Dove. The match is far from over." Spearing his rod into the earth, he pulled his shirt over his head and tossed it aside. "The vanquished party is the one who chooses whether to continue or not."

The quickening of her pulse matched the flutter of white linen. His long locks tumbled in devil-may-care disarray around his ears, the curling ends grazing the slope of his shoulders. Muscles rippled as he reached for his weapon, and light flickered over the broad stretch of chest and narrow waist.

He was magnificently male. A fact he was shamelessly flaunting.

Had she lost sight of her real purpose in the heat of a more primal battle? Focus, she reminded herself. The revelations she wanted from him were not physical.

He was watching her intently, and though his gaze was hooded, she thought she saw a peek of a smile.

Distractions were dangerous. Deliciously dangerous. She must stay on guard. "You wish another hit to your manly pride?"

"My manly pride is still well sheathed, madam. And I always take great care in guarding it from any low blows."

She couldn't bite back a laugh. "If I were you, I would not be so cocksure. I don't play by the rules."

"So I have noticed. I shall consider myself forewarned." A stirring of the palm fronds hid his face for a moment. "Ready?"

"But of course." Her hand tightened. She must keep her mind on technique and not the silky curls trailing down to the hard, flat belly and angled hip bones.

The match became a *pas de deux* of martial skills. A sensual dance. As they traded thrusts and parries, Siena was intimately aware of his whipcord strength, his leonine quickness. There was something exciting, erotic about the physical exertion. A sheen of sweat glistened on his chest, accentuating the fluid grace of his movements, the subtle contours of—

The prick of his point caught her square on the hip.

"Damn!"

"Your *filo falso* is angled a bit too low. Hold your wrist a touch higher."

"*Il Lupino* has cautioned much the same thing," she muttered.

Kirtland fell back a step. "Allegretto Da Rimini?"

Porca miseria! She could hear the fencing master's curses ringing in her ears. *No more mistakes, Volpina.*

Kirtland's gaze was far more probing than his makeshift sword. "I was not aware that he had come to England."

"Who said he had?" she countered quickly.

The earl was silent for a moment. "His training explains your extraordinary skills. Though it begs yet another question about your background."

"Which I have no intention of answering, so don't waste your breath." Ruing her slip of the tongue, Siena sought to deflect any further scrutiny of her past. "As is my right, I demand a chance to even the score."

"First you must yield the token of your defeat."

Two could wield their bodies as a weapon. Time to regain the upper hand in this war of wills. "Right." She leaned her rod against a potted palm and began loosening the fastenings of her breeches. With a slow, deliberate waggle of her hips, she peeled the buckskin down over her thighs and let the garment fall to the ground. "Satisfied?" she demanded, stepping out from the pooling of leather.

"For the nonce." He assumed a nonchalant stance, but

she read more than a casual interest in his oblique gaze. For all his austere angles and stony composure, the earl was not impervious to flesh-and-blood desire. "Ready?"

"Not quite yet." Her shirttails hung loosely around her legs. "I need a moment to dispense with this distraction." She secured the trailing linen in a knot at her waist, revealing a pair of lacy drawers that barely covered the curve of her derriere.

"Imp of Satan." His eyes ran up the length of her legs and came to rest on the sliver of midriff showing between the two garments. "It appears I am caught in a devilish dilemma. Gentlemanly honor demands that I lose, while a baser instinct urges me to show no mercy."

"Which shall win out?"

He cocked his head, throwing all but his mouth in shadow. "I warned you I was no true gentleman."

"It is a fair match, sir, for I am no proper lady."

"Then let us both be on guard."

The click of wood was not quite as same as the ring of steel, yet Siena felt the familiar thrill of anticipation as she squared off for another bout. Kirtland was as skilled as Da Rimini, but the sexual tension between them added an extra edge to the competition. She would take more pleasure in besting the earl.

This time around, she intended to try a Sicilian maneuver . . .

"Fie, sir!" she cried as her first cut struck home. "You did not even attempt a defense."

He contrived to look innocent, without much success. "You wound me, madam, by adding insult to injury." First one boot, then the other came off. "There, now we are on equal footing."

"Then perhaps we should call it a draw."

"Surely you are not feeling fatigued?" He cut a lightning flourish through the air. Several fig leaves fell to the ground. "You look to be in splendid shape."

"Oh, that I am." And indeed, she won the next exchange with little trouble. "That is quite enough," she grumbled as the earl removed his breeches. "You are making a mockery of the competition."

"It would be most unfair to quit while you are ahead." A single stride brought him within an arm's length. The scent of brandy and a distinctly masculine musk filled her lungs. "What have you got to lose, my Dark Dove?"

Everything, if she was not very careful. Did she dare continue this dangerous game with Kirtland? She had just witnessed that the difference between victory and defeat was often too slight to be seen with the naked eye.

"Nothing," she replied. A Merlin did not back down.

"We shall see." He ducked under a low-hanging ficus branch, and for an instant Siena was left wondering whether his words had a sinister shade to them. But then, there was no time to muse on nuances. His next attack was swift, sure, striking at her one weakness on the left side.

She stumbled, and still would have dodged his *debole* if not for the terra-cotta pots blocking her retreat.

"It appears as if the match is all square, madam. That is, once you shed your loss."

Siena assessed her options—which didn't amount to much. She had dressed in a hurry, not bothering with more than the bare necessities.

"Take your time," drawled Kirtland. "I'm in no hurry."

Damn the man. He was clearly enjoying this. Brushing an errant strand from her cheek, she reached back to retie her hair. As her fingers caught the curl of ribbon, her scowl took an upward bend. "You wish your forfeit?" Light as a feather, the black silk swirled in a puff of air before floating down to earth. "*Voilà*."

"Protecting your maidenly modesty?" The earl flashed a devilish smile. "There is precious little I haven't already seen, if you recall." He jabbed at the scrap of fabric. "That seems to be stretching the definition of clothing. As would be the sheath you have strapped to your calf."

She might have known he would not miss the knife, however well its flesh-colored leather fitted against her own skin.

"Very clever," he finished. "Bantrock is lucky that his cock is still attached to his ballocks."

The last thing Siena wanted was for him to dwell on her hidden blade and her reasons for wearing it. He was far too sharp at cutting through her best defenses. "I should hate to be accused of cheating, sir," she said quickly. Unknotting its tails, she whipped her shirt off and flung it at his feet. A gauntlet of linen, not leather, but holding the same elemental challenge.

"Come, let us have at it," she added. "*Mano a mano*. Winner take all."

Chapter Thirteen

"*Mano a mano,*" repeated Kirtland. Amusement warred with arousal as he stared at her bared breasts. "An interesting figure of speech." Like the rest of her lithe body, they were taut and perfectly formed, the rosy aureoles tipped with peaks that quickly darkened to a deeper red. Like points of fire. He suddenly burned to know what they would feel like beneath his palm.

Siena seized on his silence to press the offensive. "Defend yourself, sir." A loping leap carried her to the top of the potting bench. Dancing around the tiny seedlings, she dropped to the other side and came at him from behind.

He whirled. The sticks clashed.

"Quick, my high-flying merlin, but not quick enough."

She cut between two orange trees, one step ahead of his lunge. With a low laugh, Kirtland gave chase, vaulting over a row of orchids.

In the heat of battle, the drawstring of his drawers worked loose. He glanced down to see that gentlemanly propriety was hanging on by a thread. The only thing holding the garment up were his hip bones.

And his growing arousal.

"Combat stimulates the most primal of urges in men," he said, seeing her gaze drawn to his groin.

"So it would seem," she replied with dry humor, but he thought he detected a swirl of liquid heat in her eyes.

"In war there is life and death," he continued. Their weapons beat a staccato tattoo. "And very little in between."

She hesitated, which was very nearly her undoing. His rod darted in below hers, and only a whip of her hips and an arching spin saved her. The point kissed only lace.

"Bravo," he murmured, though in the same breath he sidestepped to cut off her retreat, forcing her back against the workbench.

She tossed aside the wooden sword and grabbed hold of its edge. *Impossible.* With her back to the slatted top, not even the Black Dove could manage the acrobatics needed to fly over its width. The lady appeared to agree. She swore and slid to her left.

Grinning, the earl raised his arm and stepped in for the coup de grace.

She waited under the last instant to lash out. The kick nearly took his legs out from under him, but the earl had anticipated that she might not fight fair. Matching her lightning quickness, he dodged its full impact.

"Hellion." Capturing her ankle, Kirtland twisted and pinned her up against the unyielding wood. He stepped in between her legs, crushing his heat hard against her. "Burned once, think twice, my dear merlin. This time I came ready to fight fire with fire."

Steel and flint. Tonight the clash had ignited not just

sparks but a conflagration. Its crackle was perilously close to consuming the last vestiges of his self-control.

"I'm afraid you have no choice but to concede defeat, madam." The feel of her long legs was exquisitely enticing, like steel sheathed in velvet. He must try to remember that all he wanted from her was a confession. But that was proving damnably difficult. He ran his hands along the length of her thighs, savoring the sensation.

She suddenly stilled beneath his touch. The blaze in her eyes took on a different glow. It was not the flicker of surrender, but some light he could not begin to define.

"I am in no position to argue." Her lips pursed, and he swallowed a groan, recalling how sweet they had tasted, cool and beaded with wind-whipped rain. "Though you must admit, sir, that the match could have gone either way. There is very little difference between us."

"On the contrary, *paloma*." Her loosened tresses were tumbled over her shoulders, ebony against ivory. Rare and exotic. He reached up and buried his fingers in the silky strands. "There is a world of difference between us."

She touched his chest, grazing the curls of dark hair. "Yes, you are a lord and I am . . . no one."

"I am a man, and you are a woman." Hell's fire, she was undeniably feminine. Up close, her face had a fine-boned beauty, her cheeks strong yet delicate, her chin tapering to fit perfectly in the palm of his hand. He tilted it up so that he could gaze into her eyes. She looked somehow . . . innocent. Vulnerable. As if she hadn't taken countless men inside her.

He nearly laughed aloud at the thought, but the breath had caught in his throat. He had to force himself to exhale. "Sweet Jesus," he rasped. "At this moment I don't give a damn who you are."

Her lashes fluttered, her voice wavered. "A—are you going to claim your forfeit?"

Surely no innocent could sound so sinfully seductive. Kirtland took her earlobe between his teeth. "Oh, I mean to savor my hard-fought victory before seizing the prize." He felt her shiver as he pressed his mouth to the hollow of her throat. Her skin was warm and salty with exertion, and her pulse pounded against his lips. A hunger flared deep within. Only sliding his tongue inside her warmth might slake it. "Though God help me," he whispered, "I'm not sure whether I have won or lost."

At that moment, all his carefully planned battle tactics seemed to lose their edge. Somehow, victory no longer seemed so clear-cut.

Her hands were threaded in his hair, and, as she drew him closer, he saw the same uncertainty mirrored in her expression.

"Perhaps we might, for a moment, not think of war."

Kirtland traced the line of her jaw, wondering whether he had only imagined the flicker in her eyes. Or could it be that this magnificent Valkyrie was not as certain of her own strength as she wished to seem? The thought of it sent another surge through his limbs. Not of lust, but of a longing to keep her shielded in his arms, safe from whatever enemy she was fighting.

"Cry *pax,* you mean?" Kirtland watched her carefully as he spoke, trying to discern whether he could trust this vulnerable side of the Black Dove. Was she truly offering an olive branch? Or was it the hidden hawk luring him closer with a tangle of thorns in its talons?

"*Pax.*" She sighed, her breath feathery soft on his cheek. Then her lips were at the corner of his mouth, a gossamer touch that drew a groan. "Kiss me."

Suddenly it no longer mattered what dangers lay ahead. He had survived the slashing sabers of opposing armies. He would risk the far more subtle wounds of dueling with this mysterious merlin.

Siena felt more than naked beneath his rapier gaze. She felt stripped of all her defenses.

Yet at the same time, some primal instinct told her that the earl was not her real enemy. He did not feel . . . threatening. She had survived in the slums by trusting in her primal reactions. Did she dare go on with this dangerous seduction?

As his hands skimmed down over her thighs and wrapped her legs around his hips, Siena assured herself she was equal to the challenge. She could remain detached, her mission paramount in her mind, no matter what was demanded of her body.

The earl rocked forward, his chest grazing her breasts. She felt her flesh peak, aroused by his touch. As if sensing an unspoken need, his fingers closed around her, thumbs teasing her tips to hard little sword points.

She cried out, but whether it was duty or desire speaking, she dared not say. "Kiss me."

His mouth came down on hers, expressing the same urgent need. She opened to him, drinking in the heat of brandy and male desire. It was a far more potent mix than she had ever imagined. No classroom lectures, no bedroom lessons had prepared her for the realities of real passion.

Or the jolt of fire that lanced through her as he suddenly turned his tongue to caressing her breast.

"Do you like that, *paloma?*"

Her nails scraped across his shoulders as he teased at her nipple. Her words were now just a flutter of air.

His hand reached between them, molding to her feminine mound. As he teased a finger through her wet curls, she found her voice again. "Julian." His given name came unbidden to her tongue.

He answered with a hoarse whisper. "Say it again."

"Julian." This was all about the mission, she told herself. Seducing the earl would bring her closer to learning what secrets he might be hiding. Yet who was seducing whom? Limbs entangled, tongues entwined, the edge was blurred between their strengths.

"I cannot fight this damnable attraction," he groaned. "Not now."

"Nor can I." Siena lifted herself to meet his thrust. There was naught but a thin scrim of silk and linen between them. His ridged muscles were taut with need, his steeling shaft straining to cut through the last barrier to their coupling.

He reached for the delicate twist of silk. One finger hooked in the lace, then another.

"Yes," she urged. Was it the warrior or the woman speaking? For a moment, she wasn't quite sure.

His palm flattened on her flesh . . .

A shadow, dark against the moonlight, flickered outside the glass.

Kirtland's hand suddenly shot down the length of her leg. Snatching the knife from its sheath, he rolled to one side and landed lightly on his feet.

"Spawn of Satan." His oath was left hovering in the air as he turned and raced through the screen of palms toward the rear of the conservatory.

It took a moment for Siena to gather her wits; then she,

too, pushed up from the bench. Snatching her shirt, she followed the sound of rustling leaves and running steps to the glass door that faced the rolling lawns.

It was ajar, and the chill night breeze had knocked over several specimen pots.

Outside, at the far bend of the boxwood hedges, she could just make out the shape of a figure, but it quickly melded into the shadows. Turning to Kirtland, she asked, "Did you see who it was?"

"Yes." The earl's voice was no longer gentle.

She slipped on her shirt, though it did nothing to ward off the goose bumps prickling down her spine. "*Who?*"

"Orlov."

"Damn." The oath slipped out before she could catch herself.

"Are you upset that he was spying on us?" The curl of his lip looked carved of ice. "Or upset that I moved fast enough to recognize him?"

"What do you mean?" The dueling of duty and desire still had her off-balance.

"Let us stop beating around the bush—I have suspected for some time that you and he are in league. I commend you, madam. Whether your plan is to steal the manuscripts outright or to foment enough dissension among the bidders to win the auction, your plan is diabolically clever."

"No!" The breath caught in her throat. "I am not in league with him. I swear it."

Her obvious surprise seemed to soften his cynicism. "Yet you reacted with heat when you learned he was lurking nearby. Why?"

"There is something unsettling about his presence here," she replied in all honesty. "I cannot help but wonder whether it is books that have brought him to Marquand Castle, or something else."

"I have been asking myself much the same question. But answers seem as elusive as our Russian friend."

The earl stood still as a statue, his bare flesh pale as marble in the moonglow. Stern and unyielding, like a Greek god. Siena looked heavenward, and through the high glass ceiling she saw the faint glimmer of Venus among the stars. But there was nothing of the lover about Kirtland now. He looked like Mars, a warrior expression carved on his features.

"And then there is you," he added. "Your own words have been equally evasive."

She said nothing.

He latched the door and moved away from the mullioned panes. Raising her knife to the scudding light, he turned it once in his fingers before handing it over. "So, we are back to being at daggers drawn?"

The earl spun around so quickly that Siena could no longer see anything of him but a lean shadow. But his next words echoed clearly off the glass.

"Be warned that the next time we have it, the duel will not end in a stalemate."

Chapter Fourteen

A rather windy day for an exhibition of marksmanship, wouldn't you say, Lord Kirtland?"

The earl turned from his brooding contemplation of the distant moors to meet Orlov's sly smile.

The morning had indeed dawned cold and blustery. Hardly ideal conditions for the Black Dove's second challenge, which was a test of shooting skills. In spite of the chill, Kirtland had taken his coffee out to the stone terrace overlooking the gardens, hoping to avoid the idle chatter of the breakfast room.

But the Russian seemed to have a knack of turning up where he was least wanted.

"Let us hope there is not another unfortunate accident, like the one that befell poor Bantrock. He left for Dublin at first light, in case you had not heard." Orlov exaggerated a sigh. "Imagine, suffering such a nasty slip. The fellow's face looked like a slab of raw beefsteak."

Much as Kirtland would have enjoyed smashing the Russian's nose to a bloody pulp, he kept his temper in check. "Apparently the Irishman was clumsy. He should have been more careful. With all its twists and turns, Marquand Castle can be a treacherous place."

"True, but there are so many cozy nooks and crannies as well." Orlov took a seat on the stone railing and crossed one booted leg over the other. "Did you sleep well? Or do you find the chambers here a trifle overheated?"

The earl was in no mood for verbal fencing. Ignoring the other man's blatant jab, he took a sip from his cup and resumed his silent pacing around the perimeter of the slate tiles.

His thoughts about the Black Dove and the previous day were going in circles as well.

On one hand, the rational part of his brain was warning him away from any emotional entanglement. In the past, it had always been easy to keep a distance between himself and those around him. Even Osborne was allowed only so close.

The problem was, the rational part of his brain was only a very small portion of his anatomy. The rest of him was, against all reason, enjoying her company. Her fiery courage, her sharp wit, her physical grace, her exotic beauty—everything about her was undeniably unique. Undeniably alluring.

Undeniably dangerous.

Yet danger often sharpened the sense of being alive . . .

A well-trained courtesan would, of course, know how to enflame a man's senses so that his better judgment went up in smoke. In the army, he had never been fooled by an enemy ambush, no matter how skillfully planned. Was he now falling prey to the oldest trap known to mankind?

Kirtland lifted his face to the cooling breeze. He had assured Osborne that his eyes were open to her game. So why did he wish to see an innocence in the glint of her golden gaze, despite all signs to the contrary?

Was he an idealist? Or an idiot?

Given his recent past, maybe there wasn't much difference between the two.

Still, he was inclined to believe she was not working with Orlov. Her surprise at his accusation had been too real. Indeed, now that his anger—and his lust—had cooled down, he admitted that perhaps he had overreacted in declaring they were back to being at daggers drawn.

Strangely enough, he found he did not want to break the fragile friendship that had formed between them. At least, not just yet.

What her reaction would be this morning was another question . . .

"Ah, there you are, Kirtland." Winthrop stepped out from the Music Room onto the terrace. "Would you happen to know where the Black Dove's shooting match is to take place?"

The earl set aside his musings along with his coffee. "Her groom is setting up a series of targets in the copse of elms down by the lake."

"Lud, what a devilish choice for the second challenge." Winthrop sat down on a marble plinth and took his head between his hands. "I drank far too much of the duke's brandy last night. No doubt I'll be seeing two circles rather than one," he groaned. "Not that it matters. You and Fitz are by far the best shots among us."

"Perhaps the lady will oversleep." Orlov seized the opportunity to resume his tone of infuriating insolence. "She, too, might have overindulged in some of the pleasures that can be found in the castle."

"No such luck," replied Winthrop. "I saw her entering

the breakfast room, looking quite as magnificently awake as ever."

"And the others?" asked the earl.

"They will be down shortly."

"Well, I shall leave you gentlemen to your games." The Russian stood and brushed a bit of dust from his immaculate doeskin breeches. "What is the prize for this part of the competition?"

"A ride out to the one of the hunting lodges to enjoy a private supper of game birds and port." Winthrop grimaced at the mention of spirits. "Apparently one of the previous dukes was a great one for stalking the local milkmaids. The place is said to be decorated with all manner of erotic art."

"How very romantic," quipped Orlov. "Assuming that dove is one of the delicacies on the menu."

"Would that it were so," said Winthrop. "But like the Psalters, the Black Dove's favors are under glass, as it were, until the final bids are in and a winner is announced."

"So you believe she is not spreading her wings, as it were, when you are not looking?" Orlov's brow arched upward in a blatant show of skepticism. "I admire you English gentlemen. You have such refined notions of honor to trust in a lady's word. We Slavs have a rather more Byzantine outlook on life."

"It's no wonder, seeing as treachery and intrigue seem to run as a matter of course in Eastern blood." The earl's murmur was no louder than the gusting breeze.

If Orlov heard the comment, he chose to ignore it. Clicking the heels of his boots together, he bowed. The fluttering tassels of his Hessians seemed to mirror the off-hand arrogance of his movements. "Still, it sounds as if one of your group is in for a real treat."

"Prick," muttered Winthrop as the Russian walked

away. "Someone ought to cut off his cods. And stuff them down his throat."

The thought of the Black Dove and her blade turning that mocking baritone into a shrill soprano brought a curl to the earl's lips. But then, he reminded himself that her loyalties were still questionable, despite her denials.

As for the Russian, his motives seemed clear enough. "You ought not to let Mr. Orlov get under your skin," replied Kirtland. "He, too, is playing at games. And much as he thinks he holds the winning hand, I wouldn't bet on it."

Siena checked the priming of the pistols before handing them over to Oban. "The course is set?"

"Aye, ma'am. All is arranged as you ordered. There are five stations set up along the path, a hundred paces separating each one. The targets are hung among the trees according to your layout, and these weapons will be placed atop a barrel. In between rounds, I will make the circuit to reload and collect the results."

"Excellent." She tucked the diagram back in her notebook, satisfied that everything was precisely as she had planned. Still, she felt a small flutter of nerves at the prospect of facing Kirtland.

Back to being at daggers drawn? His last words had implied that their tentative truce was over. Which perhaps was just as well. Last night she had allowed things to become too . . . personal. In wielding her body as a weapon, she seemed to have found a tiny weakness in the earl's defenses. If she was to exploit it, she must not let her emotions get out of hand.

Oban shifted slightly.

Tightening her grip on her book, Siena turned to a fresh page. "I will be accompanying each man on his round, to keep track of how long it takes him to complete the course." And to observe how well he performed a difficult task under the pressure of a time limit.

"Aye, ma'am," answered her groom. "All is ready."

After a last look at the shadowed trees, Siena returned to the clearing where the members of The Gilded Page Club were waiting.

"Gentlemen, as you know, today's challenge is a test of how well you handle a loaded weapon."

Amid a few scattered chuckles, the men gathered around her.

"The course follows the footpath through the woods and loops back to finish here. You will have to move quickly in order to finish your five shots in the allotted time of ten minutes." She held up her pocket watch to emphasize the announcement. "Those who are slow will be penalized by having points deducted from their scores, and those who fall behind by more than a minute will be eliminated entirely. On the other hand, those who finish ahead of schedule will earn bonus points. Are there any questions before we start?"

No one spoke up. Perhaps it was the threat of rain hanging over their heads, but the men seemed more subdued than usual. Or perhaps she had simply scheduled the game a trifle too early in the day. Winthrop, in particular, looked under the weather.

"You will draw straws for the order of shooting. The longest will go first, and so on."

"Stand aside," quipped Dunster. "It goes without saying that the longest will be me." His bravado had quieted somewhat since his confrontation with the earl, but he still managed to give the appearance of being supremely sure of himself.

The earl made no move to choose for himself.

It was Jadwin who won the starting honors. Kirtland was to go last.

"Are you ready to begin, sir?" asked Siena.

Jadwin removed his muffler and handed it Leveritt. "I'll be back shortly," he said with nonchalant shrug.

"I start counting the time from here, though the first target is set beneath that elm." She indicated a large tree straight ahead.

At her signal, Jadwin chose a brisk walk over a run. "A rapid heartbeat can throw off one's aim," he said as she fell in step beside him.

Siena had deliberately designed a difficult first shot, and she watched the way he handled the pistol very carefully. Every little nuance was important. A man could, of course, feign clumsiness, yet a seasoned shooter had a certain natural grace that was difficult to disguise. Most of all, she was looking for a steady hand. The traitor was a man not easily rattled. To pull off the string of betrayals, he needed to possess nerves of steel and the ability to work quickly and unerringly.

"An excellent weapon," observed Jadwin as his bullet struck near the center of the target. "The duke's?"

"Yes. Stoneleigh lent me a set from the armory," she replied. "You like them?"

"Oh yes—*très jolie*." He turned smartly for the next station, setting the same deliberate pace. "The burled-walnut stock is lovely, and silver scrolling is a fine piece of craftsmanship. I would guess it was made by Purdey, rather than Manton."

His second shot was also on the mark. As was his third. The fourth missed the bull's-eye, but only barely.

"I hadn't expected such prowess from a man of the arts," she murmured as they looped around to the last target. For the most part, Jadwin seemed content to stand in the shadow of his older friend Leveritt. It was easy to overlook him—he was of average height and average build, with light brown hair and fine-boned features that made him appear younger than he really was. He was also the quietest member of the group, but she had noticed that his eyes were always alert, always watchful.

Touching his sleeve, she added, "What other special talents are you hiding, sir?"

Jadwin looked at her sharply, then laughed. "I like being well versed in a good many things. It's important to have a certain *joie de vivre,* don't you think?"

"But of course."

His step took on a slight swagger as he returned to the group. "I believe my performance was quite adequate." He winked as he took his muffler back from Leveritt and draped it over his shoulders. "Let us see if any of you gentlemen can best it."

As Siena entered his time in her notebook, she also made a mental note to review the details of his background. Was the slip of the French phrases a mere affectation? Or could it have deeper implications? A mistress, perhaps, from across the Channel. It was an interesting possibility . . .

Seeing Oban signal that all was ready for the next round, she turned her attention to the others.

One by one, the rest of the club members took their turn through the course. Leveritt looked as if he barely knew the butt from the barrel, while Dunster was surprisingly smooth in his actions. Fitzwilliam badly misjudged his aim on the last shot, putting him out of the running, but Winthrop scored very well, despite his claims of an aching head.

"Well done, sir." As the last puff of smoke dissolved in the breeze, Siena checked her pocket watch. "So far, you have the best round, and each of your shots appeared to find the mark."

"I fear that last one only clipped the outer edge of the target." Winthrop blew out his breath. "It is not always easy to perform under conditions like these. The higher the stakes, the harder it is to relax."

"If your score holds up, I shall see to it that the tension is eased from your bones."

He watched her smooth the skirts over her hips. "The thought is enough to tempt me to wet Kirtland's powder." His tongue flicked over his lower lip. "Almost," he amended.

Although Siena had already eliminated him as a suspect, she was curious to hear his opinion of the earl. "You are afraid of Kirtland?"

Winthrop's smirk disappeared. "I'm not afraid of *any* man. I respect him. And his temper. There is a difference."

"Indeed, there is," she said thoughtfully. "Yet from what I have observed, Lord Kirtland is not given to unreasonable outbursts of anger. Quite the opposite in fact."

Winthrop looked a trifle uncomfortable. "Rumor has it he is dangerous to cross."

Rumor. Innuendo. What was truth and what was lie? Siena had no chance to pursue the subject as they came to the end of the course.

The others had returned to the comforts of the castle. Only the earl stood in the clearing. Despite the darkening skies and the gusting wind, he wore no coat or gloves, giving the impression of a man impervious to the elements.

No wonder his fellow club members were a bit intimidated, thought Siena. He was not a man who invited intimacies. And yet . . .

"Are we ready to begin?" he asked brusquely.

"My groom requires a few more minutes to reload and reset

the targets, sir." Following his lead, she replied in a clipped voice. "Do you care to know the time you must beat?"

"Not particularly."

Tucking his hands inside his coat, Winthrop excused himself from the field of battle. "I shall await the outcome inside the castle with the others, if you don't mind. Hot coffee holds more allure at the moment than hot lead."

"From daggers drawn to pistols primed," murmured Kirtland, once the other man was out of earshot. "Dare we begin another duel? There is no telling what may happen when our flint and steel strike together near real gunpowder."

Was it merely a waggle of shadows through the branches, or did the earl's lips twitch?

"I have things under control," she replied. Save for her wicked, wayward thoughts. Ignoring her earlier mental reprimand, her mind kept picturing the earl nearly naked in the moonlight.

"It did not appear so last night."

Unwilling to meet his gaze, Siena made a show of writing a few lines in her notebook, then snapped the covers shut. In the light of day, there would be no errant sparks, no unexpected explosion. "Brandy is a volatile substance. It tends to set fire to a man's imagination. Now that your head is clear, I trust you will make a real attempt at this test of skill."

Kirtland lifted a brow. "Why?"

She hesitated. "Because I'm curious as to just how good your aim is."

"I thought I had displayed my aim well enough already."

"With a certain weapon," she said tartly.

This time, there was no mistaking the quirk of his lips. "I assure you, madam, my trigger finger is quite practiced. Some say it is smooth as silk."

Siena realized she was blushing like a schoolgirl. Raising her pocket watch, she used the smooth gold as a shield from further distraction. "I think it is safe to begin."

"Do you?"

Damn. The earl kept surprising her. She had expected outright hostility, not dry humor. Why was he trying to throw her off-balance?

Siena shifted her stance and set a hand on her hip. "You *do* know the rules, sir—you may walk or run from station to station, as you please. Points are given for speed. But accuracy is most important."

He shrugged. "You are calling the shots, madam. You may start the game whenever you wish."

"On the count of three . . ."

At her call, he set out with a loping stride. Siena had dressed for the occasion in wide-cut walking skirts and a frogged spenser to assure ease of movement, yet she still had to race to catch up with the earl. He had already squeezed off the first shot by the time she reached his side.

From where she stood, it appeared as though the bullet had hit dead center. But she had no time for a closer look. Kirtland was on the move again.

"A clever choice of angles," he said as he broke into an easy jog. "Are you as adept with firearms as you are with a blade?"

"Yes," she answered, taking care to match him stride for stride.

"What the devil did this mysterious protector of yours think he was doing—training a private army?"

Only his steadying grip on her arm kept her from tripping over her own feet. "He was of the opinion a lady should know how to protect herself."

"In case she encountered Attila the Hun?"

This show of whimsy was yet another side of the earl. She shot him a sidelong look. "You are in a rather strange mood."

"As I said before, you seem to have an enchanting effect on me. A merlin full of magical powers, stirring up all manner of odd emotions."

In truth, it was her own nerves that were still slightly aflutter. She drew in a deep breath, unwilling to betray any weakness. "Or perhaps the brandy has not yet worn off."

The earl laughed softly as he took aim and fired. *Another bull's-eye.* And another at the third station. Ignoring the footpath, he ducked under a low-hanging branch and cut straight for the fourth station.

"Why don't you take the next shot?" Turning abruptly, he offered her the pistol.

"That's not how the game is supposed to be played."

"Since when do you care about breaking the rules?" he countered.

"You are wasting precious time, milord."

"I'll forfeit the seconds to see if you are as good as you say you are." The twinkle in his eye turned more intense. He edged a step sideways. "Come, you aren't going to refuse a challenge?"

"That is unfair to—"

The air was suddenly slammed from her lungs as the earl's shoulder hit her square in the chest. The full force of his weight followed an instant later, knocking her sideways.

At the same moment, a loud *crack* reverberated through the trees.

A bullet whizzed overhead as she fell to the ground, with the earl sprawled atop her.

"Roll to one side, sir," she wheezed with her first breath. "You are in the line of fire."

His arms remained locked around her. "That's rather the idea."

He meant to shield *her* from harm? No one had ever risked life and limb for her.

Quelling the urge to stay sheltered in his embrace, Siena kept up her struggles and managed to slither out from under him.

"Don't be daft," he growled, keeping hold of her wrist. "If you are as well trained as you say, you know it's foolhardy to go charging off in blind pursuit of an enemy. You know nothing about how he is armed, or how many accomplices he may have."

"I know," she snapped. "I was merely making a quick surveillance. I suggest we take cover behind that log. It gives a better vantage point."

Kirtland glanced to his right, then rolled, taking her with him. "Very observant." He, too, made a survey of the surroundings. There was no sign of movement, no sound, save for the rustle of the leaves. "Your plan for revenge appears to have drawn someone's ire. Again, I ask who?"

Siena refused to meet his eyes.

"Hell and damnation." He sounded truly angry. "How in the name of Lucifer can I help guard you against more attacks if I don't know who the enemy is?"

Kirtland wished to protect her? Siena's heart stopped for a beat. She was a trained warrior. A killer if need be. Softer sentiments had no place in her arsenal. Nor did a friend. Ever since she could remember, she had been used to standing alone.

And that, she warned herself, was not about to change.

"I don't need your help."

He captured her chin and forced her to face him. "Then

you would have preferred to have your brains splattered against yon oak?"

"It is a matter of *honor*. I'm willing to take whatever risks are necessary."

"There is nothing honorable about being dead."

"That depends, sir. I feel there is a great deal of honor in dying in the line of duty. You, of all people, ought to understand that."

His look of initial surprise softened into a grudging glint of respect. "You speak like a soldier."

"You speak as if that amazes you. Do you think it impossible that a female might possess the same commitment to higher principle as a man?"

Kirtland leaned closer, the heat of him prickling against her tensed body like points of steel. "I have ceased to be amazed by *anything* about you, madam."

She was saved from having to answer by Oban's shout.

"I am here," she called back.

"Sorry, ma'am." The groom tore through a tangle of brambles, his breath coming in ragged gasps. "I tried to give chase, but the brush is too thick. I never got close enough to see who fired the shot."

"Too late now." Siena surveyed the silent woods. "You might as well gather the pistols and take the barrels back to the barn."

Oban nodded.

She turned to Kirtland. "I would rather you didn't say a word to anyone about this."

"I agree that would be best." He brushed a bit of dirt from his sleeve. "The duke might well cancel the auction if he thought a madman was on the loose at Marquand Castle."

If there had been any question about the earl's coolness under pressure, she thought wryly, it had been emphatically answered. "Good. Then we best hurry back to the others, before they begin to question what's keeping us."

"Right." Kirtland suddenly turned and retrieved the uncharged target pistol from the underbrush. "Just in case someone is counting," he said, firing it heavenward.

Siena bit her lip. She should have thought of that. Was she missing anything else? She closed her eyes, trying to concentrate on Da Rimini's rules of warfare rather than the musky scent of the earl's cologne or the whisper-soft stirring of his breath on her cheek.

"Don't think to escape so easily, Madame Dove. We need to talk," murmured Kirtland as he matched her hurried steps toward the clearing. "In private. The duke's hunting lodge would provide the perfect opportunity."

"You are suggesting I announce you as the winner?"

"Who else? You just said you wish to go on as if nothing untoward has happened. And you have to admit I would have bested the others by a handsome margin."

Kirtland had a point. The announcement would surprise no one. And he was still a prime suspect, she rationalized, along with Dunster, Jadwin, and Leveritt. However, logic and reason said she ought to choose one of the others. The earl had already received more than his fair share of attention.

Sometimes you must take a bold gamble, Volpina. Was it *Il Lupino*'s exhortation she heard? Or that of her own inner voice.

"Very well, sir. Meet me in the stables at six o'clock."

Chapter Fifteen

*D*angerous.

With the sound of the shot still loud in his ears, Kirtland shrugged out of his muddy shirt and splashed water over his shoulders and chest, the chill sluicing over the still tensed muscles, the old saber slashes. Getting close to the Black Dove was proving perilous to his person as well as his peace of mind. He shook away the drops. But it was not so easy to shrug off the fact that the game had just taken a deadly turn.

And at stake were more than a pair of painted prayer books. It seemed that someone knew about the Dove's plan to play the avenging angel. Someone who was determined to clip her wings.

Gritting his teeth, he reached for a towel. *What of it?* It wasn't his business if she wanted to get herself killed. She had chosen a risky profession. A courtesan invited intrigue and betrayals by virtue of seeking out gentlemen who were rich and powerful—and ruthless. She could have no illusions about the fact that some of them saw it as their right to take advantage of women like her.

But whatever wrong she was seeking to redress, the Black Dove had proved that she could take care of herself. He had only to recall what had happened to Bantrock.

I don't need your help. Her words echoed in his ears. He ought to take them to heart.

The earl stared in the looking glass, his gaze lingering on the faint scars of past conflicts. They should serve as a warning about the risks of charging headlong into the fray. He ought to distance himself from the Dove, and quickly. Allowing his life to become entangled with hers was putting himself in the line of fire. For a cause that had nothing to do with him.

He had his own battles to fight. He had come here to win the St. Sebastian Psalters. Nothing else should matter. Certainly not some teasing temptress, some mysterious merlin who refused to reveal her true reasons for being at Marquand Castle.

Other than her ultimate intention of selling herself to the best bidder.

He reminded himself that she had initiated these dangerous challenges. There was an old adage—one who lives by the sword must be prepared to die by the sword.

But even as he repeated the platitude, the earl could not quite dismiss her from his thoughts. Something about her inner fire—the flame gold flash of her eyes, the hints of her hellion courage—had kindled an answering spark inside him. That she had steadfastly refused all his offers of help made its burn even harder to stamp out.

What had started as a challenge to his pride was now something far different, far deeper. At the beginning, he had been determined to prove her presence here was part of some sordid chicanery. But somewhere along the line, his own motivation had taken an unaccountable turn. He now found himself wanting above all else to believe her intentions were honorable.

Guilty or innocent? Truth or lies? It all came back to one basic conundrum—*who the devil was she?*

So many damn questions. Tonight he would not rest until he got some answers.

Too unsettled to sit cooped in her room for the rest of the afternoon, Siena changed quickly out of her shooting attire and headed for the Central Tower. She needed a distraction to clear her thoughts for the coming confrontation with Kirtland.

Dangerous.

She didn't need a bullet to warn her of the danger in getting too close to the earl. There was a fine line between seduction and being seduced. She couldn't allow the slightest slip.

Looking up, she found that her steps had brought her to the room where the St. Sebastian Psalters were on display. It was deserted, save for the two footmen standing guard at the doorway, so she decided to go inside. Art offered a temporary respite from war.

As she leaned close to the glass case, Siena felt her tensions ease in light of the wondrous pages. It was impossible not to be captivated by their allure. She could not articulate the scholarly nuances of technique or style as well as the earl, but on a purely visceral level, she felt the power of their beauty. There was a purity of vision, a clarity of color and devotion that was evident in every exquisite detail.

Entranced by her study, Siena was not aware of having

company until a voice sounded close by her ear. "Pretty little things, aren't they?"

She did not look up. "Such a description hardly does them justice, Mr. Orlov. Aren't you just a little bit interested in art?"

"I am interested in accomplishing my mission here. What about you?"

Was she only imagining the double meaning to his words?

"I have had little opportunity to become acquainted with exquisite art, and the sensibility that inspires it," she replied. "I think I should enjoy learning more about the subject."

"Really? And here I was under the impression that you were a very pragmatic person."

Siena met his mocking gaze, but not before noting the bits of mud still clinging to his Hessians and the tiny tear in the sleeve of his coat. "Who sent you here, Mr. Orlov?"

He placed a careless elbow on the glass. "We all have our little secrets."

"Are you saying I have something to hide, sir?" She could almost hear the clash of steel as they parried each other's advances.

"I am merely offering a word to the wise—and you *do* strike me as a lady who is not lacking in intelligence. I would not get too close to the Earl of Kirtland. He is rumored to be a dangerous man."

"People are saying the same about you, sir."

"You see, there is some truth to rumors."

He had his hair tied back, and though some of the strands had escaped the ribbon, Siena saw he was wearing a gold earring. A wolf's head. Was it grinning or growling? Like the Russian, it reflected well-chiseled lines and a polished patina, but its expression was impossible to discern.

Despite her misgivings, she met his gaze with an unflinching show of calm. There was no denying that he was an extremely attractive man, radiating a whipcord grace and rampant masculinity. And yet his charms left her rather cold. Unlike the earl, who from the first moment, the first touch, had sent a sizzle of heat through her.

Kirtland was fire, Orlov was ice. Elemental forces of nature. Both could be deadly.

The Russian lifted a brow. "You seem pensive. I trust I have not frightened you."

"No. I was simply wondering . . ." Siena decided to test his reaction with a direct thrust. "Was it you who shot at me?"

"Did a shot go astray this morning?" He contrived to look shocked and did not succeed.

"A bullet came rather too close for comfort."

"What makes you think it was meant for you?" he said with a softness that belied the hard glint in his eye.

Her gaze skimmed over the painted pages before she countered with her own question. "A bit of pigment and paper is worth killing for?"

"That depends on the item, wouldn't you say?"

A leading question, if ever there was one.

If Orlov were indeed the enemy, he was being very blatant about it. What game was he playing? He was far too skilled to give himself away by mistake. Siena felt her lips thin. Damn Lynsley for being so oblique in his warning. Damn herself for being unable to cut through the web of intrigue. Every way she turned, it seemed to be drawing her ever tighter within its strands.

"You believe that the concept of right and wrong is not absolute?" she finally asked.

"An interest in philosophy as well as art? You are an intriguing female, *golub*. But much as I would enjoy debating the fundamentals of morality with you, I must not be late for my interview with the duke."

Siena looked back at the Psalters as the Russian left the room, but the painted pages had suddenly lost a touch of their luster. Try as she might to focus on the brilliant colors of the illuminated letters, she could not help wondering whether she had a prayer of unraveling the truth from the tangle of lies and innuendo.

She was so engrossed in her thoughts that Leveritt had to clear his throat before she noticed his presence in the doorway.

"Might I enter? Or would you prefer a bit of privacy?"

"I should be delighted to have you join me. We have had little chance to enjoy a moment alone together, sir."

He leered, but it was not lust she read in his eyes. Some deeper, darker emotion was at play beneath the swagger and smile. What was the man afraid of? "I admit to being curious as to what all you gentlemen see in these manuscripts," she added. "Perhaps you might explain their significance to me."

The shadows seemed to lighten somewhat. "The St. Sebastian Psalters were created by an extraordinary monastery in Burgundy." His voice was reverential, more like a caress than a simple commentary. Whatever else he was feigning, Leveritt was a true lover of art.

"Are you as passionate about other things as you are about books and architecture?" she asked, recalling his equally erudite lecture on the decorative detailings of the castle.

He smoothed a hand over the exquisite embroidery of his waistcoat. "I enjoy my pleasures as much as any man."

It seemed an odd reply, though she could not quite say why. Perhaps it was only her own overstretched nerves that had her imaging a certain shrillness to the words.

"I am glad to hear it. Then let us see if we can contrive to have you win the next challenge. I should like that above all things."

"As would I."

A teasing stroke to his groin said otherwise. His first reaction was to shy away, but he covered his initial flinch with a low laugh. "Grasping little minx, aren't you. But however much I'd like my pego in your hand, we had best not risk offending the duke with such a public display of lewdness."

Siena made a moue of disappointment. "Oh, very well." She drew back. "Are you good at hide-and-seek?"

Leveritt wet his lips. "Yes, I suppose I am."

"Good. Tomorrow is a day of rest from the challenges, but when it's time for the next game, be prepared to have some fun."

"I can't wait." And yet his tone had the same doleful ring as the tall case clock that suddenly began to chime out the hour.

If she lingered any longer, she would be late for her meeting with the earl. Setting her skirts in a frothy swirl, she took her leave from Leveritt with a coy kiss and quickly crossed the carpet. But as she turned for a last, luring look, Siena came away with the impression that he was not sorry to see her go.

The flint struck up a spark, and the wick flared to life.

"It appears that the charms of the place have not been

exaggerated." As Kirtland held the oil lamp aloft, the first flicker of light illuminated the interior of the hunting lodge. A shingled cottage crowned with the thatched roof, it stood in a secluded grove of pine and spruce, several miles from the castle. But in contrast to its rustic exterior, the inside furnishings were obscenely opulent. "Nor has the collection of art." He paused to look at a series of framed woodcuts that hung on the near wall.

"Do you find them interesting?" The Black Dove, he saw, hardly gave them a glance.

"Are you referring to the technique of the artist or the subjects?" he asked dryly. The brightly colored prints showed men with impossibly large phalluses performing a variety of highly graphic sexual acts with nubile young women. "To my eye, both are rather crude."

"I thought men found that sort of thing stimulating."

"Is that your experience?" he countered. "Do you always use such titillations to arouse your clients before you take them to bed?"

Surprisingly, a faint blush came to her face. But she merely shrugged and turned to her coachman without answering. "You may put the hamper on the table, Oban. That is all for now."

The groom nodded, and after shooting the earl a hard look, took his leave from the lodge.

"An unusual name," murmured Kirtland as he lit the logs in the hearth.

"Is it?" She uncorked a bottle of claret and began unpacking the contents of the picnic hamper.

He leaned an elbow on the mantel, nudging aside a statue of a leering satyr with a monstrous erection. There was a strange sort of tension to her tonight. A maidenly reserve? His lips twitched at the notion. The juxtaposition of innocence and experience was no doubt part of her practiced allure.

And it was a potent mix. He found himself unable to take his eyes off her as she poured the wine.

"What is yours?" he asked abruptly, after accepting his share.

"What do you mean?"

"Your name," he replied.

"Why do you ask?" The Black Dove looked at him over the rim of her wineglass. Despite the winking of the cut crystal, Kirtland thought he detected a flutter of surprise.

"Because given the increasing intimacy of our acquaintance, it feels ridiculous to be calling you 'madam.'" The earl sipped at his claret. "Besides, I am curious."

She speared a slice of hothouse melon and put it on his plate.

"Mary? Catherine? Elizabeth?" he prompted.

Though she tried to hide it by fussing with the shaved ham, her cheeks turned a rather beguiling shade of pink.

The Dove on the defensive? He kept up his probing. "Allegra? Constantina? Hecate?"

"Not even close." She calmly arranged the mushroom pastries on a silver platter. "You must try some of these. The duke's chef is from Paris and has a sublime way with his sauces."

Kirtland refused to let the subject be submerged in a swirl of butter and minced morels. "Come, give me a hint."

Siena countered with a cool smile. "And what will you give me in return?"

He leaned in a bit closer, watching the light flicker over her cheekbones. "What do you want?"

She set out a plate on the side table before answering.

"You are the only member of The Gilded Page Club who has not regaled me with an example of artistic expertise. Do you, perchance, know any poems by heart?"

"A great many." He knew she was trying to distract him, but for the moment was willing to play along with the game. After musing for a moment, he made his choice.

> *"Twice or thrice had I loved thee*
> *Before I knew thy face or name,*
> *So in a voice, so in a shapeless flame*
> *Angels affect us oft, and worshipp'd be.*
> *Still when, to where thou wert, I came,*
> *Some lovely, glorious nothing did I see.*
> *But since my soul, whose child love is,*
> *Takes limbs of flesh and else could nothing do,*
> *More subtle than the parent is*
> *Love must not be, but take a body too,*
> *And therefore what thou wert, and who,*
> *I bid Love ask, and now,*
> *That it assume thy body, I allow,*
> *And fix itself in thy lip, eye and brow."*

"It's lovely," she whispered after a second of silence.

"It's Donne."

She hesitated. "What about Blake?"

Kirtland leaned back on the soft leather sofa, enjoying the dance of the flames in her fire gold eyes. "What do you know of William Blake?"

"Only that you seem to enjoy his work."

He straightened. "How do you know that?"

Siena ducked her head. "I know a great many fascinating details about you."

"Go on."

"You own a very spoiled cat named Lucifer, and a great hairy dog—or perhaps it is a pony or a basilisk."

"Mephisto's great hairy nose would be out of joint to hear you cast aspersions on his pedigree. He is a Scottish deerhound, bred from Highland stock renowned for its fierce loyalty and tenacious strength. And if his bark is now worse than his bite, I would never have the heart to tell him so." The earl shifted his weight. "Anything else?"

"You sleep in the nude."

He was no longer feeling quite so amused. "Do you mean to say you were *spying* on me?"

"It seemed only fair. After all, you had seen me in a rather compromising position."

"Only because you presented yourself on a proverbial platter." He could not bite back a smile. "You were a feast for the eyes."

"As were you. But do not get too swelled a head about my attraction to your physical charms. It was merely . . . business. You were not the only gentleman I observed. The five other members of The Gilded Page Club also received a midnight visit."

Back to business.

It was just as well. He must not lose sight of his earlier resolve in the flame-kissed curve of her lips.

"So, you were not entirely forthcoming the other afternoon." He edged forward in his seat, intent on finally forcing the truth from her. "One of us is, in fact, the dastard you seek?"

"I have yet to find the evidence I need to prove it, but yes, I am fairly certain."

"What proof?"

"That is not your concern, sir."

"The hell it isn't. You can't deny that I have been drawn into this dangerous game you are playing. I need to know who you are and where you have come from."

"We did not come here to discuss me or my past."

"I do not recall agreeing to any such rules." Seeing he had her on the defensive, the earl quickened the thrust of his questions. "Seeing as I nearly took a bullet to the brain this afternoon, I think I have a right to demand some answers from you. Let's start with the real reason you are here."

"I told you why I am here—to avenge a betrayal. And to be certain it never happens again."

His eyes narrowed. "Why do you care so passionately?"

"I have a duty to care."

"Duty?" He gave the word a mocking edge. "Being a courtesan is an odd choice of professions, given such noble sentiments."

Her jaw clenched. "Go to hell."

"You may join a long list of people who wish me to the devil." Kirtland softened his sarcasm. "But whether you care to believe it or not, I do understand idealism."

"Not many people do."

"No. And even fewer have the heart to stand up for their beliefs. Because at times it hurts, and leaves you wondering whether it is worth the pain."

Her hands clenched into fists.

Sensing that he had touched a raw nerve, Kirtland kept up the attack. "So, is there actually a chink in your armor?"

Siena rose abruptly and turned for the door. "We have nothing more to discuss, Lord Kirtland. Enjoy the fruits of your victory for as long as you wish, but I am returning to the castle."

"Not so fast." His hand caught her wrist.

Siena spun around. A physical confrontation? Somehow she had let the earl get the best of her in their verbal duel. She had been distracted, her edge dulled by his personal questions—and by the play of the light upon his face. It wouldn't happen again.

Anger gave added force to the twist of her shoulder, the flip of her wrist.

"Damn." Kirtland stared up at her from the floor. "Gentleman Jackson himself has never knocked me to the canvas."

"Because boxing is too crude a sport," she replied. "There are far more effective disciplines. I could easily put you on your arse again."

The earl was upright in an instant, a martial light in his eye. "You think so?" It appeared that he, too, could not resist rising to a challenge. "I have a few tricks of my own."

"Feel free to try them. No holds barred."

The gleam of his gaze dimmed slightly as he surveyed her skirts and slim form. "I am afraid I might hurt you. Superior size and weight give me an unfair advantage were I to fight dirty."

Siena made a rude sound. "You should know better than that by now. It's you who will be dusting the seat of your breeches. Come, try to overpower me."

"You asked for it." He circled warily, feinting several times before rushing in low and hard.

Her own limbs were a blur of motion. *Block. Spin. Twist.*

THUMP.

"How the devil did you do that?" asked the earl admiringly as he rubbed his bruised elbow.

"By employing an ancient Eastern discipline called *tai chi*. The principle is actually quite simple. It uses an enemy's strength against him."

Kirtland rose, this time a bit more gingerly. "Show me."

"Very well. Come at me again, but this time very slowly." Siena demonstrated the footwork and technique she had used to knock him down. "Now, say you were to grab me from behind . . ."

He obliged.

"It's a matter of timing, but if I shift my weight like this, and like this, I could easily flip you into the coals."

He practiced a few of the moves. "I think I grasp the essence of it." His hand suddenly shot out, and with a deft lunge, he knocked her back onto the sofa.

Bloody hell. She should have known he would prove a quick study. "That was an underhanded trick, sir."

"There is an old saying—all is fair in love and war."

"This is neither," she retorted quickly.

"No? Yet you are waging a deadly battle. Perhaps to the death, if what happened this afternoon is any indication."

His tumbled locks softened the harsh planes of his face. Candlelight caught the flicker of concern in his gaze. She closed her eyes, willing herself to ignore the curve of his cheek, his lips, as he crouched down beside her.

"I am aware of that." She tried to pull free, but he kept his hands on her shoulders.

"Stop fighting me, if only for a moment," he began.

"I have been fighting my whole life," she whispered.

"It is . . . a part of who I am. I don't expect you to know what I mean."

And yet, Siena saw from his face that he did. "You are up against a dangerous man."

"I am willing to accept the risk."

Kirtland swore under his breath. The stirring of air tickled her lashes. "You are too brave for your own good, my bold Valkyrie." She was suddenly aware of a warmth on her brow. His lips, light as a whisper of poetry. "Tell me your enemy. And let me help you beat him."

Speaking of risk.

"Please," she managed a ragged reply. "You have no idea what you are asking."

His mouth moved down to the hollow of her throat. Her pulse began to pound wildly.

"Trust," he said softly.

Tai chi was no defense against this. Nor were any of her other finely honed skills. The only thing that might save her now was—

A brusque knock sounded on the door.

Siena seized the moment to slip free of his embrace. "Oban has returned." She shook out her tangled skirts and grabbed for the candle. "It is time to go."

"Trust," repeated Kirtland as she hurried away. "What I am asking for is your trust, *paloma*. How many times must I say it—you have nothing to fear from me."

Chapter Sixteen

Kirtland helped Siena down from the open carriage. A cool silence had cloaked the drive back to the castle. If she had heard his last words, she had chosen to ignore them.

"Thank you, Lord Kirtland," she said as he took her wrap and handed it to the porter. Her tone was even chillier than the night air, the note of dismissal unmistakable. "And good night."

He followed her across the entrance hall. "It's still early. You are sure you would not care for a stroll to the conservatory?" He knew her answer would be no. Indeed, he was counting on it. "We were having such an interesting conversation at the hunting lodge. I was hoping we might pick up where we left off."

Her mouth thinned at the half-mocking edge to his voice. "I think we have had enough intimate contact for the evening." A piano sonata drifted out from the Music Room. "I prefer to take tea with the other guests and listen to the Mozart recital." She took another step, then paused. "And you?"

The earl slanted a look at the main stairs, then gave a nonchalant shrug. "In that case, I think I shall join the other gentlemen for port and billiards." Without a backward glance, he walked down the corridor and entered the Game Room. But he lingered in the haze of cigar smoke and male laughter only long enough to ensure that the Black Dove had time to settle down with a cup of oolong.

She thought to brush him off so easily? He flexed his fingers and allowed a grim smile. The lady was indeed skilled at fighting. But so was he. And she was not the only one who possessed some underhanded tricks. During the drive back to the castle, he had decided that the time had come to strip off his scruples and use a few of them. If she would not reveal any information about her true identity, he would search her rooms. There had to be some clue of a personal nature, some telltale hint that would betray her real reasons for being at Marquand Castle.

Perhaps he should not care so passionately. He had been disappointed, disillusioned in the past. Yet he could not help feeling more and more certain that she wielded her strength for something more lofty than personal greed. Her words on fighting—spoken with such a heartfelt edge—had resonated with the courage of her convictions.

Or so he wished to believe. But there was still a whisper of doubt.

Retracing his steps, the earl angled a peek through the Music Room doors. *So far, so good.* The Dove was sitting on the sofa, conversing with the plump Swedish countess from Stockholm.

Hurrying up a back stairway, he made his way to the second floor of the East Wing. The corridor was deserted, with only a single sconce lit near the door to her chambers. Kirtland tested the latch, not at all surprised to find the lock firmly in place. It was, however, an ancient model, not one of the complex military mechanisms that had guarded her London residence. A flick of his penknife coaxed the bolt free.

The scent of verbena hung in the air, along with the earthier, exotic spice he had come to identify as uniquely her own. Once he had lit the branch of candles by the doorway, he looked to the dressing table and saw only a single perfume bottle, a simple set of wooden brushes, several small bottles of cosmetics, and a box of hair ornaments—all arranged in parade ground precision. A rather spartan array for a lady of her profession. Indeed, there were very few of the frilly feminine touches that were usually found in a courtesan's boudoir.

He picked up one of the hairpins and twirled it between his fingers, curious to discover that the shaft was steel, and stiff as a rapier. Setting it aside, he moved to the escritoire. Ink, paper, the poems from her first challenge . . . Lud, had Winthrop really penned such painfully prosaic rhymes?

But no personal papers. Not a letter, not a card from a Bond Street shop, not a dressmaker's receipt. He checked the drawers and beneath the blotter to make sure he had not overlooked anything. *Nothing.* It was as if she had not existed before her recent appearance in London.

A search of her dressing room only underscored the impression. All the elegant dresses were new, as were the assortment of petticoats and undergarments. Only a pair of well-worn riding boots and the dark breeches and shirt looked to have had much use.

Frowning, the earl returned to the bedchamber. Rather than shed any light on the Black Dove, his clandestine foray had only deepened the aura of mystery surrounding her. He leaned against the carved bedpost and made another slow sweep of the room with his gaze. What the devil was he missing? His eyes fell to the crisp folds of the counterpane, the plumped pillows. More out of frustration than expectation of finding anything, he thumped a fist to the eiderdown and turned down the sheets.

"Bloody hell." Hating to retreat empty-handed, he got down on his hands and knees for one last look under the bed skirts.

If not for the wink of light off the brass catch, he might have missed the slim black box. It was heavier than it looked and took a moment to maneuver out to the center of the rug. Several tries at forcing the lock proved futile. It was a far more sophisticated design than the duke's old latches, but he was not about to be defeated by a few bits of metal.

Suddenly recalling the steel hairpin, he plucked it from the pile and set to work. His reconnaissance missions with the Spanish partisans had given him experience in such shadowy skills. On the third try, his efforts were rewarded. With a soft snick, the lid popped open a fraction.

Kirtland moved the candles closer and folded back the velvet cloth.

The cavalry saber and brace of pistols he had seen before. It was the rest of the weaponry that caused the breath to catch in his throat. Needle-thin stilettos, crescent-curved *jambiyas*, wide-bladed daggers—there were at least half a dozen different knives of various shapes and sizes. Not to speak of the more exotic implements. Razored throwing stars that he recognized as Indian in design, a hollow wooden pipe with several tiny arrows, and a selection of glass vials containing colored powders. He didn't dare hazard a guess as to what they were for.

As he sat back on his haunches, one other item caught his eye. Lifting the sheath from the case, he slid the poniard out from the leather. It was perfectly balanced, with a distinctive crosshatched hilt that fit snugly in his palm.

"Bloody hell," he breathed, after holding it up to the moonlight and examining the tiny initials etched on the base of the blade.

Returning the sheath to the box, the earl closed it and shoved it back beneath the bed. The poniard he kept in his hand.

Then he sat down to wait.

Siena joined in the polite applause. The duke had arranged for a noted Viennese musician to play for the guests, and the man was superb. However, as he paused to change his sheet music for the next set of sonatas, she quietly excused herself and slipped into the corridor.

The noise from the Game Room had grown louder, the crack of the billiard balls punctuated by the chink of glasses and rumble of laughter. She strolled closer, hoping the door was open enough to see inside.

Damn. There was no more than a crack, and that was clouded with smoke. But as she turned, Fitzwilliam came out, staggering slightly but looking to be in a jovial mood. "Er, thought I'd get a breath of fresh air," he slurred, tapping a bit of ash from his cheroot. "The terrace . . ."

Siena pointed him in the right direction. "Is Lord Kirtland still playing?" she added casually.

"Kirtland?" Fitzwilliam's brow furrowed; then his expression smoothed to a smile. "Yes, yes. Just saw him there in the corner."

She watched the baron pass through to the garden entrance hall before continuing on to the side corridor and making her way back to the East Wing. Aware that Kirtland was not wont to linger too long with the other gentlemen, she knew she would have to hurry. Even so, it was a calculated risk. She would have to trust her luck.

Trust.

The word pricked at her conscience. The truth was, she *wanted* to trust the earl. From the very beginning, she had viewed his austerity, his refusal to compromise his principles, in a favorable light rather than shadowed in suspicion. But perhaps she had gone too far in allowing feelings rather than facts to affect her judgment.

That was a cardinal mistake for any soldier.

Siena slowed, her stride no longer so sure. Her mission was clear, but was she fighting her own desire as well as the unknown enemy? Her heart wanted very much to believe that Kirtland was innocent, while her head warned that she must keep on the attack.

She drew to a halt at the archway, her shoulders pressing back against the molding as she looked down the row of doors. Behind one of them was a traitor. Did she have the mettle to match his strength and cunning? He was a master of deception.

But she was a Merlin.

Steeling her spine, Siena was just about to cross over to the earl's quarters when the sound of footsteps caused her to freeze. The notes of a Mozart melody echoed off the walls as the gentleman's whistling grew louder. A key rattled in the doorlock. Venturing a quick peek, Siena saw Orlov enter his rooms, leaving the door slightly ajar.

Sometimes the best plan of attack is to retreat, Volpina.

Siena edged back the way she had come. It was too risky to try a search of Kirtland's quarters. She would have to find another time or another way to know for sure whether he was friend or foe.

There was no need for stealth once she reached the main staircase. Still brooding over the earl, she hurried to the next floor, anxious for a safe haven in which to regroup her thoughts. Given the recent turn of events, she could not afford the slightest slip of her guard. She had been careless and clumsy earlier in the day. On the fencing field, Da Rimini would be exhorting her to keep her weapon raised, her wrist firm—

It took her only a second to realize that the door had opened at the first touch, but by that time it was too late. A hand had yanked her inside and slammed it shut.

The room was dark, save for a sliver of moonlight. But she instantly knew who had hold of her. His touch, his scent, his strength were by now intimately familiar.

She made no attempt to struggle.

"Have a seat, Madame Dove. The bed would be the most appropriate place, would it not?"

Siena turned slowly. The sight of her own poniard hovering just inches from her face was a shock, but she sought to cover her confusion with a verbal parry. "If you are in an amorous mood, Lord Kirtland, perhaps you ought to try flashing another sort of blade."

His laugh had no trace of humor. "My mood at the moment would not be described as amorous."

"No? Then perhaps you would explain why you are here."

"With pleasure."

The earl waited until she obeyed his command before he went on. "You seem quite fond of games, so let us play one now. A guessing game." With slow, deliberate steps, he took up a position directly in front of her. "Here's the question—why does a mysterious beauty suddenly appear in London and offer herself to a group of wealthy book collectors?"

"Lord Kirtland—"

He silenced her with a curt wave. "Let me finish. You have not yet heard the key clues. Though she claims to be a courtesan, she is in possession of military equipment that is issued to only the most elite cavalry regiments. And she is highly trained in its use. Indeed, she has learned how to handle a sword from none other than Allegretto Da Rimini, a renowned rascal but one of the best blades in all of Europe." The earl saw her fingers fist in the counterpane. "Not to mention that her town house in London is secured by a specialized locking system unavailable to most civilians.

"And then there is this . . ." Kirtland pressed the point of the poniard to her breast. "A perfectly balanced throwing knife crafted by Artemis Chandler. As far as I know, only military men are privy to his expertise." His litany finished, he allowed a flash of teeth. "Now you may speak."

Siena regarded him with a tight-lipped stare.

"You don't care to hazard an answer? Then let *me* make a guess." The blade slowly cut through the top lace of her bodice. "On the basis of the official arsenal, I would say you were working for the British government."

"That is absurd." Her voice was a touch more brittle than usual.

"At first blush," he agreed. "Yet I ask myself, who else would know of secret military suppliers?"

Once again he was met by silence. She looked as though she didn't trust herself to speak.

"If you are not working for our side, then a logical surmise is French intelligence." A second silk ribbon yielded to the blade. "So perhaps you are an agent of Bonaparte, sent to assassinate someone here. But The Gilded Page Club hardly poses a threat to the French. Nor does the guest list include any government official. So that seems unlikely." Her bodice had slipped low enough to reveal the black tattoo. Kirtland stared for a moment before going on. "Another possibility is that you have come to steal a critical document. The Psalters? I would not think so. So that begs the question of whether the duke holds some other secrets that might be valuable to the Emperor?"

"I am no traitor," she shot back. "Are you?"

"No." He drew the sharpened steel up so that it was kissing her neck. "But it is not my actions that are under discussion; it is yours."

"You are mad. Or mayhap someone has spiked your wine with tincture of opium." Unlike her sword thrusts, her denial did not ring quite true.

"Am I? My head may be spinning, but only from the flurry of your lies. It's high time you told me what your *real* mission is, *paloma*."

For an instant there was a flicker in her eyes—something akin to longing? Then her lashes spiked, and she tilted her chin, causing the blade to prick the flesh. "Am I to be subjected to the Inquisition?"

"I shall forgo thumbscrews or the Iron Maiden."

Threats were not the way to wrest information from her, he reminded himself. He pulled back, anger now fueled by a different heat. "I've other ways of seeking to plumb the depths of your secrets."

"The red-hot poker?"

The earl could not help the curl of his lips. Any other female would be using tears as a weapon, not irony.

"You arouse a hellfire flame in me," he answered slowly. "I am not sure whether I want to shake you until your teeth rattle, or . . ." He lowered his mouth to within a hairbreadth of hers. "Or kiss you until you cry for mercy."

Her lips parted, showing the pink point of her tongue.

"Were I marching into battle against the enemy, I would call it bloodlust." His voice turned raspy. Like metal against metal. "But this—I am at a loss as to what to call it."

"As am I," whispered Siena. Deflecting the razored steel, she touched his collar and slowly loosened the knot of his cravat. Her hand slid inside his shirt.

Kirtland felt as if his flesh were on fire. Seduction was indeed a dangerous game. He had started out with the intention of teasing the truth out of her, only to find his own weapon being turned against him.

Mano a mano? Sexual tension added a potent heat to the match of wills. It was now threatening to explode.

He caught her wrist. "You are as skilled at distraction as you are at dueling, my dear Dove. But this time, I mean to get to the heart of your deceptions." His voice was perilously close to cracking. "By God, no more lies! Tell me the truth about what you are after."

She answered with equal heat. "You ask me to trust you, Lord Kirtland? Give me a reason why I should."

"Because . . ." He drew in a harsh breath, then ever so softly feathered his lips along the slant of her cheekbone. "Because I want to believe you are innocent of any evil intentions."

"H-how can I be sure that you are not the dastard I seek? All I know for certain is that he is clever, cunning, and ruthless. You are said to be all that. And your history gives me no reason to doubt it."

In answer, the earl moved her hand to his heart. "You have nothing to fear from me. I swear on my honor."

For a flickering moment her lashes hid her eyes. "I cannot risk a betrayal. And not just for my own sake."

"I have never betrayed anyone," he said, wondering what she meant. "Not myself, not my friends, not—"

"Not your country?"

A tiny muscle twitched at his jaw. "No. Why would you ask?"

"The rumors—"

"The rumors be damned." Cupping her chin, Kirtland forced her gaze to meet his.

The martial light in her eyes was unyielding. "You are a soldier, sir. Would you betray the rules of engagement when caught behind enemy lines?"

At daggers drawn. The hilt of the poinard pressed into his palm. If ever they were to end this duel, one of them must be the first to yield. He had asked her to trust his word. Was he willing to make the same leap of faith?

There were only inches separating them . . .

Slowly lowering his mouth, Kirtland took her lips in a long, lush kiss. Perhaps she was right—he was behaving like a man possessed by madness. But all of a sudden he didn't care. Fighting his own doubts no longer seemed so important. The only battle that mattered was to win her belief in his honor. Even if it meant making himself vulnerable.

"I am not your enemy, *paloma*. But I have no proof to offer except myself, my promise."

She broke away to trace the line of his jaw, her hand blessedly cool against his flesh. "Julian."

At the sound of his name, a smoky, sensual sound from deep in her throat, all earlier thoughts of strategy, of tactics, gave way to something far more elemental. His hands found the last fastening of her bodice. Threads snapped. Silk slithered down from her breasts, their curves molding perfectly to his touch.

Kirtland groaned at feeling her hardening nipples against his palm. *Her steel matched with his.* He gladly surrendered the last little grip on his emotions.

She cried out as he took her nipple between his teeth. Her voice was rough, almost desperate with feminine longing, as if she hadn't played out this game of passion countless times, with countless men.

He thrust the idea of other lovers from his mind. The past didn't matter, only the present moment and the exquisite ecstasy of her supple body yielding to his. The poniard fell to the floor. *Be damned with cold steel.* He tugged off his shirt, feeling clumsy as a schoolboy, and somehow managed to kick out of his boots.

"Lift your hips, *paloma*."

She arched beneath him, allowing him to strip her dress and drawers down to her knees. A last little arch sent them frothing to the floor. His will to resist went with them. She was all soft flesh and willing curves.

"Julian." Her voice was like liquid fire.

Bracing himself on his elbows, he edged his steeling shaft higher.

With a boldness that wrenched the air from his lungs, she took hold of his cock and guided it to the entrance of her passage. "Don't stop this time," she urged. "No matter if a whole regiment of Russian Hussars is lurking outside the window."

An entire army could not have held him back from closing the last little distance between them. *So close, so close.* The scent of her was all around him, the sweetness of verbena now musky with an earthier spice. Somehow, he found enough breath to groan.

"*Contrapostura,*" she whispered, skimming her hands along the slope of his shoulders.

Kirtland was only dimly aware of her voice over the pounding of his blood. It was on primal instinct alone that he altered his angle.

"I yield to your *forte.*"

With a shuddering swiftness, he thrust forward, sheathing himself in her liquid heat.

Naked desire. The gleam in Kirtland's eyes lit a wicked fire inside her. But it was nothing compared to the sensation aroused by the feel of his mouth on her cheeks, her throat, her brow.

Siena cried out, wondrous of what had taken hold of her. Somehow her strategy of seduction was spiraling out of control. She had mastered the use of blades and bullets, but wielding her body as a weapon was proving far more demanding. Aware of the dangers, she stilled for an instant under his weight.

"Did I hurt you?" Beneath the rough rasp of male arousal, the earl sounded surprised. "You are so tight. I—I did not expect it."

"It's been ages since . . . I have had a **man inside** me."

He lifted slightly.

"No!" Siena gripped his back, reveling in the hard slabs of muscle, the cording of sinew tapering to a lean waist. "I—I shall adjust in a moment," she said, sliding her hands down over the taut swell of his buttocks.

A hoarse laugh. "It's not you I am worried about, *paloma*. I, too, have gone a long while without the company of a woman. I should like to go slowly and give you pleasure."

Pleasure did not begin to describe the feeling of him inside her. Strange, but it was as if a missing piece to a puzzle had been put into place. Steel interlocked with steel, his strength completing hers. It was her duty to distract him from her mission, but she could no longer lie to herself. This had gone far beyond training and tactics. It was no longer professional, but personal. Intensely so. Her hands skimmed to his hips, his ribs, the lithe line of his spine. She wanted to know every inch, every contour of him. His smell, the texture of his hair.

Everything.

"Not quite so fast, Valkyrie," he gasped, his voice hovering on the brink of control. "I fear my sword cannot keep up with your moves."

Curling one leg higher around his hips, Siena flexed her body, giving herself completely to desire. "With the proper heat, a blade can be forged anew."

"Unless it has been burned to a crisp."

What fire consumed her own flesh, she could not say in words. She kissed him full on the mouth, teasing his tongue to twine with hers. The lush curling of his caresses sent spiraling shivers to her core. So fierce and yet so tender. She was reminded yet again that he was a warrior, a man who, like her, understood both triumph and pain.

She had come to think of them as evenly matched. But all of a sudden she realized that it was not quite so. From the first clash of hands, Kirtland had taken hold of her, overpowering her guard. Oh, how she had fallen—spinning, twisting, head over heels. And yet she felt safe in his arms. How to describe the sensation?

Love.

The word took shape from the shadows. All her martial skills and mental strengths were no defense against the elemental force of love. As for trust . . .

Principle or passion. Whose side was she on?

In the next moment she must make a choice.

As the question cried out for an answer, it was joined by an echo from Kirtland's earlier interrogation. *If you are not working for our side, then a logical surmise is French intelligence.* In the heat of the moment, he had spoken with a righteous anger.

Our side.

Were words strong enough proof of the earl's innocence? Perhaps not for Lynsley's liking. But Siena was suddenly so certain she could trust her intuition that she was willing to stake her life on it. Kirtland had taken the first leap of faith, allowing his belief in her innocence to overpower all his suspicions. She was willing to meet him halfway.

But what about her mission, her country? More than her own life was at risk.

With a muffled groan, Kirtland cut through the last of her lingering defenses and buried himself to the hilt. *No more thoughts.* It was one of Da Rimini's first rules of engagement. *Once you have committed to a strategy,* Volpina, *you must believe in yourself.*

Siena arched into his thrust. If she was wrong, she would face the consequences.

Rising, falling, their bodies quickly found a perfect rhythm together, moving with the animal grace of two skilled fencers. A duel of desire. She had never felt so gloriously alive.

His hands were coaxing her higher. Heat was spiraling through her legs, seeking some sort of escape. Trembling, she clung to him. "What is happening?" she cried in wonder. "I fear I am falling—"

He covered her mouth with a bruising kiss. "Trust me, *paloma*. I won't let you go."

Trust. She yielded to his need, and hers. "Hold me, Julian. Steel me with your strength."

Her whispered urging spurred him to quicken his strokes. Harder, faster, his thrusts drove her to the very edge of reason. And then she was over it, her cries like cracking crystal as her senses shattered in a myriad of sparkling shards.

Kirtland's voice, a hoarse, husky shout of exultation, crackled in her ear as his body held rigid for one last instant, then shuddered and softened against her spent limbs.

Though the soft coverlet lay beneath her, Siena felt as if she were floating on some sun-kissed current of air. Weightless, careless. Light as a feather. Pressing her lips to the earl's shoulder, she tasted the sweetness of his salty heat and wished that she might not come back down to earth for a long, long time.

Chapter Seventeen

"Come, you are shivering."

Untwining his limbs from hers, Kirtland reached for the eiderdown quilt that had fallen to the floor. He shook it out and nestled the length of her glorious body in the puff of feathers. Her eyes, still heavy-lidded with passion, glinted in the candlelight, and as he stretched out beside her, their naked flesh took on a rosy hue in the flames and afterglow of lovemaking. He drew her close, reveling in the silky splendor of her unruly tresses, the wanton glow of her whisky-gold gaze. Warm, intoxicating. A man could drown in their depths and die happy.

"You are so beautiful," he whispered. "So alive with a mysterious, magical essence. It defies my skill with words to define."

"Your skill with other forms of expression is not lacking in sharpness, my lord."

He chuckled, enjoying the new tone of teasing in her voice. "It is heartening to hear it has not grown too dull from disuse."

"Mmmmm." A musky murmur tickled his ear. "It seemed honed to perfection. But perhaps I should test its edge, just to be sure."

The earl sucked in his breath as her fingers danced with gossamer lightness over his cock. "I fear I am not quite prepared to show to advantage."

"You need have no fears on that score." Her grip slowly curled around him, exerting exquisite pressure. "Lie still. There are several more steps to perform to ensure all is in working order."

"Sweet Jesus. I . . ." Whatever he was about to say was swallowed in a throaty groan. Pleasure—a word he thought easy enough to explain—took on a whole new meaning in her hands. A gliding exploration ran up and down his length, touching him in ways he had never dreamed possible.

"Do you like this?" She leaned low over his hip, her hair like the fluttering of silk against his skin. Then her lips were tracing the jut of bone, the tip of her tongue igniting sparks of fire. He thought he might go mad with ecstasy.

Kirtland was sure he sounded like a bedlamite, for another groan—or was it now a whimper—was his only answer.

"And this?"

Already aroused, his cock grew hot and heavy against his belly as she drew her circling, stroking caresses ever tighter. Just when he was sure he could not hold himself under control a moment longer, she stilled her stroke.

He sunk his teeth into his lower lip, the throbbing for release shuddering through every fiber of his being. "Enchantress," he whispered. For indeed his body was under her spell. It was hers, to do with as she pleased.

Straddling his hips, she ran a thumb along his hooded tip, conjuring one perfect milk white pearl. "Don't fight your passions, Julian. It's a strength, not a weakness, to be made of flesh and blood rather than soulless steel."

He had already surrendered to her first touch. "I could not fight what you do to me, even if I wanted to."

With a bewitching swirl of her fingertips, Siena once again brought him to the brink. This time, the earl was sure there was no going back. His pelvis lifted from the sheepskin in arching anticipation of her next stroke. And once again, she took him by surprise. Moving faster than the flicker of firelight, she raised herself to meet his urgent thrust.

Enveloped in her warmth, Kirtland wasn't sure whether to laugh or cry. A shout, exultant in its wonder, slipped from his lips as he spilled his seed deep within her.

A tremulous rise and fall, then Siena's voice joined with his. Her hair, tumbled in a shimmering curtain of polished ebony, hid her face for a moment, but as she rolled off him and settled her head on the crook of his arm, he caught a glimpse of a smile, sublime in its sweetness.

Gasping for breath, he lay utterly spent, the pounding of his pulse so furious that he feared his chest might explode. Its echo made his spinning thoughts even harder to sort into any coherent order. It should not come as any surprise that the Dove was a seasoned seductress. And yet, a short while ago he would have sworn she had never experienced a climax. While now . . . Surely no innocent would know such tricks to bring a man to pleasure.

"Where did you learn that?" he asked, once he was capable of speech.

"In school."

"That's not exactly the sort of subject they teach at boarding academies for young ladies."

"Oh, but they do. The class was between archery and dancing."

Kirtland laughed, albeit softly. "Perhaps at some point you will stop titillating me with lies and tell me the truth."

"I have learned not to trust anyone with my secrets."

Whatever hidden secrets lay between them, they were not nearly so strong as what drew them together, thought Kirtland. The realization had come to him over time, building slowly, like their strange friendship. He could not put a finger on the exact moment when his intuition had won out over his suspicions. But when the moment of truth had come—when he had pressed the point of cold steel up against her throat—he had known she was not the enemy.

Perhaps the key was that he had come to trust his own heart as well as hers. They were both people of principle, no matter that most people thought otherwise. She was seen as naught but a whore, and he was considered a coward. But outward appearances did not begin to define their true spirit. They were alike in so many ways. He had never imagined he might find a match for both body and soul.

Kirtland drew her closer. Even though their bodies were no longer joined as one, he could not help but feel a bond still connected them, one far more lasting than a momentary coupling of flesh. He had come to admire her courage, her conviction, her humor.

Everything about her.

He drew in a deep breath. Even the air was redolent with the mingled scent of their passion. Two as one. "You have nothing to fear from me."

She flinched. "You keep telling me that. But can I truly trust you?"

He drew in a breath. "That is for you to decide."

The faint hiss of the wicks made her silence seem louder. Kirtland dared not exhale. He had thought that books and art were the only real passions in his life. But now the thought of having only paper and pigment as company in his life sent a chill through him. What had come over him?

Love?

Surely he was far too worldly to believe in *that* emotion. True love only happened in the pages of a book—fairy tales, epic poems, *chansons de geste*. Real life was not so romantic.

Kirtland found himself achingly sorry to be so cynical.

Siena stirred and finally spoke. "I—I did go to school."

Her halting words gave him a flicker of hope.

"A special school," she continued. "Whose ranks are filled from the legion of orphans who roam the London stews. The man I spoke of as my protector chooses only those who appear tough enough, clever enough, and fearless enough to stand up to the rigorous training and discipline." Her mouth crooked. "We learn how to act like ladies. And like men, for the curriculum includes riding, fencing, and other such martial arts."

The earl drew a measured breath. "A strange choice of study that this protector of yours set up," he said, hoping to draw her into further revelation.

"Yes, but . . ." She broke off. "Before I tell you about that, I have a question about Orlov. Any idea who he is working for?"

He shook his head. "I was going to ask you the same thing. All I know is that he claims to have been sent here to buy the Psalters."

"I have been warned that he may be dangerous."

"In what way?"

"I don't know." She reacted to the curl of his lip with a small sigh. "Truly. My superiors aren't sure what he is after." She hesitated just a fraction before adding, "By the by, I believe it was Orlov who fired on us. He implied the bullet was aimed at you, not me."

He wondered how she had managed to learn *that* little nugget of information, but he schooled his features to remain impassive. "Why me, and not one of the other members of The Gilded Page Club, I wonder."

"He did not say. I imagine he sees you as the greatest threat." She hesitated. "I would."

"A threat to what? His lust for the Psalters?" The earl prided himself on his logic, but as yet, he was still having a devil of a time trying to fit all the pieces of the puzzle together. "I find it hard to believe that he was sent here with orders to kill for the manuscripts. And even if he was, how does it tie in to you? None of this is making a great deal of sense."

She flattened her hand against his chest. "I asked before whether I could trust you, Julian. And . . ."

He could feel his heart thudding against her touch. Again, there was nothing between them save for a sliver of silence. He closed his eyes and waited for her decision.

"And . . ."

The single syllable continued to resonate in the air.

Could she trust her feelings enough to risk not only herself but also her country? Beneath her fingertips, the beat of his heart was strong and steady, echoing her own inner resolve. And her own inner certainty. Julian Henning was no traitor. He was an honorable man. A chivalrous man, despite his cynical denials. Despite their vastly different backgrounds—he a peer of privilege, she a product of poverty—they were more alike in spirit than she could ever have imagined. The linking of bodies had joined them in ways far deeper than flesh.

Trust. Intuition warred with reason for an instant longer before her head surrendered to her heart.

"And no matter that Da Rimini would likely expire on the spot, I have decided to tell you everything." His slow exhaling of breath was warm against her hair. "Your guess was right. I *do* work for the Crown. I have been sent here to flush out a gentleman who is passing military secrets on to the enemy."

She felt his muscles tense. "Sent by whom?"

"Someone at Whitehall. His name is not important." She shrugged. "He would deny all knowledge of me. As would anyone connected with the government. We work strictly undercover—"

"We?"

"I was not joking about that school."

"Good God." The earl made a choking sound from somewhere deep in his throat. "There are more of you?"

She touched her tattoo. "At present, there are six of us who have graduated from basic training into the Master Class. Though we have all been schooled in a variety of disciplines, each of us has different strengths. Such flexibility allows for a better match to each mission."

The moonlight cast Kirtland's face in harsh relief. Still, the shadows could not hide the fierce flicker of his gaze. It was a moment before he spoke. "These missions . . . what happens if you fail?" he asked.

"The odds are that we die." Aware he was watching her very closely, Siena allowed a ghost of a smile. "You have experience in battle, Julian. Defeat and death often go hand in hand. We, too, are soldiers, though our existence is a closely guarded secret. My sisters-in-arms and I understand and accept the risk."

"As a military officer, I may call in reinforcements," replied the earl slowly. "And you?"

She shook her head. "We are on our own. Those are the rules."

The touch of his lips sent shivers up her spine. "To hell with the rules."

"But—"

He silenced her with a soft caress. "As you know from your scrutiny of my past, I believe in doing what is right, not what is written. This is war, a far more dangerous one than is waged by conventional armies. Don't deny that you could use an ally."

As well as a friend and a lover?

Swallowing a sigh of longing, she nodded. "I, too, believe there are times when the rules must be broken. If you really wish to help, let us join forces." For the moment she would take what he offered.

Kirtland shifted slightly. "If we are to be comrades, I ought to know your real name."

"It is . . . Siena."

"Siena," he repeated. "Yet another reason I felt a bond between us from the start." He spun a lock of her hair around his finger and held it to the candlelight. "It's a beautiful name, and fits you like a glove—a sinuous curve of syllables, sensuous as honey on the tongue. How did you come to be called that?"

"Few of us have a name when we come to Mrs. Merlin's Academy. So when we are first brought to the headmistress's office, we are put before a globe, a great, glorious orb of gilded wood and wondrous lettering. It is set to spinning, and we are told to choose a city." She crooked a smile. "A new name for the new world we enter."

"Like you, it is unexpected. And unique." The earl

paused. "You are even braver than Boudicca. Stronger than a Valkyrie."

"Oh, I have my weaknesses," she murmured.

"Name one."

Siena was not sure she was ready to reveal quite that much. "Only mythic figures have no frailties, no faults."

His jaw tightened. "God knows, I can attest to that."

She could not help but ask, "Did it wound you when the military questioned your loyalty?"

"I cannot deny it. Of course it hurts to be misunderstood. But I don't regret my choice. It was the right thing to do."

"You see." His reflection in the darkened windowpanes accentuated the chiseled planes of his face. "You *are* an idealist, willing to risk all for what is right."

"And so are you." A smile flickered on his lips before he assumed a more military face. "Getting back to business, Siena, I take it you have a plan for identifying the enemy."

"Yes. These games have all had a purpose. They are designed to draw out traits in each man that might unwittingly reveal a telltale clue."

"I figured as much. Have you eliminated any of the six?" He drew a breath. "Aside from me?"

"Fitzwilliam is left-handed and cannot have written the sample I have been shown. And my search of Winthrop's room revealed that he has a firm alibi for the time when one piece of incriminating evidence was stolen. I cannot rule out the others. Though Dunster strikes me as a man of weak will beneath all his bluster."

"Still, you cannot count him out." His mouth pursed. "So that leaves three. What is your next strategy?"

"Another challenge, as quickly as possible. You see,

my mission has an added sense of urgency in that we think the traitor has brought a stolen dispatch here—one that would destroy England's alliance with Russia if it reaches the wrong hands. I must at any cost see that does not happen."

"Such stakes will make the man you seek even more dangerous. What is the next game you have in mind?"

"As to that, I have—"

The slight rattle of the iron latch was softer than a whisper, but Siena shot up in a flash and raced to the door. On whipping it open, she saw only shadows and the steady flame of the wall sconce.

"Naught but a draft from the windows," murmured Kirtland. He was at her shoulder, the poniard in hand.

"Perhaps." After another look up and down the dark corridor, she eased the door closed. "But you cannot stay here any longer. We must not be caught conspiring together." Goose bumps prickled her flesh as she moved away and slid her silk wrapper over her shoulders. Was her decision to confide in the earl already coming back to haunt her?

"The strategy," he began.

"There is no time to talk now. You must hurry. Already the servants are beginning to stir." She tossed him his shirt. "The details will have to wait until later."

To her relief, Kirtland did not argue. He dressed quickly, pausing only long enough to hand over her blade and press a kiss to her brow.

"Until later."

Chapter Eighteen

*L*ynsley removed his spectacles and pinched at the bridge of his nose. He was tempted to pour a drink from the decanter behind his desk. Not claret or port, but a strong Islay malt, redolent of the harsh seas and smoky peat of Scotland. After reading over the note that had just come from Marquand Castle, he needed some sort of fire to melt the chill forming in the pit of his stomach.

Instead, he rose, paper still in hand, and went to stand by the hearth. Oban had served him well in a number of past missions. The former pugilist possessed a sharp eye, granite fists, and a loyal heart—a good man to have in a fight. However, subtlety was not his strength. And he had never worked for a woman before. It was possible that he had misinterpreted a word, a gesture. The marquess stared out at the Thames, then slowly shredded the missive and let it fall onto the coals. He considered himself an astute judge of character, but the young woman called Siena had always been something of a mystery to him. A Renaissance beauty, with a dark sensuality shading her luminous gaze. Did she also possess a streak of de Medici cunning?

Unwilling to trust anything to chance, he locked up the sheaf of documents on his desk, then gathered his hat and overcoat.

Driven by a growing sense of urgency, Lynsley found his thoughts becoming more and more unsettled as his carriage sped out of Town. So much was riding on the success of this mission. If the Russian Tsar did not trust in the secrecy of the negotiations and pulled out of the alliance . . .

He pressed his fingertips to his brow. No, he would not contemplate failure. Not just yet.

But as his lathered team of horses raced through the Academy gates, he had to admit that he might have to consider what other options were at his command.

"Good morning, Thomas." The door of Mrs. Merlin's private office was opened by the lady herself. Her eyes crinkled at the corners, the only outward sign of surprise at his unannounced visit. "I take it something is amiss."

"I am not sure," he admitted. "I thought I had best come here and discuss the matter with you in person."

"Do have a seat. I'll ring for tea."

"All the tea in China will not drown the deuced problem," he murmured, sinking into the sofa pillows.

"Right, but I think better with a cup of oolong in my hand." She snapped open a notebook. "What is the trouble?"

"Siena. I received word from one of my sources at Marquand Castle that she may be consorting with the enemy."

"That was rather the point, was it not?"

"Yes." Lynsley matched her ironic smile. "But she may have crossed over the line."

Above the crackle of the coals, he heard the rapid-fire click of desk drawers and the shuffling of papers. "Hmmmm." Mrs. Merlin adjusted her spectacles. "Her records are faultless. But then, you knew that. I would not have suggested Siena had I harbored any reservations." She scribbled a few lines. "The only weakness, if it may be called that, is an inclination for introspection."

"Which can be a two-edged sword in our profession. Thinking too much can sometimes be more dangerous than thinking not at all."

"You don't trust her?"

"I don't trust anyone." The brutal truth of it gave edge to his sigh. "Save for you, of course. Which is why I wish to hear your opinion of her heart."

The elderly lady tapped her pen to her chin. "How reliable is your source?"

Lynsley made a face. "I do not question his observations, merely his interpretation. A word, a gesture . . ." He threaded a hand through his hair. "You have seen far more of Siena than I have over the past few years. Do you think her capable of betraying all her training?"

The headmistress did not answer right away. Her gaze flitted from the portrait of Francis Walsingham, Elizabeth I's secret spymaster, to the collection of Turkish daggers atop the curio table. When she looked back at him, her eyes were shaded with a certain sadness. "We train the girls to lie, to deceive. To kill without compunction. And while we believe we can tell the difference between acting for good or for evil, who can say for sure when the line becomes blurred?"

"An eloquent speech, as always, Charlotte."

"But of no damn practical use to you," she added, with a faint twinkle in her eye. "However, when you get to be my age, the urge to pontificate is sometimes hard to resist."

He sighed. "At the moment, I feel old as Methuselah."

"At four-and-forty, you have some years to go to match his 964 winters, Thomas."

Lynsley allowed a wry chuckle. "I will settle for weathering this current crisis."

Mrs. Merlin flashed a smile before turning deadly serious. "Then we had better get down to specifics. Why does your source think Siena has betrayed her mission?"

"Because she was overheard telling one of the prime suspects all the reasons why she is at Marquand Castle. Every last detail, including the existence of this school." He paused. "The conversation—or confession—came after an interlude of torrid lovemaking."

"Ah. So the question is, who has seduced whom—"

A sound at the door caused her to cut off. As she turned sharply, Lynsley saw the point of a dagger slip out from beneath her cuff. "Whoever is out there, show yourself this instant!"

It was Siena's roommate Shannon who entered the study, her hands grey with gunpowder, her face sheened in sweat.

"Shouldn't you be in ballistics class?" asked Mrs. Merlin.

"Yes, ma'am. I—I was. But Mr. Musto sent me to ask you to order a fresh shipment of mercury fulminate."

"Then perhaps you would explain to us what you were doing standing outside the door."

Shannon did not flinch from the question. "I was listening to what was being said about Siena."

There was a fraction of a pause. "In that case have a seat, my dear. You are acquainted with Lord Lynsley, of course."

"Of course." As she turned, her gaze shot from the floral chintz to her sweat-dampened shirt and muddy boots. "I think it best if I remain standing."

"How much did you overhear?" asked Mrs. Merlin.

"Enough to know Siena is in trouble."

Lynsley thought for a moment. "Have you any reason to think that she may no longer believe in the mission of the Academy?"

"You doubt her heart?" Shannon's chin shot up. "Tell me why!"

"It is for Lord Lynsley to ask the questions," said Mrs. Merlin softly, though there was no missing the note of authority.

The iron fist in the velvet glove. Despite her age, thought the marquess, the elderly widow had not lost her touch. He steepled his fingers, hoping that he could prove as adept at dealing with the crisis. The traitor must not be allowed to slip through his hands.

"It is fair for her to ask, Charlotte." He met Shannon's spark with a show of calm. "I have received information that may indicate Siena has been seduced by the very man she was sent to stop. To be blunt, we fear she has abandoned her mission and gone over to the side of the enemy."

"Never!" The cry resonated like steel against steel.

Lynsley felt his mouth thin to a grim line. "In our business, I have learned never to say never."

Shannon colored slightly but did not lower her gaze.

Mrs. Merlin broke the taut silence. "Have you anything to say that might prove your assertion?"

She shook her head.

"Then you may return to your class."

"Wait!" Shannon defied the dismissal to voice one last defense of her friend. "I would stake my life on the fact that she would *never* betray the Academy or her country. No one is more loyal than Siena."

"Thank you," he said. "Your own loyalty reflects well on what you have learned here."

She looked loath to go, but a discreet gesture from the headmistress checked any further outburst. Squaring her shoulders, she snapped a salute and marched from the room.

"What do you think?" asked Mrs. Merlin, once the door fell shut.

A sigh escaped Lynsley's lips. "I think that like most of the dilemmas we face, there is no clear answer. So I have a choice—either terminate the mission right now and pray that the earl is our man . . ."

Mrs. Merlin's sober expression left no doubt that she understood the full import of his words. Difficult, dirty decisions were an integral part of their world.

"Or trust that Siena knows what she is doing."

"And have you made up your mind?"

He shook his head. "Given the gravity of the situation, I think I had better head straight for Marquand Castle rather than return to London. I will assess the situation for myself before coming to a final decision."

The notes of a Bach piano suite were nearly drowned out by the shuffle of cards and the drumming of rain against the windowpanes. Bad weather had canceled the outdoor activities planned for the afternoon, forcing the gentlemen to wander through the display rooms or while away the hours until supper at whist.

Like the skies, the jovial mood of the gathering had turned more somber. With the auction fast approaching, everyone's nerves seemed more on edge. Siena had already overheard several heated arguments arise over trifling points of card play. She looked up from her reading and slanted a glance at the drawing-room doors, impatient for the earl to return from his private audience with the duke. The unremitting downpour had also forced a last-moment change in her next challenge, and though she was anxious to inform him of the details, there had been no opportunity for a council of war.

So far, their only encounter had been a meeting of the eyes from opposite ends of the breakfast room. Even from afar, his presence had brought a rush of warmth to her face. Last night . . .

With a swallowed sigh, Siena forced her eyes back to her book. She could not allow herself to daydream about Kirtland. The sound of his voice, the feel of his body at one with hers.

"Do you play the pianoforte, madam? Or was your schooling limited to skills of a more practical nature?"

The shadow that fell across her page was a chilling reminder that the traitor was still at large. Her suspicions were still only vague shapes, and time was running out to give them a name and a face.

Steeling her expression, she looked up. "Most ladies might well take offense at what you are implying, Mr. Orlov."

"Most ladies do not possess your singular strength of character or sense of humor. Not to speak of your other, more obvious, charms."

"You seem to take a perverse delight in trying to provoke me, sir. Is there a reason?"

Orlov assumed a look of injured innocence. "Why, to see the unique shade of pink that suffuses your cheeks when you are annoyed."

Unsmiling, she met his gaze with a steady stare.

"You *are* quite provocative, madam."

Enough, thought Siena. Setting her book aside, she decided it was time to rise to his challenge. "As a matter of fact, sir, I do play the pianoforte. Quite well I am told. Would you care to form your own opinion?"

If her change of tactics took him by surprise, the Russian hid it well. "It would give me great pleasure."

Seeing Siena approach, the Swedish countess rushed through the last stanza of the melody and quickly tucked her sheets of music away. "I am sure the guests will be delighted to hear another style of play," she said, lingering only long enough to flash a grateful smile.

Engrossed in their cards, the gentlemen did not look as if they would notice an artillery salvo going off in the room, much less a change in musicians, thought Siena. Which suited her own plan of attack quite well. "Have you a particular piece you wish to hear?" she asked Orlov as she took her place on the bench.

"Perhaps something by Beethoven. I find his *Sturm und Drang* so much more interesting than the music of Bach. Don't you?"

"Actually, I prefer order and harmony to thunder and lightning, sir." She set her fingers on the keys. *Black and white.* If only her dealing with the Russian could be so defined.

"Ah." He rested a hand upon the instrument. "Are we speaking of music, madam? Or something else?"

Siena gave a guarded smile as she nodded at the gentlemen engaged in whist. "Rather than keep playing a game of blindman's bluff, I am suggesting we lay our cards on the table, Mr. Orlov. Who knows, perhaps we can work together, rather them distract each other from pursuing the prize we have come for."

"An interesting proposal." The Russian picked out an imaginary tune on the polished wood. *Scarlatti*. So he knew his way around the keyboard. "What is it you seek?"

"I have made no secret of it—a rich protector."

"Such as the Earl of Kirtland?"

"He *is* extremely wealthy."

"And extremely unreliable, according to his superiors in the British army. Who also used such words as *unpredictable*, *unsteady*. And most of all, *untrustworthy*."

"His past is of little concern to me." Siena could not help coming to the earl's defense. "Besides, it seems to me that his transgressions were more deserving of commendation than of censure."

He cocked a sidelong look at her. "Dear me, have you fallen in love with him? That could present a complication."

Her fingers suddenly stumbled over the smooth keys, striking a wrong note. "To what?"

Orlov did not answer her directly. "If it's protection you are seeking, the earl may not be the wisest choice."

"Is that a threat?"

The Russian took a moment to toy with his watch. *An Imperial eagle, a gilded bear, a carnelian wolf.* The man seemed to enjoy the subtle flashing of talons and teeth. "Call it a friendly warning. Allowing your feelings to come into play may interfere with your ability to perform the duty you have come here for."

Caught between Lynsley's oblique orders to be on guard against Orlov and the Russian's deliberately ominous double entendres, Siena knew she had little room for mistake. "Duty? That is a rather strange choice of words."

"Ah. My English is sometimes suspect."

Despite the air of nonchalance, Siena sensed a coiled tension in him. Like a predator ready to strike when the moment was right. "Not to speak of *your* reasons for being here," she countered. "I am curious, Mr. Orlov—just who is this mysterious collector you represent?"

"Let us just say, someone who is concerned with the earl and a certain piece of parchment."

"I am tired of riddles and innuendoes, sir. I don't mean to let anyone stand between me and my objective here. So if we cannot be frank with each other, I shall have to assume that you are not only Kirtland's enemy, but mine as well."

The Russian shifted slightly, a rippling of wool stretching across the breadth of his shoulders. The show of muscle belied his silky pretense. "I should hate for you to think that."

"What are you looking to gain by eliminating the earl?" she pressed.

"One less skilled competitor."

"There are others." Taking a gamble, Siena seized the offensive. "I, too, have a warning. Some of them may be more dangerous than you think."

For an instant, his arrogance looked somewhat shaken.

They eyed each other, wary, watchful, waiting to see who would make the next move.

"Might I be allowed to enjoy the music, too?" Dunster approached, a scowl marring the symmetry of his features. "Or is this a private duet?"

Segueing from Beethoven to Bach, Siena quickly composed her expression to a welcoming smile. "Not at all. Indeed, if you have a piece you wish to hear, I shall be happy to play it."

"The lady is making free with her talents," quipped the Russian. "But alas, not for long, I imagine. By the by, how is your private competition coming, Lord Dunster? Any clear favorites?"

Siena answered for him. "Not as of yet. All the gentlemen are still in the running."

"That certainly makes the last few challenges even more intense." Orlov fixed the other man with a smile. "What is the next one?"

"As you say, it's a private affair." The marquess tossed back the last of his port—not the first, to judge by the redness rimming his eyes. "I believe I would like to hear something decidedly English."

She switched in midnote to a country ballad.

"I should not have thought 'The Rose of Sharon' would be in your repertoire, madam." The Russian raised a brow. "Sentimental songs seem rather out of tune with your usual pragmatism."

Siena added a crescendo to the refrain.

"On that note, I shall take my leave." Rising with a languid grace, Orlov performed an elaborate flourish that allowed his lips to linger by her ear for a fraction. "I am not your biggest worry, madam. For that I suggest you look closer to home."

"Mongrel," snapped Dunster as he assumed the vacated seat. He appeared to have recovered much of his usual bravado, yet the lingering bouts of brooding were out of character. Perhaps the mostly masculine company did not agree with him, or perhaps the stress of the auction was taking its toll.

Or perhaps there were other pressures coming to bear.

Wondering whether she had been too quick to dismiss him as the prime suspect, Siena decided to try to smooth over their differences. "Thank you for coming to my rescue, sir. I feared you might still be harboring some resentment over our earlier misunderstanding."

He replied with a sulky grunt, neither yea nor nay.

"Come, let us have no hard feelings, sir." A flutter of lashes fanned the sultry heat of her tone. "Surely a man of the world like you understands that I could not afford to show favorites so early in the game."

Dunster preened, his pride proving easy to placate. "You might have managed to be a bit more accommodating."

"Sometimes anger can serve as a certain spice, making reconciliation all the more tasty."

"What is planned for tonight?"

"On account of the weather, I have made a change to the order of the challenges. Instead of venturing outdoors, we will have a more intimate interlude. One by one, the six of you will meet with me privately, in a room I have prepared specially for the occasion. We will be telling fortunes."

"Are you predicting that my chances at victory are going to improve?"

"We shall see what secrets the crystal ball reveals. I trust you won't be disappointed."

Dunster looked to be savoring the prospect, but his grin abruptly gave way to a grimace. "Let us hope the glass reflects that Kirtland's luck is on the wane. For one who was adamantly opposed to your proposal, he seems to be having a change of heart about playing to win."

"Don't worry about the earl." Siena didn't need to look up to sense he had entered the room. Even from a distance she felt the vibrations of his presence resonate through her fingertips. "He squeezed off several good shots, so I was in no position to deny his victory in the shooting match. But he is not really any competition to you."

Kirtland approached the pianoforte, two drinks in hand. "Your glass appears empty," he said, offering one of them to Dunster.

"It won't be for long." The marquess did not bother to repress a snigger. "In the meantime, however, I shall avail myself of your hospitality." The port was gone in a gulp.

Siena left off playing. "If you gentlemen will excuse me, I must begin preparing for tonight's game. The duke's secretary has kindly consented to let me gather a bouquet of flowers from the conservatory, and I wish to take advantage of what little light is left in the day."

She hoped the earl would take the hint. Orlov's words had added an even greater urgency to her mission. There was now little doubt in her mind that he had been the intruder at her London residence, the one who had tossed her the hint of Kirtland's guilt. But who was he working for? Lynsley must have some suspicions . . . If only he had been more forthcoming.

Somehow she must find a way to cut through the shadows and fight her way to the truth. Fencing with phantoms was beginning to sap her strength.

"I don't believe it!" The knifepoint dug into the wood with a satisfying *thwack*. "Not for an instant."

Sofia eyed the quivering blade. "That's ten demerits for damage to school property, you know."

"Sod school property."

"And ten demerits for language unbecoming to a lady." Seeing Shannon on the verge of another oath, her roommate hastened to add, "I'm not making light of the matter. I am as concerned as you are about Siena. But carving the wainscoting into kindling won't serve any useful purpose."

Shannon bit her lip.

"And you—I swear, you are even more headstrong than she is. I worry about both of you."

"Neither of us has your steady disposition," she said, sighing.

"If you are implying I have no fire inside, I shall turn that blade on your backside. I must have a steady nerve and an even temper to keep you two out of trouble."

Much of the anger faded from Shannon's face. "You are a true friend, Fifi. I know I am a trial at times."

"Yes, but things would get dreadfully dull around here without you challenging authority." Sofia pulled the knife from the paneling. "So, tell me what is happening."

"Lord Lynsley fears Siena is now allied with the enemy."

Sofia frowned. "Like you, I cannot believe that of her."

"Siena would *never* be seduced by evil."

"And yet," said Sofia slowly, "we are taught never to say never."

"That is just what Lynsley said." Shannon wanted to object, but the arguments seemed to die on her lips. "You think it possible?" she whispered after a long moment.

"I—I cannot say."

"There is only one way to know for sure—and that is to go and find her."

"Impossible!"

"She's in trouble. She may need help."

"Lud, you will be, too, if you attempt such a thing." Sofia pulled a small dog-eared manual from the desk drawer and slapped it against her palm. "Need you reread the Academy's rules of engagement? By now, we all should know by heart the risks involved when we undertake a mission."

"Yes, but I have also read the great Sun Tzu, who said that war was an art as well as a science. Sometimes one must ignore all the standard tactics and act on intuition."

Looking torn between two codes of honor, Sofia let the

book slip through her fingers. "Even if I agreed with taking such a dangerous risk," she said slowly, "Mrs. Merlin is not about to offer you the details of where Siena is along with a fresh-baked strawberry tart."

"She doesn't have to. I overheard where Siena is." Shannon set her jaw. "Marquand Castle."

"For God's sake, Nonnie! You are already on disciplinary probation. If you break yet another rule . . ."

"To hell with the rules." Shannon already had her chest of weapons open and was sorting through the choices. "If they wish to give me the boot, let them." A snub nosed pistol went into her saddlebags, along with several iron batons, a thin poniard, and a set of picklocks. "I'm not afraid of having to survive on my own in the outside world if it comes to that."

"You won't be alone. Though it's a pity to throw years of rigorous training out the window." Sofia tossed over a set of grappling hooks and a coil of rope from her own supplies. "Here, you may have need of these."

"Thanks, Fifi. Anything else you can think of?"

"Merlin's magic wand?" Though her friend essayed a game grin, she looked as though a noose were tightening around her neck.

"I shall have to settle for Excalibur." Her sword, a sleek sliver of Damascene steel, cut back and forth through the air.

"Having seen you in action, I have high hopes that our futures are riding on more than a wing and a prayer." Sofia blew out a breath. "I trust you are planning to wait until dark before sneaking out to the stables."

"I mean to go after the grooms sit down for their supper." Shannon sheathed her blade. "It's a pity that Guillermo is the instructor on duty. He doesn't like me very much these days on account of that little incident with the smoke bomb."

"I'll come with you. He owes me a favor—a rather large favor—so he'll have to turn a blind eye."

"As for Mrs. Merlin and the others . . ."

Sofia dismissed the concern with a shrug. "Don't worry about that. I shall consider it a test of my oratorical skills to convince them your absence is the result of some silly wager." She tapped at her chin. "I am sure I'll come up with a suitably outrageous one by morning."

"In other words, you shall lie through your teeth."

"That is part of our training, isn't it? And practice makes perfect."

"That's the spirit." Shannon grasped her friend's hand and gave it a hard squeeze.

"Just one last thing, Nonnie. If I am going to end up on my arse over this, I expect to go out in a blaze of glory."

"I won't let you—or Siena—down. No matter what it takes."

Chapter Nineteen

I have read somewhere that there is a special language to flowers," murmured Kirtland as he watched Siena add a cluster of bougainvillea to her collection. He had not missed her message and had joined her in the conservatory as quickly as he could. "Though I could not tell you what such an exotic species is saying."

"I am bloody tired of trying to decipher hidden meanings."

There was a brittleness to her tone, at odds with her usual note of confidence. As he moved a step closer, he saw that a stray curl had come loose from her topknot, its ebony hue accentuating the pallor of her cheek.

Damn the dastard who sent out a lone young woman, however well trained, to do England's dirty work. At that moment, Kirtland found himself wishing he might hang the fellow from the tower battlements and watch the circling hawks feast on his liver.

"Steel, at least, rings true. While words are a far more dangerous opponent." She sighed, and rather than the usual fire in her eyes, he saw a flicker of doubt. "Perhaps I am not quite as sharp as I thought."

"Did Dunster say something to alarm you?" He, too, was suddenly on edge.

"Not really," she confessed. "It's more just a feeling that I may have missed something important. And Orlov seems to know far too much about my real reason for being here," she went on. "From the start, my mission seems to have been compromised."

The earl frowned. "What do you mean?"

"You were not the only one who was seen lurking around my London residence at night."

"The Russian?"

"Oban couldn't say for sure. Orlov certainly fits the size and strength of the intruder he spotted scaling the garden wall." She plucked a thorn from her thumb. "Whoever it was, by leaving a packet of evidence that pointed to you as a traitor to England, he also sent a second message that the true nature of my activities was known to him."

"Bloody hell, you never mentioned that." His words came out harsher than he intended. "You should have alerted your superior—"

"And abandoned the mission?" Her profile mirrored the clenched angle of his own jaw. "No doubt that would have suited the enemy's purpose. There was no time to come up with an alternate plan."

"Damn." Kirtland left the oath dangling, and for a moment there was an uneasy silence between them. "That does not mean you have to engage in unreasonable risks. The shot is evidence enough that you must move quickly to—"

"I am well aware of my duty, Lord Kirtland," she

snapped. The martial light was back in her eyes. "I can handle the challenge."

That was the problem, he thought to himself. She was too damn brave for her own good. Fear for her sharpened his own tone. "Must you be so bloody stubborn about accepting help?"

"I'm trained to work alone."

Rain ricocheted off the ceiling glass. The earl tried to read her expression in the hazy half-light. "Even the best soldiers are sometimes in need of reinforcements." He could feel the thud of his heart against his ribs. "What is holding you back? Is it still a question of trust?"

"Hell, no." For an instant her steely glare softened. "But this is my fight. If anyone is to fall to a blade or bullet, it should be me."

The irony of the situation drew a ghost of a smile to his lips. "Siena, allow me to—"

"My mind is made up. So allow me to save my strength for fighting the enemy rather than expend it brangling with you."

There was nothing he could say in way of argument. As a soldier, he knew she was right. Still, he found it took all of his resolve to remain silent.

"As for moving quickly, I have already decided on a new challenge for tonight's game. The sudden change may surprise the traitor into giving himself away," she went on.

"What have you planned?" he finally asked.

"A game of gypsy fortune-telling. I have found a suitably mysterious spot deep in the cellars."

"Cards? Crystals?"

"And a bit of palmistry." Clipping the last of the bright blooms, Siena placed them in her basket.

"Have a care," he said softly. "If pressed too hard, the man you seek could snap."

She cracked a smile. "I would actually welcome it if push turned to shove."

"At least let me hide close by, in case of trouble."

Siena shook her head. "I would rather you stay away. In fact, I think it best that you skip the game entirely. Your presence would only be a distraction. I will arrange the sessions so you are scheduled last. That way, no one will notice when you don't show up for your appointed time." She looked away. "I can't afford any mistakes right now."

"Very well. Then I shall see what I can glean from Orlov." He forbore to add that whether she wished it or not, his gaze would not stray too far from her gypsy lair.

Rose knotted off the last gauzy sheet of silk. "When the candles are lit in the wall sconces, the effect will be dramatic."

Where her maid had procured the gold-threaded fabric was a mystery, but Siena was beginning to think that the older woman possessed mystical powers that rivaled those of Merlin. "You are a magician, Rose," she murmured, surveying the artful fall of fabric that had transformed the rough cellar room into a shimmering Bedouin tent. "The place looks straight out of a tale of *The Arabian Nights*."

"Aye. A few more velvet pillows for the floor and another sheepskin rug should suffice." Rose consulted her notes. "The attics have also yielded an ornate brass brazier and a Chinese dragon carved out of jade. As for special effects, I've added some attar of roses to the lamp oil. A pity we do not have more time. I could have sent for some hashish. The drug is quite useful at relaxing a man's inhibitions and inducing him to speak freely."

Siena toyed with one of the brightly painted tarot cards. "I shall have to use other tricks to coax them into revealing more than they might wish. 'The Prince of Pleasure.'" She held up the image from the Italian *Tarocchi* deck and lowered her voice to a throaty whisper. "He will tell you a naughty secret, but first you must yield one of your own."

Rose cocked her head. "Very good. But stand a step to your right so that the light casts half your face in shadow." After rearranging the flowers flanking the jade dragon, she seemed satisfied with the effect. "I'll finish off the last little details here, then come up and help you finish dressing for the part."

Siena's costume, also scavenged from items packed away by the duke's ancestors, consisted of an even gauzier silk for harem pants, a sleeveless chemise snugged at the waist with a crimson sash, and a profusion of brass chains linked around her neck. A flowered scarf wrapped around her tresses topped off the exotic garb. To her eye, she looked more like a pirate than a Gypsy, but she doubted the gentlemen were going to split hairs over such details. Not with a goodly amount of cleavage distracting their attention.

Crooking a wry smile, she retraced her way up one of the hidden circular stairwells that Rose had discovered. She would have to guard herself against the same danger. Even without his physical presence, Kirtland was a powerful distraction. The line of his jaw, the curve of his cheek, the small scar grazing the arch of his brow—his every intimate detail had become a part of her, committed to memory, to touch. *To longing?*

She dared not think of such things. He would soon return to his books and art; she would return to gunpowder and steel. Pressing her palms to her eyes, she held disappointment at bay. No matter their fleeting interlude of entwined limbs and shared passions, he was merely a temporary ally.

That she had drawn the earl into danger added to the weight on her shoulders. Along with Lynsley's expectations, she bore the burden of her own regrets. If anything happened to him . . .

It had not been pride but fear that had triggered her earlier sharp words, her edging away from his touch. To keep Kirtland out of the line of fire, she must cut to the heart of the enemy. And quickly.

Andiamo, Volpina! *Attack, even when you are weary to the bone.* The recollection of Da Rimini's exhortations urged on her own faltering step. She was one of Merlin's Maidens. She had tasted the salt of sweat, had suffered countless knockdowns, and had always risen to the challenge.

Love might be a far more dangerous opponent than any she had ever faced, but she would survive its blade as well.

"Very artful." Dunster, the last of the club members on her schedule, appeared captivated by his own reflection in the polished brass. The billowing silk and burnished light gave his fair looks an added gleam. "I do hope you will prove as creative when you decorate our love nest in Town."

"You need not worry about that," cooed Siena. A low marble plinth had been centered in the circular swirl of silk. She took a seat on the pillows surrounding it and motioned for him to do the same. Her theatrics had not teased much of interest out of Leveritt and Jadwin. She hoped to have better luck with the marquess.

Up close, Siena saw that the odd intensity in his eye was fired from within as well as from without. He exuded his usual cockiness, along with the strong scent of brandy and an edginess she could not quite define. But then, everyone, including herself, was affected by the air of anticipation hanging over the castle.

"Care for a drink?" Several decanters sat beneath the jade dragon's lolling tongue. "Brandy or whisky."

He took a moment to decide. "I'll take whisky. It has a more fiery bite."

As he reached for the glass, she took up his other hand. "Mmmm, I see deep lines, indicating strength of character. This small one here indicates luck with ladies. And this one a coming financial expense."

He gave a taut laugh as he swallowed a mouthful of the spirits. "I don't need a Gypsy to tell me that."

She humored him with a smile. "Ah, but now things become a touch more intriguing." A long pause allowed him to take another drink. "This central line hints at a wicked secret."

He snatched his hand back, spilling the last drops of whisky into his lap. "Damn slut," he snarled, swiping at his trousers.

No question she had struck a raw nerve. She must now try to soften the blow enough to learn what he was hiding. "There's no need to get upset—we all have secrets. Sometimes it's titillating to share them."

"I've had about enough of your bloody games." He tried to rise, but his legs were too unsteady.

Siena caressed his clenched fist. "I like a man who isn't afraid of breaking the rules to get what he wants."

"Enough!" he cried wildly.

His fury appeared fueled by fear. Intent on learning why, she leaned forward. "Don't worry. I will—"

As his other hand whipped up from the folds of his

coat, Siena found herself staring down the snout of a small pistol.

"You will keep your bloody mouth shut, save to answer my questions." Dunster's face, distorted with desperation, loomed just behind the cocked trigger. "Who hired you?" He was sweating profusely. "Was it Lord Netherton? I should have guessed! You were too good to be true."

Who the devil was Lord Netherton?

"I assure you, I have never met any gentleman by that name." Her own weapon, hidden beneath the skirting of the brass brazier, was just out of reach. She had made a careless mistake in underestimating the marquess. She must try to recover and not pay for it with her life. "I am just what I appear, sir. A courtesan who is looking for a rich protector. My games are just that—naughty, perhaps, but most men like to be provoked."

"I don't believe you!" His voice was shrill, savage. "He wishes to destroy me!"

"Unfairly, I am sure," she soothed.

"It wasn't my fault."

"Yet some men cannot let go of a grudge, can they?" Keep him talking, she told herself. The gun barrel was only inches from her forehead, but that could change in a flash.

"Quite right." He sounded just a trifle calmer. "It was his wife who wanted the dalliance in the first place. The baron is a country bore, more interested in his sheep than sex. What's the harm in satisfying a randy lady?"

"None that I can see," agreed Siena.

"As for his sister, she threw herself on me, I swear it." He mopped at his brow. "Forward little minx. How was I to know she was a virgin? I assumed she had been rutting with the grooms for ages." He was blabbering now. "Had Netherton kept her on a tighter rein, it never would have happened. But the girl had a rash streak. Couldn't be controlled. Wasn't *my* fault she rode out in a rainstorm to pursue me. Lud, I'd left the inn the day before."

Siena had to exercise considerable control to keep her disgust from showing. She had not been wrong about the marquess's nerve. He was not only a cad, but also a craven coward.

His voice began to tremble. "Her horse must have strayed too close to cliffs . . . the rock crumbled. Her death is more on his head than on mine."

"I see your point."

Dunster suddenly pulled himself together. "Grasping wench—I'm sure you do. Thought you were being clever, drawing the story out of me? Well, if you have blackmail in mind, think again. I've no intention of being squeezed for blunt by a manipulating little slut."

"I would be a fool to risk that with such a prominent peer." Seeing his finger tighten on the trigger, Siena sought to steady his mercurial mood. "I have no desire to end up in Newgate."

He bit his lip. "Still, I can hardly afford to take the chance that you'll keep quiet."

"Yet a shot could well cost you your neck," she pointed out. "Even a marquess will hang for murder."

"No one would hear it." However, Dunster looked uncertain as he peered up through the scrim of silk.

"Stone amplifies sound. The echo would likely reverberate throughout the house."

"Shut your mouth." He managed to rise and signaled her to do the same. "There are other ways to get rid of your meddlesome presence. I could lock you in one of the dungeon rooms. No one would ever find you." He gave a nervous laugh. "And I doubt anyone would think twice about your absence. All I would have to do is drop a word or two about hearing you say you had grown bored with our company. They would all assume you had flown off to a better offer."

Siena switched tactics, hoping a sudden show of tears might throw him off balance. "I—I swear to you . . ." As she feigned a hysterical sob, she moved ever so slightly to her right. "I will never say a word . . . I'll even come to you for free."

Dunster considered the offer. "It is a shame to waste your charms. But as Leveritt says, there are plenty of other pretty sluts." He waved the pistol. "March."

"Wait! I could pay you—" It was the oldest trick in the book, but worth a try. Staring over his shoulder, she widened her eyes. "Oh, thank God you have come!"

The marquess jerked his head around.

At the same instant, her fist hit the back of his neck, throwing him forward. As he scrabbled to recover his footing, she leapt up, grabbed hold of the hanging silk scrim, and swung forward, lashing a hard kick that caught him flush on the skull.

With a sharp grunt, Dunster fell headfirst against the stone wall, then slid to the floor.

"Men," she muttered, dropping back down to the ground and nudging his unconscious form with her bare foot.

"I hope your disgust does not include the whole of our sex."

Siena whirled around to find Kirtland standing in the doorway. He had set down his pistol and was clapping softly. "An artful display of acrobatics. But then, I expected no less," he added rather casually. He looked extremely cool and calm, save for a small quirk of his mouth. "I would have intervened earlier, but I thought you would prefer to hear his whole story."

"Easy for you to say," she muttered. That he appeared so cavalier about how close she had come to death hurt more than she wished to admit. "At any moment, a twitch of his finger might have set off the trigger."

"No matter. His weapon wasn't loaded."

"H—how did you know?"

"Seeing how agitated he was at supper, I took the precaution of searching his room." He moved around the jade dragon and stepped over the Dunster's splayed legs.

Something in his expression, a strange intensity she had never seen before, made her step back.

"Siena." His smile turned tentative. "Don't retreat."

She stilled.

"God knows, it isn't easy for me to speak from the heart. I may be able to recite a wealth of poetry, but my own feelings are not nearly so easy to articulate. My tongue trips, the words fall unsaid."

She watched the light flicker across his face. "Like fencing and boxing, all skills take practice to master." Her voice was also a little uncertain. "The first attempts may be clumsy, but I have learned that you must pick yourself up, ignore the pain of the bruises, and try again, until you get it right."

"Practice," he repeated. "An excellent suggestion." He pulled her into his arms and kissed her. A hard, hungry embrace that ended all too soon. "Siena, we must—"

Dunster began to stir.

"Damn," she swore. "This is going to present a problem."

"I've an idea. Let me handle it." Kirtland brushed a last kiss to her brow before moving to the marquess and taking hold of his collar. "Rouse yourself, Dunster. The game is over."

Dunster groaned. His lids fluttered open. "Y—you?" His face twisted in dismay as he stared up at the earl.

"Yes, me. It was lucky for the lady that I, and not you, was the last man on her schedule."

Still groggy, the marquess felt at his head. A whimper replaced his earlier bravado. "*You* hit me?"

"Who else? Count yourself fortunate that she stopped me from thrashing you to within an inch of your miserable life."

"I had no choice! I didn't want to harm her, but . . ." He fell silent at seeing Kirtland's expression. "W—what do you intend to do?" he asked. "Please, if word gets out about any of this, I'll be ruined."

"From what I overheard, you should be."

The marquess paled. "I beg of you, Kirtland. Have mercy. We all make mistakes in life."

"You mean to say you are sorry for your sins?"

"Yes, by God," he babbled. "Exceeding sorry."

"Then you will wish to do penance for them."

"Anything!"

Kirtland hauled the marquess to his feet. "Very well. If the lady is agreeable to it, I have a proposal."

She gave a slight nod, signaling him to go on.

"You will use the money you set aside for the Psalters for another purpose." He thought for a moment. "To establish a shelter for fallen women. In St. Giles."

Dunster let out a gasp. "But—"

Siena, too, felt the breath leach from her lungs.

"No buts," snapped Kirtland. "Not only that, you will continue to fund it every year. And money is not the only contribution you will make. You will involve yourself personally in the programs. Talk to the girls. Attend meetings. Enlist other benefactors. Perhaps it will give you a different perspective on seduction and the casual cruelty women endure from men."

Dunster wet his lips.

"It's that, or having your perfidy made public. Think on it. I doubt you would ever be received in Society again. Widows and wives are one thing, but innocents are not fair game, even for you."

"Very well," croaked Dunster. "I agree."

"If you fail to live up to the bargain, all of London will learn the truth as to your character. You will answer to their wrath. And mine. Do we understand each other?"

The marquess nodded.

"So be it, then. Now that you know what your immediate future is, take yourself off."

Siena waited until Dunster had slunk away into the darkness. "Perhaps I can find a suit of armor down here among all the other ancestral debris. It may need a bit of polishing to knock off the rust, but your sense of honor is already shining through, despite all your avowals to the contrary."

"I am not some storybook knight, but a man, Siena. One with too many flaws to write on a page."

"Yet you keep rescuing a damsel in distress."

He looked embarrassed.

"That was a noble idea," she continued. "I don't care what denials you make, you *are* an idealist—a man who cares about defending those who can't help themselves."

The earl shrugged off the praise. He needed practice in receiving heartfelt emotion as well as giving it, thought Siena. If she had any say in it, the training would be rigorous.

He quickly changed the subject. "Did your fortune-telling turn up any other revelations?"

She shook her head. "No, though it is quite astounding how nervous people get when the subject of secrets is mentioned. I suppose we all have private peccadilloes we are afraid will come to light. But as for learning any specifics, there were no other confessions of guilt." Forcing her thoughts from the glimmer of Kirtland's eyes in the lamplight, she added, "If I had to guess, I would say that Leveritt is the one worth more scrutiny. The next challenge should allow me the opportunity to take a closer look at his quarters. I wish to follow up on something he let slip."

Suddenly aware of the damp chill pervading the cellars, Siena shivered and her bare arms pebbled with gooseflesh. "Let us extinguish the lights and make our way back upstairs." She turned, only to find Kirtland was blocking the doorway.

"A moment before we go," he said, tugging the headscarf free of her tresses. "What of you, Siena?" he asked, smoothing the tumble of curls back from her brow. "What secrets do you wish to keep hidden?"

Whereas an instant ago she was cold, a hot flush now suffused her limbs. She had never dared voice her innermost doubts to anyone, not even Shannon or Sofia. But a look at his face, strong yet vulnerable in the stubbled light, gave her the courage to go on.

"I—I fear letting anyone know how often I feel unsure. How at times I wonder if I am tough enough . . ." She drew a breath. "A true warrior should never feel doubts. It is a sign of weakness."

"You are wrong, my valiant Valkyrie. It is a sign of

strength, for it shows you are thinking, questioning, challenging yourself. Only a fool never feels fear."

Siena wondered how she had ever thought the chiseled angles and faint scars of his face forbidding.

"Anything else troubling your heart?"

Surely her new feelings must be painfully obvious. Still, she tried to keep a brave face. "I am supposed to be asking all the questions."

A low chuckle. "I had forgotten your claim to Gypsy talents, seeing as you look more like a corsair than a Romany princess."

"We had to improvise." She gave a wry laugh. "Perhaps I do have a special knack for reading palms. I did, after all, predict that Dunster would soon be required to spend a great deal of money."

"Ah." His smile drew into a more serious expression. Taking her hand between his, Kirtland turned it upward. "Tell me, what do you see for your own future?"

She didn't dare meet his gaze. "Right now, I can't think of looking beyond my mission."

He looked as if to pursue the matter, then simply nodded and released his hold. "Very well, we'll wait and see. But not for long. Things have taken too dangerous a turn of late. I want you to set up the last challenges as quickly as possible."

Chapter Twenty

$\mathcal{K}$irtland was right. There was no time to lose.

Siena stared out her bedroom window. The rain had finally given way to scudding sunlight, and the mist had receded, leaving the moors sparkling with a hard-edged clarity. In contrast, the clouds within the castle were growing more ominous.

Dunster had departed at dawn, leaving a message for the others that an urgent matter called him back to Town. The explanation had raised no overt comment, but at breakfast, the tension was palpable among the remaining club members. Winthrop had even suggested that the games were becoming too much of a distraction from the auction.

She had agreed to consider changing the rules. Her masquerade was wearing thin. Orlov, she knew, already saw through the low-cut bodices and transparent silks. Whether anyone else suspected that the Black Dove was not what she seemed was . . . uncertain.

Rose opened the armoire. "What dress shall you be needing for the afternoon?"

"My riding habit, please," she replied, hoping a good gallop would help clear her head for the challenge ahead. At breakfast she had pronounced Fitzwilliam the winner of the previous night's challenge, with the prize being a ride out to the romantic ruins of a medieval abbey. Although he was no longer a suspect, she had wanted the time to consider how to deal with the two remaining suspects.

Leveritt and Jadwin. One of them had to be the traitor. And she was almost certain as to which one it was. Something the older gentleman had said during the fortune-telling session had sparked yet another question, but she needed to work out an exact strategy for confirming her suspicions.

Or dealing with the alternative. Either way, by the end of the night, the enemy would be unmasked.

"You anticipate trouble?" Rose looked up, alerted by the click of the lock on the weapons case.

"It's best to be prepared," Siena answered evasively as she opened the lid. She was not sure how much her maid knew of what took place during the games. Or how much Rose guessed. She herself had said nothing about Orlov's bullet or Dunster's attack.

Or Kirtland's lovemaking.

Her fingers tightened on the hilt of her poniard, matching the clench of her body. The thought of his touch sent a dagger of desire through her.

"A wise strategy when one isn't sure who the enemy is." Was there a hint of warning in Rose's tone?

Siena slipped the extra blade into her reticule, then put away the case. "Speaking of strategy, I've decided to change the timing of the next game." Making a spur-of-the-moment decision, she went on, "Instead of tomorrow, it will take place tonight."

"Which one do you have in mind?"

"The treasure hunt. We need to map out a route through the castle, one that will keep the men busy for at least an hour. Perhaps you can take a look around some of the more out-of-the-way areas and decide which ones might suit our needs."

Rose nodded. "I already have some ideas."

"I will be back in several hours, and we can work out the final details." She would make the announcement when the gentlemen gathered for drinks before supper. Even if the enemy was suspicious of her role here, the sudden change in plan might throw him off-balance. "Just keep them far away from their own quarters."

Kirtland shaded his eyes from the sun. From the shelter of the rock outcropping, he had a clear line of sight across to the abbey ruins. Siena had eliminated Fitzwilliam as the traitor, but he wasn't taking any chances. None of the members of The Gilded Page Club had seemed particularly threatening before now. Yet one was a dangerous traitor.

He had been forced to look at everyone—including himself—in a whole new light.

At the sound of hooves thudding over the wet ground, he checked the priming of his pistol and peeked down from his aerie to see Siena and Fitzwilliam dismount. Even from afar, she drew his gaze. *Like a moth to a flame.* He couldn't take his eyes off her.

Despite all their differences, they were, at heart, kindred spirits. Both of them had been indelibly marked by the hardships of life, he with the scars of an enemy saber and she with a secret tattoo. They wore them as badges of honor, outward signs of a commitment to duty, to principle. He was born a peer, she a pauper, and yet some unknown alchemy, more magic than science, had bonded them together in defiance of all rational logic.

How to explain a flash of lightning? A clap of thunder?

Or the feeling of profound peace he had experienced in her arms, despite the storm raging all around them.

Kirtland pressed back against the jagged stone, feeling a warring of desire and regret. Now that he knew she was not really a courtesan, he would not treat her as one. She might not be a real lady . . . but that was a distinction he did not care about. She had earned his respect.

And far more.

A sudden glint of sun on steel drew his attention from Siena and her escort to the trail leading up from the lake. It took a moment for his eye to focus on the approaching rider.

Orlov.

Deciding that the Russian was far more of a threat than Fitzwilliam, the earl hurried to mount his stallion. Cutting through the copse of pines, he cantered to the crest of the hill and picked out a path through the gorse and granite that led down into the wooded ravine.

"Out hunting?" Kirtland waited until the other man came abreast of the trees before spurring forward to join him. The trail was narrow, forcing them close enough that their boots brushed.

The Russian didn't bat an eye. "I thought I might shoot some birds, if the opportunity arose."

"It won't." Kirtland let the pause linger before adding, "Out of season, you see."

"You did not ask which species I was considering."

"It doesn't matter," answered the earl.

"It appears we have different customs on the Continent."

"So it does. But as you are in England, I would advise you not to risk breaking the rules."

"Then perhaps I'll set my sights on bigger game," said Orlov blandly.

They rode on in silence. The terrain flattened, yet still the earl clung like a nettle to the Russian's side until they reached a fork in the trail. After a small hesitation, Orlov reined his mount toward the south fields, away from Siena.

Satisfied that he no longer posed any immediate threat to her, Kirtland touched the brim of his hat. "Good hunting. But have a care. The weather looks to be turning, and the moors of Devon can be dangerous for those unfamiliar with the territory."

Orlov turned in his saddle. "Be assured, Lord Kirtland, I have hunted in far more treacherous environs than these."

Suddenly tiring of all the feints and probes, the earl decided to bare his steel. "Whatever it is you are after, I don't intend to let you have it."

"Then perhaps I shall have to take it by force."

"You may try."

They glared at each other, both unyielding, until the Russian flashed a mocking salute. "How sporting of you to offer a warning, Kirtland. I would not have expected it. A lofty set of scruples is not rumored to be one of your strong suits."

"Perhaps you have had an ear cocked in the wrong direction."

There was a momentary ripple in the flat blue gaze. Satisfied that he had made his point, Kirtland spurred his stallion into a brisk canter. Not that he had won any great advantage from the engagement. Orlov's reasons for shadowing Siena were still as mysterious as ever. *Friend or foe?*

Or something in between?

The earl slowed to negotiate a tricky turn. Could there be any grey area when it came to treachery? He wondered. Though he had not voiced his thoughts to her, Kirtland was now of the opinion that Orlov's shot had been fired as a warning, not a death warrant. In analyzing the incident, he had decided that the shot had been aimed high enough over their heads to be a deliberate miss.

Why?

Swearing under his breath, Kirtland wished once again that he, like Osborne, had been asked to lend his expertise to military intelligence. In mulling over the few bits of information his friend had told him about Orlov, he had come up with even more questions about the Russian's motives. However, to find answers, he would have to do his own reconnaissance. A search of Orlov's rooms was in order, but he would have to be very careful. The man's movements were unpredictable.

As was everything about the gathering at Marquand Castle.

The Psalters be damned. Come hell or high water, the earl decided he must spirit Siena away from its walls as soon as possible. Even if that meant taking matters into his own hands.

*   *   *

The light from the drawing-room chandeliers seemed a bit more subdued than on previous evenings. As did the colors of the floral arrangement and the tone of the voices. Even the clink of crystal seemed muted as the guests gathered for the daily ritual of drinks before supper. The duke's relatives seated themselves on the velvet sofas by the hearth, while the others broke off into several small circles of their own. The remaining members of The Gilded Page Club stood on their own in front of the mullioned windows.

"I have a surprise for you, gentlemen," announced Siena as she joined them.

Fitzwilliam raised his glass and composed a quick rhyme. "Dare we hope the Dove has chosen a nest. And is now willing to spread her wings to the best."

"With such puling poetry, you have not a chance of warming your cockles beneath a blanket of downy softness," said Winthrop.

"As if your words would coax a crow into your bed—"

"Don't jump to conclusions just yet." Siena cut off the gibes before they could turn too ugly. "What I meant was, I have decided to change the rules."

The four gentlemen around her exchanged speculative looks. Kirtland alone appeared more interested in the conversation taking place in one of the alcoves.

"What say you to one final challenge?" She had not yet told the earl of her idea and hoped he would not raise any objection. "To take place tonight. Winner take all."

"An excellent suggestion." To her surprise, it was Kirtland who voiced first approval. "Why wait any longer?"

Fitzwilliam seconded the sentiment. "Aye, it's high time to come to the point."

Winthrop's snigger quickly took on a more speculative

edge. "Let us hear what you have in mind before we come to any agreement."

"Fair enough." Siena indicated the bejeweled pendant nestled between her cleavage. "You see this golden dove? By midnight it will be resting in a different place. You will all receive a set of riddles at that time. Each one you solve will lead you a step closer to its hiding place. The first man to return to the Map Room with it will come away with two birds in hand."

"So this time, the winner will not be open to interpretation?" asked Leveritt.

"No," agreed Siena. "The outcome will leave no doubt as to who stands out from the others."

Jadwin had remained silent up until that moment, but on hearing the others murmur their assent, he shrugged. "Well, if even Kirtland is on the same page this time, who am I to object?"

Siena signaled for more champagne to be served all round. "Then we are all in agreement. We will gather in the Hunt Room at midnight. There you will receive your set of riddles and the final instructions. Dress for a stalk, gentlemen. Although the trail will not lead outdoors, there will be a number of thorny obstacles to overcome before reaching the prize."

"And you, madam, should come attired for a tumble," suggested Winthrop with a wink. "After putting us through a merry chase, I am sure the winner will not wish to waste any time in claiming victory."

"Good things come to those who wait," she replied.

"So they say. But when the moment is right, one must be ready to seize it." Kirtland's words were cryptic, like the crescent curve that had come to his lips. What message, if any, did he mean to convey?

She had not long to ponder the question, for as the footman came over to refill their glasses, he contrived to murmur in her ear, "The Weapon Room. At eleven."

His whisper stirred a flutter of her lashes, a silent assent. Strange how she knew he would sense its meaning. A look, a gesture—there was an understanding between them that went beyond words. Their bodies were in tune. Even now, she did not need to look around to know he had moved a half dozen paces to her right, his shoulders squared to the marble hearth.

A moment later he was gone, drawn away to converse with the duke's secretary at the far end of the room.

Siena turned slightly, letting her gaze linger on the spot he had just vacated before looking to the open French doors. Torches were lit along the terrace, and several of the gentlemen had stepped out to enjoy a smoke in the lingering twilight. The carved balusters had mellowed to the color of amber honey, and she suddenly felt the need to seek a sliver of solitude.

She slipped from the room and found a spot at the railing, far from the rumblings of male laughter. Like distant thunder that presaged a storm, it stirred a thrumming awareness that her mission was drawing to a head. The very air seemed charged with the crackle of coming lightning. Drawing a steadying breath, she sought to channel its force deep within her.

Her hands pressed hard against the weathered stone. The flex of muscle rippled through her limbs, in perfect harmony with balance and focus. She trusted her body, her physical training. If it came down to a test of strength or stamina, she was a match for any man.

As for a battle of wills? Siena stared out at the purpling moors. Her belief in the principles of the Academy was unflinching as well. She would fight to the death to defend them.

Never hesitate, Volpina. When the time comes to thrust the blade home, you must think of nothing else. Da Rimini had taught her well.

Her arm was poised, her steel was honed. The only possible weakness was her heart. She had let emotion come into play, stirring feelings that had no place in a warrior's world. Distractions could prove deadly.

And love was perhaps the most dangerous of them all.

Love. It was a two-edged sword. She loved her profession and all the noble ideals espoused by Lord Lynsley. But Julian Henning had made her realize that love was more than an abstraction. He embodied all that she held dear—strength, honor, compassion. He had also awakened her to other elemental passions. The pleasures of lovemaking, the nuances of art, the power of poetry.

As a lone child in the slums, she had seen men as threatening brutes. As a student at the Academy, she had learned to view them in a more admirable light. They were teachers, disciplinarians, leaders who set an honorable example. They had molded her mind and her body. But until now, she had never imagined a man could be trusted with her heart.

Duty and desire. If only . . .

Siena thrust such musing aside. There was still a battle to fight before she tried to sort out her inner conflicts. It wasn't as if the earl had asked her to choose between her world and his. Their alliance was only temporary.

"Your face is far too lovely to be wearing such a pensive frown." Fitzwilliam, bearing a fresh bottle of champagne, perched a hip on the stone balustrade and refilled her drink.

Sentiment gave way to a steely smile as Siena turned.

"Come, let us toast to the striking sunset. And the coming dawn. By tomorrow, you will have settled on your new protector. I should think that the prospect would be a pleasing one, for no matter whom you choose, you have a good deal to gain."

And a good deal to lose.

She raised the glass to her lips. "To the new day."

Would that she and Kirtland lived to see it.

The surrounding steel of the Weapons Room— centuries of razored blades, hammered shields, and daggered points—gave the clock chimes an added edge. Her nerves already sharp with worry, Siena moved deeper into the recess between the display cabinets. Row upon row of Roman knives lay upon pristine velvet.

She forced her eyes away.

The earl entered, his dark evening dress blending in with the night shadows. A glance around, and he came to her with a silent, stalking step. His features, chiseled to a harsher angle by the reflected light, betrayed his own tension. He said nothing as he slipped into the narrow space beside her, his mouth set in a hard line.

And then, suddenly, his lips were upon hers, softening for just an instant into a searing kiss, before resuming their martial slant.

"This change in strategy—what have you planned?" he asked.

"The treasure hunt will allow me to search Leveritt's room first, then move on to Jadwin's if need be." Somehow she managed a show of composure despite the fluttering of her heart. "Rose and I have routed the trail through the far reaches of the attics. The riddles should keep them occupied for well over an hour."

"Give yourself no more than half an hour," he replied. "After that, the risk grows too great."

"The timing should be no problem." She sketched out the logistics, and though his frown deepened, Kirtland raised no objection until she had finished.

"I cannot say I like what you are proposing. There are too many things that may go wrong."

"No battle plan is foolproof. If need be, I will improvise."

"I will drop out of the hunt and come back to keep track of Orlov. He poses as great a threat as the others." He touched her arm. "Promise me you will stay away from his quarters."

"I am not so rash as to walk straight into the lion's den."

"Knowing your unflinching courage, I would not put it past you to charge straight through the gates of hell."

"Only if Lucifer stands between me and the paper I have been sent to recover." She wished to say more, but to speak now of personal matters might weaken her resolve.

His jaw clenched, and for a moment, Kirtland looked on the verge of voicing a more vehement protest. But then, he seemed held back by the same reticence that gripped her. "Be careful, Siena." A low murmur and a last light brush of his lips to her forehead were all he allowed before disappearing back into the shadows.

"And you, Julian," she whispered into the darkness.

Chapter Twenty-One

$\mathcal{K}$irtland doubled back through the gallery corridor, pausing every few steps to check for footfalls behind him. Feigning puzzlement at the first of Siena's riddles, he had been the last to leave the Hunt Room, and from there, it had been easy enough to drop away from the rest of the group as they hurried for the attic storerooms. Still, he could not shake off a feeling of unease. An unseen threat shadowing his steps.

Taking cover in the doorway of the Renaissance Room, he checked again for any sign that he was being followed. *Silence.* Not a scuff or a flutter of movement, save for the noiseless flicker of the wall sconces. And yet, the hairs on the nape of his neck stirred a prickling warning.

He forced a measured breath. The rasp of his nerves was no doubt due to rust. He was out of practice—that was all. And in the past, his fears had been for himself and his battle-hardened troops, not a lone young female. That she was trained to take care of herself did not still the thud of his heart. She was in danger, and his instinct was to rush to her rescue, no matter that their strategy demanded that he guard the flanks.

Damn. Despite Osborne's teasings, he had never thought of himself as a *parfait chevalier* in a *chanson de geste*. He had too many chinks in his armor. Yet armed with naught but his heart, he would gladly joust dragons, demons, or the devil himself to keep Siena safe from harm.

All the more reason to locate Orlov, he reminded himself. And quickly. Her change in strategy had made a search of the Russian's rooms less important than finding the man himself. Knowing Orlov was in the habit of lingering over port and cigars, Kirtland decided to head for the small studies on the floor below. Wherever he was, the Russian was soon to acquire a companion. A shadow to his every move.

Hurrying his own strides, the earl slipped down one flight through the servant stairwell and picked his way past a row of decorative plinths. The first few rooms were dark, deserted. He came abreast of the Coin Room and, finding the fire banked and the candles extinguished, turned for the East Wing. A move that would bring him closer to the Russian's quarters. And to Siena.

"Looking for something?"

The sudden sound froze Kirtland in his tracks. "A drink," he replied.

Orlov, his brows a golden gleam of mock surprise, clucked in dismay. "Have the duke's servants let all the decanters go dry at the same time? How shockingly lax. But then, it is so difficult to come by good help these days."

"I find myself in the mood for something other than brandy or port."

"Indeed? Have you ever tasted Russian vodka?"

"No." The earl kept his voice deliberately neutral.

"I have a bottle in my room. Would you care to try it?" An invitation, or a challenge? "I warn you, though, it is an acquired taste."

"Like you?"

Orlov laughed softly. "You are not the first to imply that I am best enjoyed in small doses."

The man did possess a dry sense of humor, admitted the earl. To go along with his insolent arrogance.

"The same might be said for you, Lord Kirtland," continued the Russian. "But despite our apparent distaste for one another, why don't we put aside our differences for the moment and have a friendly chat. Who knows, perhaps we will come to some sort of meeting of the minds."

"Perhaps." Kirtland nodded his agreement. "Very well. Let us raise a toast. To the hope of continued goodwill between our two countries, if nothing else." Not that he trusted the man's sudden civility for an instant. But the opportunity gave him a perfect excuse for being close at hand to the rooms of Leveritt and Jadwin in case Siena ran into any trouble.

"Just so. A spirit of international cooperation between St. Petersburg and London."

However silkily the Russian dressed his words, they had a hint of menace to them. What did Orlov really want, other than a handsome sum for his services? Until Kirtland knew the answer, he must assume the worst.

He would be vigilant if the other man tried any tricks.

They walked in silence, the slide of the Russian's velvet slippers matching the whisper of the earl's soft-soled evening shoes. Like a panther and a lion, thought Kirtland. Prowling through a gilded jungle.

It was not until they had entered the East Wing that Orlov started up again with his usual small talk. "How strange that you have chosen not to compete for the pleasure of buying the Dove's services. Or mayhap . . ." He stretched the pause out for several steps. "You have other arrangements with her. Mayhap you are getting them for free."

"I am not sure why my decisions should be of any interest to you, Mr. Orlov."

"We are engaged in our own competition, are we not? Your choices may affect my own strategies. Rather like on a battlefield."

As if he needed any reminder that he was treading on dangerous ground.

They turned into the corridor, and the earl could not keep from tensing every muscle. The Russian kept pattering on with his sly innuendoes, but Kirtland was only paying them half a mind. Most of his attention was focused on the closed doors and what might be taking place behind them. There was no need to be so on edge, he assured himself. It was far too early for any of the club members to be returning from the hunt.

A click of the latch and Orlov entered his rooms. "Wait here, I'll light a taper for the candelabra." He returned, the single flame in one hand, a bottle in the other. "The glasses are on the sideboard."

Kirtland took a step, then hesitated.

"*Na Zdorovie,*" announced the Russian, lifting his arms in some impatience. "That is, unless you are having second thoughts about trusting my hospitality. I assure you, the drink is not drugged."

Still thinking of Siena and her dangerous games, Kirtland darted one last glance to the corridor. Was there a shifting of the shadows? His eye was off the Russian for hardly more than a heartbeat.

Just long enough for the heavy glass to come crashing

down upon his head. As he slipped into blackness, he heard
Orlov add, "But the bottle has rather nasty aftereffects."

Leveritt's door was locked, but Siena had anticipated as
much. The ancient iron was no match for the blade of her
pick. The door opened and closed so quickly it appeared
naught but a stirring of the corridor shadows. As a precaution, she took a moment to throw the tumbler back in place.

His room was inordinately neat, the brushes on the
dressing table perfectly aligned, the bottles of Macassar oil
and cologne in a straight row, the dressing gown already
laid out in precise folds upon the bed. Siena smoothed
a hand over the paisley silk, then moved to the dressing
room. Elegant coats of the softest superfine wool hung
paired with tailored waistcoats of costly brocades. Pantaloons, trousers, formal breeches—all bespoke an exquisite sense of style. Her gaze fell to the buttery-soft leather
boots and embroidered slippers. Apparently no expense
had been spared on achieving such sartorial splendor. Leveritt was a gentleman who did not overlook details.

Next she checked the bureau drawers. Scented shirts,
starched cravats, silk stockings. Everything in exact order.

Not a hair out of place.

Siena paused for a moment, slightly puzzled as to why
this perfection was stirring a prickling at the back of her
neck. Then, acting on instinct, she turned to the desk.

Surely it couldn't be quite that simple. And yet, a methodical mind might well stick to its ordered routine. As *Il
Lupino* had constantly reminded her, an enemy's strength
could often be turned into his ultimate weakness. Opening the letter case, she found only a correspondence from
Leveritt's banker and a bill from an antique dealer on
Bond Street. The contents of a notebook proved equally

bland. Several scribblings regarding a recent art exhibit, a sketch for a silver epergne, a reminder of a forthcoming auction of Italian paintings. Nothing out of the ordinary.

Pressing her eyes shut, Siena focused her thoughts on all she had read of the men, the mission. What was it that tied all the elements together?

The answer seemed so obvious as to be absurd.

Books.

Turning slowly, almost casually, she moved to the bed-side table. The book was, ironically enough, a thick tome on Russian religious icons, lavishly illustrated with hand-tinted engravings. Its binding fell open to reveal a folded paper, nestled between a grim-faced St. Sergius and an unsmiling Madonna and Child.

God in heaven. Siena ran a finger over the broken wax seal, tracing enough of the double-headed Imperial eagle to know she had at long last found what she had come for.

Her elation had little time to take wing, for as she lifted the document from its hiding place, hurried footsteps sounded in the corridor and a key rattled in the lock.

Siena shoved the paper inside her shirt and bolted for the open window. The thin ledge provided a precarious perch, but balanced on her bare toes, she began inching as fast as she dared toward the decorative arch. Another few feet, and she could climb to cover—

Damn. Up ahead flashed a glimmer of fair hair. Like a bad penny, the Russian kept turning up where he was least wanted. A swirl of smoke explained his presence at the open casement. But where was Kirtland? Her foot slipped as she shifted her stance. *Steady,* she warned herself. The earl had come unscathed through a brutal war. He knew how to take care of himself. Still, she could not keep from wondering if he was close. If he was safe.

Her mind clouded with questions, she nearly missed the tiny flare of orange as Orlov tossed away the butt of his cheroot and flexed his shoulders. In another instant he would turn her way.

She could not go forward; she could not go back. The only choice was the mullioned glass at her shoulder. *Jadwin's room.* The latch gave way to her hip, and she rolled silently onto the carpet. For a moment she lay still, honing her senses to a fighting edge. Victory was so close. She must not allow it to be snatched away at the last moment. *Keep your mind and your eye on the opponent's blade until it is lying in the dust, Volpina! Desperation gives men an added strength.* She must use Da Rimini's words to steel her own nerve for the final flurry.

Her fingers pressed to her left breast. She would draw courage from not only the hawk, but from something deeper within herself. *Love.* She had come to understand that it was not a weakness but a strength.

Stilling the racing of her heart, Siena angled a glance around the room. Jadwin's trunk was unlocked, his portmanteau propped open against a chair, offering a tantalizing peek at a jumble of papers. But there seemed little point in snooping through his personal effects. Whatever his faults, she decided to let them remain private. Her mission was to unmask a traitor, and the proof of perfidy was in her possession.

Her hand was on the door latch when it suddenly rattled in her grasp.

"The devil take it . . ."

Siena fell back, narrowly avoiding a blow from the door.

Jadwin stared in shock at her black shirt and trousers. "W—what game is this?"

There was nothing to do but brazen it out.

She arched a leg and gave a sultry look. "Take a guess, sir." She toyed with the top fastening of her shirt. "I had a feeling that you would have no trouble with the riddles." It was odd that both he and Leveritt had returned sooner than she expected, but perhaps Rose had not reckoned with the linguistic talents of the club members. They were, after all, particularly skilled with words. "Did I make them too easy?"

"No—that is, I felt a trifle unwell and decided to come lie down."

Her palm slid suggestively over the curve of her breast. "I am sure I can cure any malady that ails you."

He grabbed for her hand. "I fear I must—"

His fingers snagged in the silk, ripping loose a button. The dispatch fell to the floor.

Before she could react, Jadwin picked it up. "What's this?" he stammered, staring at the red wax seal as if it were a pool of blood.

"Nothing," she assured him. "A *billet doux* I found under my door." Plucking the folded document from his grasp, Siena covered her concern with a quick laugh. "You don't want to read it. The prose is quite embarrassing. Why, I am sure the fellow who penned it is already regretting his folly of putting pen to paper." The crackle mimicked her own inward warnings as she wedged it into the hidden pocket of her trousers. *Keep your concentration as sharp as your blade, Volpina!* She had let her mind wander, her step slow a fraction.

"Pour us a drink." She turned, taking care to expose a goodly amount of cleavage.

Jadwin paled, and his hands were shaking as he turned for the decanter.

A sip, a smile, and she would think of some excuse to slip out for a moment—

He suddenly whipped around, a small pistol in his hand. "Give it to me."

"What?"

His voice rose. "Now! Or I'll blow a bloody hole through your heart!"

"No need for violence, sir," she soothed. "There must be some misunderstanding, sir. I—"

The latch clicked, and Leveritt entered. "There is no misunderstanding," he said, closing the door behind him. "Well done, Johnny. You were right to move so quickly."

Both men?

She felt a bit light-headed. Of all the possibilities she had considered, this one had never entered her head.

"I don't know how you stumbled onto our secret," continued Leveritt. "But if you think to blackmail us, you are far too late in the game. We have grown sick and tired of it all."

"The lies, the pretenses," growled Jadwin. Sweat had curled the tips of his shirtpoints. "But in another few days, we will be safe."

"But why?" asked Siena. "Gentlemen such as you have everything."

Smiling, Jadwin touched his friend's arm with an easy intimacy. "I should think it would be obvious."

Realization suddenly dawned on her. "For *that* you would betray your country?"

"Why not?" countered Leveritt. "Our country despises our sort. They would put nooses around our necks if the truth were known."

"This last delivery is our ticket to freedom." In the glow of moonlight, Jadwin's face appeared white as chiseled marble. Bloodless. "Our contact in France will pay a king's ransom for it, seeing as the Emperor will be able to use it to break Russia's alliance with England."

In spite of the initial shock, her training quickly took over, and Siena kept probing for information. "If it is so valuable, I wonder that you tarried here."

"Art has always been our passion, and the Psalters are a treasure worth taking considerable risk to possess," he replied.

"Indeed, this fortnight's delay only adds to the price we will get for the dispatch. Napoleon is champing at the bit to have it." Leveritt looked immensely pleased with himself and the opportunity to display his cleverness. "And the beauty is, once we outbid the others for the Psalters, they will cost us no more than a small deposit, for the duke will trust our bankers to complete the transaction once we have returned to Town."

Jadwin, too, seemed eager to expound on their cunning. "Rather than return to London, we will be off to the coast and a fast cutter to Le Havre. And from there, perhaps Sicily or Greece. Wherever men of a sensitive nature can enjoy art and life without censure."

"If one is discreet here," she began.

"What do *you* know of discretion!" Leveritt's slightly effeminate mouth pursed in a petulant pout. His tone turned ugly. "A woman who prances around naked, inviting men to fight over the privilege of rutting between her legs. Your wicked ways are applauded and overlooked with a wink of an eye by the *ton*. You offer your flesh for money, not love, and earn a pretty penny for your lewdness. It's bloody unfair."

"Unfair?" In some ways she could understand their dilemma. She, of all people, knew how primitive instinct could turn savage. No matter whether they were highborn or lowborn, men were quick to attack those who were weak or different. But it galled her to hear such self-pity from men of wealth and title. "It is you who had the good fortune to be born to a life of privilege, who don't know what you are talking about. Given your advantages in life, you could have come up with an alternative to treason."

"You sound like a sniveling Methodist," snarled Leveritt. "How dare you preach at us. You don't understand a thing about being different."

There was little point in correcting his conceit. She must instead find a way to use it as a weapon, seeing it was the only one at hand. "I don't suppose I do." Bowing her head, Siena hoped to appear suitably chastised. "Clearly your intellect sets the two of you apart. I would guess, by finding the government dispatch hidden in a book bearing The Gilded Page Club bookplate, that you passed on your information using such rare volumes."

"You *are* a smart little slut. Too smart by half."

"Not really. I would never have been clever enough to conceal my dealings with the enemy from the other members."

"Bah. It was easy enough," he answered. "Dunster was far too busy with his womanizing to notice aught but his own reflection in the glass. And the others, they, too, were wrapped up in their own interests. Kirtland was the most worrisome of the lot. His intellect and his military training made him dangerous. But given his own problems with authority and his increasing absence from London, we figured it a safe bet that he would not notice anything amiss."

"As for you . . ." The snout of Jadwin's gun pressed up against her chest. "How did you come to discover the truth?"

"Mere chance," she bluffed. "I always search the rooms of the gentlemen I choose as my marks. The risk is usually worth the reward."

"So we are not the first who you have targeted for blackmail?" A harsh laugh. "Be assured we are the last."

Leveritt smiled grimly. "The Black Dove will not be flying away from this particular encounter. In fact, you have made it inordinately easy for us to deal with the matter."

So she had, thought Siena, cursing her naïveté for not having interpreted the subtle signs correctly. She had been right to sense something odd about them, but dead wrong as to the reason why.

"Exactly." Jadwin seemed to be savoring the scenario as he would a fine wine. "I heard a noise. I saw an intruder slip in through my window. Bang." He blew a whiff of imaginary smoke from his fingertip. "Who could blame me for protecting myself?"

"Before you do so, I am curious. How were you drawn into treason?"

The two gentlemen exchanged looks. "I suppose there is no harm in telling it." Leveritt's shrug held not a twitch of remorse. "During the Peace of Amiens, we journeyed to Paris, to partake of its legendary pleasures. There was a party in St. Germain. Champagne. Girls. Boys. Anything our hearts desired. Our host, an old friend of Paul Barras and Josephine de Beaharnaise, was very Continental about such things. *Chacun à son gout* was how he put it."

Each to his own taste. "How very accommodating," said Siena aloud.

"Yes, we thought so, too," replied Jadwin, missing the note of irony in her tone. "The fun went on for several days, with our new French friend taking us from one grand hotel to another, each offering more outrageous entertainments. When we finally had to take our leave, the three of us had formed a true bond that went deeper than mere nationality."

"Or so we thought, until last year, when a man approached us outside the town house of The Gilded Page Club." Despite his seeming nonchalance, Leveritt had paled, and a sheen of sweat glistened upon his brow. "At first, the information he demanded did not seem so very bad. A question of which regiments were being sent where, along with their numbers and their commanders. It was easy enough to come by through conversation at White's."

"Then the demands grew greater." Jadwin took over for his friend's flagging nerve. "We had no choice but to go along with them. He had incriminating letters that would have ruined us."

Siena longed to slap the sulky smugness from his face. Instead she merely said, "Yes, you did have a choice. You could have done what you are doing now. As you said, there are many parts of the world where the moral strictures of society are not so rigid. You could have made a new life, free from fear or censure."

"And give up the glittering social life of London? Sacrifice all the comforts of our clubs, our rank, our fortunes?" Leveritt's laugh held a hint of hysteria. "Not until we had accumulated enough ready blunt to live in the manner to which we had been born." Suddenly seeming to tire of explanations, he mimed squeezing off a shot. "But enough talk. Go ahead, John. Pull the trigger."

Jadwin cocked the hammer, then slowly lowered his sights. "Wait," he murmured. "A shooting, no matter how justified, will bring a magistrate here, nosing around, asking questions, bringing unwanted attention to us. I have a better idea. Let us put a gold watch and some other valu-

ables in her pockets—a set of diamond shirt studs, a few
gold fobs that we need not admit are ours. Then we'll
take her up to the battlements. It's a long fall down from
there." The gun barrel traced a spiraling curl through the
air. "And the beauty is, everyone will think her a common
thief as well as a slut. There will no connection to us."

A grin eased the tautness of Leveritt's features. "That
is one of the things I like so much about you, Johnny. You
do have a delightfully diabolical mind."

"Which is why you must not worry so, my dear Ran
dall. I have told you, they are not nearly clever enough to
catch us."

Out of the corner of her eye, Siena saw the butt of the
pistol rise. She angled her head just enough to blunt the
full force of the blow. Letting out a low groan, she crumpled to the floor. For the moment it was wiser to feign un-
consciousness. They were confident, contemptuous—an
attitude that led to carelessness.

She would marshal her strength and be ready to strike
back when the moment was right.

"I have a few things in my dressing case that will suit
the purpose," called Jadwin. "It's there, on my bureau."

It took considerable restraint to lie limp as Leveritt
yanked the hard-won dispatch from her pocket and shoved
the trinkets in its place. The brush of his hand made her
skin crawl.

"Fetch a cloak," added Jadwin. "If we run into anyone
on the way, we can say Winthrop is three sheets to the
wind and needs a breath of fresh air to clear his head."

"Dead drunk." Leveritt laughed. "I like the irony of it.
Here, let us splash some spirits over her for good measure." The cloying scent of port soaked through her tangled curls.

"Now lift her."

"Plaguey female," huffed his partner. "She's heavier than she looks."

"Her fall will be that much swifter," assured Jadwin. "Hurry. We need to get her though this corridor before any of the others return. From the entryway, there is a shortcut to the main tower. Once we reach the spiral stairwell that leads to the battlements, we should be safe enough."

Stiff with cold and fatigue from hours in the saddle, Shannon stumbled down from the hillock where she had hidden her horse. The thorny gorse tore at her sleeve, leaving a trail of scratches across her arm. *Steady,* she warned herself. She had managed to come this far without mishap. But now, with every step, the way grew more dangerous.

Cutting through a walled orchard, she paused to survey the castle up ahead. The crenellated crest rose out of the fog, a somber outline of slate and shadows. Shannon lowered her gaze, noting that the only flicker of light appeared in the second-floor windows of the Central Tower. The two wings were dark, deep in repose.

She would have liked to study the details a bit longer, but a muffled bark sent her loping along the privet hedge that bordered the drive. She had spotted the watchman earlier, patrolling the outer grounds with two great mastiffs. His rounds seemed to follow a regular pattern. Her breach of the castle defenses would have to come from the rear.

The fanciful expanse of glass, pearly white against the dark stones, immediately caught her eye. Ducking in closer, Shannon crept along the perimeter of the conservatory until she came to a set of brass-framed doors. In a matter of moments she was inside, the soft snick of metal leaving no trace of her entry.

Cutting quickly through the greenery, she slowed to a stealthier pace as she came to a darkened corridor. *Where to look for Siena?* The castle offered a maze of possibilities. But one errant move . . .

Giving sharp echo to her own mental warnings, a door swung open and a maid, staggering under the weight of a silver tea service, crossed through the corridor up ahead. Shannon waited a moment, then followed. Another door, this one painted sage green, fell closed.

Her manual on martial arts was far more familiar than the primer on Society etiquette, but Shannon forced herself to recall what she had been taught about the workings of a titled household. The list of guests and their appointed quarters would be among the schedules and menus held by the housekeeper. Along with the butler, the woman would have a small room of her own, located somewhere near the pantries . . .

A short while later, armed with a suite name and a rough sketch of the castle floorplan, Shannon set out in search of Siena's quarters. Given the late hour and the dim glow of the few lamps left burning, she decided to risk traversing the main rooms rather than navigate a more circuitous route through the servant passageways. She padded down a long corridor, ascended a set of stairs, then crossed an octagonal entry hall and entered what the map called the Little Ballroom.

There was no worry that her steps might echo through the cavernous space. The thickness of the Turkey carpet, soft as velvet underfoot, could have muffled the tread of an elephant. Still, she had to take care not to trip as she stared up at the magnificent carved ceilings and gilt framed oil paintings that graced the colonnaded walls.

A bit breathless, she passed through the far doors and

hurried up the main circular staircase, her hand barely touching the Rococo railings.

Another darkened hall, another sharp turn, and she found herself peering through the portico of the sculpture gallery. In the low light, the multitude of shapes took on an eerie life of their own—headless Roman antiquities at play with naked Greek gods, writhing Renaissance serpents ready to strike at terra-cotta Chinese warriors. Silent sentinels of centuries past.

Halfway through the room, Shannon heard a whisper. She froze as a flicker of movement caught her eye. A pair of men—there was no mistaking the flesh-and-blood forms that materialized from between the inanimate statues. Their profiles did not pale in comparison to the smooth marble gods. Dark and light angels. *Lucifer and Gabriel?* Not only were they opposed in looks, but in words. For as they came closer, it became clear they were in the midst of a heated argument.

"You are wasting your time. I don't have it."

"So you say. But I'm not convinced."

Shannon saw the glint of a knife pressed to the throat of the dark-haired gentleman. He did not flinch. "Kill me and be damned about it. But I tell you again, the lady is innocent of any betrayal. If you harm her, I'll crawl back from the bowels of hell and tear out your heart."

"A touching speech. So you are actually in love with the lady? I would not have expected a man of your hard nature to be capable of softer sentiment. A pity it will come to naught. I don't believe in love. Or avenging spirits, whether they come from heaven or hell." The blond god tightened his grip on his prisoner's arm and turned him roughly toward the far wall, where an arched alcove led off from the main gallery. "So save your breath. You are going to need it."

Though the quarrel looked to be taking a deadly turn, Shannon didn't dare interfere. Whatever the dispute, it was obviously personal. Slipping her own knife from its sheath, she hid behind a winged Venus and waited for them to pass. Still, she felt a twinge of regret that the dark-haired gentleman appeared to be marching to his doom. Chiseled into his angled features and imposing height was a certain strength of character, evident even in the gloom. An intangible aura that commanded respect. It was hard not to admire a man who faced death without the slightest frisson of fear.

As for the fair-haired gentleman, he had a swagger that set her teeth on edge. Apollo, with an arrogance to match.

He suddenly whipped around, as if aware of another presence.

She held her breath as his gaze locked with the marble eyes overhead. Though he passed over her, unseeing, the glint of aquamarine ice sent a shiver through her sword hand.

"Your misdeeds already beginning to haunt you, Orlov?" There was an edge of ironic humor to the dark-haired gentleman's voice.

A low laugh. "You know, under different circumstances, I could almost come to like you. However, business is business."

Shannon watched the two of them disappear in the shadows of alcove. The clank of a key was followed by the rasp of rusty hinges. Then silence.

She could not afford more than a passing moment of sympathy for the stranger. Not with Siena's life at risk. Once she was certain they were gone, she slipped from her hiding place and hurried into the East Wing.

Chapter Twenty-Two

*I*f you are considering any tricks, don't bother." The knife pressed hard enough against the earl's flesh to draw blood. "I know them all," added Orlov. "The slightest jiggle of the candle or slip of your step, and I will slice your jugular clean through."

Still a bit groggy from the blow to his head, Kirtland nonetheless managed a quip. "Messy but quick. Perhaps I ought to consider it, depending on what grisly fate lies below." He had no doubt that the Russian was proficient in the use of any number of deadly weapons.

"I am not a barbarian. I am going to take no pleasure in killing you. As I said, this is merely a matter of business."

"If that is the case, then I, too, can cross your palm with gold. A great deal of it."

The earl felt Orlov stiffen. "Unlike you, Kirtland, my loyalties are not for sale."

"You wish me to believe that you do what you do for principle, and not money?" It was his turn to scoff.

"Somehow I am as skeptical of your sentiment as you are of mine."

Orlov surprised him with a show of emotion. "Think what you will. My services are for hire, yes. For a great many things that may be illegal and immoral. But by all that is holy, I would never sink so low as to sell out the country of my birth." Recovering his usual nonchalance in the next sentence, the Russian gave a gruff laugh. "For a man, honor is a bit like a maiden's virginity. Once you yield it —whether for pay or passion—it is lost forever."

"Thank you for the lecture on morality," said the earl. "And biology."

A shove hurried him down the last few steps. The flickering light revealed a small chamber hewn out of ancient rock. The air was dank, and from a grating below his feet came the gurgle of water.

"Let us see if your sarcasm is dampened by the prospect of an uninterrupted interlude of intimate conversation. I doubt we shall be bothered down here. Indeed, I am counting on it."

"Don't let me keep you from a more interesting engagement. Like having sex with a sheep, perhaps? Or do you just like to watch?"

"I would watch my tongue, if I were you." Taking the candle from Kirtland's bound hands, Orlov wedged it into a crack in the wall. Wax dripped, mimicking the faint splash of drops from sweating stone. "As you see, the duke's ancestors must have had a touch of Mongol blood in their veins. Did you know that water torture is a favorite method of the Chinese for extracting information?"

"I told you—you are wasting your time," he replied. "I've none to give."

The Russian snapped a rusted manacle around one of

Kirkland's wrists before cutting the rope. "You may soon have a change of heart." After snapping the second one shut, he stepped back and crossed his arms.

Hanging spread-eagled against the rough stone, Kirtland was in no position to argue. Looking around, he could not escape the bleak truth. Like a damnable fool, he had blundered straight into a trap. He had never felt so helpless, so hopeless. He had failed in his promise. Siena was alone, left to face the danger by herself. That she expected no more cut even deeper to the quick.

Should he throw himself on the Russian's mercy? The man had all but admitted he had none. Emotion did not come into play. He must try to keep despair at bay by maneuvering as best he could for a bargaining position. "What is it you want to know?"

"Everything about your network. Your contacts, your bolt-holes, your route of transporting the information." The Russian leaned back against the wall. "I'll make a deal with you. Tell me all the details and I'll show some mercy, no matter that it compromises my orders."

"You will let me go?" The earl did not believe it for a moment, but wished to test just how forthright the Russian intended to be.

"No. You will die. However, I'll do my best to help the Black Dove escape Lord Lynsley's wrath. You don't really think he will go easy on a rogue agent, do you? No government can afford to allow such betrayal to go unpunished."

Lynsley. Like the damp chill, a visceral anger knifed through to his very marrow. By Osborne's account, the marquess was an honorable man, doing the best he could to keep evil at bay. But at the moment, Kirtland hated him with a vengeance. "The cold-blooded bastard, sending a young woman to do his dirty work."

Orlov ran his thumb along the knife blade. "The same might be said of you, for seducing the young woman to certain doom in order to try to save your own traitorous neck."

"I never . . ." He swallowed hard, aware of an unpleasant taste in his mouth. There was a grain of truth in the accusation, for however unwitting his actions, he might have sealed Siena's death warrant with his passionate lovemaking.

"Never what?" Orlov arched a mocking brow. "Never thought about the penalties of disobeying an order? Yes, I have heard that about you. Unfortunately, the Black Dove does not have a lofty title and noble heritage to shield her from the consequences of conceit."

"Sod you." Kirtland could muster little vehemence to the insult. What was left of his anger cut inward, a knifing pain that left him bereft of further speech. His muscles sagged, his head drooped, his lips formed a ragged whisper. "And damn me to eternal hellfire." Everything blurred into the same unremitting shade of ember grey, save for the bleak realization that he had likely cost Siena her life.

"No doubt we both have a date with the devil." Strangely, Orlov's echo had lost a touch of its sarcasm. "If you have a shred of honor left, give me some tangible reason to save the Black Dove. A bargaining chip, for in this dirty game we play, nothing is given for free."

"I would gladly hand over the information, if it were in my possession," he said wearily. "All I can offer is the truth." Eyes narrowing, he tried to make out the wildly flickering cast of Orlov's features. Light and shadows.

Hide-and-seek. He was not thinking clearly, else he would have realized before now that he had missed seeing a key clue. "But first I have a question of my own. Why do you need to know the French network, when it is yours to begin with?"

"You think *me* an agent of Napoleon?" He seemed genuinely surprised.

"Why else would you be seeking the document?"

The Russian closed the gap between them. Standing toe-to-toe, his gaze slitted to a razored edge, like the blade that pressed once again to his throat. Both probing for a weakness. "Enough of spinning in circles," he demanded. "Of games within games. As it happens, I'm being paid to keep the document from falling into French hands. By whom is no business of yours. What should concern you is the fact that I will do whatever I have to, whether it means slicing your throat. And that of the lovely lady, much as I would hate to do it."

"Then you ought not be wasting your time down here, carving me into trout bait. You ought to be helping her trap the true culprit." Kirtland decided to take a calculated gamble. He had nothing to lose. "She is no traitor. And neither am I. We have narrowed the suspects down to a pair."

Orlov's gaze betrayed a flicker of indecision. "Who?"

"Leveritt or Jadwin. Even as we speak, she is looking for the proof."

"If what you say is true . . ."

"You need not take my word for it. Why not go see for yourself?" Sensing a weakening of the other man's assumptions, the earl mustered some force to his words. "*Now,* damn it. What are you waiting for? I'm not going anywhere. If I'm lying, you can return and cut out my liver at your leisure."

The sharpened steel scraped against his skin, then pulled back a fraction. "Very well. And if you are telling the truth, I'll see to it that you are released." Metal jangled against metal as Orlov dangled the key from his knifepoint. "I shall leave this here. Call it a gesture of goodwill." He hung it on one of the spikes sticking out from the wall.

"God, how odious to think I must hope that the enemy does not put a bullet or blade through your brain."

"Or my heart." Orlov patted his breast as he turned away. "Oh yes, I do have one, and as you see, it's quite a sensitive organ."

The slap stung her cheek. "Wake up."

Siena let out a whimper.

"Hit her again." Leveritt seemed to take pleasure in giving the order.

She opened her eyes and for an instant saw only hazy slabs of mossy stone.

The pistol jabbed into her ribs. "Climb up the steps." Jadwin forced her back against the parapet.

"Unless the Black Dove can, by some miracle, spread wings and fly, I advise you to say a last prayer," sneered Leveritt. Holding the document in gloating triumph, he waved it under her nose. "You should have been content with spreading your legs, you hen-witted little harlot, rather than trying to soar above your station in life. As you see now, a bit of feathered fluff is no match for a pair of eagles."

Siena swayed slightly, all the while gauging distances and trajectory. From her previous trip to the Tower, she knew there was a narrow ledge, perhaps fifteen feet below, where the stones of the crowning battlements jutted out to join the wider base walls of the castle.

A leap of faith, for in truth, she had never attempted anything half so dangerous.

"Jump," ordered Jadwin with a menacing wave of his weapon. "Else we will give you a helping hand."

May Merlin guide her flight.

As she dropped to a deep crouch, Siena snatched the document from Leveritt, then launched herself into a high back somersault. The instant her head cleared the top railing, she tightened her arc to bring her legs in line for a landing. Everything was spinning, a vortex of slivered stone and the jagged shadows of the ground below. No time for thought, for logic. She must trust in her intuition.

Her toes caught the lip of the ledge. Barely. She teetered for a moment, caught her balance and kicked out again, dropping down a few more feet in order to grab a handhold. From there, she could shimmy around the corner and swing into the shelter of the sentry niche carved into the center of the wall.

But the granite, weakened by age and the elements, crumbled beneath her grasp. Siena hit heavily against the mortised facing and began to slide down the rough stone. Somehow, her flailing hands snagged a crack, stopping her fall with a shuddering jolt. Hanging by her fingertips, she barely dared to breathe.

Jadwin fired. The bullet hit scant inches from her head, sending up an explosion of shards.

She heard Leveritt shout, "Don't be a fool. She's done for in any case. We must cut our losses and make a run for it."

Glancing down, Siena saw he was not far wrong. Her fingers were slowly slipping, and the drop was a straight plunge, with no other ledge or cornice stone to break her fall.

"Hold on!" cried a familiar voice.

No, it was the wind playing tricks against the stone. Her grip slipped another fraction. Or wishful thinking.

"Another moment, and I'll have a rope to you."

Shannon?

Siena hiked her chin up a notch, hardly believing her ears.

Sure enough, a knotted line slithered down the wall. She managed to grab hold and wrap it around her wrist. Setting her feet to the stone, she inched her way to the window opening.

"How the devil—" she began.

"You know the old saying. Birds of a feather flock together." Shannon took hold of her arm and pulled her into the shelter of the alcove. "You're hurt," added her friend, wasting no more time in preliminaries.

Siena brushed her off. "Never mind about that." Ignoring the blood on her face, she looked to the archway. "The traitors—they must not get away. But . . ." *Where was Kirtland?* Torn between duty and a desperate fear that the earl was in trouble, she let her voice trail off.

Shannon's face tightened to a mask of misgiving. "But *what*?" She leaned in close, so close that her bared knife blade touched Siena's breast. "Why do you hesitate? You haven't been seduced by the enemy, have you?"

"By all that is holy, no!" Her voice, she knew, was brittle, but it did not come close to cracking. "How could you ever think such a thing?"

"*I* didn't. But Lynsley fears the worst. He received word that you were in bed with the enemy."

Siena was glad that the darkness hid her telltale flush. "It was not what it appeared. The earl—the suspect—has turned out to be a trusted ally, a true friend." She drew in a ragged breath, straining to hear any sound of footsteps over the thudding of her heart. "The shot should have brought him running. I'm worried that something has happened to him."

She felt her friend stiffen. "Is he tall, dark, handsome as sin?"

"Yes," she whispered, her own muscles going taut.

"Damn." Shannon added another oath. "I think I saw him . . . being forced at knifepoint into the cellars by a blond Adonis—"

"*Where?*" She tried to keep her fear in check.

Shannon quickly described the exact location of the door. "If only I had known."

Siena wasted no time in recriminations. She broke away. "To hell with the others. I must help Kirtland. I have Lynsley's precious document. The culprits are no further danger to England. If he wants my head for letting them get away, he may have it on a platter."

"Leave them to me." Her friend pulled the pistol from her belt. "You had better take this, in case you run into the sun-kissed Satan."

"You keep it. I'll murder the devil with my bare hands if he's harmed Julian." She gave her fellow Merlin's arm a hard squeeze. "You are a true friend, Nonnie. Be careful. These men won't hesitate to use deadly force, and neither should you. I will explain everything later." Hesitating, she added, "There is a small statue of Athena in the gallery you just described. I shall hide the dispatch under its base." It was unnecessary to say any more.

Their eyes met in silent salute. "Godspeed," said Shannon. "And may Merlin's wings carry you safely through the night."

After watching Siena disappear into the darkness, Shannon turned and hurried down the circular stairs of the stone turret. She dared not pause to consult her sketch of the castle layout, but she recalled enough of the details to decide her best chance of intercepting the enemy lay on the floor below.

Easing the landing door open, she found herself in a long corridor. The flickering oil lamps, their flames turned down low for the night, cast barely enough light to make out the doorways lining both sides of the carpeted parquet. She paused to listen . . .

It was the gleam of golden hair that gave him away.

Shannon quickly slipped behind the suit of armor that stood guard in the Medieval Gallery, wondering how a man so tall and broad could move so noiselessly. His feet were like cat's paws on the carpet. Silent, stalking steps.

Her jaw hardened. The hunter was about to become the prey, she vowed, thinking of Siena's stricken face. Another few strides, and the Russian would be forced to answer for his misdeeds. She would see how *he* liked the bite of steel against his neck.

Tucking the pistol away, she drew her knife.

He slowed, but only slightly, as he passed her. Perhaps it was the faint sound of stirring in the central Tower that spurred him on. A murderer would not wish to be caught red-handed . . .

Her breathing stopped for an instant as she saw the

streak of blood on his sleeve. And then her lungs began to move, as did her feet. With a vengeance.

She feared the pounding of her pulse might give her away as she crept to within an arm's length of him. Ahead, the double doors opened to yet another bewildering maze of corridors. He would have to halt and survey the surroundings before choosing his next move.

He had scoffed at the notion of spirits and specters. *Ha!* Let him laugh now. He was about to discover that avenging angels did indeed tread the earth. She raised her knife, poised to strike.

Another step . . .

He whirled, quick as a wild dervish, and grabbed her wrist, giving it a wrenching turn that twisted sinew from bone.

Her blade slipped into his grip.

Biting back a scream of pain, Shannon spun out of his grasp and threw a hard punch at his kidney. It landed square on target.

Only to bounce off with a sickening thud.

"Well done," he said, touching the tip of her own dagger to her breast. "A perfect move, a well-aimed blow. I would be at your feet now, writhing in agony, save for a bit of luck on my part." It was only then that she saw the faint outline of a package beneath his coat. "That being said, I must ask you to step back and place your hands atop your head. Otherwise, I shall be forced to do something extremely ungentlemanly."

"Bloody bastard," she said as the prick of steel pressed deeper against her flesh.

Orlov gave an infuriating smile as he untied the coil of rope from her belt. "I've a thick skin, sweeting, so you may keep that sharp tongue of yours sheathed within those lovely lips."

"I'll do as you demand," she said through gritted teeth. "But only because Siena has sworn to kill you with her bare hands for murdering the earl. Hopefully, she'll allow me to watch."

"I left Lord Kirtland quite unharmed. Otherwise, I would be quaking in my boots." He grinned. "On the other hand, the thought of close combat with your comrade-in-arms does provoke a number of intriguing possibilities. I might just take my chances."

"Mortal combat," corrected Shannon. "You would not be intrigued. You would be dead."

He laughed, lightly and without malice. "Perhaps," he replied, raking her with a head-to-toe glance. "The rumors do not do you justice. Lord Lynsley's flock of Merlins is magnificent."

"Who are you working for, that you know about . . . us?" she demanded.

"Someone who has paid me to take him a bit of paper. Just not the one that everyone here thought. I take it your comrade recovered the document?"

"Yes." She took some small measure of satisfaction in telling him that.

"Ah, well, if I have to concede defeat on that score, it couldn't be to a lovelier opponent. Do give my apologies to Kirtland for any discomfort I have caused him." He paused. "And accept my sincere regret for your injury. I trust your wrist is not too painful. Had I known it was a young lady who was creeping up on me, I would never have taken advantage of the mismatch."

She fixed him with an icy glare.

Orlov shook out the rope and hammered the grappling hook into a lacquered Chinoise cabinet.

"I hope that isn't a priceless piece of Ming Dynasty art," she muttered, watching splinters fall to the floor. "I'm in enough trouble as it is."

"A later copy, not nearly as valuable." He shifted the knife to his other hand. "Tell your comrade not to be too angry with me. Indeed, I have done her a great service, which she shall soon discover."

With that cryptic statement, he leapt lightly to the windowsill, performed a jaunty bow, and disappeared into the night.

"Damn you to hell." Shannon rushed to ledge, hoping to rip the iron claws loose and send him plummeting to the ground. With any luck, he would break every damn bone in his arrogant body.

Fortune, however, was not on her side. Her hands hit the casement in frustration as she watched him lope away into the woods. A wolf, right down to the grinning gold earring she had spotted amid the tangle of fair hair. And to add insult to injury, the rogue had not only used her own rope to escape, but he had also taken her favorite knife—a silver-handled Andalusian beauty—as a parting memento of his triumph.

Someday, she vowed, he would pay for this night. And dearly.

But grudges would have to wait. There were other dangerous predators still on the prowl.

Chapter Twenty-Three

$\mathcal{F}$rom somewhere deep beneath his feet came a shuddering crack, then a gurgle that sounded like demonic laughter.

Kirtland's head snapped up. Was it only his imagination, or was the clammy air growing even damper? He had not long to wonder, for in a matter of minutes the guttering candle stub revealed a chilling sight.

The underground cistern was suddenly rising, and fast. The recent rains had been heavy, and one of the ancient sluice gates must have given way. Water was now licking at his boots. Uttering a low oath, he glanced at the spiral stairs, shadowed in gloom. Shouting, however, would only be a waste of breath. Buried deep within the bedrock of stone and mortar, the chamber would not allow a sound to escape.

Silent as a grave.

He would have to pray that the Russian, for all his faults, was a man of his word. His own pitiful efforts were proving mockingly useless. He twisted again at the chains, but the metal, though pitted with age, held fast in the stone. His wrists were raw, bleeding.

The water, cold and dirty, was now to his thighs.

With a faint sputter, the wick gave up the last of its light, leaving him shrouded in darkness. It was, he thought, an irony that his life was to be snuffed out now, just when a spark had been lit within. His regrets were not for the past, only the future.

But at present, one mistake overshadowed all the others. He wished he had told Siena that he loved her. He wished he had said the sentiment aloud, no matter how strange it felt on his tongue. Lud, he was fluent in so many languages, ancient and modern, and yet the one word—a single syllable—had proved so diabolically difficult to master.

Love.

He found it was not so very hard after all.

"Love," he whispered, and somehow its echo rose above the roiling waters.

"*Amore.*" It sounded even lovelier in Italian.

Damn. He wished he had shouted it from the battlements, signaling an end to the siege of loneliness and bitterness that had kept him in hiding within himself.

Too little. Too late. But there was still a ray of hope for Siena. Perhaps Orlov could help her escape to Italy, and she would have a chance to see her namesake city. To experience its magical Tuscan light, its monumental beauty, its glorious art.

He smiled, but the idea of her experiencing it with another was cold comfort indeed.

Siena hesitated on the landing. Orders were orders. Lynsley had made it clear that the document was all that mattered, whatever the cost. Her head called for a retreat. Yet her heart rebelled against leaving a comrade on the field of battle.

And heart was everything.

She had been true to her code, her country. She drew a steadying breath. For that to have any real meaning, she must also be true to herself.

Lynsley, she hoped, would understand.

Wrenching open the door to a side stairwell, she raced down two flights and cut across the central entrance hall, taking care not to rouse the sleeping porter. She had just reached the corridor connecting the Tower with the East Wing when a piercing cry shattered the stillness of night.

"They are gone!"

Flattening herself against the wall, she saw the butler, his shirttails hanging loose from half-buttoned trousers, come rushing down the main stairs, brandishing a cudgel.

In his wake stumbled a half dozen footmen, some still in their nightshirts.

"Spread out," he bellowed. "Search the woods. Find them!"

Siena did not pause to puzzle out how or why the hue and cry had been raised so quickly for the two men. Leveritt and Jadwin were no longer of primary concern. In the commotion, she slipped through the side portico and up the East Wing stairs, taking the treads two at a time. It was the enigmatic Russian whose motives stirred a sense of dread. No doubt there was a rationale behind all his actions. She should be able to figure it out. But the pumping of her heart drowned out all logical thought.

Let Kirtland be alive, she prayed, her cheeks suddenly wet with tears.

Knocking aside a potted palm, she vaulted over the

banister and charged down the side corridor. A marble
faun teetered as she pushed through the Greek antiquities.
Ignoring the thud, she ducked under the snaking tendrils
of a stone Medusa and darted into the alcove.

Pausing only long enough to secrete Lynsley's dispatch
beneath the marble Athena, Siena kicked at the door, but
the lock, thick with rust, was stuck in place. *Improvise,*
Volpina! It was one of Da Rimini's favorite refrains. A
look over her shoulder showed a row of classical deities.
Uttering a silent prayer, she hoisted a bust of Mars and
ran back at full tilt, ramming it headfirst into the paneled
oak.

A last tug freed the bolt from the shattered molding,
and she slipped through the crack. It was pitch-black, and
the stairs were slippery with mold, slowing her pace to
a maddening crawl. Shivering, she struggled to strike a
flint to the candle she had grabbed from one of the wall
sconces. The sound of roiling water rose up from the circular stone well, like the rumblings of some malevolent
serpent. Dizzy with fear, she cried out his name.

"Kirtland!"

No answer, save for the deathly pounding in her ears.

"JULIAN!"

"HISSSSSSSSSS." Was the faint echo naught but a
mocking taunt?

Light flared as the wick caught a spark, and with it
a ray of hope that she was not too late. "Hold on! I'm
coming."

Water, black as ink, lapped over the last step. The weak
pool of light showed swirling currents . . . a hand half-
submerged . . . then another. And between them an upturned brow, pale as death.

Wedging the candle between the stones, Siena plunged

in. The cold hit her like a fist, driving the air from her lungs. Gasping in shock, she drew on her yoga training to regain control of her breath. *Mind over matter.* Ignoring the pain, she fought her way through the eddying vortex. The swirling waters were disorienting, but she kept her focus on the far wall. Finally, her numbed hands framed the earl's face and lifted it above the brackish current.

"N-now who is riding to the rescue," said Kirtland through chattering teeth. His lips barely moved; his flesh felt like ice beneath her touch. "T-too dangerous. Leave me, before the cold saps your strength. Your duty is to—"

"Damn duty!" One hand holding him up, Siena struck frantically at the chain bolts with her knife, but the stone was unyielding to her steel.

"The key," he managed to whisper. "Hanging there."

The light was dying fast, and in the dance of deathly shadows, she nearly missed its jagged outlines. "Hold your breath," she shouted in his ear. "Don't you dare give up the ghost now, my love, or I swear, I shall follow you to hell and duel with the devil to get you back."

She didn't dare wait a fraction longer. Clawing her way along the stones, Siena snatched the ring just as the water swallowed the spike.

Fingers fumbling, freezing, she jabbed blindly at the manacle lock. *Your thrusts must be strong and steady,* Volpina. She had fought fear and fatigue before, she reminded herself. Keep a steel wrist, an iron will.

The first cuff surrendered with a dull *click.*

Siena nearly sobbed at the sweet sound. "One more moment," she cried, attacking the next one with renewed fury. The earl had not responded. His head, now slumped against her shoulder, was like a deadweight . . .

No, she would not think of defeat. Not now.

Pain shot through her hands as her skin scraped stone and metal.

"*Twice or thrice had I loved thee, Before I knew thy face or name,*" she gasped, repeating a bit of the poetry he had recited to her. Her strength was ebbing.

"*I bid Love ask, and now, That it assume thy body . . .*" His breath, a mere zephyr, stirred a faint warmth.

Resolve. Redemption. She found the opening and drove the key home.

The shackles fell away.

"Kick!" she urged, striking out in what she hoped was the right direction. It was now pitch-black, and the whirling, slurping crosscurrents had grown even more disorienting. "Kick!" She could not hope to keep them both above water for much longer.

By some miracle, her feet found the submerged stairs, and she summoned a last burst of energy to drag Kirtland up the first bend and out of immediate danger.

"Julian!" Brushing back the tangle of wet strands, Siena pressed her lips to his brow. "Damn it, don't leave me." She kissed the drops from his lashes, the hollow of his cheek, the dark stubbling of his jaw. "I fear I could not bear it, my love."

The endearments gained added force as her fist pushed down hard between his ribs.

A weak sputter, but it was enough.

"Julian."

"Lud, I've come close enough to drowning without having yet more water splashed on my face." His mouth curved beneath hers, his smile tasting of her salt.

"I seem to have turned into a watering pot. Just like some silly, simpering schoolgirl."

"Are you really crying?"

"Yes." Embarrassed, she tried to pull away. "No."

Kirtland caught her hand and kept it hard on his heart. His sodden shirt was like ice entwined in her fingers, but the thud of his flesh pulsed with heat. "Was I delirious, or did you say 'love' just now?"

Why deny it? "Yes. God help me, I have tried to fight it, but I do love you, Julian. More than I can say." Siena was trembling, and not from the chill air. The truth was, after tonight, they would go their own separate ways. He was a lord, and she was most definitely not a lady. She had no illusions about what that meant. "Not that it matters."

He whispered something, too softly for her to hear.

"Come, we must get you into dry clothes and in front of a fire," she urged. "Exposure can kill as surely as a sword thrust."

"You, too, are shivering, so I will wait a bit longer before stripping my soul bare, my valiant Valkyrie. I wish to see your lovely face and luminous smile when I speak of . . . of feelings I have kept hidden away for too long."

The door was slightly ajar. Shannon eased through the crack and quickly crossed to the shadow of the large pianoforte. *The Music Room.* Slowly, silently, she crept forward. A gilded harp, spectral in the scudding starlight, cast a delicate weaving of dark lines across the carpet.

But not dark enough to obscure the figure crouched by the open terrace doors.

Her hand shot to her boot and withdrew the hidden stiletto. Stealing another step closer, she angled its edge a touch higher—

The clouds shifted, and for a fleeting moment the figure's face was shown in clearer relief.

Their eyes met.

"Sir!" A strangled whisper slipped from her lips. "W—what are *you* doing here?"

"I might ask the same of you." Wiping the blood from his fingers, Lynsley stood up. "Your handiwork?"

"No, sir." Shannon looked away from the two bodies lying by the threshold. Leveritt, whose throat had been cut, was sprawled beneath his fellow club member. Jadwin, too, was dead, a knife sunk to its hilt in its heart. "Nor that of Siena," she hastened to add. "Indeed, I am quite certain it was the work of another guest, a fair-haired gentleman with a trace of a foreign accent."

"Hmmm." The marquess carefully folded his ruined handkerchief and tucked it in his pocket. "Where is he now?"

"Gone, sir. I'm afraid I let him get away."

A silence, save for the faraway shouts from the gardens. "Which leaves just you here for me to deal with."

Her chin rose. "Yes. And I'm fully prepared to take the consequences for my actions."

"You disobeyed an order."

"Actually, I did not. No one specifically said I was not to help my comrade."

"That's rather splitting hairs."

"Yes, sir. But given that Siena's head was in danger, I thought it the lesser of two evils." She rubbed at her wrist. It ached abominably, as did the idea of being drummed out of the Academy. Even so, she could not regret her actions. "If you wish to court-martial me, I understand."

"Discipline is the cornerstone of our organization, Shannon. Without it, we cannot hope to succeed in our missions."

"So is loyalty, sir," she said softly. "And the ability to make difficult decisions in the blink of an eye."

A knock sounded on the door.

He sighed. "We shall have to continue this discussion later. My carriage is down by the gatekeeper's cottage. Wait for me there. And do have a care not to be seen. I have enough to smooth over with the local authorities without having to explain a fully armed female Fury prowling the grounds."

"Yes, sir." She hesitated just a fraction. "Just so you know, Siena succeeded in her mission—she has whatever it was you sent her to find."

Lynsley gave a tiny nod. He waited until she had vaulted the terrace railing before admitting the magistrates, two neighboring squires who had been roused from their beds by his messenger.

"Dirty business," muttered one of the gentlemen, quickly averting his eyes from the pooling blood.

His associate, one hand holding back a retch, could only nod.

"Any idea what happened, milord?"

"I did not arrive soon enough to witness what actually transpired, but it appears that the two gentlemen quarreled, and it took a violent turn," answered Lynsley. "From the angle of the bodies, I would guess that during the struggle for the knife, a wild slash to the neck felled the unfortunate Lord Leveritt . . ." An earlier rearranging of the original positions now supported the surmise. "And though in his death throes, he managed to knock down the fleeing Lord Jadwin, who must have stumbled and fallen on his own weapon."

If either of the two magistrates bothered to look closely, he would see a number of details that contradicted such a scenario. There had been little time to create a more elaborate cover-up of the murders and eliminate the telltale signs of a third party. Lynsley could only hope that his own government position would distract the other men from too careful a scrutiny.

His strategy seemed to pay off, for the next comment was a brusque cough. "So it seems to me as well, milord."

"Aye. Tempers can flare when gentlemen are in their cups," added the whey-faced squire. He eyed the bottles of brandy that the marquess had added to the room. "A dirty business, indeed."

"And likely to become even messier, given the identities of the deceased." Lynsley pursed his lips. "That is, unless we move to handle the matter quickly and discreetly."

The two men exchanged baleful looks. "God preserve the duke and our district from scandal."

"I cannot offer divine intervention, but if you like, I may be able to offer some assistance in keeping this matter quiet. My position at the ministry has given me some experience in dealing with unpleasant matters."

"Harrumph." After a few moments of huddled conference, the magistrates accepted the offer without further question.

"Then you may leave all the details to me." In fact, Lynsley already had Oban making arrangements for the removal of the bodies to London. By first light, he planned to have all traces of the crime, along with any potentially embarrassing evidence from the rooms of Leveritt and Jadwin, removed from Marquand Castle. "As there are no eyewitnesses, I'm sure that a written statement from the duke's secretary should suffice for your records. I'll see that it is transcribed and sent to you by the morrow."

"How fortunate for us, milord, that you happened to be in the neighborhood."

"Yes, fortunate indeed," replied Lynsley blandly. "After dining with friends at the Blue Boar Inn, I felt the need to ride out and clear my head. As luck would have it, I chanced to hear shouting from the woods and came to investigate."

"Luck," repeated the whey-faced squire. "What a night!" He pressed a handkerchief to his lips. "Er, is there any reason for us to remain here? It seems we also have a theft to deal with. Someone has made off with a pair of the duke's precious books."

"None at all."

Nodding gratefully, both magistrates were quick to retreat and leave the marquess to the gruesome task of tidying up.

The worst was over, mused Lynsley as he sidestepped a darkening pool of blood and took a seat upon the window ledge. Judging from Shannon's report, the mission had, against all the odds, been accomplished. There were just a few loose ends to tie up.

Chapter Twenty-Four

I assume you are waiting for this, sir." Looking more like a waif than a warrior with an old holland cover draped around her shoulders, Siena handed over the document. On discovering the house in an uproar when they emerged from the cellars, she had refused all suggestions of blankets and brandy, demanding instead to report immediately to the marquess, whose presence had been mentioned by the agitated butler.

Lynsley took a cursory look beneath the wax wafer, then tucked it into his coat. "Well done," he murmured.

"Is that all you have to say?" growled the earl.

Siena, bruised and bleeding from the cheek, managed only a lopsided grimace. "Julian—"

Kirtland shook her restraining hand from his sleeve. "Nothing more? No *bon mot,* no pithy pearls of wisdom?"

The marquess's show of placid patience was far more provoking than any retort.

"Then allow *me* to express my sentiments." The punch, a right cross to the jaw, knocked Lynsley to the floor. "*That* is for sending Siena alone into a nest of vipers, knowing full well the dangers." He rubbed at his bruised knuckles. "The next one will be for questioning her loyalty. And mine."

"I can't say I blame you for being upset." Lynsley still wore a look of unruffled calm. "I don't like it any more than you do, but I do what I must. Some things are worth fighting for."

Slanting a look at Siena, the earl could not help but agree.

The marquess got to his feet, rather more quickly than Kirtland expected. Perhaps Osborne had not exaggerated the cursed fellow's credentials. His movements seemed a great deal more nimble than those of any deskbound bureaucrat. "It isn't often that I am delighted to discover that I was wrong," went on Lynsley as he dusted the seat of his trousers. "My apologies to you, Kirtland. Might we declare a truce before any more shots are fired?"

"You ought to be apologizing to Siena," he muttered. "She is the true hero of all this."

"Indeed. She has come through with flying colors. A true Merlin." Lynsley turned slightly. "I will need a full report, of course, but it can wait until morning." He angled a glance at the two corpses. "As you see, I have several more pressing matters to clear up. The physical evidence must be removed, and an explanation for the events must be decided on. Though I confess I am still searching for one that will suit."

"You might call it a lover's quarrel," ventured Siena.

Lynsley blinked. "An interesting suggestion. That would certainly be grist for the gossip mills. Especially if there is a grain of truth to the story."

"There is, sir."

"Again, you have made my job a little easier."

"Speaking of which." Siena could not contain her curiosity. "How *did* you come to be here?"

"Having heard conflicting reports about your actions, I thought it best to come see for myself. I have been enjoying a few days of leisurely fishing along the River Ex. While at night Oban and I have been keeping watch on the castle. I told the magistrates that I heard shouting while out for a late ride and came to offer my assistance." Lynsley turned.

"Sir—a last question. Did Shannon . . ."

The marquess shook his head. "No. Not that I would not consider it a black mark against her if she had. It seems it was Orlov who administered the coups dc grace."

"Orlov?" she exclaimed. Kirtland saw a war of emotions wage across her features. He suspected she had a softer spot for the rogue than she cared to admit. "But why?" she asked, half to herself.

"For the same reasons as you," answered the earl. "He told me he had been hired to steal the government dispatch and was willing to go to any extremes to get it."

"Then why didn't he simply cut your throat and come after me?"

"I do not pretend to understand what game he was playing," replied Kirtland. An inquiring look at Lynsley elicited naught but a shrug. "He did, however, claim it was to keep it out of the hands of the French."

"Perhaps. Then again, there is the chance that he was using the document as a distraction, and his true intentions were always to steal the Psalters," said the marquess in answer to the unspoken question. "They have, by the by, disappeared. As has Orlov."

"The devil you say!" Was it a touch of jealousy that gave an extra edge to his disappointment? Kirtland decided he was in no frame of mind to grapple with that question. "It seems I have more than one score to settle with that spawn of Satan."

"Whether he is in league with Lucifer or not, the fellow has proved hellishly hard to pin down," said Lynsley with a tight-lipped grimace. "My sources still cannot say whom—if anyone—he is working for. And though I have sent out alerts to the towns along the coast, I doubt we shall catch him."

All thoughts of the Psalters were suddenly forgotten as he watched Siena's face. No gold-leafed Madonna, no pigment made of powdered jewels was half so precious to him as the curl of her dark lashes, the curve of her lips. The courage of her convictions.

The earl suddenly quirked a smile. "It doesn't matter."

Her eyes widened slightly.

"Let him have the blasted books and be damned. Considering the stakes, I consider myself the winner by far."

Lynsley looked thoughtfully to Siena and back again. "Your personal loss has been England's gain."

"We shall see," he said, a reply that won a cryptic smile from the marquess. "The final tally has yet to be made."

"If punishment is to be dealt . . ." Siena's voice dropped a notch. "I should not be here if not for Shannon. Nor would the dispatch. I know that her passions sometimes get the better of her. But she has the heart of a Merlin. Please do not clip her wings."

"She said much the same of you." The marquess clasped his hands behind his back. "I shall take your support into account when making my final decision."

"Might I add—"

Kirtland touched her arm. "Duty can wait until dawn."

"But—"

He cut her off with a request of his own. "If you don't mind, Lynsley, I would like a few words in private with Siena."

"Of course." The marquess coughed. "But before I go, I would like to extend one last apology, Kirtland. And an offer. That is, if you would consider putting your considerable talents to future use for your country."

Still a bit wary of Lynsley's wiles, the earl was slow to answer. "How so?"

Strangely enough, the marquess was looking at Siena rather than at him. "There is a good deal of unrest in Italy at the moment. I could use an experienced eye to take a firsthand look around and report on the situation. Seeing as the two of you seem to work well together, I am hoping you might agree to continue as a team. A rich gentleman taking the Grand Tour would be the perfect cover. And a female companion would add to the appearance of its being merely a personal pleasure trip."

"You are proposing that Siena and I take on another mission?"

The marquess replied with a straight face, but Kirtland thought he detected a shade of a smile. "Just a thought. In case it might dovetail with a more private proposal."

"Two birds with one stone?" The earl arched a brow.

"In a manner of speaking." There was now no mistaking the twitch of Lynsley's lips. "No need for an answer right now. I will leave the two of you to talk it over."

A brief bow, and he was gone, leaving only the echo of his last words.

Siena seemed hardly aware of them as she continued to fret over her comrade's future, rather than her own. "If I have caused Shannon to lose—"

Kirtland silenced any further recriminations by sweeping her up in his arms. "Enough, *amore*. You have done your duty. And far more." Seeing that he had her full attention, he followed in Lynsley's footsteps and hurried through the door. "From what you have told me, your friend is quite capable of fighting her own battles. Right now, I don't want to speak of war, or of others, but of *us*."

Whether it was the dizzying pace as he veered off sharply and started up the stairs, or the fact that his lips were teasing a trail of kisses across the nape of her neck, Siena replied with only a soft sigh. He reached the first landing before she recovered enough of her equilibrium to speak.

"D—did you just say 'love' in Italian?"

"Would you care to hear it in Greek or Latin? Mitteldeutch? I can even manage it in Russian—*lubov*."

"I would rather hear it in plain English." Her fingers threaded through his still-damp hair, twining them closer. Their cheeks touched. "Unless, of course, you are merely playing word games."

"It is no game, Siena. It never has been, this powerful attraction that had drawn us together from the very first."

"Magic. There is no other word for it."

"Yes, there is." He spun in a circle, his heart feeling light as a feather. "Love."

"Julian—"

"Ah, that's another word that sounds delightful on your lips. Say them both again, Siena. Together, in concert, if you please."

"I love you, Julian."

Sweet music to his ear. For all the cuts and bruises, the shivering doubts and painful memories, his world was suddenly in perfect harmony. "And you, my midnight merlin, are the light of my life. I love you."

* * *

The sparkle of his eyes, the lilt of his laugh. It was, she knew, a moment she would always treasure, no matter how quickly it might pass. No one had ever said those three words to her before. Nor had she ever uttered them aloud. Such a simple string of letters. How was it they changed everything?

Everything and nothing. They dwelled in different worlds. He lived in light, she in shadow. Their paths from here must eventually take them apart.

And yet . . .

She stifled such wishful thinking in a small sigh. Lynsley's proposal, however enticing, would only prolong the moment.

"Just a little longer." Kirtland seemed to sense the tension taking hold of her. "We are almost there."

"W—where are you taking me?"

"To your bedchamber. You need warm blankets and a swallow of brandy to bring the color back to your cheeks." He grinned, looking sinfully handsome despite his disheveled state. "And perhaps a bout of heated lovemaking, once I have your glorious limbs tucked in among the silk sheets and eiderdown pillows."

Her eyes clouded, dimming for an instant the gleam of his gaze. What else could he offer her but to continue in the role of a courtesan? It was, after all, what the marquess had suggested. The prospect should not hurt, but it did. "You are asking me to be your mistress?"

He pressed a kiss to her brow. "I am asking you to be my wife, Siena."

"The earl and the urchin?" She dared not let hope take wing. "Or worse, the lord and the lightskirt. Think of the scandal. Your name would be savaged by the gossips. You can make so much higher a match."

"I have weathered far worse slander. Let the tabbies talk. You know how little I care for their opinion." He stopped, set her down, and took her face between his hands. They were rough yet warm, scarred, yet strong. So like the rest of him. "I learned on the battlefield that title and pedigree mean nothing. It is heart and soul that are the true measures of a man—and a woman."

"The challenges will be daunting."

"Perhaps. We are both unused to letting down our guard. Expressing our feelings does not come so easily as wielding a sword to keep others at a distance. But I am willing to try. What say you, Siena? I think we match up quite well—I shall teach you a proper *rompere di misura*, and you shall show me the footwork of a tai chi flying dragon."

She started to speak.

"There is just one catch."

Her lips stilled.

"We shall have to put off a conventional wedding trip until later. I would like to take up Lynsley's offer of the Italian mission. The chance to serve King and country plays some part in the decision, but I have some very selfish reasons as well. I want to ride through the streets of Siena with you, meander through piazzas of Florence, float along the canals of Venice, with arias of *amore* serenading our ears." His face was alight with a warmth that no Renaissance master could ever capture with paint and canvas. "What say you?"

"Yes." Siena wished to sing to the heavens, but barely managed a whisper.

"To Italy or to me?"

"I think," she said softly, "that both sound wonderful beyond words."

Epilogue

Coals cracked in the hearth, setting up a cheery blaze that was only partially blocked by the great mass of grey fur curled in front of the hearth.

"Good of you to share a spark or two with us," murmured the earl as he settled down upon the sofa and propped his boots on a stack of books.

Mephisto raised his shaggy head and gave a low *woof*.

Kirtland smiled, a sigh of contentment slipping from his own lips. He did not need any outward spark to warm his bones. He had an inner flame.

The fire within.

Not bad for a first line of poetry. Perhaps he would take a stab at writing an ode to his new bride, though her singular spirit seemed to defy description in mere words. It would, he decided, take a lifetime for her moods, her mysteries to become commonplace. Maybe two.

"I am waiting." Siena's raven tresses tickled his cheek as she leaned her head on his shoulder. "A teacher should not be tardy to his own class."

"Where did we leave off?"

"William Blake." She handed him the book. "*Songs of Innocence and Experience.*"

"Hmmm. I'm afraid we were neither last night. If I recall correctly, the lesson on meter came to a rather abrupt end when the pupil insisted on asking for a more detailed demonstration."

"Do not deny your experience, my lord. You seemed quite conversant on the subject."

"With you, it takes on a whole new meaning. However, at this rate, it will take us quite some time to cover all the basics of English poetry."

"I will try not to distract you again," she said primly. "I am beginning to understand the nuances of coupling rhymes."

"Rhyming couplets." He grinned.

"What are we studying tonight?"

"I'm sure I'll come up with an interesting topic once we begin." He hesitated a fraction. "You are sure that you are not growing too bored with books? Lynsley promises we shall soon be leaving for Lombardy."

"You could never be boring, Julian." Curling her fingers with his, she lifted his hand to her lips. "I love learning more about art and literature, though I do confess that I am looking forward to testing my mettle in a new mission."

His palm cupped her chin. "But this time we go together from the start. You will never again face danger alone, Siena. Never."

"Together," she whispered. "I never dreamed such an ordinary word could sound so poetic."

After a last, lingering caress, Kirtland cleared his throat and opened the leather-bound volume. But instead of his silver bookmark between the pages, he found a folded piece of vellum.

Eyes narrowing, he smoothed it open.

If you are still interested in a certain collection of manuscripts, I am of the opinion that they would be most at home in the library of someone who appreciates beauty and intelligence. It will, of course, cost you, but no more than you were willing to spend in the first place. If the offer is agreeable to you, bring a portmanteau with the money to The Hanged Man Tavern on Wilmot Lane, tomorrow at precisely 4 in the afternoon. Ask for the room of Mr. Smythe. Leave it there. The books will arrive at your town house later that evening.

You will have to take a leap of faith. The question is, who do you trust?

It was signed with a slashing "O" written in red ink. Below it was a postscript.

By the by, felicitations on your recent nuptials. Your bride is indeed a most remarkable lady. Indeed, were I ever to find her match, I might even consider matrimony myself—a state I have assiduously avoided at all costs. But the odds are, I will enjoy my bachelorhood until I shuffle off this mortal coil.

"I'll be damned," muttered Kirtland.

"That does not rhyme." Brows quirked, Siena looked up.

He handed the note to her.

"Hmmm." Her expression was equally inscrutable.

"Perhaps Lynsley can nab him," mused the earl.

She thought for several moments. "Do you want the manuscripts?"

He made a wry face. "Pragmatic, as always, my love. Are you suggesting that I ignore the possibility of capturing the rascal and simply hand over the amount he is asking for?"

"Why not?" Siena pursed her lips. "I don't think Lynsley would disagree. The matter is finished, and Orlov, for all his faults, did us a favor." She tilted back her chin, and batted her lashes. "Do you, perchance, hold a grudge?"

"No doubt I am being terribly petty to feel just a touch of resentment toward a man who tried to feed me to the duke's trout."

She laughed, a carefree sound that warmed his heart. "He *did* say he was sorry. As for feeling any hesitation over edging out the other bidders, consider the Psalters a reward of sorts from a grateful government. Do you mind that you must bear the actual cost?" A mischievous smile played on her lips. "Perhaps I could put in a voucher for expenses."

Kirtland chuckled. "The expression on Lynsley's face would be priceless. But no, I will not ask the government to pay a penny. I will consider it my penance for past mistakes to pay Orlov's price. And then, of course, I shall have to settle up with the duke."

"Are you sure the cost is not too high?"

"You, my brave and bold avenging angel, are worth every illuminated manuscript in Christendom." He kissed her upturned lips. "How could I begrudge the cost of the Psalters—even if it's going to that imp of Satan—when you turned out to be the answer to all my prayers?"

About the Author

ANDREA PICKENS started creating books at the age of five, or so her mother tells her. And she has the proof—a neatly penciled story, the pages lavishly illustrated with full-color crayon drawings of horses and bound with staples—to back up her claim. Andrea has since moved on from Westerns to writing about Regency England, a time and place that has captured her imagination ever since she opened the covers of *Pride and Prejudice.*

A graduate of Yale University, she works in New York City as the Creative Director of a lifestyle sporting magazine, a job that lets her combine her love of the printed word with her master's degree in Graphic Design. Her work lets her travel to a number of interesting destinations around the world—but her favorite spot is, of course, London, where the funky antique markets and used-book stores offer a wealth of inspiration for her stories.

Please visit Andrea's Web site at www.andreapickens online.com. She loves to hear from her readers!

Enjoy a sneak peek of
Andrea Pickens's
sizzling new romance!

Please turn this page
for a preview of

SEDUCED BY A SPY

AVAILABLE IN SPRING 2008.

Chapter One

*T*he wind whipped against her cheeks, a hard, biting cold that cut down to the bone. Ignoring the pain, Shannon ducked low in the saddle and spurred her lathered stallion toward the high stone fence.

"Fly, Ajax, fly," she whispered, feeling her own muscles tense at the sight of the rocks standing in sharp silhouette against the scudding mists. "NOW!"

Soaring high into the air, the big animal hung for a heartbeat above the jagged teeth before thundering back down to earth in a blur of heaving flanks and flailing hooves. The ground was slick with rain, and the stallion stumbled, but Shannon gathered the reins, steadied its head, and angled for the narrow path between oak trees.

Faster. Faster. A mere fraction of a second could make the difference between life and death.

Despite the chill, her face was sheened in sweat. *The gun.* Surely it was just up ahead, where the trees thinned to a small clearing. Straining, she caught sight of the telltale glimmer of steel among the fallen leaves.

Shannon leaned forward. Gripping the leather pommel with one hand, she kicked a leg free of its stirrup and swung low. Thorns scraped her fingers, but she managed to snag the weapon. A hard twist, a turn of her hips, and she was back upright.

Steady. Steady. No mistakes—not now. Not with all that was riding on her ability. Her pulse was racing nearly as fast as her stallion's gallop. Her heart thudded against her ribs, its rapid-fire beat echoing the cacophony of pounding hooves and snapping twigs. Drawing a deep breath, she willed herself to see only the leering face up ahead—the coal-dark eyes, the menacing snarl, the broad bulk of shoulders cloaked in black . . .

Without hesitation, Shannon took aim and squeezed off a shot.

A hoarse cry rang out as the bullet exploded, tearing a gaping hole in the figure's chest. She slowed to a trot and circled back, the acrid smoke of the gunpowder still heavy in the air. From the corner of her eye, she caught a ripple of movement in the trees. A young man stepped out from the sheltering branches.

"Is he dead?" she demanded as he crouched down over the jumble of cloth.

"Dead as a doornail." Giovanni grinned as he poked at the singed straw. A tall, well-muscled Milanese mercenary, he served as the Academy's assistant riding instructor. "*Bravissimo.* You hit him square in the heart."

"No real harm done." She repressed a twitch of her lips. "Jem will fashion him a new one by morning."

"*Sì,* but God help any flesh-and-blood enemy who stands in your path." He consulted his pocket chronometer, and the pearly flash of teeth stretched wider. "A *magnifico* time, *Signorina* Shannon." He gave a jaunty salute as he snapped the gold case shut. "You've shaved another second off the Academy record. None of the other students come close to matching your equestrian skills." Standing in profile accentuated the artful tumble of his dark hair. It curled in Renaissance ringlets around his open collar, looking soft as silk in contrast to the sculpted muscles of his broad shoulders. The very picture of masculine beauty.

And well he knows it, she thought wryly. The Academy—a small school hidden in the pastoral countryside outside of London—required both its teachers and students to possess a unique range of talents. Giovanni was apparently picked not only for his finely honed skills in riding and fencing, but also for his perfectly chiseled body. The young Italian was often called upon to model for the advanced drawing classes, a position he flaunted with shameless bravado.

Giovanni held his pose for a touch longer before turning with a suggestive cock of his hips. "Now, if you wish to have expert instruction in the art of swordplay, come by my quarters after supper. A private tutorial is yours for the asking.

"Steel yourself for disappointment. If we crossed blades, you would not come out on top."

"All the better, *bella.*"

"I doubt you would be singing the same tune as a castrato."

Giovanni accepted the set-down with a good-natured laugh. "I can't help myself, *cara.* We Italians are born with a lively appreciation for beauty."

"Keep your lively appreciation buttoned in your breeches. Mr. Gravely would not be at all amused if he were to get wind of you trying to cut a swath through his students."

His face lost a touch of its waggish cant. "*Porca miseria!* You won't . . . hay on me, will you, *Signorina?*"

She bit back a laugh. "No, I won't grass on you, Giovanni. I stand by a friend. Even when his boudoir braggadocio threatens to get out of hand."

"*Sì.* We all know of your steadfast loyalty." Suddenly serious, he kicked at a wisp of straw. "It is a pity that *Signorina* Siena has taken her leave from our ranks."

Shannon swallowed hard, trying hard not to dwell on the fact her own departure from the Academy might also be imminent. The difference was, her friend and former roommate Siena had taken up an even more challenging position, while she . . .

She looked away to the shadows, loath to let anyone see a flicker of pain in her eyes. She was, after all, one of the select few who had made it through to the Master Class. Its badge—a black-winged merlin tattooed just above her left breast—marked her as a hardened warrior, a trained killer.

Softer sentiments had no place in such an arsenal of talents.

"I miss her," mused Giovanni.

"As do I."

He slanted a searching look at her. "It will only take me a bit longer to finish up here. Wait, and I will ride back with you."

"If you don't mind, I'd rather go on alone."

Before he could argue, Shannon gave a flick of the reins and spurred her stallion for the stables. Her body relaxed, instinctively matching the rhythm of the canter. Would that she could exercise such easy mastery over her mind, she thought. Daredevil acrobatics came naturally to her. The steel of a sword or pistol fit her hand like a second skin. But when it came to controlling her tongue or her temper, she was awkward, unsure. Damnable inner demons, they seemed to have a will of their own.

"Bloody hell." The oath slipped from her lips as the whitewashed walls and peaked slate roofs of the stable took shape from out of the fog. Her fears, sharp and pointed as the weather vane crowning its center cupola, formed into a palpable presence in her chest. Like the talons of the weathered copper hawk, they clenched and would not let go.

Would Lord Lynsley expel her from the school? She had broken a frightening number of rules by interfering in another Merlin's mission. But as of yet, the marquess had been ominously silent as to her future.

Looking around her, Shannon felt regret, recriminations, dig even deeper. The shooting ranges, the fencing field, the spartan classrooms and dormitories—all were so achingly familiar. It was hard to imagine an existence outside the ivy-covered walls. After all, it had been home since . . . a life she did not care to remember.

The fears, the filth, the violence had been left behind in the slums of London. Even her real name, if ever she had possessed one, lay buried in the shadows. Like all new students, she had been ushered into the headmistress's office, a skinny, frightened little girl uncertain of what to expect. One of the first things Mrs. Merlin had done was show her an ornate globe, and as the orb was set to spinning, she had been told to pick out a name from the myriad cities dotting its surface.

A new name for the new world she was about to enter . . .

Seen from afar, Mrs. Merlin's Academy for Select Young Ladies was indistinguishable from the other boarding schools that polished highborn daughters of the English aristocracy into Diamonds of the *ton*. However, outward appearances could be deceiving. The difference was . . . day and night.

Shannon's grip tightened on the reins. Here, the students were not pampered young misses who were admitted on account of their family's pedigree and purse. They were streetwise orphans, handpicked by the Marquess of Lynsley from the rookeries of Southwark and St. Giles.

Shannon wondered what had he seen in her. A surly toughness that refused to knuckle under to the grim realities of the stews? Even as a small child, she had been awfully good with a blade.

With her fists and her fury, she had fought her way to the top of the class. Unlike the other finishing schools, the Academy's curriculum was not designed to cast its students in a rosy light but rather to thrust them into the heart of darkness. To be sure, there were instructors to teach dancing, deportment, and all the other social graces. But while other girls studied the art of watercolors, Merlin's Maidens studied the art of war. Their master classes included rigorous training in the traditional martial arts of fencing, shooting, and riding, along with the more exotic Eastern disciplines of self-defense and yoga.

Would that she had paid a touch more attention to the lessons on self-control. Action came so much easier than introspection.

Blinking the beads of moisture from her lashes, Shannon forced her chin up. She would not surrender to self-pity. Discipline, duty, and a dispassionate detachment from emotional excess—those were the rules that Merlin's Maidens swore by. If her superiors deemed her unworthy of the name, she would go out with her head held high.

Disobeying orders was a serious transgression. It was understood by all that a Merlin was on her own when dispatched on a mission. But on learning that her roommate was in dire danger while trying to trap a deadly traitor,

Shannon had slipped away from the Academy without permission in order to ride to the rescue.

But while she had violated the spirit, if not the letter, of the law, she could not truly say she was sorry. Part of the extensive training taught that in their profession, there were no rules. And so, she had obeyed her heart rather than the Hellion Handbook that each student was required to memorize.

Right and wrong. Discipline and duty. That her intervention helped defeat a dangerous traitor did not, according to the headmistress, diminish the gravity of the offense.

No one questioned her courage, merely her character.

"Shall I rub 'im down fer ye, Shannon?"

Roused from her reveries, she shook her head. "Thank you, Jem, but no. I shall see that Ajax has his oats before I go in to my own supper." She patted the stallion's sleek neck before slipping down from the saddle. Her legs wobbled a bit as her boots struck the cobbles. She had pushed herself at a punishing pace all afternoon— fencing, karate, and the cross-country shooting course. As if pain could make amends. But exhaustion kept her from thinking too much about the future.

Her hands were rough as well. Stiff with cold, they fumbled with the buckles of the bridle. "You will find barley vastly more tasty than hair," she murmured, fending off the velvety nuzzling to her neck. Ajax's nickering formed soft puffs of vapor in the twilight chill as she untangled the loosened strands of her chignon from the leather and brass.

After currying the stallion's coat to a gleaming chestnut sheen, she pitched a few forkfuls of hay into the stall and latched the door. Duty done, there was nothing to keep her from joining her comrades in the dining hall. And yet she lingered, loath to see the glimmer of sympathy in their eyes. Pity only piqued her wounded pride.

Dipping into the stone cistern, Shannon splashed a handful of water over her brow. Its ice was a well-needed slap in the face. She threw back her head, determined to shake off the maudlin mood, along with the grey grains of gunpowder still clinging to her cheeks.

"Need a hand?"

She watched her roommate slip out from the shadows. Sofia always appeared so assured, so elegant, moving with a natural grace that would have been right at home in the ballrooms of Mayfair—save for the foil and saber tucked under her arm.

"It looks like you have had a rough afternoon."

"Not bad."

"Don't beat yourself up. You made the decision you thought was right and would do it again in a heartbeat."

"Thanks for not saying I told you so." Shannon essayed a smile.

Sofia uttered an unladylike oath. "I'm not such a fair-weather friend as that." She quirked a wry grin. "Besides, it isn't as if I'm entirely innocent of wrongdoing. Giovanni still hasn't forgiven me for sneaking your stallion out of the stables."

"You are the best of comrades, Fifi. And you shouldered more than your share of the blame. I'm sorry you were stuck with so many demerits."

Her friend cut a jaunty flourish through the air. "I am learning a great deal about the fine points of weaponry, seeing I have been set to polish the whole damn armory."

She winced. "Lud, Da Rimini is a bastard—"

"Shannon!"

She snapped to attention at the sound of the stablemaster's stentorian shout. Hopkins did not often raise his voice above a growl. "Here, sir!" she answered.

"You are wanted in the headmistress's office."

Mrs. Merlin wished an audience? Her heart gave a lurch, hope warring with trepidation.

"NOW!"

Muddy boots and cockleburred buckskins did not help to inspire much confidence. She would have preferred to appear more polished and poised, rather than as a bedraggled gun rat.

"Good luck," murmured Sofia. "And Godspeed. You heard him—march!"

Turning smartly, Shannon maintained a military stride until rounding the barn door, then broke into a hell-for-leather run.

"*Na Zdorovie*."

Alexandr Orlov accepted the glass of clear spirits. "Cheers," he murmured, tossing back the potent vodka in one gulp.

Prince Yuri Feodor Yussapov, head of Special Intelligence Services for the Imperial Russian Ministry of War, chuckled as he switched to a bottle of ruby port and poured them both another round. "I trust you enjoyed your sojourn in England?"

"It had its high points, Yuri."

And its low ones as well. Orlov pursed his lips, aware of a slightly sour taste in the back of his mouth despite the sweetness of the wine. The covert mission had not gone quite as planned. In truth, he considered it somewhat of a personal failure, though the end result had proved satisfying to his superiors.

He had been dispatched to London to retrieve a stolen

document. The fragile alliance between England and Rus
sia depended on keeping it out of French hands, and the
Tsar had been unwilling to trust Whitehall's agents to ge
the job done.

Perhaps because not in the wildest flight of fancy would
anyone in Russian Intelligence have imagined what shape
and form the English counterattack would take.

Orlov stared moodily at his port. The paper had indeed
been found—but not by him. Though to be fair, he had
made a certain contribution to the success of the venture
The two traitors would not be sending any more state secrets across the Channel. Still, the thought of being out-
maneuvered by a rival operative stuck in his throat.

Swearing a silent oath, he drained the rest of his drink
in one gulp.

Never one to hold his punches, Yussapov threw in another sly jab. "Don't look so glum about being bested by
a female, *tovarisch*. Lord Lynsley's winged ladies are said
to be birds of a unique feather."

"They are that." Both he and the prince had been as-
tounded to discover that Whitehall's most trusted agents
were a secret force of highly trained women warriors.

And they were good. Damn good.

So was he. Yet it was only by the skin of his teeth that
he had eluded the embarrassment of being captured. Sitting here, in the comfort of the Stockholm embassy, it was
easy enough to crack jokes. But at the time, it had been
no laughing matter.

Taking up the prince's Cossack dagger, Orlov spun its
point upon the leather blotter. "However, you might have
given me—and Lord Lynsley—fair warning that the mission was a joint venture. As it was, the wrong man nearly
ended up with his throat cut."

"*Bah.*" Yussapov brushed off the retort with a cavalier wave. "All's well that ends well. Is that not how your famous Bard put it?"

"As I am half-Russian, I am wont to look at things from a more melancholy perspective," he replied dryly. "It is easy for you to laugh from the comfort of your stuffed armchair and sable lap robes, but the whole affair came dangerously close to disaster on account of not knowing who was friend and who was foe. If we are allies with the British, should we not try to work together a bit more closely?"

"We are uneasy allies, Alexandr. The Tsar is not quite certain he can trust the Mad King and his ministers."

"Still, it is cork-brained not to share intelligence with Whitehall." Light winked off the razored steel. "While we circle each other with daggers drawn, Napoleon's agents steal a march on us."

"You have a point." The prince stroked at his beard. "I shall raise the issue with His Imperial Highness."

Orlov felt marginally better for having voiced his opinion. Yet his mood remained surprisingly discontented given the superb quality of the aged port and Turkish cheroots. Leaning back, he propped a booted foot on the desk and, hoping to rid himself of his black humor as well, blew out a ring of smoke. It hung for an instant in the air, a perfect oval in harmony with itself, before disappearing in a sinuous swirl of ghostly vapor.

Ashes to ashes . . . What strange musings had come over him? His Slavic penchant for brooding introspection was usually balanced by the devil-may-care English side of his nature. His mother, a lively Yorkshire beauty, had proved a perfect foil for his Muscovite father's proclivity for solitary sulks.

Orlov drew in another lungful of the pungent tobacco. He was aware that many would say he had inherited the worst traits of both parents. His cynical outlook on life and acerbic wit offended most people. Deliberately, he conceded. He was the first to admit that he was an unprincipled scamp, a rapscallion rogue. A man possessing a finely honed sense of honor would have great difficulty doing the things he was called on to do. Lies, thievery, seduction . . . and yes, even murder. His conscience—if ever he had had one—was certainly long dead to remorse, recrimination.

"Another drink?" Yussapov was eyeing him strangely from beneath his shaggy silver brows. "You appear—how do the English say it?—red-deviled tonight."

"Blue-deviled, Yuri." Forcing a sardonic smile, Orlov held out his glass. "Stick to Russian if you wish to employ subtle sarcasm. It loses something in the translation."

"*Moi?* Sarcastic?" Assuming an air of injured innocence, the prince toyed with the fobs on his watch chain. "I am merely concerned for you, *tovarisch*. As a friend. fear that of late, we are asking too much of you."

Orlov nearly choked on a laugh. "I am greatly touched by your tender sentiment," he replied, after swallowing the port. "Not that I am fooled in the least by what motivates it. I take it you have another job?"

A flicker of hesitation and what seemed to be a flash of warmth. But Orlov quickly dismissed it as a quirk of the candlelight. Or a figment of his own overheated imagination. For when Yussapov spoke, it was with his usual ruthless candor. "As a matter of fact, yes. This one will not require your celebrated charm with women."

"You are skating on dangerous ice, Yuri," he growled. "That particular joke is wearing thin."

"You are in an odd mood." The prince folded his large

ands upon the desk. "But I shall take heed of the warning
nd skirt the issue—"

Orlov's glass thumped down beside the fallen dagger.

"My, my, such a sensitive skin tonight, *tovarisch*. But
ery well, I shall refrain from any further mischief." His
xpression sobered. "There is, after all, nothing remotely
musing about this next mission."

"Which is?"

"Our head of intelligence in Brussels was murdered
ast week. We have good reason to think it was done by
D'Etienne, the same fellow who dispatched the Prussian
nvoy in Warsaw."

"I have heard of him," murmured Orlov. "He is said to
be the most dangerous agent the French have. And very
good at what he does." A wry grimace thinned his lips.
"Apparently the rumors are not much exaggerated."

"Good, yes." Yussapov swirled his ruby port. "But not,
trust, as good as you."

Muscles tensing, he straightened in his chair. "What is
t you want me to do?"

"Kill him, of course."

"Of course," repeated Orlov softly.

"As you know, we have resumed negotiations with
England about forging an alliance between us and our
Eastern compatriots. D'Etienne hopes through murder
nd mayhem to disrupt any agreement between our
countries."

"Where is he now?"

"In Ireland. He's staying for several weeks to foment
rouble with the Irish nationals. From there, we believe
he is scheduled to move on to England, in order to assassinate Angus McAllister."

"The Scottish ballistics expert?" Orlov frowned. "That

would indeed be a blow to the British efforts to improve
their artillery units."

"So you understand the gravity of the situation."

He stared at the bloodred refractions of light from the
crystal. "You have no need to offer moral explanations. I
am far from fainthearted."

"You are human, Alexandr. As am I. I do not ask you
to take a life lightly," said Yussapov quietly. "But however
repugnant, the action may save a great many good men."

Orlov merely shrugged.

"You look tired, *tovarisch*."

"I'm not getting any younger," he snapped.

A wink of gold flashed in the candlelight as Yussapov
toyed with his signet ring. "Perhaps the time has come to
think of settling down. Of getting a wife."

"God. Forbid." He grimaced. "Can you really imagine
me legshackled to a proper little London belle or Muscovite miss?"

The prince contemplated the question. For all of five
seconds before giving a bark of laughter. "I confess, I cannot picture you leading such an ordinary life."

"Work may be a hard mistress, but it's far preferable
to the boredom of matrimony." A sardonic curl lingered
at the corners of his mouth. "I trust you have the logistics
for this assignment arranged."

"A sloop is ready to sail on the next tide."

"Ah, and here I thought I would have a chance to explore the Nordic delights of Stockholm. A pity—a blond
Valkyrie would be just the thing to appeal to a man of my
tastes." He rose. "Perhaps next time."

The prince pushed a packet of papers across the desk.
"All the background details are there, as well as maps and
a list of contacts."

Orlov slipped it into his coat pocket. "When do you
return to St. Petersburg?"

"I still have several more meetings with the Minister of
War and his deputies regarding the Polish question. After
that . . ." He shrugged. "God knows where I shall be. Like
you, I am dispatched to wherever it is necessary to fight
fire with fire."

"Do have a care not to get singed, Yuri."

"And you, Alexandr. Contrary to what you think, I am
sentimental old fool. I would be greatly upset to hear of
our demise. So do try to return in one piece rather than
to out in a blaze of glory."

THE DISH

Where authors give you the inside scoop!

♥ ♥ ♥ ♥ ♥ ♥ ♥ ♥ ♥ ♥ ♥ ♥ ♥ ♥ ♥

From the desk of Andrea Pickens

After watching all the old James Bond movies more times than I care to count, I began to think . . . why is it that the boys get to have all the fun? They always get to be the spies. Or the pirates. Swashbuckling swagger, daredevil heroics, drop-dead good looks—yes, Johnny Depp and Orlando Bloom cut a fine figure with their flashing swords, but I found myself secretly wanting Keira Knightley to pick up a saber and kick some ass, too. So, I decided to turn tradition on its ear and create a trio of leading ladies capable of beating the men at their own game.

Select Young Ladies, a secret school for Hellion Heroes. I chose to set it in Regency England because that era is so richly romantic. It was a world aswirl in silks, seduction, and the intrigue of the Napoleonic Wars. A time when old ideas were constantly clashing with new radical ones. What better place for an unconventional female to test her mettle?

Siena, the star of THE SPY WORE SILK (on sale now), is given a perilous assignment: unmask a clever traitor lurking among London's wealthiest peers before he strikes again. Her only clue is that the man she seeks belongs to an exclusive club of art collectors. And so, armed with only her wits, her blades, and her body, she journeys to a remote castle where the club's members have gathered for a special auction. However, her prime suspect, the enigmatic Earl of Kirtland, proves a far more dangerous opponent than she ever imagined. Is she a match for his steel?

My research included a good deal of poking around Portobello Road, that delightful stretch of antique markets in the Notting Hill section of London, where one can spend hours poring over all the wonderful vintage jewelry, engravings, weaponry, and fashions of the time. And for those who wish to get a peek at the wilds of Dartmoor, check my Web site www.andreapickensonline.com for photos of the estate that inspired Marquand Castle.

Enjoy!

Andrea Pickens

♥ ♥ ♥ ♥ ♥ ♥ ♥ ♥ ♥ ♥ ♥ ♥ ♥ ♥ ♥ ♥ ♥

From the desk of Candy Halliday

The fun part in writing any series is the opportunity to reunite the characters from the previous book. That was certainly fun for me in the Housewives Fantasy Club series.

Revisiting Woodberry Park and being back together with sassy Fantasy Club members Zada, Tish, Jen, and Alicia was a reunion I didn't want to miss. However, in the second book of the series I wanted to make sure outcast Alicia in YOUR BED OR MINE? finally got her chance at happily ever after.

So . . . THEY'RE BACK!

In the sequel DINNER FIRST, ME LATER? (on sale now) the Housewives Fantasy Club is back in session—turning up the heat and keeping life steamy in Woodberry Park. A little too hot and steamy if you ask Alicia!

How can she possibly tell her best friends and neighbors that the new hunky celebrity who moved into their quaint little cul-de-sac was once her secret fantasy crush?

No way! Alicia vows.

Her Fantasy Club pals would never let her live it down. Besides, that fantasy ended when Jake "The

Rake" Sims went from respected Cubs baseball sta
to infamous playboy and underwear model—NOT
the type of man Alicia wants on her gotta-have-
him list!

Or so Alicia didn't think.

But what would you do if your celebrity fantasy
crush (and admit it, we all have one) offered you:

A. One night of passion.

B. No strings attached.

And, C. He gave you his promise no one would
ever know?

Would you go for it? Or would you chicken out?

I'm not going to tell you what I would do i
Matthew McConaughey made me that offer. Bu
I do hope you will visit Woodberry Park again, o
choose to meet the Housewives Fantasy Club for
the first time in DINNER FIRST, ME LATER? See
for yourself if Alicia fulfilled her fantasy with the
new bad boy from across the street.

One thing, however, you can be assured—once
the Housewives Fantasy Club calls the meeting to
order, the nights in Woodberry Park are always hot
and steamy.

Happy reading!

Candy Halliday

www.candyhalliday.com